100   125   150   175   200   225

2.50   BOOK RACK   275

USED PAPERBACKS - SELL - TRADE

2201 W. PARK ROW

300   ARLINGTON, TEXAS   325

274-1717

5210 RUFE SNOW DR.

N. RICHLAND HILLS, TEXAS

656-5565

350   375   400   425   450   500

New Orleans ER

Robert Mickey Maughon, M.D.

This book is dedicated to all my patients,
who made it possible.

Chapter One

Alight drizzle covered New Orleans. Only the lights of the French Quarter cut the night's darkness. Dr. Robert St. John drove his 1965 Jaguar XKE convertible up Royal Street, turned on Poydras and drove by the Superdome. Parking in his space at New Orleans Hospital, he grabbed his white coat and headed to the E.R.

A commotion at the back entrance caught the young doctor's eye as he approached the hospital.

"Hey," he called. "What's going on?"

"You cock-sucking doctors!" yelled a struggling young black man.

Two large, burly New Orleans policemen, both black, attempted to control the steel-muscled youth.

"Calm down, brother, or we'll have to beat the everloving crap out of you!" said the larger of the two officers as he struggled to cuff the youngster.

"Those goddamn doctors cut my brother to pieces!" the young man screamed.

The police officers now had him mostly controlled, but he continued to yell obscenities and threaten Robert. He had struggled so violently he was literally foaming at the mouth, reminding Dr. St. John of a rabid dog.

"Sorry Doc," the smaller cop puffed, exhausted from the struggle. "He's been going on about his brother being killed at the hospital, spouting nonsense about...oh hell...just crazy stuff about his brother...about him having his heart stolen...something crazy like that."

The now-silent youth had been put in a choke hold. The

two officers drug him kicking to the squad car and pushed him into the back seat.

"Damn crack cocaine," said the larger cop. He looked at Robert. "This is what they do when they get hopped up on that shit," he explained.

"I'm glad you guys were here to wrestle him. I couldn't have handled him by myself if he had jumped me," Dr. St. John said.

"Glad to help, Doc, just part of the job."

"Just another night in New Orleans," his partner shrugged as they pulled away from the emergency room, the youth kicking at the back window of the patrol car.

With a knot of dread rising in his chest, Robert walked into the chaos called New Orleans Hospital E.R. Henry Simms, a fellow E.R. doctor, motioned for Dr. St. John to join him at the first cubicle.

"Robert, can you sew up this guy? He was hurt on the docks earlier tonight."

"Sure, Henry, be glad to," he answered, surveying the gaping wound on the worker's arm.

"Thanks. I've got to get to an Alzheimer's patient they just wheeled in. Hey, did that nut attack you outside?"

"Yeah, he tried, but the cops hauled him off before he could get to me."

"I think if I hadn't been a brother, he would have tried to kill me, too," Dr. Simms whispered above the constant E.R. noise.

"Crack," they mouthed simultaneously.

Dr. Simms wandered to the back of the E.R. in search of his next patient.

"Help me, Lord!" an old man's voice cried from the back cubicle.

"Who is that?" Dr. St. John asked an intern, as he sewed up the dock worker's arm laceration.

"Ah, it's just an old Alzheimer's patient they brought in. He repeats everything over and over."

"Help me, Jesus!" came the voice again.

2

Robert ignored the voice and continued his work.

"Help me, Jesus. Help me, Lord. Help me."

"Shut him up, okay?" the doctor asked the intern as he placed a dressing cover on the dock worker's wound.

The intern walked back through the usual E.R. bedlam and approached the old man.

Robert gave wound instructions to the worker and shook his hand. "I'll see you back in ten days to remove the stitches."

Nurse Sally Ortiz wheeled in another patient: a chronic lung disease case who was a frequent visitor to the New Orleans Hospital E.R. "He's old," she said as she pulled the wheezing old man into the first cubicle.

"Let's use some aminophylline and place him on oxygen," Dr. St. John immediately ordered.

The intern brought over an oxygen mask.

"Hey, what'd you tell the old man to shut him up?" asked Robert.

"I told him this was a Buddhist hospital and he was making people mad by praying to Jesus, so stop it."

"Help me, Buddha!" came the old man's voice from the back. Robert and the intern laughed.

Dr. St. John pulled the oxygen mask up and over the old man's nose, coaxing the elastic contraption to snugly fit his weathered face. The patient acknowledged his gratitude by nodding his head.

"Breathe slowly and evenly," Robert instructed.

"I know," was the answer, followed by a deep cough.

Dr. St. John smiled weakly. The old-timer had been here before. Chronic lung problems don't heal themselves.

Flipping through the medical chart, he saw that his good buddy Dave Wyatt had treated this one before. Dave had treated all of the regulars—that group of people who just couldn't get well.

"You know Dr. Wyatt, sir?" he asked the patient.

"Yes sir, Doc." The old patient pointed with a bony finger. "Look-they want you."

"What?"

"Look!"

The old patient was pointing toward the front door of the emergency room. A group of nurses were scurrying around at the nurses' station.

"There's probably another patient who needs help, sir," Robert said.

"Well, they want you—look!"

Robert looked up. Sally Ortiz was looking at him in a peculiar manner. He continued to write on the chart, expecting her to wheel another patient to his station.

"Doc, I'm telling you—they want you over there," the old-timer said, lifting his oxygen mask enough to emphasize his statement. It snapped back so crookedly on his face that Robert couldn't help but chuckle.

"Okay! I'll go see what's up." As he strode toward the nurses' station, he realized what the patient meant. Sally was alternately waving for him and burying her head in her hands. The seven or eight nurses at the station seemed to be comforting her.

As he approached the group, Sally sank into his arms sobbing.

"Sally! What in the world? What's upset you so?" He looked around the group. All the other nurse's heads were hung—all eyes looking toward the floor.

Sally sobbed. "It's Dave—Dave is dead. There's a policeman…"

"What?"

She looked up at him. "Dave is *dead*! He's at your apartment. There's a policeman here who wants you to go with him to—" She could barely speak between gasps.

"What?" was all he could utter. He looked around again. The room seemed to spin

"Dr. *Wyatt*?" He asked incredulously.

A police officer stepped through the crowd of nurses and asked, "Are you Dr. Robert St. John?"

"Yes, I am."

4

"Please sir, can you step with me outside the hospital? Please sir, come with me.

As the doctor and the police officer left the E.R., rain began to pour over the eaves of the hospital.

The officer said, "Wait here, and I'll pull the car over."

After he pulled the blue police car under the eave, Robert jumped into the passenger side. The officer introduced himself as Sergeant Sandy Elliott of N.O.P.D.

"I know this is a shock and it's difficult, Doc, but we found Dr. Dave Wyatt at 1304 Royal Street about three hours ago, an apparent suicide."

"Are you crazy?" responded Robert.

"Doc, please. You gotta identify the body and help us any way you can. As you probably know, suicide is considered homicide for various reasons."

"Look, Officer Elliott, I just left Dave a few hours ago and he's supposed to relieve me in an hour. I'm his best friend. I'm treating an old-timer who is his patient. Either you're crazy, I am, or this is the Twilight Zone."

"Dr. St. John, I know this is really tough, but we found him—"

"How? Why? How did he do it? He couldn't have...I don't believe it...Why? Do you... have any other information?"

"No. He left the gas on in the apartment and, you know, *expired* that way."

Dr. St. John shook his head slowly.

The policeman continued, "Look Doc, just go with me to identify the body. The neighbors say you were his roommate and his friend."

"Yes, I was—am—his best friend. Let me check out with the nurses. I'll be right back."

Robert stepped back into the emergency room. His hand trembled as he waved for his charge nurse, Sally.

"Sally, I have to go with the officer to the apartment to see if this is true. Can you take care of everything and call Dr. Simms to cover for me?"

5

"Sure, Robert," she said, embracing him. "I'd go with you if I could."

"No," Dr. St. John replied. "Stay here and I'll be back ASAP. I don't know what to say except that hopefully this is some kind of nightmare that really isn't happening."

He removed his white coat as he left the emergency room and held it over his head to stay dry as he walked to the patrol car. Officer Elliott opened the door. Robert said, "Let's go."

As they pulled out, Dr. St. John said, "I'm not going to believe this until I see Dave."

"Doc, we consider this a suicide preliminarily because the doors were locked, there was no sign of forced entry, burglary…you know, no evidence of foul play. The gas had been left on. As I said earlier, we'll investigate it as a homicide because that's the law. Tell me, was Dr. Wyatt depressed?"

"Hell no," replied Robert. "He was a happy guy. He *loved* his work! We were raised together in Tennessee. Turn here, Officer, on Royal Street. Listen, I have a question."

"Sure, what?"

"Was there any sign of trauma, violence?" Robert wiped away a tear. He had not cried in a long time, even though he had seen many sad things in his career.

"No, Doc. That's why we'll basically view this as a suicide unless some evidence or witness turns up to make us assume otherwise. Of course, we'll have to perform an autopsy to determine the exact cause of death. Look, I know this is no consolation, but I've been doing this a long time and this happens a lot, to the person you least expect. At N.O.P.D., if it looks like a duck, walks and talks like a duck, it's a duck until considered otherwise. This is suicide—routine business."

The officer stopped short, noticing Robert had his head in his hands as tears flowed down his face. "Maybe I could see Dave," he gulped.

"Look—trust me—this does happen all the time. Look at it this way—Did Dr. Wyatt have any enemies—problems—gambling debts—drug problems, etc., to suggest foul play?"

"No!" Robert replied emphatically. "He was very down-to-earth. No problems. Just a great guy."

"Look, we're two blocks away, Doc. If you can't do this, we'll get somebody else."

"No! I want to see for myself or I won't believe this."

The apartment the two young doctors had shared was an old shotgun flat in the Vieux Carre, or as the tourists called it, the French Quarter. A group of bystanders were milling about outside of the residence. The yellow police tape denoting and delineating a crime scene had already been set up.

Officer Elliott said, "I'll go in first. You follow me."

Robert noted his neighbor Jim Marshall on the right side of the street as he got out of the car.

"Sorry, Doc," Jim said. "I smelled gas, so I called the cops. I told them he was your roommate. I didn't know what else to do. I knew you were at work, so I assumed it was Dr. Wyatt they had found."

"That's okay. Thanks, Jim," Dr. St. John said. Both men lowered their eyes, not looking at each other again.

As they crossed the doorway into the apartment, Robert smelled the distinct odor of natural gas, even though all the windows had been opened.

Officer Elliott said, "This way, Doc. He's in the bedroom. First, let me introduce you to Lieutenant Sheldon. Lieutenant, this is the deceased's roommate."

Robert shook hands with a portly man with black, bushy eyebrows and dark eyes.

"Doctor, this is never pleasant. We hope you will identify the body and answer any questions we ask. Okay?"

"Okay. May I see Dave now?"

"Yes sir. This way." They walked over the threshold from the sparsely decorated living room to Dave's bedroom.

Dave Wyatt's expressionless face stared up at the slowly rotating ceiling fan, oblivious to the pain he had caused his closest friend.

"I can't believe this," a shocked Robert said, tears again coming to his eyes. "Are you sure this is a suicide? Dave

7

wouldn't do this!"

"Well, we can't be absolutely sure until the coroner investigates and the autopsy is done," Elliott answered, "but the doors were locked and the gas was on from the inside. Sure looks like a suicide to me. Um, Doc, anybody else have a key?"

"No," Dr. St. John said. "Do you guys have a handkerchief?"

"Officer Elliott produced one and asked, "So this is Dr. Dave Wyatt?"

"Yes sir, this is him."

Elliott continued, "Okay, we'll notify next of kin. Now, do you have a place to stay tonight?"

"Yes. I can stay in the residents' quarters in the hospital."

"Okay, just so long as we have a place to find you. Come on, I'll give you a ride over in the patrol car. Does—did—Dr. Wyatt have any close friends?"

"Yes. Ann Finn is, or was, his closest friend, probably. By that, I mean his most intimate friend."

"Where can I find her?" Elliott inquired.

"She's in administration at New Orleans Hospital. She probably doesn't know about this yet, Officer. I really don't look forward to telling her. Do you mind contacting her, or having one of your men contact her? I don't feel like talking to her."

The officer noted the confused and hurt look on the doctor's face.

"Okay—don't worry about it—as we told you, we consider this an apparent suicide. The question is purely perfunctory, if you know what I mean."

They stepped back outside. The crowd had grown. Robert noticed one of his regular alcoholic patients in the throng.

"I'm sorry, Doc. Anything I can do?" the emaciated man offered.

"No, no. Thanks." Robert slowly shook his head. It did make him feel somewhat better to know a patient actually cared, even if the guy was a street bum.

As they walked to the black-and-white Chevrolet Caprice police car, Officer Elliott patted him on the back. "Look Doc, you'll question your not knowing how to prevent this," he said. "It's normal."

"I know what I'll go through."

"Yeah, I know you doctors. You're think you're supermen. Might as well listen to me. You're human, just like anyone else and if you two were as close as I think you were, you'll go through the grieving process. I just want you to know it's okay to be human. Hey, cops are human too, believe it or not."

"Thanks, Officer Elliott. I appreciate that. Hopefully, I can think this through closely and not get depressed—but I have pretty good insight. If I need help, professional help that is, I know where to find it."

"Yeah, Doc, you're right. Just remember, we have a counseling service through N.O.P.D., too, if you need it." As he pulled up to the E.R. entrance, he asked, "Is this okay? Can we contact you here?"

"Yes sir. Just call the administrative offices. They can get in touch with me anywhere."

Dr. St. John got out of the car. "I'll call Dr. Wyatt's family in Tennessee."

"You don't have to do that. One of our men will do it."

Robert continued, oblivious to the officer's words, "No, I have to talk to them. I've known them since I was a kid, and Dave was my best friend. I'll call them later."

"Okay, Doc, but we'll still have to contact them—police protocol."

Extending his hand, Robert said, "If there is anything I can do, let me know."

Officer Elliott shook his hand and said, "Okay."

"Okay, Officer. Goodnight."

As Dr. St. John entered the E.R., Sally Ortiz ran immediately over to him and pulled him over into the patient check-in office.

Robert asked, "How are things going in here? Did you get back-up for me?"

"Just the regular mayhem and gunshots. What happened? Is Dave—?"

"Yes, Dave's dead. He killed himself. I was his best friend and I had no clue."

"Clue to what? What happened!" Her voice was close to a scream.

"Hell, he killed himself...committed suicide...and I thought he was the happiest guy in the world! Shows what a friend I was. I can save the lives of total strangers here, but I don't even know my roommate's suicidal. Some M.D. I am."

Sally sat down in a chair, dumbfounded.

"Killed himself? They told us he was dead but I had no idea—suicide! I thought foul play or something."

Big tears formed in her eyes. "Our E.R. director killed himself..."

"Don't feel bad, Sally. I was the closest one to him and I had no idea. Look, can you guys handle things down here? I need to go upstairs and call his family—I really don't want to be down here tonight."

"Sure. Go on upstairs. What room will you be in if we need you?"

"I'll be in 201," he said, indicating the break room for chief residents and E.R. doctors.

"Okay."

"Hey, Sally, have you seen Ann Finn?"

"No. She flew through here—looked like she was in a big rush. All the guys stopped to stare at her as usual." Sally rolled her big brown eyes jealously. "Robert, are you going to tell her? yourself?"

"No, the police said they would do it. But hell, Sally, I know I should." He reached over and hugged her hard and walked away from the frenzied E.R. in a daze.

Chapter Two

Dr. St. John took the elevator up to the old part of New Orleans Hospital, the rooms where M.D.'s in training in the '30s and '40s actually lived along with their families, thus the name *residents*. Reaching Room 201, he thought back to memories of Dr. Dave Wyatt and himself as young interns. They were good memories.

As he stepped into the room, the telephone on the side table brought him back to the present as he realized he had two telephone calls to make: one to Dr. Wyatt's family and the other to Dave's friend, Ann Finn. He really didn't want to make either call.

I've got to call Ann. It's the least I can do, he thought. After repeated calls and reaching only her answering machine, he decided to call Dave's folks. *Boy, this is tough.* Another tear fell, dropping onto his shirt.

"Hello, Mr. Wyatt?"

"Yes. Robert? Robert, is that you?"

"Yes, Mr. Wyatt. It's Robert St. John in New Orleans."

"Robert, N.O.P.D. just called twenty minutes ago. Please...forgive me if I break down...you know, Mrs. Wyatt and I are taking this hard..."

"Mr. Wyatt, I don't know what to tell you."

"What happened? What in the world could have gone wrong? We just spoke with Dave two weeks ago and he seemed happy and optimistic about the future. There seemed to be no problems—he had a good girl—we just can't understand—" A sob came through the phone.

"Robert, is it possible the police are wrong and this really isn't suicide?"

"Well, Mr. Wyatt, the coroner will do an autopsy."

"Oh? Do they have to? I don't know."

"Yes sir, it's the law."

"I see—well, if it has to be done, then we want to be absolutely sure."

"Yes sir—I can't believe this myself. I just left him three hours before his body was found."

"But what happened?"

"The neighbors smelled gas and called the police and—well, that's it."

"My word, we're just dumbfounded, confused and hurt." A few more sobs came through.

"Mr. Wyatt, is there anything I can do for you myself?" Robert heard two loud knocks on the door. "Hold on, Mr. Wyatt. Someone is at the door."

He opened the door and waved in Sally Ortiz with his open hand. He pointed to the foot of the bed. The stocky Hispanic nurse sat down.

"Okay, Mr. Wyatt, I'm sorry, I'm back."

"Robert, there's something you can do. Will you be coming up here for the funeral?"

"Yes, I'll try to. I'm sure we'll have a memorial service here in New Orleans. I'll do my best to come."

"Thanks, Robert, and God bless you—see you soon."

"Bye, Mr. Wyatt."

Hanging up the phone, Robert turned to Sally. "Is there a problem in the E.R.?"

"Just the usual chaos. I came to check on you."

"Sally, how could this have happened?"

"The one thing you can't do is blame yourself. This is not your fault. I got you a sedative from the hospital pharmacy to help you sleep."

"I really don't need anything."

"Well, I think you do, so take this and go to sleep," she said, handing him a Valium. "It's okay for even a tough guy like you to be a patient on a night like this."

"Okay. Thanks. I tried to call Ann Finn but couldn't reach her."

"There'll be plenty of time to talk to Ann in the morning if we can't reach her tonight."

"Yeah, I guess you're right. Boy, Sally, what a jolt, you know? When you're a doctor, you think you've seen it all and nothing can possibly shock you. But this is unbelievable. I don't know how to act or feel about this. It's horrible!"

"You'll get through it. We'll all get through this together. Okay?"

They hugged and then she headed for the door.

"Go ahead and try to get some sleep. I'll make sure the E.R. and the hospital pager don't bother you tonight."

"Thanks, Sally. I guess I will try to sleep. I am feeling kind of tired and drained."

"I'll see you in the morning." Sally closed the door.

Dr. St. John opened the window next to the bed and looked out over the city. The sounds and sights of New Orleans appeared totally different to him. He lay down, took his sedative and drifted into a restless sleep.

He awoke with a start although he was groggy. The benzodiazapine had sedated him well. The morning sun drifted into the room, and he remembered the night before. The idea of seeing Ann Finn this morning made him shudder.

As he looked in the mirror, he thought, *Lord, life goes on. Poor Dave.* A tear formed. *No, I don't have time for this.* After showering and shaving, he put on his laundered blue scrubs and a white coat with *Dr. St. John* embroidered on the lapel.

Well, hopefully Ann knows and I'm not telling her for the first time, he thought as he walked down the hall. Interns and residents were scurrying about, hurrying to their many rounds. As he reached the elevator, he thought he overheard a group saying, "Did you hear? Can you believe?" The reality of Dave's death came crashing down on him. He thought about the shame the suicide would bring to the memory of Dave—a guy who through sheer determination and hard work had become a truly remarkable emergency room physician. That is how he would be remembered...the doctor who killed himself.

Damn! That's horrible, he thought. *The doctor who killed himself.* As the elevator reached the second floor, the location of the administrative offices, he looked in the shiny metallic door that reflected his white-coated image. As he stepped out of the elevator and knocked on Ann Finn's door, he took a deep breath and said to himself, *I'm ready.* He knocked on the door.

"Come in."

As he walked through the door, he immediately saw the figure of Ann Finn in the back of the office. Even from where he stood, he could see her bright red eyes and the handkerchief she held in her left hand. He sighed. *Thank God, she knows.*

Jerri, the secretary, looked at him. "Do you wish to see Miss Finn?"

"Yes, Jerri—I'd like to see her if I may."

As he looked up, Ann Finn answered his question by walking toward him.

"Ann, you know then?" he asked as they embraced.

"Yes, Robert, I know. Come on into my office and we'll talk."

"Okay."

"Jerri, please allow Dr. St. John and myself some privacy."

"Certainly, Miss Finn." Jerri closed the door behind them.

"Ann, I don't know what to say."

"I knew Dave as well if not better than you." She used the handkerchief she held in her left hand to dry the tears that had formed in her eyes.

Dr. St. John walked over to her and put his hand on her shoulder.

"Well, you know, Officer Elliott who was here yesterday said this happens more than one would expect and to those you least expect. As a physician, I would probably concur, but it doesn't make it any less difficult, especially if it's someone you know."

Ann moved closer to him. "Oh, Robert," she embraced him tightly. "I cried all last night after the police contacted me. I kept expecting a call from you."

"I tried to call you!"

"I know, I know."

"Is there anything I can do for you, Ann?"

"Well, Robert, actually there is."

"What? Anything!"

"Mr. Levitz, the NCHO-appointed hospital administrator, and I would like for you to have dinner with us tonight at Commander's Palace."

"Why?"

"We need a new emergency room director, and you're the logical choice."

"God, I dreaded telling you this so much, and now I get a job offer instead? This doesn't feel right."

"Put yourself in my place. If I were a man and this happened to my girlfriend, would I be given any latitude on my job performance? Hell no! I'd be expected to perform and do my job well, no matter how badly I was hurting. I am going to do my job. Do you understand? It'll make my life easier if I stay with the structure and sanity of the daily routine here. Okay?"

"Yeah, I guess. It's just that Dave and I were so close."

"I know, we were close too, but right now we have to fill this vacancy that's been created. Life goes on and this is the obvious time to discuss this. Will you meet us tonight?"

"Of course I will!"

"Okay, Doctor. Seven o'clock?"

"Seven o'clock is fine. You know Commander's is my favorite restaurant."

"I know. Don't be late. On your way out, tell Jerri I'm expecting Mr. Levitz to call and to put him through, please."

"Sure Ann. I'm going to work today too."

"Are you sure you're up to it?"

15

"Well , I think you're probably presenting a good example to everybody."

"Well, I hope so."

"Good. See you tonight then."

He gave Jerri Ann's message on the way out, adding "Jerri, there may be some people trying to contact me today—if so, I'll be in the E.R."

"Okay, sure, Robert."

Dr. St. John took the stairs down to the floor level toward the emergency room. He met Sally one flight above the E.R.

"Robert, how are you? Did you sleep last night?"

"Yeah, Sally, thanks. I'm going to work. Are you?"

"Yeah, but why don't you take the day off? We'll take care of everything."

"Well Sally, Ann Finn is in her office, working and planning a restructuring meeting for tonight, so I'm going to follow her example."

Sally drew up her face and skewed it in obvious contempt: "Ann Finn!"

"I know, I know. You girls don't like Ann because she's a good-looking girl who plays hardball with the guys. But, Sally, she's right. Life goes on."

Sally still had the look on her face. "I don't care, Doctor. If my fiancé just killed himself, I'd be home in bed or at my mother's crying my eyes out. Ann is a cold-hearted, calculating bitch who thinks only of advancement and what everybody else can do for her. Hell, she only liked Dave because he was a doctor, and you know it."

"Oh, Sally! Give it a rest."

"It's true, Doc, whether you like it or not."

"Sally, are you jealous?" Dr. St. John stifled a mock laugh, then guffawed for the first time in almost twenty-four hours.

"Look Robert—*trust me.* I'm Latino and we Latino women know each other. You'd better watch that Ann Finn or she will have you seduced before you know it, just because you're a doctor!"

"Sally! What a thing to say! I know you're jealous now." Sally broke away and moved up the stairwell. "Trust me, Doc man, watch Ann Finn and do what I tell you. Take the day off!"

"I'll see—but I'll probably be in the emergency room working if you need me."

"Bye. See ya."

Dr. St. John laughed on the way down the stairwell to the E.R. Sally always spoke her mind, no matter the circumstance or consequence.

Entering the emergency room from the stairwell, he noticed Officer Elliott talking to Dr. Simms, who had replaced him on the previous shift. As Robert approached them, he overheard the officer thanking him for his cooperation.

"I'll see you soon," the officer told Dr. Simms. Then noticing Robert, he said, "Hey, Dr. St. John."

"Good morning, Officer Elliott."

"Dr. St. John, could I talk with you in the office for a minute?"

"Certainly. Hold on a moment." Robert turned to Dr. Simms, who was examining an elderly woman. "Is everything okay for now while I talk to the officer about Dave?"

Dr. Simms stopped his examination long enough to nod."

Robert and Officer Elliott headed for the office. Elliott closed the door behind them.

"You were right, Doc," Elliott said. I thought you'd want a follow-up on our investigation."

"Sure, what did you find?"

"Nothing. It's just like you said. Everyone we asked said Wyatt was happy. No great career problems, well-liked—the least likely case for suicide that you could imagine. But it's like I told you last night: Sometimes it's those who are the least likely or suspect who commit suicide. You just can't see

17

inside a person's mind or heart."

"Yeah, I know. That's basically what everyone keeps saying," Robert stated slowly.

"And Doc, also as I told you, there was absolutely no evidence of foul play, so, unless something shows up on autopsy today, this will be ruled a suicide and there will be no further investigation."

Dr. St. John said somberly, "I would attend the autopsy today, but you understand."

"Oh Doc, Lord no. We wouldn't expect you to be there. That's above and beyond the call of duty. Oh by the way, you can go back to your apartment if the autopsy doesn't show anything."

"Thanks. I do need to go by there or send somebody to get some clothes."

"Sure," Elliott answered. "I can understand that. As a matter of fact, I'll take you by right now if you want."

"Let me check," Robert said, "to see if Dr. Simms can work for me again this shift."

"Okay, I'll be in the squad car out back."

Dr. St. John walked out to the emergency room and looked for Dr. Simms. He found him in the third cubicle, repairing an arm laceration and asked, "Henry, can you cover for me while I go back to my apartment for a few minutes?

"Go ahead, Robert. You know I've got everything covered."

"Thanks, buddy—I'll owe you."

Dr. Simms looked up and smiled, waving him on with a suture in his hand.

Dr. St. John walked to the patrol car and got in with Officer Elliott. "Let's go," he said.

"You know," Officer Elliott said as they drove through light mid-morning traffic, "you guys have great reputations. Everyone, from the people in your neighborhood to the orderlies in the E.R., thinks highly of you."

"Thanks, Officer."

"This whole thing is a shame, Doc. You know a lot of people think doctors make too much money and are conceited. But you guys obviously weren't in it for the money. I mean, being E.R. doctors and all—working in a charity hospital like you do. You ought to hear people talk about you! Well, you're to be commended."

"Yeah, we could make a lot more money in private practice, but this is what we wanted to do. It isn't like work. Sure, we get tired. I don't really know how to explain it. It's fun in many ways."

"Good. That's good news, Doc. You know, police work and your type medicine are similar."

"Really, Officer? How?"

"Well, we deal with people who need us and who don't always appreciate us, right?"

"Yeah, you're right, Officer. Hadn't thought of it that way." Robert looked at the officer curiously. "Why, what's the point?"

"Well, me and the other homicide detectives downtown—remember, I told you that legally this thing has to be considered a homicide until the autopsy is negative? Well, we had another suicide yesterday. A businessman who did the same thing. Everyone thought he had it made. Beautiful wife, family—everything—and he used a thirty-eight caliber to the head." Elliott said, pointing his finger to his temple and making a trigger-pulling motion.

"Who was it?"

"Ah, a guy in the import-export business. Guy seemed to have it made. His wife is in shock. And you know, that's another thing that probably makes our type of work similar. His wife went absolutely to pieces. Had to be sedated. Have you talked to Dr. Wyatt's significant other, Ms. Finn?"

"Yeah, this morning."

"Totally different attitude, huh, Doc? A few tears, yeah, but she's at work today going about her business, right?"

"Yeah, I know. I talked to her and we're going to have supper tonight."

The officer looked at the doctor with a big grin.

"Oh no, Officer. That's not it. It's strictly business— about replacing Dave in the emergency room."

"Oh Doc, I'm not implying anything."

Your look said everything, Robert thought.

They turned off on Royal Street and headed toward the apartment.

"Yeah, well, she's a looker, Doc."

"Strictly business, buddy. Strictly business."

"Well, that's my point. How different people handle things differently. The businessman's wife is a basket case and your doctor buddy's friend is having a business dinner tonight. See what I mean? Don't some people in accidents go hysterical and others take it in stride?"

"Yes, that's true."

The officer looked at Dr. St. John. "Here we are, Doc."

"Dave's body has been removed, hasn't it?"

"Of course! Last night. I'll go in with you."

"Yeah, okay. Thanks. I guess I would like for you to come in with me." They walked by the yellow crime scene tape. "When will this come down, Officer?"

"Probably tomorrow, after the autopsy is performed today."

"And I can come back to stay in the apartment then?"

"Yes, if you want."

Robert hesitated, "I'll probably get another place."

Officer Elliott opened the door to the apartment and looking over his shoulder replied, "Many people do move after something like this happens."

The smell of gas permeated the apartment but was much less pronounced than it had been yesterday.

"By the way, Dr. St. John. Don't touch anything in the apartment other than your clothes."

Robert shot a puzzling glance.

"Don't worry, Doc. Understand, until the investigation is over, this is still considered a crime scene. You couldn't come in here unless I was with you."

"I see," replied Robert, looking around. "I understand."

"I'll be back in a minute. Wait, okay?"

After a moment: "You can come on in now. I just wanted to be sure everything was in order."

The officer disappeared somewhere into the apartment, off toward the kitchen. Dr. St. John crossed the living room, passed Dave's bedroom and entered his own. The last image of Dave, lying in his bed just before Robert went to work the previous day, haunted him as he got some clothes together for his meeting that evening. Tears nearly rose to his eyes again. *No,* he thought, *I'm not going to do that.* But tears burned his eyes anyway. He scolded himself, *Stop it!* But the image wouldn't leave his mind: his best friend, suicidal. Something he should have picked up on, but didn't. *But,* he consoled himself, *Officer Elliott seemed to be a smart, compassionate guy and he said this sometimes just happens.*

"Here I am, Doc," Elliott announced as he returned to the small foyer of the apartment. "Let me help you with those things."

"Thanks," Robert replied solemnly.

As they stepped outside, one of the neighbors walked up behind the doctor and put his hand on his shoulder.

"Sorry, Doc," the neighbor whispered. "We're all in shock."

"Thanks. I am too," was Robert's only reply.

The neighbor continued in his very low tone, "Anything we can do?"

"Watch the place for me for a few days," Robert requested.

"Sure thing, Doc," the neighbor blurted, in a braver voice.

Elliott locked the front door and then helped Robert load his clothes into the patrol car.

"Let's go," Elliott said. "Now, where to?"

"Back to the hospital. I think I'll stay in the resident's quarters upstairs for a while."

Robert reminisced as they drove past Brennan's restaurant on Royal Street. He flashed back to the times he and Dave, and occasionally Ann, would leave the hospital after a long day and go to one of New Orleans' famous landmarks. He saw numerous tourists filing into the pink-facaded building, mindless of the pain he was experiencing. As they drove closer to the hospital, Ann Finn's beautiful face flashed in front of him. "Life goes on," she was saying, tossing her chestnut hair. Robert snapped back to reality as the patrol car pulled up to the E.R. entrance. The officer turned to Robert and offered his card.

"Here's my card, Doc, just in case you need anything."

"Thank you, sir."

"If anything comes up at the autopsy, I'll let you know."

Robert looked startled.

"Don't worry, Doc. I don't think anything will show up out of the ordinary. If it does, I'll call."

Deciding to avoid the E.R. crunch and scrutiny, Robert slipped up the back stairwell of the hospital. He hoped to avoid the inevitable questions that would come from being seen getting out of a patrol car. He had thought enough and answered sufficiently for now. Besides, he needed to get ready for tonight's meeting. Officer Elliott had made a very valid point about the beauty of Ann Finn. Dr. St. John smiled to himself. Dave and he were good friends. He had even accused Dave of sleeping with her so he could be appointed E.R. director, but he hadn't been serious. It did seem to get under Dave's skin, though and that had been good enough reason for the teasing.

As he entered his room, the phone was ringing. He answered, "Hello, this is Dr. St. John."

"Doctor, this is Jerri, Ms. Finn's secretary."

"Hi Jerri, what can I do for you?"

"Ms. Finn asked that I call and remind you about tonight."

"I haven't forgotten."

"She also said to remember to wear a coat and tie and if you didn't have one to stop by her place to see if she couldn't help."

"Thanks, Jerri, but I already went by my apartment to get some clothes."

"Good, Doctor. I'll let Ms. Finn know."

"Thanks. Bye."

As he hung up the phone, he mused about how the officer had been correct about this woman: beautiful and all business. Something he found very attractive.

He lay down to take a short nap and remembered a time when he was a teenager and he had desperately wished that a year would lapse as he slept so, as the adage went, time would cure all pain. This is what he prayed for as he lay down to sleep.

He awoke with a start and looked at his watch. 6:30 p.m. *Oh no*, he thought, *Ann will kill me if I'm late.* He showered, shaved and dressed with the speed of a doctor used to being on call.

"My car!" he thought out loud. He remembered he had parked his Jaguar in the parking garage. *Good God. If they've towed it, I sure as hell will be late. Great!*

Running to the garage, he found the car covered with parking tickets but not towed. He drove as fast as he could without smashing into the trolley cars on St. Charles. He turned into the parking lot of Commander's Palace in time to see Ann entering.

While trying to find a place to park, he thought, *Dave, if they want me to take your place, I'll do my best, but I think they could respect your memory for just a few days anyway.*

He finally found a parking place and approached one of New Orleans' most beloved culinary citadels. As he walked up to the steps of Commander's Palace, memories flooded over him and he momentarily forgot the present. This place was his and Dave's favorite. Dates and celebrations were all reasons to venture to Commander's. They were on speaking terms with virtually all of the staff.

The voice of the maître d', Silas Arlington, quickly brought Dr. St. John back to reality. Silas grabbed the doctor's arm and whispered, "Ms. Finn is waiting over at your favorite table." He pulled him over to the side and continued, "I wanted to offer my condolences to you. She told me about Dr. Dave."

"Yes," Robert whispered. "It's been difficult." He changed the subject: "Where did you say Ms. Finn's seated?"

"Over here, Doctor," Silas gestured, courteously extending his hand toward the table. He then patted the doctor on the back.

"The usual, Doctor?" Silas inquired formally.

"Yes, Silas, please."

Silas Arlington was a descendant of New Orleans slaves. His entire family had frequently used the pediatric unit of New Orleans Hospital and had also been patients of his and Dave Wyatt's in the E.R. Silas always seated the two of them at their favorite table, overlooking the courtyard, where they could have a full view of all the pretty ladies in attendance. Silas Arlington was a true friend.

Ann stood up as Dr. St. John approached the table.

"Please, Ann, sit down," Robert said. "Where's Mr. Levitz?"

Ann sat down. "He asked that I meet with you alone. He had another appointment."

"Well, I thought he was going to be here!" Robert protested, looking at her sternly. His annoyance at having made such a rush to get there began to show, but he quickly curtailed his emotions.

"Relax, Doctor! He gave me permission to act on behalf of the hospital administration."

"Okay," Robert said, adjusting himself in his chair. With that, Silas reappeared, bringing the drinks to the table.

"Here you go, a Southern Comfort for the lady and a Jack Daniel's for the gentleman. The waiter will be around in a moment. May I do anything else for you?"

Robert looked up, smiled and shook Silas' hand. "You're still going to let us be your doctors even though Dr. Dave isn't with us anymore, aren't you?"

"Of course, Doctor," Silas said evenly. "My family will always come to see you if we need help. You can count on it. You've never let us down before, sir."

"That's good to know, Silas. Of course we want you to stay well."

"Of course, sir. That's what you call preventive medicine, I believe I recall," Silas said, bowing slightly as he backed away from the table. "No eggs, no grits, no butter, no smoking." Silas stifled a smile. He turned on one heel and walked away. They could hear him repeating the list of no's as he faded into the restaurant. As Robert returned his attention back to Ann Finn, he was chuckling under his breath.

"That Silas," he said, shaking his head.

"He likes you, Robert," Ann replied. "That's why we want to keep you happy and contented at New Orleans Hospital, now that your best friend is gone."

His brow tightened as he looked at Ann and said, "Why do you think I would leave? Hell, you were closer to Dave in many ways," he said, shuffling awkwardly in his chair. "Are you going to leave?"

A slight redness crept up her neck.

"No," she said coolly. "The administration at the hospital wants to make sure you are given the support and encouragement you need during these difficult times."

With that comment, she slowly took a sip of Southern Comfort and watched his eyes, never raising her glass above a point at which she would lose eye contact with him. He raised his glass also, not to mimic her gesture, but to have time to respond. This lady had just lost someone very close to her and she was as cool and detached as anyone he had ever seen.

It was as if there never had been someone by the name of Dave Wyatt. Sure, she had shed a few tears this morning in her office, as evidenced by the reddened eyes, but even then, she was all business. He couldn't help but admire her. Jesus! Her looks added to his admiration, but there was something else. She was too reserved, too businesslike, too something he couldn't put his finger on. Maybe he was making too harsh a judgment. As she had said earlier, if she were a man, she would have been expected to act exactly as she had. He lowered his glass a little and swallowed hard.

"Well, Ann, as I understand it, you and administration want to fill the E.R. directorship and I'm your choice. Is that why you wanted to see me?"

"Yes, to be fairly direct, that is it. We need you right now!" She extended her index finger from her glass as she took another sip, still making sure she did not lose eye contact with him.

"As I said earlier—" she continued.

He interrupted. "I know, business and life go on."

Her eyes widened a little bit. "Exactly," she said petulantly. For the first time, she allowed herself to lose eye contact with him and to soften a little bit. He began to wish he hadn't been so harsh.

"Robert," she spoke, leaning forward as if letting him in on a secret. "I will allow myself some lowering of this veil of indifference in your presence for a moment, but just a moment," she sighed, glancing down and back up again. "I was closer to Dave than anyone in the world. However, since I was a little girl, I have not been able to allow myself the privilege of caring about circumstances beyond my control. I have had to have the structure of my schooling and then my career to promote stability in my life. Dave's death is just another tragedy in a long line of events that reinforces that I will not allow my emotions to be swept away." She held up her hand as if to say "Don't ask if you don't want to know."

She took another gulp, finishing her drink, and waved at

Silas, pointing to her drink and to Robert's to signal refills. "Besides," she continued, "being a woman in the South, and honey, this is the Deep South, I have to be twice as good as any man to keep the respect of my peers, not to mention their confidence in my ability."

Dr. St. John realized the conversation was going in the wrong direction. He instinctively tried to change the subject. "Ann, did you know Dave and I were raised together in Tennessee?"

"Of course. Dave told me."

"Did he tell you about the time he and I were only seven or eight years old and we got into the only fight of our lives?"

"No."

Laughing louder than the situation called for, probably due to the emotions of the past two days and the Jack Daniel's he had consumed, Robert continued.

"I remembered this last month when Silas brought his children to the emergency room with the chicken pox." Stopping to take another sip of his Jack to gain a little composure, he rubbed the rim of his glass with his finger.

"Well," he continued, snickering a little bit to himself, "Silas' boys were arguing that they both wanted to be the New Orleans Saints' quarterback, but the older one said the younger couldn't because the Saints' quarterback was white and that made it impossible. The younger one's only rebuttal was that he was pretending and anything was possible when you are pretending. He had completely forgotten to offer the fact that the older child was black also and would similarly have to pretend."

He peeked to study Ann's face, which had shown no sign of amusement. However, he was too far into the story to back off now.

"So?" was her only reply.

"Well, you're from the North, aren't you?"

"That's right."

"Well, Dave and I both wanted to be Condredge Holloway, who was the University of Tennessee quarterback, and well, um—" He felt a slight flush run up his face partly from the booze and partly from the thought that the story was not going over well. He forged ahead.

"Anyway, we both wanted to pretend to be Holloway in the neighborhood pick-up games, and one day we got in a fight, the only one we ever had. Dave said I couldn't be Holloway because I wasn't black. Of course, Dave failed to see the logic that he was as white as me. Well, that's the story of our only fight. What do you think? "

"That's quite an amusing story," Ann said, obviously not very impressed.

Trying to salvage some of his male Southern pride, Dr. St. John offered, "I think it would be a lot funnier if you had been raised in the South, and understood about little white boys wanting to be black."

Silas had slipped up behind him unnoticed with another round of drinks. "Oh, Robert, I think you're telling Ms. Finn about my children both wanting to be the quarterback of the New Orleans Saints."

"Yes, Silas, I was, although I'm not much of a storyteller. I was also telling her about Dave and me similarly wanting to be the quarterback of the Tennessee team but needing to be black."

"Well sir, since you aren't much of a storyteller, let me recommend the blackened redfish tonight, which will be an improvement over the recantment of your childhood."

Ann and Robert smiled at each other.

"Silas, that's a wonderful idea," Ann said.

"Count me in too, Silas."

"Allow fifteen minutes for your meal. And if I might interject my own personal views, you both need to let your hair down a little. There is too much seriousness and tragedy recently." Silas paused. "You folks relax and let me take care of you tonight. I'll return momentarily to see if your drinks need refills."

With that, Robert did relax.

"Boy, that Silas is a real card, huh, Ann? Did you know

we attended Tulane University together as undergrads?"

"Really?" replied Ann, stoically.

"Yes," Robert asserted. "He was restaurant management and retail business and I was pre-med."

"How fascinating," were the only words Ann could muster.

As their conversation began to drift effortlessly from subject to subject, with no mention of Dave by either side, the fifteen minutes needed to prepare the redfish passed. When Silas brought the food, both were ready for the diversion of dinner.

Dr. St. John took the first bite of his meal. *You dumbass*, he thought, remembering how his first story had fallen flat. *Of course she was offended by the stories of Dave. He's dead! She may protest that she has to be tough and all that for her job, but she's still a woman. And here I am jabbering on about a dead man."*

His thoughts caused him to smile. "Is something funny?" Ann asked.

"Oh no!" he responded between bites of food. "This is delicious. Silas always has the best culinary creations."

Ann was giving him the once-over as he raked his fork through the last vestiges of his wild rice. He felt awkward as he wondered if it was a physical attraction or if she was examining him purely on a business level. Silas approached and again saved the day. "How is everything?"

"Wonderful," they answered in unison.

"How about dessert?"

Again both nodded spontaneously in the affirmative.

"Pralines and cream?"

"Of course," they both giggled.

"Coming up in five minutes."

Finally, Ann broke the ice. "Would you care to discuss the job offering?" This somewhat disappointed him, as her earlier observations now took on a more professional cast.

"What's there to discuss? If you offer the job, I assume I'll take it."

Ann seemed to actually sigh with relief. "Would you like

to know any of the benefits or extras that come with the position?"

"Well, I assume I would do quality assurance, monthly reports, the usual kind of stuff that any E.R. director would do."

"That's right, but what makes the job at New Orleans Hospital different is the close affiliations administration maintains with the department heads. That's how Dave and I became so close in the first place."

"The Commander's Palace specialty dessert of all time," Silas announced. "Anything else I can get for you right now?"

"No thank you, sir. We're just fine for right now. Check back with us in a little while," Dr. St. John replied.

"You got it." Silas spun and sped away back into the crowd.

Dessert gave Robert time to retreat for a minute and clear his head. *Now,* he thought, *I know women, or at least I think I know them as well as any man might assume to. Is she trying to seduce me?* He brought his spoonful of the sweet confection back up to his face to mask an obvious search of her eyes. He caught a glimpse of her attempting to gracefully scoop the last bit of remaining cream in her bowl.

He caught himself feeling that desire that occurs when there's attraction between two people. *She's trying to seduce me. Seduce me? She's doing a damn good job. Boy, I'm confused and this Tennessee Tea isn't helping,* the doctor confessed to himself. He swallowed more Jack Daniel's with his last bit of dessert.

"Are you curious, Robert, why this directorship is a little different from others when it comes to potential and responsibilities?" Ann asked. "You see, New Orleans is one of the few hospitals in the world where transplants and special procedures are processed with the blessing of the National Health Care Organization. With this greater assumption of advanced medical procedures comes much greater scrutiny and monitoring. Therefore, it's imperative that we fill the vital E.R. chief's job immediately. NHCO certainly allows no time off for deaths and sickness, which are just part of the human condition. They mandate this on record-keeping. Protocols have to be top priorities, or we lose our special privileges. Do you understand?"

"I see. So this is your total approach to the situation...as a businesswoman?"

"Absolutely!" she flashed a smile, then allowed her hand to rub the tips of his fingers. "I'm so glad you under-stand what makes the speed of this transition so imperative. I'm not heartless. I'm just taking care of my people's jobs—keeping the administration happy in order to maintain our special license for medical assignments."

"Ah," he said. "I'm beginning to see, Ann. Is this the reason so many autopsies are performed on apparently nonsuspicious deaths? By this I mean, M.I.'s, cancer deaths, strokes—in other words, anything with a normality. Is this why so many autopsies are authorized?"

"Absolutely!" she whispered, leaning toward in a move-ment that allowed her blouse to open slightly. "But, I want to warn you, Robert. If you take this job, what I have just told you is very confidential."

"Why?"

"Well," she laughed softly. "I can't really say. That is, I'd like to, but I really don't totally know myself. Perhaps it's the controversy surrounding certain procedures and the government's involvement."

"But look," Dr. St. John intervened, "I'm not a Washing-ton insider. I just do what I'm supposed to do."

"I know. But do you see, Robert, why it is imperative to me personally to replace Dave as soon as reasonable, not just for me, but for the good of the whole institution?" She squeezed his hand.

"I'm beginning to understand," he said cautiously.

Silas approached and saw them holding hands. He

abruptly turned around in case he had interrupted something. He looked over his shoulder and offered to come back
later to check on them.

Ann caught him. "Don't go, Silas. I'll take the check
now."

"Oh, no ma'am. Your meal is on the house tonight."

"Silas, you're such a dear, but I can't allow you to do
that."

"Ma'am, it's management's pleasure. Please relax and
enjoy the rest of your evening." Silas smiled gracefully and
slowly retreated from the dinner table.

As they got up to leave, Ann extended her hand and
asked directly, with no hesitation: "Would you come to my
house to further discuss this position? There are some special
considerations you need to be aware of."

He could feel his pulse pounding, redness escaping from
his neck to his face. Stammering slightly, he attempted to
maintain his composure as he looked directly into her eyes.

"Sure," he squeaked in a manner that he deemed embarrassing. As he gained his composure, he mumbled that he
thought they had covered most of the necessary job description.

"No, Robert, not at all. As a matter of fact, you haven't
asked the most important question about the job."

"What's that?" he asked with a blank stare.

"Your salary, silly!

"Whew," he stammered, under his breath, thinking, *This
lady knows exactly what she wants.*

The memory of his good friend slowly faded from his
mind as Ann ushered him out of the restaurant toward his
car. They slowly sauntered away from the small twinkling
lights that encircled the restaurant.

When they reached his Jaguar, she said, "I like your
wheels. Follow me. I live in uptown only five blocks away."

No problem," he said, pulling out of the parking space
and following closely behind her Mercedes. He reassured
himself that they would have one more drink, discuss the

upcoming job situation and then he would make a hasty retreat back to the residents' quarters. He didn't dare look in the rearview mirror to adjust his tie, coat lapel or hair for fear of what he might see in his reflection.

Ann lived in an antebellum home only a few blocks from Commander's. She had renovated and decorated the home, which dated back to the 1850s.

"Here we are," she said as she popped out of her car onto the sidewalk.

"This is nice! Did you decorate this yourself?" Dr. St. John asked as they entered her home.

"Yes, interior design is a hobby of mine. What would you like a drink? The same as earlier?"

"Sure. Jack on the rocks is fine."

She brought his drink to him. He broached the subject of his salary by beginning: "How much more money can I make?"

"How much would you like to make?" she smiled.

He thought quickly to himself. He didn't want to mention Dave or make any comparisons to him. Although the drinks had clouded his judgment a bit, he was still an astute observer. He deliberately opted not to bring up Dave, especially during this conversation. The mention of his name at dinner had obviously agitated her, and he did not want to repeat that during this delicate topic. He wanted to keep the rapport he had established with her at dinner, and much as he might hate to admit it, he was basking in her attention. Her relationship with his best friend had lost its importance for now. Something told him he should keep it that way.

"Sit down on the couch with me," Ann coaxed flirtatiously."

He sat down next to her on the large, overstuffed sofa. "Ann, I really hadn't thought about the money."

"Robert, did you know we have our own special status within the federal government system?"

"No, I didn't know that." He allowed himself to relax on the couch.

"Oh yes, it can be quite lucrative, if you have an understanding of the kind of results they expect. But that can wait until tomorrow when I introduce you as the new E.R. director!" With that, she raised her drink as if to toast the decision.

"Hey, I kind of like that idea."

"Well, I would definitely say a celebration is in order." They clinked their glasses together in a semi-exuberant manner. A small amount of liquid spilled accidentally down Robert's chin, and they both laughed at his clumsiness. Ann reached over with a napkin as if to dry his chin and hesitated slightly, catching his eye. She kissed him lightly on the cheek, dropping the napkin from her hand and touching him lightly. Her kiss moved to his lips, and what had started as an action on her part became a joint effort with no protest from him. Their kiss and embrace became more passionate. Breaking slightly from the embrace, Ann took his hand and led him from the couch into her bedroom. All remembrances of people past and present had slipped from his consciousness as they resumed their embrace in her bed.

He slowly removed her clothes. Her body was much more beautiful than he had imagined from the conservative business suits she wore at the hospital. They made love passionately for several hours. Exhausted, they fell asleep in each other's arms.

Dr. St. John awoke not with a start, but with a slow realization of his whereabouts. He imagined his breathing to be as loud as the most obnoxious snore. After assessing his situation, he thought it best to beat a hasty trail to his room at the hospital to think about what in the hell he had done and how he was going to handle it.

Slowly, he kept reminding himself, as he slipped from under the sheets of Ann's bed, groping for the clothes he had discarded hastily the night before. His goal was to get out of that house unnoticed, reevaluate his situation and get a handle on his feelings. *A good strong cup of coffee would probably do the trick,* he thought.

After finding his shoes, he was close to succeeding in his mission of getting out of the bedroom door unnoticed when he heard the rumpling of the sheets as Ann rolled over in bed. As he quietly closed the door, for an instant he felt like a heel. He shuddered slightly at the thought of confronting Ann later at the hospital. After the events of last night, he would most certainly be the new E.R. director if his disappearing act didn't spoil his chances. What he needed most right now was to just get away and sort out all of these confusing feelings.

I do have to admit one thing, he said to himself with a hint of regret, *I like Ann Finn. She's a hell of a woman.* Sliding out the front door, he made a dash for his car. Fumbling for his car keys, he realized, *I'm still smashed, but I've got to get out of here.* He fired up the Jag and scooted down the road, parting the fog with each acceleration and looking for St. Charles.

* * *

"Code Blue in the I.C.U. Code Blue in the I.C.U." Dr. Henry Simms scrambled with a couple of nurses toward the back of the E.R. They hustled upstairs to the I.C.U. on the second floor. New Orleans Hospital's system for handling codes required that all resident physicians split duty to help with intubations and defibrillation wherever they were needed. Dr. Simms was currently on call for all codes in the hospital.

He and the two nurses rounded the corner to the I.C.U. The group of physicians, nurses and medical students that had gathered to help was slowly dispersing.

Dr. Simms spotted head nurse Sally Ortiz leaving the I.C.U. "What happened?" he asked her.

"Hi, Dr. Simms. It was a cardiac arrest. One of the patients admitted last night from the E.R."

"Which one?"

"I think it was the kid who had OD'ed."

"That kid was stable when we sent him up. Good grief…this place is turning into a morgue. I've been a resident here for three months and there are more 'crash and burns' in our admissions, especially off the streets, than I can ever recall at Cook County Hospital."

"You know how these indigents are," Sally said. "This is the way it is here at New Orleans Hospital. The people we treat generally don't take good care of themselves...any little event can precipitate tragic results."

"I know, but this..." He waved his hand at the body being rolled out of the I.C.U.

"Well, we can wait on the autopsy, along with the morbidity and mortality reports," Sally interrupted.

"Yeah, but we don't see them for six or eight months. They all go to National Health Care in Washington. Shoot, by the time I get mine back, I don't even remember some of the patients...much less what was wrong with them."

Sally Ortiz patted the young physician on the back. "I know, Dr. Simms, I know. Do the best you can."

Dr. Simms stood all alone in the hall outside the I.C.U. with his hands on his hips, frustrated. Sally left him and headed down the hall.

He turned around and walked slowly back to the E.R.

* * *

Dr. St. John actually slid onto St. Charles Avenue because the speed at which his car was traveling caused his tires to lose traction. It was a good thing it was early morning, with no traffic, or he would have been an accident waiting to happen. He was glad to have been with Ann, but out of the fog and the mist he was hurling through came the worst remorse he had ever known. *Damn, damn,* he thought. *My best friend is dead for forty-eight hours and I'm sleeping with his woman.*

An anger within him began to surface as he increased his acceleration to forty, fifty, sixty miles per hour through a twenty-mile-per-hour zone. He began to curse himself for betraying his best friend, and Ann Finn for making him weak. *How dare she screw me, if she had loved him so much?* His anger was inflamed by the alcohol in his system. Laughing outrageously, he pulled the steering wheel sharply to the left, crossing the grass median and the streetcar tracks centered on the median of St. Charles.

"Up the down lane!" he yelled, as he had so many times to his staff when a car wreck had come into the emergency room. "I can't believe that bitch. I can't believe me!"

Just in time, he crossed the median back into the right lane as he heard the clanging of a passing streetcar that would have most certainly sent him to heavenly ruins. It wasn't really himself he was concerned with. It was the image of his beloved Jag crumpled beyond repair under a three-ton streetcar. He quickly came back to his senses. He slowed down and congratulated himself on his good luck while driving like a drunken fool, until flashing blue lights reflecting in his rearview mirror shocked him back to reality.

Damn, the cops! I'm drunk, I think my license is expired and I almost crashed into a cherished New Orleans landmark, "A Streetcar named Desire." What next?" he thought as he pulled his car over.

An informally clad officer slowly approached the car. Robert squinted hard through the rearview mirror. He thought he recognized the lanky man coming up from behind in the mist.

"Well, Dr. Robert St. John, what a surprise," came a sarcastic quip. "Won't your chariot mind you this morning?" The officer chuckled.

Robert did a visual double take when he peered through the window. "Officer Sandy Elliott!" he said, as he rolled down his window. A hint of a smile appeared across his face. "You did say you would contact me. Have you been following me?"

"As a matter of fact, I have."

A jolted Robert dropped his jaw, completely astonished.

"Doctor, your driving stinks," he said as he moved

closer to the opened window. "Whew! And your breath does too. Get out of the car."

"Yes sir."

"Get in the patrol car," the officer demanded. Both men walked toward the car. Robert started to get into the rear.

"Get up here with me," the officer commanded.

Dr. St. John entered the patrol car on the passenger's side and slid in.

"I'm probably going to give you a break this time, Doc."

"Great. Oh thanks, you don't know what this means to me."

"Shut up and listen to me, okay? Have some coffee."

"Yes sir." The officer handed him a thermos of coffee. Robert gladly accepted a cup. "Just what I needed," he said.

"You're not really as drunk as I thought you were by the way you were driving down St. Charles. Man, you're crazy to drive like that. Hell's bells, man! You're a doctor. You're supposed to be an example. Christ, what if you had killed somebody? Do you think that would have helped anything? No!"

"Wait a minute, Officer," Dr. St. John said, suddenly remembering that Elliott had been following him. "You've been spying on me. I've got rights too."

"Cut the crap or I'll haul you into the drunk tank and have your face on page one of the *New Orleans Times Picayune* as 'The Saw Bones Sot' so fast you'll—" Elliott's face was turning red from anger. "You were on a public thoroughfare. Need I say more, Doctor?"

"Okay. Okay, but I'm curious. Don't misunderstand, I'm thankful you're giving me some slack by allowing me to go free. But why were you following me?"

"I need your help, Doctor St. John."

"My help? What do you mean? I'm confused."

"I need your help for the same reason that I've been following you for the past ten hours."

"What are you talking about?"

"I need your help in a possible murder investigation."

"Murder? Murder! You mean Dave? But you said he committed suicide. Everybody said so!"

"Notice I said 'possible' murder investigation."

"You mean I'm a suspect? Are you even daring to hint that I killed my best friend?" Robert's sobriety had returned, along with a great deal of anger.

"Damn!" Elliott rolled his eyes in exasperation. "How did you ever get through medical school? Do you honestly think I would be here talking to you about helping me if you were a suspect in this? You told me you weren't guilty simply by your behavior yesterday."

"Oh." Robert cleared his throat, embarrassed by his anger and confusion.

"Doctor, this thing probably is a suicide. My boss, Lieutenant Sheldon, would have my badge right now if he knew I was sitting here talking to you. First of all, I'm letting you off an obvious D.U.I., and second of all, I'm entrusting your help in what probably is a suicide."

"I don't understand, Officer? Why?"

"The autopsy, Doc! Or did your shenanigans last night with the lovely Miss Finn make you forget that?"

"Hey," Robert interrupted, his shame surfacing. "You don't have to get so personal."

"Doc, your alibi jives with the time of death and the nurses confirmed your presence in the emergency room at the time, making your involvement impossible as confirmed by the autopsy's time of death."

"Well, did the autopsy show that Dave was murdered instead of killing himself? Well! What the hell, man? You're confusing me."

"Now, hear me out, Doc. I've been doing this a while. This man had no reason to kill himself: no psychotic history, a model citizen. It's just a hunch really. I'm a good cop. If I turn over a few stones and nothing shows up other than the guy fooled us and just decided to kill himself, so be it. But what if my gut feeling is right and he was done in? If I didn't research this thing, go the extra mile, I would never forgive myself."

"How do I fit in?" Robert asked.

Elliott reached for the thermos. "My boss, Lieutenant Sheldon, thinks this is a suicide all the way. He really might pull my badge if he knew I was talking to you right now. He doesn't want me wasting my time researching this thing. Well, I've got my reasons."

"I see, Officer. You know I'll help. I'll help anyway I can. In a way, I hope your hunch is right. Dave is dead and that feels bad enough, but in a strange way, it would somehow make me feel better, you know, considering his family and his reputation. It would make me feel better to know it wasn't suicide. Do you understand?"

"I thought you'd feel that way, Doc. That's why I've asked for your help. But you've got to promise me that you will tell no one, and I mean absolutely no one and that includes breathtakingly beautiful women. I've already observed how easily you can be seduced."

Okay, okay. You don't have to get so personal. But has anything else happened that has made you suspicious?"

"No, or at least not anything I can tell you, Doc."

"Well, if we're going to be partners in this thing..."

"Who said I wanted a doctor to be my partner? Do you remember me asking you to be my partner?"

"Well, no. I just assumed."

"All I'm asking you to do is to look for any suspicious happenings—changes—something you don't feel comfortable with. Okay?"

"Yeah, I understand. Do you think I'm in danger?"

"Lord, you never answered me: How did you get through medical school? Did I ever say you were in danger? Do you think I would be confiding in you right now if I honestly thought you were in danger?"

"Hey, Elliott, I'm just out of my field a little here. I just want to understand. Okay?"

"Sorry. Look, Doc. Your friend in all probability committed suicide, but New Orleans is an unusual place filled with

40

unusual people, and stranger things have happened."

"You're just a good cop, aren't you, Officer Elliott?"

Sandy Elliott stammered at the compliment. "I'd like to think so."

"Yes sir, I think you are." With that, Robert extended his hand and the two of them shook.

"Listen, Doc. Are you going to the funeral?"

"Yes, I am."

"Good, I want you to be on the lookout for anybody who doesn't seem to quite fit in. Do you know what I mean? Someone who doesn't have a legitimate reason to be there."

"Okay. I know what you're saying. Anything else?"

"No. Here's my phone number." Officer Elliott handed Robert a piece of paper. "It has a beeper number on it too."

"I understand," the doctor said.

"Any questions?"

"No." The doctor released his grip from the officer's hand and stepped out of the car.

"Call me the minute you get back from…wherever it is you have to go."

"Tennessee…Knoxville."

"And especially call me if anything unusual happens."

"Sure thing, Officer. Thanks."

"Keep it under your hat, Doc, and be careful. Are you sure you're okay to drive?"

"Yeah, I've sobered up. I'll call you."

"You do that."

Dr. St. John tried not to wobble on the way back to his car. At first he felt immediate relief, but as soon as he started to drive away, he was overcome with a huge wave of confusion and concern. He groped the wheel. "Murder! What in the hell is going on?"

Morning traffic had begun to swell as he approached downtown. Robert almost ran off the road as he fumbled with his glove box. He stuffed the card Officer Elliott had given him into the crowded jumble of parking tickets and registration papers. As he pulled into his parking space at the hospital, he glanced over at Ann's reserved space.

"Good, she's not here," he thought.

He slipped past the E.R. entrance into the back stairwell to return to his room. Entering the hallway to his temporary quarters, he saw Sally Ortiz round the corridor, heading for the morning E.R. shift.

"Hey Doc! Come here!" she called.

He didn't really want to talk to her this morning. He felt a pang of guilt. Sally stopped dead in her tracks approximately three yards from him.

"Well, look what the proverbial cat dragged in. You look awful! You need to shave and change your clothes. Did you sleep in them?"

"No, Sally! But thanks for your interest," he retorted.

"The rumor mill has it that you're going to be the next E.R. director." Sally hugged him in congratulations. "Whew! You stink like a brewery! Are you drunk?" She pushed him away. "It's a good thing Dr. Simms is going to double up the next two days for you, because you sure as hell can't work like this."

Sally Ortiz came from an extended Mexican family. She looked at the emergency room members as an extension of that family. Everyone took her overbearing and protective manner in stride. She was the mother of the unit.

"Thanks for all you've done, Sally. It means a lot to me. And tell Dr. Simms thanks for covering for me so I can go to the funeral. I guess I'll be the new director when I get back. Ann offered me the job last night at Commander's Palace."

Sally jumped back. She stood erect with her mouth open. She stuck out her index finger and moved it in a side-to-side manner, indicating that she strongly disapproved.

"Is that where you're coming from, smiling and looking like this?" she exclaimed, drawing in a huge breath.

Dr. St. John offered no protest.

Sally gasped again. When she got extremely excited, she started speaking half in Spanish and half in English. He didn't understand a word, but she was obviously fiercely upset and heartily disappointed in him

She turned to walk down the hall and, maintaining her mother's role, continued to let him know she strongly disapproved.

"I told you I didn't like that woman and for you to be mindful of her, and you come here looking like this—our new director and *this* is how he behaves." As she rounded the corner, he thought he heard her say, "...and Dave's not even buried yet."

As he opened the door to the residents' room, he noticed the message light blinking on the telephone. The operator gave him the message that Ann Finn wanted to see him in her office, so he dialed her number.

"Hello, Ann Finn's office."

"Jerri? It's Dr. St. John."

"Dr. St. John, Ms. Finn wants you to come to her office as soon as possible."

"Okay," he sighed. "Tell her I'll be right there as soon as I change and shower."

"Okay, Doctor, I'll tell her."

What was that in her voice? he wondered as he hung up the phone. *Does the whole hospital know I slept with Ann last night?* He slipped out of his clothes and into the shower. *Showers are the allies of all physicians*, he thought as the invigorating waters flowed over his body. "Yeah," he said out loud, berating himself, "especially for a doctor whose best friend has just killed himself and he gets plastered and sleeps with the dead guy's girlfriend. Great!" As he opened his mouth and let the water cleanse the nasty taste on his breath, he thought how wonderful it would be if shower water had a healthy dose of Prozac in it. He could use it.

Dr. St. John slipped into clean scrubs, checked his face, and practically ran down the hall toward Ann's office. He didn't want to see anyone else who would chastise him for his behavior like Sally had. He didn't knock on the door but just strode in.

"Hi, Dr. St. John," smiled Jerri. "She's waiting in her

office for you. Go on in."

If Ann was mad at him, she hadn't let Jerri know, because Jerri had smiled at him, he thought as he entered Ann's office. He had already rehearsed his apology speech on his way down the hall.

"Ann," he said softly as he approached her.

"Robert!" Rising from her desk, she walked around it to greet him. If she was mad, she didn't show it. A large smile illuminated her face. He wasn't sure how to address her. Should he shake her hand or kiss her?

As she reached him, he began to offer an explanation. "Ann, about last night, uh, this morning I had to..."

Before he could finish, she had embraced him and was kissing him passionately. The nature of the kiss caught him off guard. Soon, however, he was taken away by her ardor.

As their lips parted slightly, she breathed deeply and began. "Darling, there's no need to explain this morning." She kissed him again. "We've both been through an ordeal." She looked at him, and for the moment he completely lost his sense of guilt concerning the circumstances of their relationship.

"But Ann," he protested. "Dave. What about Dave?"

"Robert, there's nothing wrong with us consoling each other. We're suffering a great loss but there is nothing we can do to bring him back. Don't feel guilty. I know what you're going through but we will make it through this together."

Dr. St. John felt horrible for turning her luminous smile into a plaintive call for support.

"Robert, I just want to know one thing. Do you care about me? That's all I want to know. It's more important to me than you might think. I've lost so much. Please don't think I'm cold-hearted or bad. It would really hurt me if you thought of me that way."

"Oh no, no, Ann. I'll support and help you any way I can. You should know that. I don't want you to worry about anything. Promise me."

"You're a godsend."

They kissed again. *I like this woman—and she likes me,* he thought, then said: "Ann, we have to make plans to go to the funeral."

Ann hesitated momentarily, diverting her eyes. "I don't know if I can. Robert, hold me." She pulled him tightly to her. He was only aware of her breasts pushing against his chest.

"You don't have to if you don't want to," he said, holding her as tightly as she was holding him. "But don't you think it's the right thing to do? I'm his—I *was* his best friend, and you were—" he stammered, searching for the correct word.

"Perhaps you're right," she agreed.

"That's right, Ann. We have to be strong now. After all, I'm your E.R. director, and we have to stay close."

"Yes! Okay, we'll take your car and on the way, I can explain everything you need to know about your new position and the protocols and special responsibilities. It takes twelve hours to get to Knoxville, doesn't it?"

With that, she coaxed him out of her embrace. She reached around him to touch the message button on her desk. "Jerri?

"Yes, Ms. Finn."

"I will be going to the funeral with Dr. St. John after all. Please cancel all my appointments for the next—" She turned back to him, "How long will we be gone?"

"Three days," Robert responded.

"Did you hear that, Jerri?"

"Yes, Ms. Finn."

Ann released the button, smiling at Robert. "Good, it's settled. We have so much to discuss!" She kissed him again. "Besides, we still have a lot to learn about each other."

Chapter Three

ulling the XKE up to Ann's front door, Dr. St. John turned off the engine and sat in the car, contemplating the events of the past few days. He laughed out loud remembering driving over the streetcar median on St. Charles and grew sad when he thought about Dave. When he thought about Ann, he smiled but thought she must be Rasputin to have totally captured his imagination so quickly. He spontaneously felt a twinge of unease when he remembered his roadside conversation with Officer Elliott.

Shaking his head, he consoled himself. *Sandy is a nice guy, but he's wrong,* he thought. *After all, there was no struggle and Dave was strong as a mule. He would have fought if there had been an intruder, and the guy had no enemies. I'll put that thought out of my mind and make as much good as I can out of a horrible situation.* As he got up out of his car to get Ann, she came bounding down the front steps with a small suitcase. "Don't bother," she said, as he attempted to help her with her suitcase. "I'm a strong woman."

"Well, hop in and get comfortable. It's going to be a long drive, " he said, looking at her in amazement. Gone was her ever-present career suit. She looked resplendent in a tight body suit and boots. She could have easily been a Las Vegas showgirl instead of the health care executive that she was. He started the car.

"Wait! She protested so loudly that he surged up from his seat slightly.

"What?"

She twisted her torso in the seat and asked incredulously, "Aren't you going to kiss me, Doctor?"

Smiling, he slid his hand behind her neck and leaned forward to kiss her. Before his lips reached hers, a petulant finger prevented their lips from touching. "On second thought, Doctor, it's going to be a long trip. Maybe we should save that for later."

He kissed her anyway, and they became so amorous in their embrace that he felt they should return to her house to complete their obvious desire for each other. She pulled away from him in a demure way. "Let's go. We have an awfully long drive ahead of us."

Reluctantly, he pulled the car onto the street and began the difficult journey home. "Do you want to take the scenic route or go by interstate?"

"Interstate makes more sense this trip, doesn't it, Robert? We'll take the scenic route next time."

"Have you ever been to Tennessee before?" he asked, quizzing her in a circuitous manner to avoid asking if she had ever been to Tennessee with Dave.

"Never been," she said coolly, apparently picking up on the inference and resenting it.

"Oh. Well, it's beautiful this time of year. The leaves in the areas around the Smoky Mountains are just about to change colors, and the flowers are really magnificent, if you're interested in that sort of thing."

The interstate loomed forward, and he passed familiar signposts on what was normally a happy trip. He had left the top down on his car, as the rain of the previous days had disappeared. Beautiful Louisiana sunshine beamed overhead. "So, what do you want to talk about?"

Ann didn't respond immediately. Her chestnut hair whipped behind her in the open car. "Oh Robert, let's not talk about anything for a while."

"I understand," he said and touched her hand. She jumped slightly, apparently startled by his touch. But she turned and smiled at him with her almond-shaped eyes. Then she turned her head away and continued to let her hair blow wildly in the wind. Robert turned his attention toward the road in an attempt to leave her to her own thoughts.

Several minutes passed, and the mesmerizing narrow lane lulled him into a state of comfort.

"You think I'm a bad girl, don't you? Don't you?" Her words shook him.

All he could manage was, "Huh?"

"It's true," she pouted, pulling a handkerchief from her purse and wiping a tear from her cheek.

He took a hard look at Ann Finn. She was not the person she had appeared to be for all of these months. Physically appealing, no doubt, but instead of the businesslike professional he had perceived, she was warm and sensitive. Perhaps an emotional chameleon. She continued, "I know your friend Sally Ortiz doesn't approve of us being together and…" she stopped, choking back words.

"Ann," he said, stroking her face. Suddenly he felt as if he were the superior force in their brief relationship. "Don't pay any attention to Nurse Ortiz. What did she say to you?"

"Nothing, Robert. She didn't have to."

"Ann, it's probably just that our relationship evolved so quickly and under such tragic circumstances. Everyone is upset, that's all."

"Reassure me. Tell me you want to be with me, no matter what the circumstances." She glanced at him with tear-reddened eyes.

His heart melted. He pulled her shivering body against him. "I want to be with you no matter what and regardless of the gossip," he whispered. He kissed a tear that had slid down her face to her lips. "Do you understand me?"

She nodded her head affirmatively against his shoulder. Her confession concerning their affair put him at ease with himself at last.

The droning of the road and Ann's emotional release

had quieted their situation. He continued driving with her head tucked under his right arm. She slowly fell asleep against him.

Ann awoke from her sleep with a start. "Where are we?" she asked abruptly.

"About one third of the way there," Robert responded, without losing view of the highway. "We've made good time, and you had yourself a good rest."

"I really did!" she said as she extended her tan arms over the top of the car, yawning and stretching.

"Are you hungry?" he asked, finally looking her way.

"I could eat. How about you?"

"Sure thing. What do you want?"

"Robert, I like seafood. Is that okay with you?"

"Absolutely. You must have read my mind. I think there's a seafood place up ahead near the state line." With that remark, a broad smile appeared on Robert's face.

"What is it?" she quizzed him.

"Nothing."

"Then why are you smiling if it's nothing?"

"Well, it just occurred to me. I'm riding down the inter-state with my boss, with whom I'm sexually involved."

"That's it?" she asked with a grimace. "That's not funny."

"Well, it is to me. I've never had sex with any boss of mine before. Never had the urge to."

"Will you shut up?" She leaned over and kissed his cheek and nibbled his ear. "Did you think that was sexy?"

Robert laughed. "Look, there's the restaurant!"

"Great! I'm starving, aren't you?"

He nodded in agreement as he took the exit leading to the World's Greatest Seafood Restaurant. He pulled into the nearly full parking lot.

"Look at the people!" he said in amazement.

"I don't care. I'm starving." They kissed as they got out of the car and then walked hand-in-hand into the restaurant.

They crossed the foyer into the massive dining hall. The

tables were almost full, but there wasn't a line.

"Great. I hate to wait in lines," Ann said. "I have no patience," she said, pointing to an empty table.

Passing by the PLEASE SEAT YOURSELF sign, they sat down and picked up the menus on the table. A waitress whisked by them and yelled, "Someone will be with ya'll in a minute."

"Thanks," they said together. Turning his attention to Ann, Robert caught himself eyeing her slyly over the top of his menu. The sun had added a touch of color to her face and arms while she had slept. Her body was accented by the tautness of her body suit. He caught himself staring at her breasts. He forced himself to study the menu in front of him.

"Alligator tail!" she exclaimed triumphantly. "That's what I want!"

"Alligator?" Robert rolled his eyes.

"Oh yes. I love it. It's delicious if it's done right."

"I believe I'll stick with shrimp."

A waitress approached their table. "Anything to drink before I take your order?" she asked.

"Beer for me," stated Robert.

"Me too!" parroted Ann.

"Okay. I'll be back with two beers in just a second."

After their orders were brought to the table, Robert brought up some subjects he had been curious about but had been reluctant to mention. "Ann, where are you from?"

"Nowhere really. Army Brat. We even lived in Europe and Japan for a while."

"Oh, I see."

"Why do you ask?"

"Curious. We just don't know each other very well."

"I know. You want a taste of my alligator?" she asked, holding a piece to his face with her fork.

"No thanks. I'll stick with my shrimp."

Finally, he asked her what he most wanted to know. "How did you and Dave meet?"

Without looking up from her plate, she replied simply,

"Work."

"Were you close?"

Dropping her fork abruptly to her plate, she looked at him and said, "Robert, this has been a tragedy. I want to get through this and go on with my life. I've had enough tragedy in my life, and I don't want to dwell on it."

"Sorry," he said as he peeled another shrimp. "Dave and I were close, Ann, and he never really talked much about your relationship. I won't bring it up again." His voice trailed off to a whisper. "Just curious." He resolved that he wouldn't bring up Dave again with her.

They continued their meals in near total silence. Each ordered another beer and watched the endless parade of cars on the highway.

As he received the check from the waitress and paid her, Ann excused herself from the table and suggested they spend the night somewhere close by. They left the restaurant and found a small motel with individual cabins.

"Oh, let's stay here! It reminds me of a place we used to visit when I was a child." Her disposition immediately brightened,

"You're the boss," he enthusiastically joined in. A neon light beamed VACANCY. Robert parked the car directly in front of the motel.

After checking in, he was uncertain of Ann's state of mind toward him. *I guess I have been somewhat insensitive toward her,* he thought. He decided he would apologize as soon as they got settled into the room. Maybe he could explain his curiosity to her. He got the bags out of the car and brought them into the room.

"Ann, where are you?" He looked around the room, trying to adjust his eyes to the dark. Two hands clasped his face from behind, covering his eyes. He jumped forward, about two feet, turning toward her. "Ann! You're naked!"

"And you're not," she said as she approached him. She took off his clothes, one piece after another.

Well, so much for her state of mind, he thought. They did not stop making love for at least two hours.

"That was good," she sighed, languishing back on the bed completely nude.

"Yes it was," he concurred, admiring her body. They fell into a deep sleep, not awaking until mid-morning of the next day.

After dressing and packing the car, Robert pulled over to a gas station before returning to the interstate.

"Want some coffee?" he shouted over his shoulder as he went to pay for the gas.

"Yes, black. Thanks!"

They sat in the car for a second, sipping their coffee. "This should wake us up and get us going," she said, looking at him sweetly.

Reflecting on the past few days, he blurted out, "I like you, Ann."

"I like you too." They kissed gently. "Some people misunderstand you, I think."

He blushed as he remembered that she had been overly sensitive to his awkward statements.

"I don't give a damn about anything as long as I know you like me, and I think you do," she said.

They spoke very little as they continued northward. Ann obviously enjoyed allowing her hair to blow out the uncovered car. It whipped violently. She seemed to enjoy it, and he relished in her delight.

As they approached Knoxville, Ann leaned over to him and said, "Let's go to the graveside services only."

"Ann," he protested, "I talked to Mr. Wyatt the other night. I feel very obligated to go to see him."

"Robert, I'm begging you. If you've come to care for me at all in the past few days, you'll understand. I just don't think I can possibly go through any more pain."

One look at her face, and he acquiesced. "Okay," he mumbled.

"Oh, thank you! You're a dear, simply a love. You can visit his family later in the year, when things are less emotional."

He shook his head in a positive manner but felt full of shame anyway.

"Robert, take me to see something that I might enjoy seeing, something that tells me a little about you."

Without hesitation, he said, "Let's go to campus."

"The University of Tennessee?"

"Yeah."

"Okay," she nodded. "That could be fun."

He drove her around the campus, showing her which dorms he had stayed in as a student. "Look!" he exclaimed. "The stadium is open. Let's go in and look around. I really want to see it."

"Sure!" she said, feigning exaggerated interest.

They climbed up the ramp leading to the huge Neyland Stadium, "Home of the Volunteers." As they reached the mezzanine, Ann said, "Wow! The field looks so small from here."

This had been one of his favorite places as a child. He was careful not to mention that this had been one of Dave's favorite places too.

"Ann, I remember when Tennessee beat Notre Dame here in 1979. That was one of the most exciting days of my life. We were *big* underdogs, and—"

"Hey! You guys!" came a voice from below. "You can't stay here!"

They looked below them at one of the groundskeepers.

Dr. St. John responded, "The gate was open."

"Well, you still can't be here." The old man turned back to his work.

"Okay. We're going."

Robert took Ann by the hand and led her down the steep ramp to his car.

"I bet you had lots of girlfriends when you were here,"

Ann said slyly.

"What?" he said, looking over his shoulder at her. "You never cease to amaze me. Where did that come from?"

She continued, "And for some reason, that makes me jealous, thinking about you with another woman."

Laughing, he led her by her hand to the car. "You just don't strike me as the jealous type. Besides, with your looks, you could get any guy you wanted."

They looped around the campus and headed to the cemetery. Judging by his watch, they had just missed the church services. The cemetery was outside town, nestled in the foothills of the Great Smoky Mountains. People had begun to arrive for the graveside service as they pulled up. He caught himself almost confiding in Ann about Officer Elliott's request and the conversation they had. He stifled any thought of that as he remembered the admonition he had been given: "Don't mention this to anyone."

Southern funerals are unusual. They are times of sorrow and remorse, but these events also are a way for people who were not close to the deceased to socialize in a subdued, comforting manner. Robert talked with several old friends who offered condolences. They recollected old times and shared poignant remembrances of Dr. Wyatt as a youth. Robert kept his emotions intact, remembering very well the Southern custom of grieving only in the civilized comfort of your own home.

Robert spotted his sister Susan along the edge of the crowd. He waved for her to come forward and meet him.

"Hi, Sis." He hugged her in a "big brother who's come home" fashion.

She kissed him on the cheek. "How's my brother the E.R. doctor?"

"Okay, I guess, considering," he responded, almost losing his composure.

Susan quickly changed the subject. "Who's this with you, Robert?"

"Sis, this is Ann Finn, an administrator at New Orleans Hospital."

Ann and Susan shook hands. "My pleasure to meet you, Ms. Finn."

"Likewise," Ann smiled broadly.

Susan St. John had short hair cut like the skater Dorothy Hamill, whom she admired greatly. She worked at Oak Ridge National Laboratory near Knoxville. She had never married—"too busy" she had always said. Robert considered her a genius. She knew her brother very well, and she was extremely outspoken. She gave Robert a knowing glance, guessing that he was involved with Ann. Robert was relieved when a friend of Susan's called for her from the other side of the cemetery.

"Will I see you later?" she quizzed.

"I don't know. Ann and I have to get back to work, Sis. We'll see."

"You know I have a lot of questions concerning Dave. We all do." She looked at him in the protective way only sisters can when they hurt for an older brother.

"Okay" was all he could say.

"Good." She kissed him on the cheek, implying she was not going to pry any more. She scurried off to her beckoning friend, looking back over her shoulder. "Nice to meet you, Ann."

Ann simply held up her hand in acknowledgment.

Robert introduced Ann to others as merely a friend from work who had been close to Dr. Wyatt. Life had never seemed more real to him. He was acutely aware of everything around him.

In the corner of his eye, he noticed a very well-dressed gentleman. The man seemed to know him, but Robert did not recognize anything about him. He began to feel edgy as the man's eyes followed him.

"Bobby!" called a voice from behind him. He hadn't been called that since he was a child. Turning, he saw the pained face of John Wyatt, Dave's dad. They embraced warmly. Mr. Wyatt had been the one who had encouraged Dave and Robert as children to become doctors. He would have been an extraordinary doctor himself if his environment hadn't limited him. He had a warmth and a compassion that Robert hadn't found in any other person, and in many ways, he had been their role model. Robert felt tremendous respect for this man who had spent so much time with him and his best friend when they were young.

Their words to each other were brief. "How are you holding up, Mr. Wyatt?" Robert asked.

"As well as can be expected, Bobby."

A member of the congregation came up and whispered something into Mr. Wyatt's ear. "I've got to go, Bobby. Are you coming by the house later?"

"We'll see, Mr. Wyatt. If not, I'll come back to see you during the holidays."

"Good seeing you, Bobby," Mr. Wyatt said, as he was led toward the graveside.

Looking around, Robert couldn't find Ann. As the service began he joined the group of mourners gathered close to the prepared graveside. He could barely make out the words of the preacher due to the drove of people who had turned out to mourn the unexpected tragedy.

Ann must be here somewhere, he thought, looking around the crowd for her tiny figure. A movement in the parking lot gripped his attention. It was Ann. He could see her sitting in a car with the older, well-dressed gentleman he had seen but could not recognize. *Who in the world could that be and what was Ann doing with him?* He forced himself to maintain his composure. There was enough unease in the crowd around him as it was. He faced the graveside and the mourners and joined in the ritual of bereavement.

From where he stood, he could see that Ann and this older gentleman were having a very demonstrative discussion. He had lost track of the service, and now people were starting to move away from the graveside toward their cars. He decided to go over to the black sedan and introduce himself. Ann noticed him and quickly grabbed the man's arm and pointed to him. He warned himself, *Don't come across as a jealous, immature jerk.*

The two immediately got out of the car to greet him as he approached. Ann calmly walked over to Robert and gently took his hand.

"There's someone here I would like for you to meet," she said to him.

Dr. St. John looked up at the man expectantly.

"Robert, this is Richard Castner. He was an associate of Dr. Wyatt's through hospital administration."

Robert extended his hand and shook the older man's hand graciously. He suddenly remembered seeing this gentleman somewhere before, but couldn't put his finger on exactly where that had been.

"Don't you recognize him, Robert?" Ann quizzed. "I thought even you would recognize Richard Castner of the NHCO."

Ann smiled, trying to relieve the awkwardness of the introduction.

"Oh yes, Mr. Castner. I apologize. I've seen you on television several times. It's an honor to meet you." Robert's bluntness came forward: "What brings you to Tennessee?"

Mr. Castner patted Robert on the shoulder. "It's a pleasure to meet you, Doctor. I came for Dr. Wyatt's funeral. He was a very special young man and I don't have to tell you what a tragic loss this is for our medical community."

Robert nodded affirmatively but was a little confused by Castner's words. He looked at Ann curiously.

"Look," said Ann. "There's a lot to discuss and explain. I told you the new E.R. directorship was a very important position with many responsibilities. That's what Mr. Castner has come to explain."

Before anything else could be said, Castner interrupted,

"Look, I have an idea. Let's go and get a nice lunch and drive up to the top of the beautiful Smoky Mountains together and get to know each other a little better. Funerals never have been my strong suit," he chuckled, uncomfortably. "How about you, Doctor?"

"They're against my religion," was Robert's only response.

Chapter Four

The view from the top of the Appalachian chain summit was spectacular when they arrived. They had driven above the mist from which the Cherokee people had given the mountains their name, Smoky Mountains.

After admiring the view from inside the black Mercedes-Benz, Robert interrupted the silence.

"So, what's so unusual about the situation at New Orleans Hospital that the head of the National Health Care Organization comes to see us personally?"

"Let's get out of the car and enjoy the view," Richard Castner said. "I love this place."

The trio stepped out onto a graveled scenic overlook and surveyed the white cushion of clouds that carpeted the entire landscape below them.

"Dr. St. John," Castner continued, "I knew Dr. David Wyatt very well. I wanted to attend his funeral out of respect for him and his family. This isn't totally about seeing you and Ann."

"Why didn't Dave tell me about a lot of this, Ann? I feel now as if I didn't even know my best friend."

"Obviously, Robert, he was a very private person, more than any of us realized, considering he just took his own life and none of us had a clue that he was capable of doing anything like that!"

Robert again noticed Ann's agitation at the mention of Dr. Wyatt.

Richard Castner pulled out his National Health Security card.

"You know what this is, don't you, Dr. St. John?

"Of course. It's the health security card that all U.S. citizens have carried since the legislation passed a few years ago. All my patients at New Orleans use it."

Castner continued, "This card represents an enormous hurdle for the administration, as I'm sure you understand. "Do you have any idea what kind of political blood it took to get this program passed to protect the patients you treat?"

"Yeah, I can imagine. But what does that have to do with Dr. Wyatt, Ann, and myself?"

"Well, Dr. St. John, as Ann has informed you, the E.R. directorship of New Orleans Hospital has a great deal to do with this card. In order to get the bill passed, we had to make many, many, many compromises, as you can imagine."

"I'm not the political type, Mr. Castner, but I can imagine."

"And when I say political blood, Dr. St. John, I mean that literally. Blood."

"Okay, okay. So?

"Hold on. Did you realize, Doctor, that New Orleans Hospital is the only medical institution in the country that is being allowed to do autopsies on virtually every death in the hospital? This was unheard of at any institution prior to the passage of the bill that legalized this card. There is a crying need to perform this procedure on people who die to better understand pathology, don't you agree?"

"Of course I do."

"Dr. St. John, did you know that the National Institute of Health is allowed to do certain procedures? Johns Hopkins, the Mayo Clinic are allowed to do other procedures, and many others have certain privileges, but your institution was chosen for this one thing—autopsy."

"Damn. I didn't know that. Why isn't it common knowledge?"

"Because politically, the passage of the congressional bill that okayed this little piece of plastic," he flashed the red, white and blue credit-card—sized object in his face, "was a miracle. The conservatives didn't like it, and the liberals didn't like it. Buried in that 32,458 page document is the authority for this card to allow for special considerations such as the 'knowledge gathering' that your institution and other institutions around the country are practicing. And this knowledge gathering has to be done precisely, accurately, and follow the absolute letter of the law, which is stated in that monster of a document, or—" Castner snapped his fingers, "those privileges will be taken away by the people who watch over us and, Doctor, that includes people who watch over me too."

"The E.R. director was felt to be the best candidate to oversee the project and the paperwork for several reasons," Ann interrupted.

"Yes, Ann will explain further about the details on your way back to New Orleans, I'm sure."

"Well, I see," Robert touched Ann on her arm. "I see, Ann, why you've been so upset. This has implications far beyond what I understood." Ann stood there and silently nodded her head yes.

"I've got to get back to Washington. I feel very good about your selection, Ann." With that, Mr. Castner shook Robert's hand. "Your work is very important, Doctor. Take pride in that, and excel!"

The ride back to his XKE was slow due to traffic. The trio talked only about the sights the mountains presented and the beauty of the splendid vistas. There was no talk of responsibility, government agencies, dead friends, or new jobs to be learned. They finally arrived at the cemetery, where Robert's car was parked. Dr. St. John and Ann shook hands with Castner and wished him a safe journey.

Ann and Robert walked hand in hand back to the car. They kissed for a very long time. He felt closer to Ann now and much more comfortable in her presence.

As they left, heading back to New Orleans, the freshly covered grave of Dr. Dave Wyatt slowly disappeared.

A sense of euphoria overwhelmed Robert as he and Ann slowly made their way to New Orleans. They constantly held hands and stared at each other. Robert could not believe his good luck. The enthusiasm he had for his new job was only equaled by the way he had felt when he had been elected New Orleans Hospital's Intern of the Year as a neophyte M.D. As they approached New Orleans, Robert found himself wondering if he was falling in love with Ann.

"Let's check the hospital before we go to my place, Robert."

"Yeah, good idea."

The skyline of New Orleans loomed on the horizon.

"Robert, let me ask you something. Does the hectic pace of the emergency room ever get to you, you know, bring you down?"

"Oh, sometimes, but it doesn't last long." He looked at her curiously, "Why do you ask?"

"Because the new position will bring a lot more paperwork and detail into your schedule."

"I don't understand your point."

"Well, we don't know what made Dave do what he did. I just couldn't stand it if the same thing happened to you," she said, laying her head on his shoulder.

"Oh dear, dear Ann. Don't worry. If I start to become too stressed, I'll let you know," he said, sighing deeply as he kissed her on the top of her head. "Don't worry."

They drove over the Lake Pontchartrain Causeway, five miles of bridge over the huge lake. New Orleans Hospital loomed in the crescent city. Built in the 1930s by the Kingfisher himself, Huey Long, it now appeared to be a huge mausoleum tomb sitting beside the modern Superdome. The hospital represented a return to a different day.

As they pulled up to the hospital, Ann pointed to her

parking place. "Use mine, Robert. It's closer."

"You're too good to me," he joked.

"Are you going with me to the administration office?"

"I'll meet you there in a few minutes."

"Hurry up!"

"Okay. Sure," He politely kissed her on the cheek.

"Remember, Robert, that as the director, you'll only be required to work two shifts. You'll be spending time with me overseeing things and doing the paperwork that is required."

He nodded his understanding as he headed to the E.R. As soon as he entered the corridor approaching the E.R., he was greeted by a familiar "Code Blue I.C.U. Code Blue I.C.U." blaring over the hospital intercom. Instinctively he broke into a run and headed for the nearest stairwell, which led to the I.C.U. on the third floor. Dr. Simms, who had covered for him while he was gone, was intubating the patient. As doctors and nurses poured into the room, a controlled bedlam proceeded in an attempt to save the patient's life.

"What's the patient's status?" Dr. St. John barked to no one in particular.

"Fifty-year-old with multiple system disease. Was stable until he coded," shouted a nurse.

"I'm in!" Dr. Simms said. "He's intubated." He signaled the nurse to begin ventilation with an ambu-bag to facilitate oxygen administration.

"Do we have a rhythm yet?" one of the nurses shouted.

"Looks like ventricular fibrillation. We need to defibril-late," shouted Dr. St. John as he reached for the defibrillating paddles in the crash cart that one of the students had rolled in.

"Charge to 200, and clear!" With that instruction, every-one cleared the bedside, and Robert pressed the discharge button on the paddles that were placed over the cardiac area of the patient's chest. With a "fthum," the surge of potentially life-saving voltage surged through the patient's body, causing the thorax and upper extremities to bolt upward off the bed.

"Any rhythm?" yelled Dr. St. John.

"No pulse," said Dr. Simms, looking at Robert.

"No pulse," reiterated a junior medical student who had entered the room with an influx of doctors and nurses.

Robert said, "It looks like we have electromechanical disassociation. Any pulse?

"No," came a chorus of voices of nurses who were simultaneously checking pulse points and readying epinephrine and lidocaine waiting for his order.

"Any blood pressure?"

"No."

"Do we have blood gases yet?"

"Not yet, Doctor."

"Then let's give more epi and prepare to defibrillate again."

"Epinephrine given."

As the EKG rhythm continued to beep across the monitor, Robert and the staff continued to repeat cardiac protocol in an attempt to save the patient's life.

The medical student proclaimed excitedly: "Finally got the blood gases and they're horrible. Good thing you went ahead and pushed bicarb."

After thirty minutes of effort, Robert asked a nurse for the time.

"11:31 a.m."

Robert turned to the nurse and said, "I'm declaring this patient dead at 11:31 a.m." With that he turned to leave the room as all the personnel discontinued chest compressions and began the clean-up of the room.

"Wait!" screamed the medical student. "The patient still has a cardiac rhythm on the monitor!"

Robert returned to the room. "Your lesson for tonight is to study electromechanical disassociation," he said, patting the student on the shoulder, "because you just saw a classic textbook example."

"Oh," the embarrassed student mumbled.

Robert turned to go to the E.R. when over the intercom came: "Dr. Robert St. John. Please report to Administrator Finn's office."

He stopped dead in place and took the opposite direction to Ann's. As he rounded the corner toward administration, he heard the unmistakable voice of Sally Ortiz reaching all the way out in the hall from Ann's office.

"What's she mad about now?" he asked, recognizing the unmistakable mix of Spanish and English that indicated that Sally was pissed off. As he opened the door leading to Ann's office, Jerri rolled her eyes and said, "I don't know if you really want to get mixed up in this, Doctor."

"Who paged me?"

"I think Ann did."

"What do you mean he has to go to Mexico? Why?" Sally blared, with her hands on her hips, jutting her chin out in defiance.

"Who's going to Mexico?" asked Robert as he entered the room.

"Well, the E.R. director returns," Sally ranted while tapping her foot in staccato.

"You are, Robert," responded Ann in her most authoritative tone.

"Why?" He looked at both women with a confused smile.

"Porque?" Sally asked with her hands on her hips.

"Nurse Ortiz! Why do you mix two languages when you're angry?" an exasperated Robert retorted.

Ann interrupted, "You know why she does it, Robert!"

"You don't know anything, Señorita." Sally turned to face Ann in a threatening manner.

Dr. St. John stepped between the two women.

"Time-out!" he shouted, making the football symbol with his hands. Extending his arms from his chest, he physically separated the two women.

Turning to Ann, he asked calmly, "Why am I going to Mexico?"

"El Sexo," nodded Sally with a tilted head held in a disapproving manner.

"That is enough!" shouted Ann, her face red.

"That is enough," repeated an exasperated Robert.

"Well, I don't give a damn what you two do, but I need someone to replace you in the E.R. Poor Dr. Simms has exhausted himself working in your place."

"Good point," Robert said as he turned his gaze to Ann, still holding the women apart with his outstretched hands.

"As soon as you accepted the E.R. directorship, I had Jerri call in a replacement. Here's her resume." Ann reached across her desk, grabbed a document and threw it at Sally. "As a matter of fact, she should be checking in today with you, Nurse Ortiz."

Sally snatched the credentials from Ann's hand, reading the name Dr. Elizabeth Sheridan Johnson on the cover page, and followed this observation with a noncommittal "hmm."

"You are excused now, Nurse Ortiz." Ann waved toward the door, expecting the nurse to leave.

"I'll go," Sally shot back. "This lady doctor better be good and experienced. It's a war down there! Or have you two forgotten?"

"I haven't forgotten. It'll work out. I'll have a staff meeting just as soon as he gets back," interrupted Ann.

"Why am I going to Mexico?" Robert asked again.

"We're going to Mexico because I said so," Ann responded, smiling and looking at him lovingly. "And I'll explain as soon as we have some privacy," she added softly, quickly shifting her gaze to Sally.

"E.R. director!" Sally said with a question in her voice. "I wonder how in the world you got that title?" She turned to leave, staring at his groin on her way out the door.

As soon as Sally had left the room, Ann said sharply, "I

think I hate her!"

"I think the feeling is mutual," he said as he stared at the door.

Ann's mood totally changed. "Darling! Let me tell you the news."

"Yes!" he interrupted. "What's this Mexico business?"

"I'll explain on the way to the airport?" she said, kissing him lightly on the cheek as they walked into the front office.

"Jerri, Dr. St. John and I can be reached at the beach house near Cancun or the American Hospital there. You have the numbers, don't you?"

"Yes, Ms. Finn. What would you like for me to tell Administrator Levitz if he asks when you will be back.?"

"He's never here anyway. But if he does ask, tell him to call Mr. Castner at NHCO in Washington."

Ann winked at Robert as they left the office. She practically pulled him out the door. "Ready for some rest and relaxation, Doctor?"

Dr. St. John protested unrelentlessly on the way to her apartment and then to New Orleans International Airport. "Do you know what in the hell you're doing? What is this hospital you're talking about in Mexico? I expect an explanation."

Ann reassured him repeatedly. "You'll see when we get there. Don't worry, you'll be impressed! You're going to have to trust me. Now hurry or we'll miss our plane."

"Okay," he said with reserve. "But you sure are a woman with many surprises...and I don't necessarily like surprises."

*   *   *

They made their flight and headed to a foreign land that he had never even thought about visiting until two hours prior to take-off.

As soon as they landed in Cancun and cleared customs, he turned to her with his hands on his hips and a slightly bemused look on his face and said simply: "Okay, we're here. So?"

Ann was hailing a cab in perfect Spanish. "Oye!" She waved wildly at a passing yellow Chevrolet.

"A donde?" quizzed the Mexican taxi driver after he had pulled over to the curb and packed their two bags.

"El Casa del Mar."

"Sí! Sí! Señorita."

"Rápido!" Ann encouraged the driver."

"Sí, Señorita."

Robert looked at her in amazement. "What other talents do you have that I don't know about?"

She kissed him and whispered, "I always thought men liked mysterious women."

"Up to a point."

The driver slowed down and began to turn into a long winding drive that led up to a huge Mediterranean hacienda perched over the Gulf of Mexico.

"Wow!" Robert said. "Where are we?"

"Casa del Mar—House of the Sea." Ann said, waving her hand proudly over the expanse of the mansion. They scooted up the walk past a couple of guards to the front door.

"Whose house is this, anyway? Why are we here? Ann, you said you would explain all this to me when we got here."

"Come on," she said, grabbing his hand and pulling him down the large foyer. "I'll explain everything to you, but only after a swim and drinks in the Jacuzzi."

All he could do was trudge behind her tugging hand, "All right, all right," He sped up following her down the hallway. "But I want some answers, Ann!"

With that, they entered an expansive glass-enclosed area that housed an indoor pool and small gymnasium.

Robert could see white steam rising from the pool. It did look inviting. As they walked by the pool, he noticed two doors, one designating "hot steam" and the other "dry steam."

"Is there a masseuse in the house?" he asked sarcastically.

"Yes."

They continued their tour, walking toward another glass structure connected to the pool area. Robert stepped into one of the most lush greenhouses he had seen. As he looked out over the grounds, all he could see was an impeccably manicured landscape.

Ann pointed to a dressing room next to one of the saunas. "You can find trunks to fit you in there. Of course, if it were night, we could go skinny-dipping."

He entered the dressing room and found a rack of at least thirty trunks, just his size and style. He couldn't help but admit that this was one hell of a place. He just wondered who it belonged to and what he was doing there.

He stepped out of the dressing room. Ann shouted from behind her dressing room door, "Go on outside to the freshwater pool and Jacuzzi. I'll be there in a minute."

As he pushed the door to go outside, Ann peeked out from behind her dressing room. "Robert?"

"What?"

"There's a phone next to the Jacuzzi. Order a Southern Comfort for me and a Jack Daniel's for you. Just dial 9.

"Okay."

"Great. See you in a second."

He caught a glimpse of her naked body through the dressing room door. *God she's got a great body,*" he thought. He headed out the door over the tiles to the churning Jacuzzi.

After ordering the drinks, he settled into the Jacuzzi and relaxed. A lot had happened in the past week. "It's enough to make a man's mind spin," he muttered to himself.

Ann approached him in the smallest bikini he thought he had ever seen.

"How do you keep that body in that shape? You don't exercise!"

"Huh? Oh, I exercise like crazy, and I really don't like to

eat, or rather, I eat moderately," she said, sliding languidly into the Jacuzzi.

"Okay, Ann, what's the secret? Who is the owner of this place? When are we going to the hospital?"

Ann reached over and clamped his mouth shut with her right hand. "It's my home!"

"Yours?" a muffled scream seeped through her hand. "How could this be yours?" He tried to pull her hand off his mouth as she clamped down harder.

A tuxedoed boy approached from the side of the house with two large drinks.

"Shhhh," she motioned for Robert to be silent as the waiter approached.

"Okay. I'll be quiet until after we're served, but then you have a lot of explaining to do, young lady."

"Okay, Robert, relax. There's nothing unusual about this place." She stopped short as she looked up at the young waiter. "Gracias, Julio."

"Sí, Señorita," he responded, as he left the drinks by the hot tub.

"You can speak English, Julio."

"Okay, Miss Finn. Will there be anything else?"

"No, Julio, thank you."

As the waiter strode toward the mansion, Ann turned toward Robert and began to kiss him.

"I'm rich!" was all she said as she released him from her grasp.

"Rich? On an administrator's salary? You said you were raised as an army brat!"

Ann leaned out of the pool, grabbing one of the towels laid next to the pool. Her backside was exposed.

"No," Robert warned. "You're not getting off that easy. You know what you can do to me," he said, taking a mock disinterest in her voluptuous body. "You owe me an explanation, Ann Finn," he continued, his voice raising as he sipped his drink.

"First of all, I don't think I owe you any explanation."

70

Ann slid back into the hot tub, wrapping her hair in the towel. "But I will say this, Robert. I care for you very deeply, so—"

"So," he repeated, waiting for a response.

"I inherited a great deal of money from my parents, and I do not want anyone to know it." She raised a finger to stop his next question. "I will answer most of what you want to know, but much of this is extremely personal, and I may not want to confide in you."

"I understand. I guess."

"No, you don't understand, Robert! You may think you do, but you have no idea how many guys come on to you if you are reasonably attractive and very wealthy, and I'm sick of that scenario."

"I don't want to probe, Ann, but you can understand some of my curiosity, can't you?"

"Of course, love," she said as she kissed him again.

Before he could continue his questions, Ann interrupted. "Do you know what I want to do next?"

"What?" he asked as he sipped his drink.

"Give you the best sex you've ever had."

He almost dropped the drink as he choked on a piece of ice. "Here? Out in the open?"

"Why not?" She reached to loosen his trunks.

"But it's daylight. Someone will see," he protested as she pulled him out of the hot tub and placed him on a lounge chair and proceeded to do just what she said she was going to do.

After thirty minutes and three orgasms, he couldn't stand it anymore.

"Stop! Stop!" he shouted as he pulled her to him. "Goddamn—you're beautiful, wealthy, smart, got the best body I've ever seen...great sex.... Why do I feel that you're still hiding something from me?"

"Why do you care?" She curled up next to him and purred, "Shut up and just fall in love with me."

I'm probably already in love, he tossed around in his mind. "I just don't like surprises," was all he could say, as he felt himself falling asleep.

He awakened with Ann at his feet giving him a pedicure and a hot oil treatment.

"That feels great, Ann. After such great sex, I'm reluctant to spoil the mood."

"Well, don't then," She continued to pamper his feet. "I love the sunsets here in Mexico. I've heard that they are more beautiful than in the U.S. because the dust from the Sonora Desert heightens the beauty and the intensity of the color."

"Why didn't you mention the money before now? You said you inherited the money from your parents. Are they dead? Why are you still working?"

Ann covered her ears with her hands, and her face and neck veins began to bulge. "I'm going to scream if you don't shut up, and I mean now!"

He felt his breath slowly ooze from his mouth.

"Robert, I'm going to answer those questions tonight. Then I want you to promise me something."

He nodded yes.

"No more questions tonight or until we return to New Orleans. And do you know why?"

He nodded sheepishly.

"Because I want to have a good time. This is my home, and I want to enjoy your company in my home. Besides, someday maybe, just maybe, this will be your home too," she said, reaching up to stroke his face. "So why don't you relax and see if you like it here. Okay?"

He nodded and decided to try to relax. Within minutes he was asleep again.

* * *

Later, Ann seemed more at ease. She began to offer her life's story.

"Both of my parents died in an airplane crash when I was twelve. I lived with my aunt and uncle until I went to college.

I went to Harvard after high school. Did I tell you I made the highest grades in my class? For some reason, that was very important to me. Anyway, when I was twenty-one, I inherited my parents' estate. I decided to work because working hard had always been my greatest source of personal satisfaction.

"And," she continued, clasping his face between her hands and looking straight into his eyes, "I don't tell anyone about the money because half of the people turn out to be assholes when it comes to that. Especially guys! But you're different, Robert. You know I've admired you for a long time."

Robert blushed and he looked down at the floor.

When he looked back at Ann, she said, "I wanted to get to know you a lot better and be sure I could trust you with some very intimate details of my life. Do you understand?"

He nodded yes.

"Good!" she gently shook his face side to side, affectionately. "Now, no more questions tonight. Besides, do you know how many men would love to be in your shoes right now...to find out that their new lady friend is a multimillionaire with a beautiful beachside mansion."

With that, she laughed and turned toward a corridor. "Let's get some food!" she said as she trotted toward the kitchen. Her sumptuous bottom moved with her increased speed.

She's right, he said to himself. *Hell, it's like I've hit the lottery!*

The same tuxedoed waiter greeted them at the doors that led to a large restaurant-style kitchen. "What is your wish, madam?" Julio asked as he graciously waved them toward the central table.

"Robert, you remember when I told you that I loved seafood on the way to Knoxville?"

Before he could answer, she walked over to a large refrigerator with stainless steel doors and windows. "Look!"

73

she shouted. "Lobster, shrimp, grouper, red snapper, oysters! Which do you want?"

"Geeez, this is grrrreat."

"Please tell me you love seafood as much as I do! You can't live in New Orleans without loving seafood!"

"I do, I do. I love seafood as much as you do. You know that. I'll have what you're having. But who's going to eat all this?"

"Another question!" she continued. "All that we don't use here at Casa del Mar is donated to the hospital. What's really fun is that not only do we have our own yacht here, but we have our own fishing boat too." She smiled gratefully toward Julio. "The staff takes care of all of that. They go fishing every day, if need be. So, Robert, what do you want?

"I want the guys to take me fishing in the morning. It's been such a long time since I've been fishing."

"Okay! Julio will take my doctor friend to fish in the morning."

"Of course, Señorita Ann."

"Great! I can't wait. What do you think we can catch?"

Julio responded by holding his arms out as wide as he could, "Marlin grande!"

"Now back to the subject at hand: What do you want to eat tonight?" Ann implored. "You've got to be big and strong to bring in a three hundred to four hundred pound blue marlin that we catch offshore here," she said, stroking Robert's biceps.

"Julio," Ann continued, "How about red snapper, blackened, Cajun-style?"

"Of course," Julio answered. He turned to the task at hand.

While cooking, Julio kept them entertained by telling them stories of local people and families. After he had fed them all they could eat, Ann said, "Let's go upstairs and rest." She stood up from the table. "You have a busy day tomorrow. If you want to go fishing with the guys, you have to get up early because you have to go with me to the hospital in the afternoon."

"Okay. Thanks, Julio. That was great. I'll see you in the morning."

"Sí, Señor. Buenas nochés. Hasta la vista."

As they went to the room, Robert took Ann by the hand and said, "You know, this is weird. I don't really know Spanish, but I understand everything Julio has said."

"Yeah, it's funny, but 'good night,' 'thank you,' and 'welcome,' seem to transcend language."

They settled into the large suite, which was mostly glass and exposed wooden beams. "Whew! This is a magnificent place, Ann. You must really be proud of it!"

"Thanks, Robert. I am," she smiled. "Let's get some sleep."

They lay down together, holding each other.

Robert was awakened by the rays of sunlight that sneaked into the room. There was a knock on the door. It was Julio.

"I'll be right there, Julio," Robert whispered loudly.

Ann hadn't awakened yet. He didn't disturb her as he quietly dressed.

The house seemed even larger in the daylight, as he and Julio walked down the path to the marina. He hadn't noticed before, but the whole house was surrounded by a large white masonry terrace. As they neared the marina, Robert could make out a forty-two-foot Hatteras and a slip for a larger boat.

Julio readied the boat for their trip.

"Are we ready, Julio?" yelled Robert. "Sí Señor," Julio answered.

Robert noticed Julio's formality as he stepped into the boat.

"Is it okay with you if we speak English?"

"Yes sir," Julio grinned.

"Great, because I don't know a lot of Spanish. Your English is really very good, from what I observed last night."

"Miss Finn wants us to talk Spanish around the house," shrugged Julio.

"That's strange, but I guess it's her house. So what will we catch today?"

Julio again spread his arms wide and shouted, "Marlin!" as he steered the boat into the gulf. The sun was stirring above the horizon as Julio pressed the throttle forward to propel the boat toward deeper waters. Two miles offshore Robert noticed a boat off from the horizon flashing toward the marina.

"What's that?" Robert pointed the faintly approaching vessel out to Julio.

"Oh that's the yacht returning from the mainland."

"That boat is flying." Robert strained to get a better look at the glistening white of the approaching vessel.

"Man, that boat is really flying!" he repeated, squinting as he got a better look. "What kind of boat is it?"

"A Sea Ray 2001 Series—it's part hydrofoil. You can't buy them from a dealer. They're a special-order boat only."

"Wow," was all Robert could say as the hydrofoil slowed down and began its glide toward the dock at Casa del Mar.

"Julio, why does she need a super boat like that?"

Robert tried to catch a glimpse of the super speed boat at dock.

"I'm just an employee Doctor, I don't know."

Julio pointed to an area of turquoise gulf approximately two miles in front of them. "Look here, Doctor St. John. When we reach that spot we will begin to troll parallel to the coast along the fall of the continental shelf. That's where the big sport fish like marlin are located. Do you mind guiding the boat while I ready the Bally Hoo bait fish?"

"No. How are we going to fish?"

"Trolling is the best way to cover the most water, and we'll use these silvery needle-nose Bally Hoos. Did you notice how I hooked them through the gut and wrapped the steel leader around the elongated nose?"

76

"Yes, and what are these colorful pleated rubbery skirts?"

"They're supposed to mimic mauve creatures and fish such as squid. And of course the Bally Hoo gives a fish taste when they strike so the marlin or sailfish won't let go until we set the hook. What do you want to catch, Doctor?"

"Marlin or sailfish would be wonderful—I've never caught either."

"Are you in shape?" Julio asked suspiciously.

"Why?"

"Because if we hook a four hundred pound blue marlin you'd better be in shape for a big fight or look out!"

A touch of anxiety swept up in the doctor's throat as the prospect of a grueling two-hour fight with a half-ton fighting acrobat made him wish he had kept up his workout program more consistently.

Julio lowered the hundred-pound test lines. Robert allowed him to take over the wheel after Julio had completed the task of preparing the rods and reels.

"Now we'll approach the drop-off." Julio pointed to the depth finder on the dash of the boat. "We'll troll at approximately 3.5 knots along that break-off. The large game fish will come up for the smaller bait fish from deep water, and hopefully," he grabbed Robert's arm in a viselike grip, "we'll get them to attack our lures, and you'll land your first large saltwater game fish."

"All right! This is going to be fun!"

They began the slow trolling off the deep drop-off of the azure waters of the gulf. The occasional beep of the depth finder brought hope of a marlin strike.

"Look!" Robert pointed to the white flash of a boat leaving the Casa del Mar Marina. "There goes the Sea Ray hydrofoil again."

Julio shrugged his shoulders. "Yes sir, they use that boat a lot."

The boat appeared to jet over the gulf waters. "Would they let me take it out for a spin?" he joked.

"Oh no, I don't think so, Señor Robert. There's some kind of specialized equipment on it or something—it's a very expensive boat. But they might let you. It won't hurt to ask."

"Specialized equipment," Robert's forehead wrinkled in wonder. "Why does she need specialized equipment on a 'Porsche' speedboat?"

Julio shrugged. "I don't know. She's wealthy. Los Ricos do a lot of things we regular people don't understand."

Zzzzng! The line from the outer holder on the boat was hit by a large blue marlin.

"Hold the boat steady!" Julio shouted. "I'll set the hook!"

"Okay! Okay!"

Julio jerked the rod handle toward the front of the boat and yelled, "It's set! Now get the rod."

He sat Robert in the center seat with the swiveled rod holder at the base of the chair. Julio handed him the rod. "Put the rod handle in the holder and strap yourself in, and begin reeling. As soon as I bring in the other reels I'll start backing the boat to the fish as you reel."

Robert's line twitched from the reel toward the deep. He had never seen anyone move as quickly as Julio did gathering the rods and reels to get them out of the way. Julio ran back to the bow and began to back the boat down.

"Whoa!" screamed Robert, his biceps straining against the rod. "This son of a bitch is big!"

"He's surfacing, Doctor. Keep pressure on the line."

"Okay!"

About a hundred and fifty yards behind the boat a large marlin surfaced and leaped again and again, trying to throw the hook from its mouth.

The struggle against the big marlin continued for forty-five minutes. Robert paused several times to rest. "That's okay," Julio said, noting his fatigue. "Just keep the line tight."

As the big fish nestled up against the boat, Julio took out a video camera from the bulkhead and took pictures of the happy angler and the large fish.

"We don't kill the fish," Julio said. "We do tag them for the Bill Fish Society." He placed a rod with a plastic tag behind the dorsal fin and tagged the fish with a push.

Julio jerked the hook from the hardened bill and released the fish. It circled and began to slowly swim back to the deep.

"Good job!" Julio shook Dr. Robert's hand.

"That was fun…I think." Robert sank back into the chair exhausted. "Let's go home, Julio."

"Yes, sir."

As they approached the marina, the lithe figure of Ann could be seen against the backdrop of the cliff.

Robert waved enthusiastically as they pulled toward the slip.

"I've got a great fish story to tell you," he said as he helped Julio with the docking.

"Wonderful," she clapped her hands. "I'm glad you had a good time."

"Great time!" he clapped Julio on the shoulder. "Thanks to this guy!

"Do you feel like doing something else?"

"After I shower."

"Okay, then let's go to the Hospital of the Americas in town."

The three walked from the boat toward the house. "Julio, would you mind taking us?" Ann asked.

"No, of course not."

After cleaning up, Ann and Robert walked to the front of the driveway. Julio pulled up to them in a Mercedes.

"The Hospital of the Americas is very close," Ann said as they closed the door. "Did you know it's considered a sister hospital of New Orleans? Since NAFTA was passed several years ago, the U.S. and Mexican governments have really tried to collaborate on certain endeavors. Health care is one of them. Mr. Castner has been here several times to see the autopsy and transplant program, comparing the results with ours and correlating data for NIH to review. Also, Hospital of the Americas is a world-recognized center when it comes to heart, liver, lung, bone marrow and kidney transplants."

"Interesting." Robert turned toward her with renewed intrigue. "I had no idea."

"That's one thing about American people," Julio chimed in from the front seat. "They think all Mexicans wear sombreros, ride burros and eat tortillas. They're shocked when they find out we have hospitals and airports."

He was cut short by Ann. "Okay, Julio," she said laughing "We understand."

"Yeah," chimed in Robert. "What I never realized is you had such good fishing."

"Only the best," Ann smiled.

Julio laughed and said. "Right, right—and good fishing, too." He turned back to concentrate on the road.

"Who's the head honcho there, Ann?"

"Raphael Guttierez is the administrator, similar to Mr. Levitz at New Orleans. But unlike the U.S. hospitals, the administrator is the top surgeon on staff. Mr. Guttierez is that also.

"I see." He rubbed his chin in genuine appreciation.

"Can you see the advantages in that arrangement, Robert?"

"Yes, I can. The administrator would naturally be much more pro-staff. He would naturally be concerned about the bottom line financially, but he would appreciate the difficulties staff and doctors and nurses encounter."

"Of course!" She clapped her hands. "It's a superior way to practice medicine, and I have written a logistical research paper on institutionalizing such changes at many U.S. hospitals, including New Orleans Hospital."

Julio again chimed in with an exaggerated grin. "See, Doctor, we're superior here in many ways in sunny Mexico."

They both responded from the back seat. "Shut up, Julio."

Ann kissed Robert's neck and rubbed his leg. "I wonder

who would be one of the top candidates to take over Mr. Levitz's position as CEO of New Orleans if Mr. Castner decides to experimentally implement this system in a few hospitals in the U.S.?"

"Me?" Robert jolted toward her with genuine surprise. "Me?" he again stuttered.

She continued to stroke him in a seductive manner.

"But I wouldn't be qualified," he protested.

"Don't underestimate yourself. You wouldn't be qualified in the old American way of doing this. But you would be imminently qualified if this system is transferred to the United States."

He furrowed his brow and shook his head slightly.

"I don't know," he began slowly. "But I do see why you wanted me to come down here."

Ann grabbed his face. "You would be qualified as any body else. You're a doctor, for Christ's sake!" She squeezed his face, pulling it up and down in a positive gesture.

"Here we are," Julio interrupted, as he pulled into the hospital drive.

"Wait for us here, Julio," Ann demanded as they walked toward the entrance.

"Talk to Dr. Guttierez about this, Robert."

"This is impressive." He looked at Ann as they entered the building.

"This place looks new. It's huge!" He glanced up and down the halls that radiated from a solarium like spokes of a wheel.

"It is new, relatively speaking," Ann said as she walked briskly toward a bilingual sign that stated ADMINISTRATOR/ ADMINISTRACION.

The receptionist jumped up instantly, recognizing Ann.

"Señorita Finn." She hugged Ann affectionately.

"Is Dr. Guttierez here?" Ann looked toward the large office in the rear.

"Sí, uno momento."

The receptionist buzzed the administrator's office, then waved for them to follow her to the doctor's office. They walked in a mahogany-paneled room with a marble floor.

"Impressive," Robert marveled, as he looked around the office. The diploma on the wall above the large desk was from Harvard Medical School.

Dr. Guttierez held up his left hand while hanging up the telephone with his right. He jumped up to shake Ann's hand. "Ann Finn! How wonderful."

"Dr. Guttierez, this is Dr. Robert St. John, the new E.R. director of New Orleans Hospital. He'll also be coordinating the autopsies at New Orleans to NHCO specifications."

Dr. Guttierez's face lit up.

"Ah, how wonderful! We must get to know each other well, as the work between our two hospitals is truly extraordinary." He pumped Robert's hand.

Ann patted Robert on his shoulder.

"I hand-picked Dr. St. John for the job. I think he is immensely qualified."

"Ms. Finn has shown me the paperwork and protocols involved, but I'm not quite as confident of my qualifications as she," Robert protested.

"He's just being modest," Ann protested.

"I hope I prove to be as capable as Ms. Finn expects."

"I told Dr. St. John about the possibility that New Orleans may follow the Hospital of the Americas in allowing a doctor such as yourself to be administrator."

"Ahhh…" Dr. Guttierez nodded positively. "I think you will be most impressed with the possibilities for America after I show you the work that this hospital is doing in the nature of organ transplants."

"Yes, I've heard," Robert replied. "From Ms. Finn, of course. I must tell you that I was somewhat ignorant of your research and the work being done here."

"Let me take you on an extensive tour of the hospital. With your new duties over the autopsy records at your hospital, you will be interested in the autopsy procedures here."

"Yes, I will be interested, Dr. Guttierez."

"I was just telling Dr. St. John how the NHCO compares the autopsy findings here with those at New Orleans in hope of better understanding the pathology process in Homo Sapiens."

"But the most exciting thing that I think you will see is the research work we are doing in relation to organ transplants," Guttierez said.

Excitedly, Ann interjected: "You see, as you are possibly aware, in Mexico hospitals aren't placed in the legal handcuffs that we are in the United States."

Guttierez continued: "Your country's NHCO of course adds its advantages to many people receiving medical care. However, it jeopardizes certain new procedures and advancements, such as the transplants that are being pioneered here, because of legal and monetary considerations. We are under no such stifling bureaucracy here." His voice rose with emotion. "The very successful capitalistic system of the U.S. has failed to extend that positive influence to health care because of the rules that government has placed on the health care providers and the hospitals there."

Ann held out her NHCO card to Dr. Guttierez and Robert. "This has its advantages, but it's got disadvantages too," she said.

"Exactly." Dr. Guttierez turned the card in his fingers.

Robert handed the card back to Ann. "Of course, I'm sure most Mexicans would love to have one of these, especially the 70 percent of the people who are poor."

Dr. Guttierez shrugged. "But you are losing much of the—no, you've lost much of the lead that Debakey and Cooley pioneered in Houston, in the name of socialist equality."

"Oh really?" Robert bristled somewhat at this unsolicited political commentary.

"Doctor, don't misunderstand: I am in awe of many of your fine institutions in the U.S. Oh, enough of this stupid lecture," Guttierez smiled and pointed to the Harvard degree on the wall. "I did receive my education in the good ole U.S.A.!"

Robert noted: "You got your degree at Harvard, just like Ms. Finn."

"Yes, I did."

"Did you know each other there?"

"No!" Ann blurted out.

Robert felt uncertain, but for a second an obscure gut instinct told him that they had known each other then, and well.

Dr. Guttierez changed the subject quickly. "I want to show you the hospital, Doctor."

He turned to Ann. "Here are the financials for the majority of last year. We have nothing to hide here. Perhaps you would like to peruse them to understand how we transact business here and compare that to your hospital in New Orleans."

Ann had already adjusted his chair to a more comfortable position in order to study the documents.

"That settles it then," Dr. Guttierez declared. "The administrator will study boring financial and accounting ledgers, while the two doctors delve into the brave and exciting new world of techno-medicine."

Ann waved them out the door.

I can't help but like this guy, Robert thought to himself as Dr. Guttierez walked him back out into the solarium and down one of the corridors extending to the periphery of the complex.

"I hope you weren't offended earlier, when I was commenting on the differences between the health care delivery of our two countries," Dr. Guttierez said.

"No, no—really, it piqued my curiosity more than anything," Robert replied. "Like, how do our countries' transplant programs differ?" He was confidently trying to conceal his ignorance.

"Do you realize, Dr. St. John, that we perform almost as many heart transplants here now, at this hospital, as your whole country performs?"

Robert stopped dead in his tracks. "That's not possible." He stammered in utter disbelief.

"Oh yes! After the implementation of your national health insurance program rules limiting those types of procedures went into effect across the U.S. And the actual transplantation and even harvesting of organs have been made much more difficult by the new mega-bureaucracy in Washington.

"I know that the surgeons of New Orleans are bitching like hell against that," Robert acknowledged, remembering conversations he had had with some of his surgical buddies.

"But," Dr. Guttierez continued as they entered a pre-op area of surgical suites. "We here are free of such governmental and bureaucratic encumbrances. We can proceed in any way that we feel is feasible and scientifically rewarding. Mexico City, for instance, has possibly surpassed Houston as the advanced cardiac treatment center of the Western Hemisphere."

Again Robert stopped in his tracks: "How can that be?"

"There is so much bureaucracy in your health program that expensive and extremely extensive procedures such as transplants have mostly been dropped. We practice capitalism and free enterprise here."

With that, he opened the doors to a large doctor preparatory area to change into surgical gowns and scrubs.

Robert was somewhat numb as he put on the scrubs that were provided to him.

"Oh, I'd love to show you—if we have time—how we use much of the profits from our transplant program to treat the poorer Mexican population in our clinical outreach programs."

"Sure," Robert replied, still somewhat humiliated by what he had heard.

Looking at Robert closely, Dr. Guttierez said. "Oh, I've offended you! I'm sorry. I should have kept my opinions to myself."

Robert shook his head. "No, sir. I'm just surprised and shocked, that's all."

"All Americans are very—how do we say—Americans are self-oriented. You hardly recognize the rest of the world exists, much less Latin America. I understand how America works and thinks. For God's sake, I studied there and got my degree in your country. The United States is still the richest, greatest country in the world, and I guess I've been bragging—no, I've been boasting, absolutely boasting, about this one small thing that our country learned from yours and now in my opinion does better."

Guttierez looked comfortingly at Robert. "Just one thing," he said, holding up his index finger. "Out of millions of procedures."

He pushed open the doors marked AUTHORIZED PERSONNEL ONLY into the largest surgical suite Robert had ever seen. Eleven procedures were under way simultaneously. The operating tables were arranged in a circular fashion. The noise of the monitors was instantly distracting, as Robert stared in disbelief at the goings-on.

Dr. Guttierez turned to a prep board positioned on the back wall of the Operating Room. "Look," he said excitedly: "two Mexicans, one Canadian, one Brazilian, two Western Europeans, one Australian, one British, two Japanese, and one Chinese."

"This is unprecedented," Robert shook his head in disbelief. "Why haven't we heard of this in the U.S.?"

"Simple," Dr. Guttierez proclaimed. "Your NHCO doesn't want you to know."

"Bullshit," Robert objected.

"Well," replied a defiant Dr. Guttierez. "Why haven't

you read in JAMA or NEJM about this?"

"I can't explain it."

"Because you're not supposed to know, and the transplant surgeons of the U.S. don't really want you to know this. They don't want to lose your business down here, and quite honestly, only the wealthy can afford this." He added with a smirk: "We don't accept your NHCO cards."

"I'll be damned," Robert said, thinking: *No wonder Ann dragged me here. I wouldn't have believed it in a million years.*

"Of course, you will be primarily interested in the autopsy work. And we will be extremely interested in an account of your new position at New Orleans Hospital."

"It's boring stuff. Autopsies. I'll do some of the NHCO paperwork, but I'll really be leaving most of that up to Ms. Finn. She's brilliant when it comes to the tedious nature of those NHCO forms."

"I see."

"There's one thing, Dr. Guttierez: To do this volume of transplants, you must have one hell of a waiting list for organs."

"Dr. St. John," Dr. Guttierez leaned over to whisper into Robert's ear, "if I show you something will you promise not to tell anyone, not even Ann?"

"Yes, sure," a confused Dr. St. John responded.

Guttierez pulled him out the door, down another expansive hall.

"What I'm going to show you is the crowning achievement of this hospital, and my brainchild. We have perfected a method to store vital organs for up to one week prior to use in surgery."

Again Robert had to come to a full stop. "Incredible and unbelievable!" he shouted.

"Shhh!" Dr. Guttierez admonished. "I can't show you the procedure, only the storage. We have not shared this technology with anyone yet, until we are approved for patents in the U.S., Japan, Western and Eastern Europe, and

Australia. Only then will we do a major research paper on this subject to be released to the world."

Guttierez pushed the doors open to another area. Two armed guards saluted him. He spoke Spanish to them and they immediately opened the locked doors. Robert and Guttierez stepped into what appeared to be an observation deck overlooking a lab with approximately eight space-suited personnel at work.

"Pull up a seat," Dr. Guttierez pointed to some chairs. "Watch carefully—observe and learn."

For about ten minutes the two observed the personnel open up giant liquid nitrogen cooling containers and pull out two human hearts and a liver. They went through a long and tedious procedure of placing the organs in different collecting vessels from which the organs were quickly ushered to what Robert assumed was the operating room.

"I can't take you onto the floor of the lab, or I would be killed—literally," Dr. Guttierez said. "I think you understand the need for secrecy."

"The only thing I can tell is to think 'potassium' instead of 'sodium'. Impressive, extremely impressive," Dr. St. John allowed.

"Come on, let's go to the autopsy department and see how the study of pathology in our two countries can benefit the people of the world."

Robert was numb as he was perfunctorily led through the autopsy lab.

"We'll send you the data directly from here."

"Thanks. I'm still learning the job, and any data will help."

Dr. Guttierez patted Robert on the shoulder. "Remember, some of the great scientific advances of the world were founded on boring statistical paperwork. As Thomas Alva Edison said: 'Ninety-nine percent of invention is perspiration and one percent is inspiration'."

They both laughed at that proposition.

Ann didn't notice them as they reentered Dr. Guttierez's

office. She was at work crunching figures on the financial papers before her. Looking up finally, she gave a slow whistle.

"Impressive, Señor Doctor Guttierez."

"Thanks."

"If you think the financials are impressive, Ann, you should see the pioneering work they're doing here in the field of organ transplants," Robert said.

"I know," she nodded "Do you see why I wanted you to come down here to see this?"

"Yes, I do." He instinctively moved toward her in an affectionate manner, forgetting Dr. Guttierez's presence.

Coldly she moved away from him, diverting her eyes toward the floor.

"Now, Robert, Dr. Guttierez and I want to warn you not to mention this to anyone in the United States."

"Yes," Dr. Guttierez emphasized.

Shocked, Robert interrupted. "With what I've seen! No way!"

"Robert, listen to me," Ann looked first at Dr. Guttierez and then back to Robert. "There are political, and I mean *big* political issues at stake here. Think about it. Dr. Guttierez and I thought long and hard about asking you to see the transplant operations. But we had faith in the fact that you would be sensible in understanding the political reality of this.

"There are people in the U.S. who would tie up the implementation of this new transplant procedure for years if the news was leaked to the media. Remember, Robert, what Mr. Castner alluded to about the political blood that the approval of the NHCO card cost! This could be as controversial as the abortion issue in the United States. Do you want that?"

"No, but how is that so?" Robert asked.

Dr. Guttierez interjected. "Robert, I—we took a huge risk in showing you this. But it was a calculated risk. We felt that we could trust you."

"You can! But why not share this with the world now?

It's fantastic!" Robert was shouting.

"Robert," Dr. Guttierez interrupted. "The money involved is phenomenal; the controversy will be phenomenal also."

"Sit down, Robert." Ann said.

"I don't want to sit down!"

Ann crossed over and led him to the big chair behind the desk. "Sit," she commanded.

Dr. Guttierez interrupted. "As a person who has lived in your country, studied in your country, but has lived most of his life in a different country, I want to present a change of perspective. I want to share this political scenario with you. Ann, do you think I should continue?"

"Absolutely, Dr. Guttierez."

"Let's talk about something that is happening in your country now—abortion—and compare this to our advanced cryo-storage and retransplantation program here at the Hospital of the Americas. What I am going to tell you, as I have said earlier, can't be shared, no matter what."

Ann looked Robert in the eyes.

"Robert," she said, holding up her hand to stop Dr. Guttierez from speaking. "If you trust me, if you care for me, if you have hope to know me—promise me that you will not, *will not*, discuss this with anyone. Do you believe in me?"

He looked into her eyes.

"Yes, Ann. I'll listen and be quiet." He sighed deeply. "Go ahead. I'm listening, with an open mind."

She turned to Dr. Guttierez. "Continue, please."

"Robert, we are on the verge of being able to store, after freezing them, viable human organs up to a year prior to transplantation."

"Impossible!" Robert responded.

"Would you have thought the one-week period of storage was impossible prior to today?"

"No," he admitted, "but —"

"Be quiet, Robert! Let Dr. Guttierez continue."

"If we can store organs for up to a year, do you want to know what will happen in the U.S.?"

"Yes! It would be great."

"No, Robert!" Dr. Guttierez shouted now. "It might well tear the fabric of your society to shreds."

"You keep saying that, goddammit," said Robert. "But how? Why?"

"Think, Robert!" Ann interjected. "The health care bureaucracy NHCO set up in the U.S. has already slowed transplants in the U.S. to a trickle, because it rations—it *rations*—the availability of these mega-costly procedures, and because of the cap on expenditures for the total health care budget."

Robert's heart sank, his head heavy in understanding.

"That's right! That's right!" he repeated. "But the NHCO system has spread more health care to more people."

"But at a heavy burden," Dr. Guttierez added. "The most expensive procedures—heart and kidney transplants, bone marrow transplants—are rationed!"

Robert suddenly understood what this meant. As he slowly began to talk, he knew what he was saying was true.

"This would revolutionize this procedure, wouldn't it, Dr. Guttierez?"

Dr. Guttierez nodded acknowledgment.

"But the cost?" Robert asked.

"Unfortunately, Robert, the cost of storage actually skyrockets instead of going down, as you would hope."

"Robert, do you see the need to wait before we tell the world?" Ann asked.

He nodded. "I'm beginning to." Then: "Wait—you're doing procedures now on people as we talk."

"These are unique cases, Robert," Dr. Guttierez explained. "They have to forward $200,000 up front and another $200,000 on completion of the operation. Did you notice we have no Americans?"

"Yes."

"That's for a reason. We don't want the publicity yet—especially in the United States."

"That's right. We have to get the data together, and any interruption—" Ann motioned for Dr. Guttierez to continue.

"We're going to have to do a lot of very good preparation work to get the U.S. government to go along with this if it is to be offered to people in the U.S."

"I see," said Robert. "Let me see if I understand the extrapolation: If this procedure is available in the U.S., because of the current rationing system for organ transplantation, the intrinsic cost of the new storage system that I've just seen would create plenty of friction between those able to purchase a transplant at $400,000 and those stuck with the health card system. No, that would definitely not be politically expedient—I understand and can see that."

"This is so revolutionary, Robert, that it absolutely has to be presented to Congress and presented only after the data and studies are totally complete, which shouldn't take more than two to three years."

"Two to three years?" Robert exploded.

"Yes, and I picked you, Robert," Ann stroked his hand, "because we need to correlate pathology through autopsy reports between here and New Orleans during the next two to three years. We need you! If we can show you the morality of not offering this to the American people—to Congress—well, we should be able to bridge the bureaucratic mindset of the NHCO committee."

Guttierez interrupted. "And as happens with most procedures, the cost of this will go down, hopefully way down, in time."

"I see," Robert nodded.

Guttierez continued. "The baby-boomers of your country have turned old age, and those children of the post-War affluence who have been denied nothing in their lives are to be denied what would be a life-saving procedure, that through our process could be offered to almost everyone?"

"Mind-boggling," Robert agreed.

"At rates prohibitively expensive," Ann reiterated. "Do you see, Doctor, why I felt that by denying this to all those people who were used to instant gratification, this could be an extremely explosive issue?"

"More so," Robert responded.

"You have used your extrapolation skills very well," Guttierez said.

"I'm sorry I didn't pick up on the dilemma sooner," Robert said. "Ann, it looks like we have a lot of pathology correlation work to do when we get back."

"Yes, we do." She smiled.

"Doctor, does your offer of forwarding pathology and autopsy reports from the Hospital of the Americas still stand?"

"Of course, Dr. St. John." said Dr. Guttierez.

"Let's go to the beach house," Ann cajoled.

"Talked me into it," Robert responded.

The three exchanged handshakes, signaling the end of the brief but important meeting.

As Julio drove them back to Casa del Mar, Robert couldn't help but think about Dave Wyatt. *Poor bastard,* he concluded. *He couldn't handle the pressure of all this crap.*

Chapter Five

What a week," Robert declared as he and Ann walked hand-in-hand past the guards and through the front doors of Casa del Mar.

"Do you know how exciting this is to me, Ann?" he asked when they reached the seclusion of their private suite.

"Really, Robert?" she said teasingly. "I want you in me, darling." She grappled with his trousers.

"Whoa, get serious for a second, Ann. I really want to help you guys provide the new medical procedure to all the American people."

"I know I made the right decision then to introduce you to Raphael's Hospital of the Americas." She had his pants pulled below his waist, stroking him.

"Yeah, this will certainly be exciting." He stepped out of his pants.

"Your job will be pretty mundane, Robert. You know— the compilation of statistics for NHCO."

"I know—is that really the only way I can help advance our cause?"

"It's the best way, dear!"

"Okay, as a physician, I understand the necessity of doing a lot of so-called scut-work in order to achieve the desired result."

She pulled off his shirt.

"It's amazing," he continued, "that we have this opportunity to help the world. Will we be mentioned in the same breath as Pasteur? Fleming and Schweitzer? I can do the small repetitive job presented to me in order to better mankind."

After removing her clothes in half the time it had taken to strip Robert, Ann had positioned herself in bed. "You look like a damn fool—comparing yourself to the medical giants while you're stark naked with an erection."

Robert looked down at himself: "You're right. I'll collect the Nobel Prize for Medicine tomorrow. Tonight the medical mamba in Mexico".

"Quit the solicitation and come here, Louis Pasteur!"

"Sí, Señorita." He dove into the bed.

* * *

The sun again crept into the room, awakening him the next morning. Ann was already dressed and gone. After showering and dressing, he plodded to the kitchen. Julio was preparing breakfast.

"Are you hungry?" he asked Robert.

"You bet." Robert rubbed his hands together in anticipation. "Where's Ann?"

"She headed out early this morning," Julio replied as he prepared breakfast for the doctor.

"Do you want to go fishing today, Doctor?" Julio quizzed. "Yesterday a tourist from the Ritz at Cancun caught a 600-pound marlin."

"Yeah, maybe we'll go, if Ann wants to," Robert said, disappointed that she wasn't there. He toyed with the eggs on his plate. "I'm feeling like a homesick sixteen-year old."

Ann burst into the room with a huge sack of corn.

"I just had to go to the market and get fresh eloté," she beamed, pecking Robert on the cheek as she walked by.

"Julio, clean these, if you will, so we can have corn for lunch. I just love boiled whole corn."

"Sí, Señorita."

"Oh Julio, you and the staff can quit speaking Spanish if

you want."

Julio looked confused.

"A woman can change her mind. That's a woman's prerogative, you know, to change her mind." She winked at Robert. Noticing his somber expression, she came over and affectionately kissed him.

"Oh, what's the matter, my baby, so sad?"

Julio carried the corn to the back kitchen to clean.

"I want you around me," Robert said. "Especially when I wake up in the morning."

"Oh, darling! You know how much you've come to mean to me." She tousled his hair, and kissed him affectionately on the lips. "You were sound asleep this morning, and I just love Mexican corn! Boiled with salt and lime—it's called eloté here."

"Okay," he said, still pouting.

"I'll wake you up next time before I leave." She added: "I'll never leave your side again!" She flexed her arms in an exaggeratedly submissive pose.

"Okay." He smiled this time. "I'm just getting used to you." They kissed.

"Why don't you move in with me when we get back to New Orleans?" Ann asked. "You don't want to go back to that apartment in the French Quarter. Besides my house in uptown is so much nicer. We can ride to work together, too. Good, its settled," she smiled broadly, without giving him time to respond to any of the previous flurry of questions.

Robert looked pensive for a moment. "You're right. I never want to go back to that apartment." He hesitated for a moment, then said, "Yeah, I'll move into your house when we get home."

"Great," Ann said. "It's settled."

Robert's face brightened. "Do you want to go fishing with me and Julio? A tourist from Cancun caught a 600-pound marlin yesterday."

"I'll go if I can lay out in the sun while you fish."

"Good! It's a done deal," he exclaimed. "Julio?" he shouted at his newfound Mexican friend cleaning the corn in the kitchen alcove.

"What?" Julio poked his head around the alcove corner.

"Ann and I will go fishing today."

"Fine." Julio smiled. "Let me finish up here, and I'll get the boat ready."

"Julio, go ahead and bring the corn and a basket for lunch. Also bring beer. I'll do take some work to do on the boat while you little boys prove your manhood by catching Moby Dick."

"Yeah, Julio, let's catch Moby Dick. Sounds good to me."

* * *

The two fisherman and the sunbather moved toward the Hatteras moored at the marina. The giant Sea Ray hydrofoil was again nowhere to be seen.

"Ann, let me go out on the Sea Ray sometime, okay?"

"Sure," she said as she loaded her picnic supplies, with Julio's help, onto the fishing vessel.

"Why do you need a boat like that anyway?"

"I'm rich. I don't need a reason," was the curt reply. "I just like having the best."

Julio yelled from the pilot's deck. "Are we ready to go?"

Robert unlashed the twined rope. "Let's go."

Ann was busy in the galley. "You hungry yet?"

"Not yet, unless you are."

"When do you want to move into the house?" she asked, as she cleaned and organized the kitchen.

"I guess when we get back to New Orleans."

They leaned somewhat to the right to balance themselves as Julio headed out into deeper waters.

"Okay, it's settled then. When do you want to go back home?"

He shrugged in a nonchalant manner.

"Tomorrow okay?"

"Yeah, it's okay with me so long as I can come back down here with you before long!"

"Certainly. You can come back down here anytime you want," she reiterated between kisses.

She patted him on the butt, and pushed him toward the stairs leading from the galley toward the deck. "Now quit yakking. We'll talk about setting up housekeeping on the plane tomorrow. Go help Julio fish, or whatever you guys wanted to do."

"Hey, Julio!" He bounded up from the galley. "What can I do?"

"You can ready the Ballyhoo, if you want.

"Sure!"

The day passed quickly. They caught one small sailfish, which was fun, but no Moby Dick. They had fajitas, eloté and quesadillas with a lot of beer. Julio had become a friend in a short time.

The night and next morning flew by. Ann and he were on the Delta 747 headed back to New Orleans long before he wanted to go. The prospect of participating in an exciting medical advancement in organ transplantation as proposed by Dr. Guttierez gave him goose bumps in anticipation. He was looking forward to becoming the best E.R. director he possibly could, and to helping Ann and Dr. Guttierez in any way he could to benefit what he considered the equivalent of a medical search for the Holy Grail.

As the jet was close to landing at New Orleans, Ann began making arrangements to have Robert move to the Garden District New Orleans house. "Have the movers go get your belongings, darling. Just give them the keys and let them do it all. You don't have to ever go back to that French Quarter apartment."

He kissed her on the cheek. "Thanks, Ann, that's a great idea." He wanted to start a new life, never go back to the apartment and the haunting memories lingering there. Besides, he wanted to start his life over with Ann in her midtown antebellum mansion. His Jaguar looked better in front of that place than his old Vieux Carre apartment anyway. The thought made him laugh out loud.

"What?" Ann asked, as they were preparing to depart the jet. "What's so funny—what?" she elbowed him in the ribs.

"You're always hustling me into things, Ann. But I like the thought of my XKE out in front of your place."

After bustling through New Orleans International Airport, they hurried to Ann's Garden District home. Upon arriving at her house, the amorous new couple decided they needed to christen every room. They began in conventional manner, in the bedroom.

"How long have you lived here, Ann?" Robert asked after they had made love.

"I've lived here for two years now. I moved into this house when I came to New Orleans. Why do you ask?"

"I don't know. Just curious, I guess." Then: "I love your house in Cancun. Why didn't you move there permanently?"

"My job, silly! I'm dedicated to my work."

"Yes, your work. You really are dedicated, aren't you darling?"

"Yes I am."

"Do you want some coffee, dear?" She slipped on her gown and headed toward the kitchen.

"Yes, splendid idea! I love the way it reinvigorates me after sex," he laughed.

Sitting quietly in the kitchen sipping their coffee, Ann asked, "Are you ready to go to the hospital and get back to work?"

"Yes, I really am, in a way," he replied.

"This is going to be exciting, isn't it?"

"I think so."

"The societal implications could be enormous!"

"Enormous!" he mocked her serious tone.

"I'm serious. What?"

"I'm serious too, Ann. I was just teasing you a bit. What's the next step?" He got up to look out the large kitchen window. A squirrel played in the giant oak tree in the front yard.

Mr. Castner thinks it's a matter of compiling the data in a logistical manner, doing comparative work and then presenting Congress and the president with the data, hopefully to get the transplantation program approved here."

"Sounds like a lot of work."

"Mr. Castner thinks it will take a Herculean effort because the bureaucracy develops such an inertia. And the cost poses such a dilemma."

"But Ann, Dr. Guttierez feels the cost of the procedure will drop, as with any new process."

"Hopefully it will, darling." She joined him by the large window. "All we are to do here, Doctor, is keep our noses to the grindstone, accumulate the statistics, compare them to Raphael's mortality reports and help Mr. Castner present the facts to the NHCO and Congress. Hopefully they'll approve them."

"Yes, I guess that's all we can do for right now."

"Yes," She pulled him close.

He hugged her back. "Ann? Why don't you let Sally and some of the others at the hospital know what kind of research you're doing? They look at you as just another administrator."

She stomped her foot. "I will not explain myself to those people. Robert, you cannot tell anyone of our association with Dr. Guttierez, or the Hospital of the Americas."

"And why not?" he prodded. Her sheer gown revealed all of her body to him as she stood defiantly in front of the window.

"Mr. Castner understands politics much better than we do. He emphatically says that we have to be able to offer irrefutable evidence that this medical procedure is the way for the United States to go, or it will be shot down in subcommittee—period!"

"I admire your conviction, darling." Robert believed she knew the best course in this area. "I just thought that if the guys at work knew the implications of some of your work they would understand you better."

"Robert," she said, allowing her blouse to fall open slightly. "I'm not in a popularity contest here. I'm trying to achieve something that most people only dream of—helping people, truly helping people. Besides, I'm wealthy and I don't care what those people back at that hospital think of me or what they know.

"I'm absolutely certain that we have the chance to do something truly earth-shattering here," she continued. "The way you can best help the cause is to complete all the work, no matter how boring the NHCO forms are. It's going to be a major headache to follow my lead and get all the data compiled in a clear and concise manner."

"Yeah, I agree."

Ann sat back into a kitchen chair, sipping her coffee. She pulled both legs up to the seal of the chair, slowly allowing them to open.

Trying to suppress the feeling she was stirring in him, he swallowed hard.

"Want to christen the kitchen?" she purred. He tossed the coffee into the sink and joined her on the kitchen table.

The telephone rang after they had moved their lovemaking back to the bedroom. "Wouldn't you know it," Robert complained, rolling over as Ann picked up the phone.

"Hello…Jerri? How are you? That's okay, we just got back. Yeah, it was great. What's up?"

Jerri's voice was loud enough for Robert to make out the sound of his name.

"Yes, he's here—somewhere—" She smiled at Robert. "Let me see if I can find him."

She covered the phone with her hand. "It's Jerri. The new

E.R. doctor has Martin and Marion in the pediatric E.R. Jerri says they probably have strep throat, but they won't let anyone treat them but Dr. St. John."

"Silas' kids. I'll have to go."

"Jerri, he'll be there in a little bit."

Robert slipped into scrubs. Do you want to go with me?"

"No, sweetheart, I'm going to stay here. I'm exhausted." She rolled over in the bed.

Then, bolting straight up, she yelled: "Robert!"

"What?"

"You must not tell anyone about what's happening at the Hospital of the Americas. For all the reasons we talked about—the controversy and the timing of everything. It's too soon."

"Yeah, you're right." He sank down beside her on the bed. "Shoot, I would want to tell all the staff in the E.R. You know that work doesn't necessarily motivate these people. But this—this is *mega*-exciting."

"I know it is. I know it truly is a physician's dream—a chance to go down in medical history perhaps. But darling, please see things logically. You know how difficult is was to get the NHCO program passed. This will be just as politically explosive. And you never know who might want to see this study undermined. Are you willing to take that chance? The work is too important!"

"You're right, Ann. I just want the best for us."

"Think of all the people in the U.S. you potentially would help, Robert. And the beauty of this scenario, scientifically speaking, is only a limited number of people are really involved at this point in the scientific process, the crucial data-gathering phase, which should reduce or eliminate bias. Right?"

"You're right. Absolutely. It's just you, me and Dr. Guttierez."

"And Castner will press the issue at the appropriate time at NHCO and with Congress."

Robert stood up. "You're right. I want this to succeed as much as anybody, Ann. I've got to go. Silas' kids await."

"Okay." Ann slid back into bed. "I'll be waiting right here for you."

"I'll be back in a flash. Mum's the word." He hurried out of the house and drove to the hospital.

Robert entered the pediatric E.R. searching for his two small patients. Silas spotted him before he had time to get his pediatric stethoscope around his neck.

"Robert," Silas waved and motioned toward his two youngsters. "Thanks, Doc. I know it's a pain to come in to just see these two little fellows."

"No problem, Silas. Glad to do it." They shook hands. "I hear we have two young men who aren't feeling too well."

Marion and Martin nodded vigorously. The pediatric nurse told Robert that their strep cultures had turned out positive.

"Silas," Robert began, "we'll treat them with Amoxicillin, a penicillin derivative, which is still the drug of choice for strep throat."

"Okay Doc, whatever you think is best."

Robert removed two written prescriptions from his pad and handed them to Silas. "A teaspoon three times daily for ten days, Silas. By the way, young fellas, which one of you is the quarterback for the Saints this week?"

Martin and Marion immediately turned and pointed their index fingers at one another.

Silas laughed. "Robert, after the Saints' quarterback threw four interceptions last Sunday, neither one wants to be him now."

Robert couldn't help but laugh. Bending over he hugged his two young patients. "Four interceptions? I don't blame you—I wouldn't want to be him either! Be good, fellas, and take all of your medicine." They nodded their heads affirmatively.

"They also have decided that they can't talk since they

have the dreaded strep throat," Silas said.

Robert laughed again. "Guys, I'll let you talk, but you can't kiss girls." Both youngsters wrinkled their faces and wiped their mouths clean at the mention of kissing girls.

Silas shook Robert's hand. "Thanks again, Doc. See you at Commander's soon."

"See you, Silas. We'll probably be back in a couple of nights."

Robert laughed again at his two young patients as he walked toward the Adult E.R.

Chapter Six

Dr. St. John," Sally Ortiz's familiar voice came from behind an E.R. curtain covering Cubicle 4.

"You aren't speaking Spanish, Sally," he said as he pulled back the curtain. "That means you must be in a good mood."

An elderly woman was receiving an ophthalmological examination from a female physician Robert didn't recognize. Sally came up and hugged him.

"I'm not mad at you, Doctor." She looked behind him. "Where is she?"

"Back at the house," he confided.

"Good! Can you keep her there?"

"Okay, Sally. If you only knew." Robert bit his tongue, remembering to not say anything about the exciting revelation of his Mexican trip.

"Believe me, Dr. St. John, I know her!"

"Who are you talking about?" asked the young female doctor.

"Ann Finn!" snorted Sally in obvious disgust.

"And who is the new doctor, Sally?" Robert asked.

"Dr. St. John, this is Dr. Elizabeth Sheridan Johnson."

Elizabeth held a hand out and Robert shook it. He was still unable to see her face as she continued her exam.

Elizabeth inquired, without interrupting her exam: "What's wrong with Ann Finn?"

"Oh! You really don't want to know, Dr. Johnson." Sally rolled her eyes in contempt of the absent administrator.

"Personality clash," Robert offered in rebuttal as he grabbed Sally, pulling her to him and kissing her on the cheek.

Elizabeth completed her examination, shaking her long blonde hair as she put the ophthalmoloscope back into her pocket.

"Retinitus pigmentosa—the other E.R. doctor's diagnosis is correct. I am going to arrange an ophthalmological consult for you to receive proper care."

The elderly patient thanked her and left the cubicle.

Elizabeth turned to Dr. St. John, extending her hand in formal introduction. "I hear you're going to be my new boss."

"Yes, I guess I am." He hoped she didn't hear the rush of inhaled air he took when finally face-to-face with her intense beauty.

"Where'd you go to medical school? he sputtered like a shy prepubescent. He could feel his face turning a bright crimson.

"Duke, but I'm originally from Atlanta.

Sally, sensing mutual chemistry, pulled their hands apart. "That's enough professional fraternalization for now." She pulled him toward the E.R. office.

"I'll talk to you again soon," Robert offered as Sally dragged him away."

"Bye-bye," Elizabeth said with a syrupy Georgian accent, giving a feminine wave.

"That's all you need, Señor Testosterone, another female friend!" Sally pushed the door closed behind her, ensuring their privacy. "Officer Elliott called for you yesterday."

The mention of the officer's name brought him back to the harsh realities of the happenings of the recent past. Robert felt himself collapsing into the nearest chair.

"What did he say, Sally? Was there any news?"

"He didn't confide in me. But the tone of his voice indicated he just wanted to touch bases with you."

"I see. I had completely forgotten to call him because the Mexico trip came up so unexpectedly."

"If I were Officer Elliott, I'd have had the Mexican federales arrest Ann Finn."

"What is it with you and Ann? Oh, never mind!" he shouted quickly before she could respond. "I'll call Officer Elliott right now, but I don't have anything to tell him."

He fumbled in his wallet for the officer's phone number . He had kept it with him just in case something unusual did come up.

Dr. St. John tried to be coy. "Tell me about the new E.R. doctor, Sally."

"What do you want to know about her, Doctor—her bra size?"

"Sally." Robert stopped his search for Officer Elliott's telephone number. "Why must you be so impertinent? I merely want you to tell me if she's a good doctor, in your opinion."

"She's single," Sally retorted.

"That's not what I asked, Sally."

"I'll let you alone, Robert. You can call Officer Elliott in private."

"Thanks, Sally."

"By the way, how was your Mexican getaway?"

"Great. Ann just needed a rest, a little breather from the stress, you know."

"Okay. Just curious."

Dr. St. John called Officer Elliott after finding the number.

"Hello, Officer Elliott speaking."

"Sandy Elliott. This is Dr. Robert St. John."

"Well, the traveling doctor! How are you? Why didn't you tell me you were going to Mexico?"

"I didn't think it would matter. I guess I wasn't thinking."

"Oh, I think you were thinking, Doctor. You were just

thinking with that wrong head again."

"Officer Elliott, that's not true. Oh, there's no need to explain anything to you. I haven't perceived anything unusual or out of sorts. I was going to call you after getting back from the trip."

"That's okay, Dr. St. John. I was just teasing you anyway."

"Officer, have you had any different thoughts about Dave's death. Are you still suspicious? Did anything turn up?"

"No, nothing. Lieutenant Sheldon found out that I was snooping around this, and he blew his Cajun stack. He threatened to fire me...you know how it is."

"Yeah, I can guess." But how did he find out what you were thinking?"

"Beats me, Doc. I thought you might have turned me in. That's why I didn't like you fleeing the country to Mexico."

"Fleeing the country? Good grief!"

"Well, I think there's a suspicious death, possibly homicide, and the guy I don't suspect and actually confide in goes off to a foreign country two days later!"

"I see your point, Officer."

"Don't worry, Doc. After all, I knew which head you were thinking with. By the way, how is the beautiful Ms. Finn?"

"Oh, she's fine, Officer. Uh, I really don't like to discuss that, though. It's embarrassing, and it makes me look like a cold-hearted jerk."

"Look, who cares about appearances, Doc? You're human too, and if you and the lady help each other through this, I personally would advise you not to care what anyone says."

"Well thanks, Officer Elliott, I guess. I think that makes me feel better."

"All I'm saying is life is for the living, Dr. St. John. Okay?"

"Sure. Do you want me to still contact you if anything

out of the ordinary happens?"

"Well, considering my supervisor, Lieutenant Sheldon, is going to can my ass if I waste time on what he considers an obvious suicide, you better be sure that it is something extremely—outrageously—out of the ordinary."

"Okay, I understand, Officer. I'll probably see you around."

"Oh sure. You're going to be sure to see me, considering all the murders in this city."

"I'll probably see you in the E.R. some night, don't you think?"

"Yes sir, unfortunately you are correct. Okay, Doc. Behave yourself. Take care of your new lady friend. She's a looker."

"I'll do that, Officer. See you."

"Doctor," one of the nurses opened the room to the room. "I'm sorry to interrupt, but we have a man with a seizure disorder coming in by ambulance. Dr. Johnson asked if you would help with this one while you're here and all."

"Certainly. I'll be glad to. Give me a second to make a phone call."

"Sure, Doctor, the ambulance is still about five minutes away."

"Oh, nurse," he said before she closed the door. "Is that patient actively seizing?"

"Yes sir."

"Let's get an I.V. ready: Valium I.V. push and start a Dilantin drip."

"Yes sir."

Robert decided to call Ann, as he had spent more time at the hospital than he had expected.

"Hello, Ann."

"Robert, where are you? I thought you would be back an hour ago."

"A couple of things came up, and I'm going to help an intern with a seizure patient that's coming in now."

"Do you have to?"

"Yes, dear, it'll only take me a second and then I'll be right back."

"Okay, but hurry! Just don't drive that Jag so fast you get a ticket!" she laughed.

"Oh, speaking of police, Officer Elliott and I talked."

"What about?"

"Oh, nothing. He just confided, you know, that with the autopsy and evidence and everything, that the case was closed."

"I never knew there was a case." Ann's voice sounded agitated.

"There wasn't really. Never mind. I'm sorry I even brought it up."

"That episode of our life is over. That's the past, Robert. We have so much to look forward to: travel, accomplishments. You know all that we have to look forward to."

"Dr. St. John," the nurse burst back into the room. "Sorry to interrupt, but the patient is here."

"Thanks nurse, I'll be right there. Ann, I've got to go. I'll be there in just a few minutes."

Chapter Seven

Dr. St. John! Dr. St. John! Dr. Johnson would like you to help her in E.R. Cubicle 4, *stat!*" The E.R. nurse's frantic voice trailed away as she headed to a group of interns, nurses and Dr. Elizabeth Johnson.

One of the paramedics who brought the patient in said, "Good luck, Doc. That's one seizing son of a bitch," as he pushed the stretcher past him back to the ambulance.

"Dr. Johnson, what's the status of this patient?" Robert asked, peering into the large group of people.

"Status epilepticus. I'm finally getting some response from the I.V. Diazepam." She looked up and smiled at him. "I didn't want you to leave the hospital if we hadn't stabilized him first."

"Have you started intubation yet?" he asked.

"Just starting."

The patient on the stretcher had finally quit the jerking motions that were classically seen in a grand mal seizure.

"Thank you, Doctor." Elizabeth looked up again and smiled. "First week on the job, you know. I feel better now. Do you have somewhere to go?"

"No, not really." Robert responded, mesmerized by her smiling face.

Damn, he thought, *when it rains it pours! Three months of no women at all, then two of the most beautiful girls in the world just plunk down in front of me. That's the way it goes.*

"Continue the I.V., Doctor, get blood gases, SMAC-24, CBC and call me when the CT scan is set up for the study of the patient's head.

"Do you want to go get a cup of coffee, Doctor?" Dr. Johnson walked out of the cubicle and grabbed his forearm.

"Sure, I guess so, sure. I don't have anywhere to go," he said, completely forgetting Ann waiting for him at his new home.

"Let's go to the doctors' lounge then." She pulled off her white coat and hung up her stethoscope. She wore a black business-style dress suit. She was slightly taller than Ann and probably more voluptuous if that was possible.

The lounge was empty. An old-fashioned coffee pot was brewing fresh coffee for the staff on duty.

"So, you're from Atlanta?" He poured them both Styrofoam cups of coffee. "Cream and sugar, Elizabeth? May I call you Elizabeth?"

"Call me Betsy," she responded. "And I like my coffee black."

He handed her the coffee. "How did you wind up in the Big Easy, Betsy?"

"Let's see. Well, I'm a real daddy's girl. My father's an executive with Coca-Cola in Atlanta. I went to Duke in North Carolina. When this job offer came up, I grabbed it immediately. I think I needed to get away on my own."

He couldn't help but smile at her.

"What's so funny?"

"You're such a beautiful woman, and you're a doctor. I wouldn't think you would need to get away from your family to feel independent."

"You don't know my Daddy: Mr. Kevin Johnson of the Johnson family of Atlanta. He is all Southerner, and I'm his ultra-Southern Belle daughter as far as he is concerned." She leaned forward confidentially. "When I graduated from Duke, the whole family came to see me at my Durham apartment. I was entertaining a young gentleman friend. Nothing was going on, really. The guy was a fellow medical student. The family arrived sort of unannounced. And I thought Daddy would tear the poor boy's head off. Believe me, I needed to get away! I love my family very much, but…"

"I see," he nodded reassuringly.

"Besides, I hear New Orleans is a fun place for a single, unattached woman." She coiled her hair with her hand.

"It is! It is!" He laughed. The figure of Ann Finn with her arms crossed over her chest flashed into his mind's eye.

"Dr. St. John," Robert heard the operator's voice over the hospital intercom. "Dr. St. John, telephone."

"Will you excuse me just a minute?" He smiled at Elizabeth and picked up the lounge phone on the table.

"Dr. St. John?" the operator asked.

"Yes, this is Dr. St. John." He shifted the telephone to his right hand so he could continue to gaze at Dr. Johnson.

"Robert!" came the authoritative voice of Ann Finn.

He shifted the telephone rapidly to his left hand and cupped the right hand over the receiver.

"Ann, Ann," he repeated. "I'm just leaving the hospital…."

"The nurse in the E.R. said the seizure patient was under control and that you weren't in the E.R. Where are you, Robert?"

"Uh, uh…I'm in the doctor's lounge."

"What are you doing in the lounge? Why aren't you on the way home?"

"I am, I am. I'm just walking out the door."

He cupped his hand over the telephone and glanced back at Elizabeth, smiling at her. Betsy smiled back as if saying: "I know that's your girlfriend."

"Who's there, Robert?'

"Well, Ann, there are several people here, uh, the new doctor you hired…"

"Funny, I don't hear anyone else talking."

"They're exhausted, Ann. You know, long call day. That's it, they're exhausted."

"They're not saying a word, Robert."

He looked back at Dr. Johnson and smiled broadly.

"The new doctor is there?" Ann asked.

"Yes, she's here. I'm coming home right now."

"What's she like? Her record at Duke was impeccable, but there was no picture or description, other than that she was a single, white, 26-year-old female."

"Homely, wears glasses." He cupped his hand over the phone, not daring to look back at Elizabeth.

"Yeah, I figured as much," Ann interrupted. "With all those A's in medical school she's obviously smart. I figured she would fit in well and follow the protocols. You remember the very important work you're now in charge of, Robert."

"Absolutely. See you in a little bit."

"Bye."

Robert hung up the telephone and attempted to nonchalantly rejoin the young doctor sipping her coffee.

"Girlfriend?" Elizabeth looked up and smiled broadly.

"Oh, no—just a friend," he lied, hoping this lovely creature hadn't overheard him call her *homely*. "I really need to go, though."

She stood. "Me too."

"Do you think you need me anymore in the E.R., Elizabeth?"

"No, thanks. I'm just waiting on lab and CT head scan."

"Remember to keep the Dilantin drip going overnight."

"I will," she laughed. "I did study at Duke, you know."

"Just trying to be helpful," he added, slightly embarrassed.

"I know. Thanks." Then: "Would you like to have supper some night, Robert?"

He was taken aback by her forthrightness.

"Yes, uh, yes, I would, I guess."

"Good. When?"

"Soon, soon. I'll check my calendar at home and..." recovering his composure somewhat, "I'll talk to you tomorrow. Is that okay?"

"Sure." She beamed as they parted ways—she to the E.R. and he to Ann and his new home.

He paused at the doors leading out to the parking lot. He

turned and watched her as she opened the doors to the E.R.

"You're not shy, are you?" he called to her. "I mean for a Southern girl!"

She stopped and turned toward him. "No, not at all!" She tossed her hair in a large exaggerated motion and disappeared into the E.R.

He meandered through the parking lot. The outline of the Superdome reflected back on the walls of the old hospital. Robert paused at the XKE. He looked back at the reflection and couldn't help thinking about the contrast of the two buildings. One represented the old way of building—masonry and mortar. The new, shiny steel of the Superdome looked almost like a spaceship, a giant metallic spaceship plopped down and forgotten in this historic city. He returned to the XKE, climbed in and ignited the engine. Slowly driving past the front of the hospital, it struck him as ironic that it was in the worn, old building rather than the new that he would have a hand in developing a revolutionary new procedure that would help all of mankind. "Damn," he said out loud, "and I can't tell a soul." He sped down Poydras Street toward his new home.

Ann greeted him with a kiss as he entered the Midtown home.

"Supper is ready, darling. Do you like soft-shell crab?"

"Love it. How did you know?"

"Just guessed. That's why I was so anxious for you to get home. It's my specialty."

They talked about a lot of subjects that night. They were still getting to know each other and were curious about the circumstances of one another's lives.

Robert found out that Ann had studied business administration at Harvard. She learned that he had always wanted to be a doctor. They had both lost their parents at an early age.

"Your furniture and belongings are being moved tomorrow."

"Great!" Robert exclaimed. "I really miss my U.T. football and my baseball glove. And of course my golf clubs."

"We have a lot in common," Ann smiled at him. "I love golf also."

"Really? What handicap do you carry?"

"A seven."

He nodded in appreciation. "Not bad!"

"I am pretty good." She mimicked a golf swing. Her breasts bulged through the tight shirt she wore.

He began to playfully push her toward the bedroom.

"Uh, I see," as she glanced at him over her shoulder. "You want to discuss something with me in the bedroom."

"I just want to get to know you better," he laughed.

"Hmm," she said as she removed her shirt. "Have you ever noticed that this is about all we do?"

"It's a good foundation to build a relationship on," he said as he pulled her on top of him on the bed.

* * *

"Let's drive in together to the hospital," Ann suggested, as they dressed the next morning.

"Good idea. I have a lot of paperwork to catch up on."

"Robert, we'll work together on the NHCO forms and protocols, if that's okay"

"Okay? It's great—from what I've seen it's just a bureau-cratic bundle of—"

"Well, don't forget that our, or at least Mr. Castner's, presentation to Congress about the transplant program's implementation in the U.S. will depend a great deal on the pathology data that you present in those papers."

"I know, but minutiae is not my forte."

"Don't worry, darling." Ann kissed him reassuringly. "I'll help you remember."

"Great. Thanks, Ann. We have a lot of work to do, don't we?"

"*Lots.*"

They walked hand-in-hand to the Jaguar. "I'll drive— I'm in the mood," Robert said, jumping in the driver's seat.

"Oh, Robert, let me leave the key with Mrs. Sutton next door so the movers can get into the house when they bring your football and baseball glove."

"Hey, tell Mrs. Sutton to tell the boys to be careful with that stuff!"

Robert dropped Ann off at the front of the hospital close to the administration offices.

"Come up to see me at my office after you check in at the E.R.," Ann said as she kissed him on the cheek.

"I'll do it."

"Park in my place if you want to, dear."

Robert pulled carefully into Ann's space, making sure no car doors could open and scratch his beloved automobile. As he started toward the E.R., he noticed Dr. Johnson in the parking lot.

"Dr. Elizabeth Sheridan Johnson, how in the world are you?" He noted her stunning Chanel outfit. "Whoa! I've never seen an E.R. doc dress quite like that."

She turned around as if she were on a Paris runway. "My Daddy always wanted me to 'dress nicely,'" she said, laughing. "How do you like it?"

"Aren't you afraid blood will get on it and ruin about $1,000 worth of clothing?"

"Doctor, that's why they give us these." She lifted her hospital-issued white coat.

"I have one too," he said, holding his coat up.

"I guess that makes us twins." She bumped him with her hips in a flirtatious manner.

"How's your seizure patient doing?"

"It's funny you asked. He crashed and burned last p.m."

"You're kidding. When I left last night he was stable. I thought —"

"That's what's strange—he was stable! I put him in the unit on a Dilantin drip. His CT scan was negative, electrolytes messed up some, but nothing major."

"Probably a big drinker, huh, Betsy?"

"It's sure not a good start for me. My first seriously ill

117

patient, and he dies. I know he was a drinker and that was the probable cause of his status epilepticus...but no apparent cause of death?"

"Betsy," they stopped at the threshold of the E.R. door, "Let me reassure you, the indigent patients we treat here are the hardest to treat in the world. In no way will you be blamed." He placed his hand on her shoulder in a reassuring manner.

"Thanks, Robert, that makes me feel better."

"P.P.O.," he said as they entered into the E.R.

"Piss-poor protoplasm," both simultaneously muttered.

"What's your schedule this month, Doctor?" Elizabeth asked, as they passed the bulletin board where schedules were posted.

"Let's look." They stood shoulder to shoulder, surveying the schedules.

She pointed to a Saturday a week ahead. "We're both off then, Doctor."

He gulped. "Yes, I see we are."

"I guess it's a date then." She looked at him with big blue eyes.

"I guess so, Elizabeth."

"Good, it's a date." She turned into the E.R. "Seven o'clock, I'll meet you here."

She glanced over her shoulder: "And don't be late."

He stared at her backside and felt that sexual stirring deep in his body that only a beautiful woman as she or Ann could make him feel.

Ann! His thoughts scrambled back to his live-in boss. *What the hell am I doing?* He decided to go upstairs and check Ann's office.

Maybe Ann is going to be on the space shuttle to Mars that weekend. What am I doing, making a date with this beautiful young doctor while living with my boss? You damn fool!

"Code Blue I.C.U. Code Blue I.C.U." blared over the P.A. Robert changed direction and began to run upstairs with a group of other doctors and nurses.

Sally Ortiz met the rushing group with raised arms. "Stop. Don't bother. I'm calling the code. The patient has expired."

Breathless, Dr. St. John asked, "What happened?"

Sally just shrugged. "A patient admitted last night just coded, and I've called it. Not anything we can do."

The I.C.U. nurse was pulling a sheet over the newly deceased. Sally hooked her arm through Robert's. "Come on, let's go." The rest of the group dispersed.

Sally looked at Robert. "You like Dr. Johnson, don't you?"

"Sure, she's a nice young lady," he stammered.

Sally let go of him as she turned toward the nursing office. "Be careful," she clucked, disappearing into the office.

Dr. St. John wondered why that code had been called so quickly. "Piss-poor protoplasm," he mumbled to himself.

Stuffing his hands in his scrub-suit pockets, he ambled toward Ann Finn's office again. He knew Sally's admonition to be careful meant Ann wouldn't tolerate him messing around.

"Jerri, is Ann here?" Robert asked, craning his neck in search of her in the back office.

"Yes, she is. But I think Mr. Levitz is in the office with her now."

"I'll wait." He sat down in a chair, flipping through a *Sports Illustrated*. He kept an eye on the door to the office where Ann and Mr. Levitz were meeting.

"Look, Jerri, here's an article on the University of Tennessee football team!" Excited, he held up the magazine to a page with young football players dressed in the bright orange and white uniforms he had grown to love.

"Oh," the obviously disinterested secretary responded. "That's a pretty orange."

He began to immerse himself in the article about how the University of Tennessee had become the premier football program in the nation, in the author's opinion, under Coach Phil Fulmer. He looked at a picture of the massive stadium, with its orange and white checkered end zones. The colorful end zones reminded him of the afternoon in Knoxville when he and Ann had been thrown off the football field by stadium security.

"Ann's schedule!"

Jerri looked up. "What about Ann's schedule?'

"Do you have a copy of Ann's schedule here?"

"Dr. St. John, Ms. Finn is a very private person. She generally doesn't like other people knowing her private business. Even personal friends such as you."

"Jerri," he began, "you know that Ann and I have started a personal relationship."

"I know. Everybody knows, Dr. St. John."

Robert felt his ears burning and knew they were a slight shade of pink. He wished he didn't blush so easily. "I didn't know it was common knowledge."

Jerri rolled her eyes and parted her lips. "There aren't many secrets in this hospital."

"I'm not trying to pry, but Saturday will be our first month anniversary and I want to surprise her.

"This Saturday, Doctor?"

"Yes."

"Oh, I think that's what she's talking to Mr. Levitz about." She leaned toward as if to whisper to him.

"I'll tell you if you promise not to tell."

He crossed his heart.

Jerri barely whispered. "I think she's going to Washington, D.C. today. Something about Mr. Castner and NHCO and some kind of forms or paperwork that we're behind on."

"Oh, I see. When's she coming back?"

Jerri crossed her arms. "All men are dogs, Dr. St. John, and I'm not telling you. Nothing personal of course."

"Of course, Jerri. It's just that I want to have a surprise get-together for her, and you're invited if we have it." He played on the knowledge that Jerri loved parties.

"I think she's going to be gone a week or longer. Usually that's the itinerary when she goes to Washington."

Acting disappointed, Robert said: "Oh, rats. Maybe I can go with her so I won't have to miss our anniversary."

"I doubt it. She usually has loads of important work to do when she goes to Washington. She always takes a ton of NHCO paperwork up that Mr. Castner looks over before it goes to NIH or something. It's obviously very important."

"I see. How do you know all this, Jerri?"

"I know a lot of things, Dr. St. John. That's why I said all men are dogs a minute ago. I thought you just wanted to know if Ann was leaving because of the new female doctor."

His ears became red hot. Feigning innocence, he asked, "What doctor do you mean, Jerri?"

"The new E.R. doctor—she's very beautiful. Some of the staff say she's even prettier than Ann."

"Really, Jerri?"

"That's right, Dr. St. John, and you're a handsome single guy, so I just figured two plus two equals four. Naturally I thought you and the new doc had made plans or had eyes for each other."

"Oh, no, Jerri. It's just that I'm planning this anniversary party for Ann and myself..."

"Good, I don't include you then, Doctor, among those useless guys I've known that will treat a girl any old way. They'll be out in a minute."

Robert sat back down and leafed through the magazine pretending to read about his beloved Orange and White. After a moment Jerri interrupted him.

"I'll tell you a little secret, Dr. St. John. Ann was very mad at Mr. Levitz for recommending Dr. Johnson for the job."

"Why?"

"Because Ann didn't know what she looked like until Sally Ortiz came by and told her about fifteen minutes before you walked in."

"Sally told her what?"

"That Elizabeth was prettier than Ann was, and younger, and has a better body. You may not know this, but Nurse Ortiz and Ann don't like each other."

"No joke," he replied. "And Ann knows that Dr. Johnson is pretty?

"Nurse Ortiz used the words 'stunning' and 'beautiful' to describe her body."

"That's something Sally would do," Robert muttered to himself. "Thanks, Jerri."

"Think nothing of it, Doctor. I'm sure you and Ann will be very happy."

"We are." He sat back on the couch and tried to concentrate on the magazine. If the truth be known he didn't really feel morally comfortable with his and Ann's relationship. It was just that they needed each other so badly after Dave's death. She was so beautiful, but on the other hand, he was actually more attracted to Elizabeth. His head felt light and dizzy.

Why do women do this to me?" he wondered. *Ann is your boss—you have a chance to do exciting work in the medical field—extraordinary ground-breaking work—Ann is beautiful and wealthy, with a great body, wonderful sexually."* That settled it—he couldn't see Elizabeth.

Still, there was something about her that was drawing him to her—that was obvious, and in a way Ann never could. He felt dizzy again, and he began to hold his head at the temples with his open hands. *Good Lord. I can perform in the most pressurized medical situations without even an elevated heart rate, but leave it to two women to make me a wreck.*

"That settles it." The voice of Mr. Levitz interrupted his train of thought. "Ann, you'll leave immediately for Washington."

The door to Ann's office swung all the way open. Ann's concerned face was nodding in a supportive manner.

She caught a glimpse of Robert out of the corner of her eye. She smiled and motioned for him to join them.

"Mr. Levitz, you know Dr. Robert St. John."

"Absolutely," Mr. Levitz pumped Robert's hand enthusiastically.

"Dr. St. John is our new E.R. director, Mr. Levitz." Ann

smiled.

"I know, I know," Mr. Levitz responded.

Carlos Levitz was a thin, pale individual no one at the hospital knew very well. He obviously had many duties, including coordinating the business matters of the NHCO. Ann Finn was considered by most of the staff as the de facto administrator at New Orleans because of Levitz's long absences.

"We're expecting you to do a good job, Dr. St. John. We've evidently got a paperwork mess at the moment. I've asked Ms. Finn to go to Washington to straighten everything out. The NHCO has been informed by NIH and the Department of Health and Human Services that your predecessor, Dr. Wyatt, wasn't doing a very good job."

Robert hung his head a little, feeling embarrassed for his friend.

"No offense, Dr. St. John. Dr. Wyatt was a good doctor. But evidently his skills as administrator of the autopsy program and E.R. director were lacking."

"Don't worry, Mr. Levitz," Ann interjected. "I will personally guarantee you that Dr. St. John will get us back in the good graces of Health and Human Services, NHCO and our fellow researchers at NIH."

"Mr. Levitz smiled broadly.

"Ann, your word is good enough for me. You know how outrageously demanding all this bureaucratic mess has become since the NHCO took over the country's health care."

"We'll do it," Robert reassured Mr. Levitz.

"Good, son. The poor bastard before you evidently couldn't handle the pressure."

Although Robert agreed with Mr. Levitz's perceptions concerning Dave Wyatt, he couldn't help but feel more than a twinge of anger at this man who probably hadn't even known his best friend.

"I'll contact you the minute I get back from Washington, Mr. Levitz," Ann reiterated, leading him to the door. She sensed the anger he had brought out in Robert.

"Good, do that," he responded. "I'll be looking forward to that." Stopping halfway through the office door, he added: "Let me know how the new E.R. doctor works out. I really shouldn't have hired her without asking you first. If Nurse Ortiz complains about her behavior again, or if her mortality rate appears too high we can always make a change."

"Thank you, Mr. Levitz. I'm glad you see it my way. I'll call you the minute I get back."

Robert began to follow Ann into her office. "Robert, will you give me a moment to call Washington and Mr. Castner at NHCO?"

"Yes, Ann, of course."

"It will just take a second, Robert. I think better if I have privacy. I'll explain everything that's happened in five minutes. Wait here with Jerri just a minute more, okay love?" She kissed him on the lips.

Robert returned to his seat and again began to leaf through the football article.

"I told you," Jerri whispered.

He scooted forward in his seat and whispered back: "What's going on, do you know?"

"Ann Finn is not happy that Mr. Levitz hired Dr. Johnson."

"I thought Ann hired her."

"She did, but Mr. Levitz basically told her to. Politics or something. And remember, you two were going to Mexico and we needed someone immediately in the E.R."

"I remember."

"I'll tell you something else, Dr. St. John. Nurse Ortiz didn't say anything to Ann about Dr. Johnson, other than she was beautiful."

"Oh, really? Sally didn't say anything about her conduct?"

Jerri crept closer and lowered her voice even more. "Ann doesn't like to have other attractive women around the hospital. She considers this place her domain: she doesn't like competition. I would consider it convenient, in a way."

"Why?"

"She cares for you; she wants to make sure you're not tempted to stray."

"Oh? Aren't you getting a little personal now, Jerri? Dr. Johnson and Ms. Finn are professionals."

Jerri acted offended and threw up her hands.

"I said it before, and I'll say it again: When it comes to beautiful women, all men are dogs!"

Ann Finn opened the door, not a second too late as far as Robert was concerned.

"Come on in and I'll fill you in."

Jerri acted oblivious to the fact that he had ever been in the room. "Remember your anniversary, Doctor, when Ann is in Washington," she mouthed.

He circled her desk and walked into Ann's office. Ann kissed him after he had closed the door.

"Did Jerri entertain you while I was busy?"

"I didn't know she was—how do I put it?"

"Opinionated!"

"Exactly," he agreed. They both laughed.

"She does excellent work; otherwise she'd be fired." Ann circled around to her desk.

Dr. St. John was unable to contain his curiosity. "What's up in Washington?"

"You've seen the NHCO documentation required?" A large tear rolled down her cheek. "Dave just wasn't doing anything right—the bureaucrats—" she stopped to regain her composure.

Robert reached over and kissed the tear off her face.

Ann kissed him passionately. "All you have to do is help me prepare the work properly. I have to go to NHCO and correct a lot of things prior to going to NIH. Mr. Castner said we're in jeopardy of losing our privileges in autopsy and spinal procedures."

"What can I do, Ann? Do you want me to go with you to D.C.?"

"No!" she said firmly. "There's nothing you can do

there. I have to straighten this all out myself. I know the ropes; I know what they want. I've had to do this before. I'll probably be gone a week to ten days. I'll just hole up at the Ritz and correct all the mistakes—Dave's mistakes."

"I see." He was torn between the fact that he wanted to help Ann—out of allegiance—and his desire to get to know Elizabeth Johnson better. He had thought he might possibly be in love with her last week, but he and Ann weren't married, after all. *No, she's just my boss and I just moved into the woman's home!* he thought.

Her moist kiss brought him back from the debate raging in his head.

"You know how you can help me, baby?"

He kissed her back. "How?"

"Go through the stack of NHCO papers that I'll leave for you. I can leave them at the house for you to work on while I'm gone. It will give you plenty to do in case you get lonely."

"I've seen them before, but I don't want to mess things up."

"Robert, all you have to do is complete the first part. I've always filled in the really complicated parts of the forms later."

"Why? Wouldn't it be easier if I just did the whole thing?"

"Go ahead and try it. But these are bureaucrats we're trying to please. I know what they're looking for."

"That doesn't make sense!"

"This is government bureaucracy we're talking about, Robert. You've seen the requisition forms and all the crap you have to handle to practice medicine in the system. The whole damn thing doesn't make sense."

He nodded his head in understanding.

"Yeah, the government can screw up anything."

"Robert! What a thing to say! Watch your tongue." She couldn't suppress a little laugh. "Actually, darling, I couldn't have put it better myself."

"There's something else I want you to do when I'm gone."

"What's that?"

"Stay away from the new E.R. doctor, Elizabeth Johnson."

He felt his ears getting hot again. "Why, whatever do you mean?"

"She's already lost a patient on her first shift that she shouldn't have."

"Ann, you know these people who have abused themselves sometimes die inexplicably. It's part of providing care at a large charity hospital like ours. It just happens—it's nobody's fault."

"Well, this patient was poorly managed, that's all I can say. What's the deal between you and this Dr. Johnson anyway?"

He blushed again. "Nothing." He stumbled for words. "What I mean is that I'm sick of doctors being blamed for poor outcomes in this kind of institution. It's not the doctor's fault!"

She punched his chest with her index finger. "Well, the staff has already complained about her."

"That's not true! You're just jealous." He immediately regretted letting the words slip out.

Ann punched him in the chest. She threw herself onto her office desk and began to sob.

Their first fight, and over what? Another woman. He should have known. His remorse was immediate.

"Ann, darling..." He pulled her trembling torso toward him, kissing her face over and over in a romantic gesture.

"Leave me alone!" She pushed him away.

He was overwhelmed by her distraught actions. He felt his feelings bubble to the surface and said, "Darling, I'm in love with you!"

She stopped crying and looked up into his eyes.

"Do you mean it?" she whispered.

He kissed her passionately. "Yes."

"Don't ever hurt me, Robert."

"I won't, Ann. Never."

Ann walked over to the door and locked it. She pushed him back into the large chair next to her desk. "Don't ever betray me, Robert." She unzipped his fly. "I need you too much, and I've fallen in love, too."

Robert protested at first, but he quickly forgot everything as she brought him to ecstasy. Afterward, she helped him adjust his clothing and regain his composure before leaving the office.

"I'll see you when I return from Washington."

"Are you leaving now, right this minute?"

"Yes, I've got to. Mr. Castner emphasized that it's most urgent that I straighten all of this mess out now. Our government funding depends on me.

"I see. I'll be waiting for you then, Ann," he said, kissing her again.

"I guess that means if I call the house at night, you'll be doing the paperwork I've asked you to do."

"Yes, ma'am. I'll be a good little boy. Don't you trust me?"

"Men aren't to be trusted, Robert, unless you make the consequences such that they understand they must behave. Did you enjoy what I just did to you?"

His face broke out into a huge grin. "I loved it."

"See what I mean?" There will be a lot more of that if you prove you truly care for me."

"Yes, dear. I'll get to work on the NHCO forms tonight."

"Great. And Robert," she held his face firmly, "do you remember the Lorena Bobbitt lady, and what she did to the man she was with?"

"Oh!" He instantly grabbed his crotch, making a pained face. "Ann, you wouldn't."

"Robert, I'm just telling you I don't want to go through any more pain in my life. Remember that."

Chapter Eight

The week Ann was in Washington passed quickly for Dr. St. John. He spent most of his spare time at her house attempting to complete the mountain of NHCO forms there. He deduced that the paperwork the mountain represented was too much for any one person to complete. The complexities of the questions made reasonable answers from reasonable assumptions impossible.

He first noticed this on the second form, which concerned a patient named Thomas Jefferson Hastings. Mr. Hastings had diabetes, which in all probability had caused him to develop heart, kidney and peripheral vascular disease as well. However, the NHCO forms had requested confirmation that Mr. Hastings had died of heart disease only. This was straightforward enough; obviously this was the ultimate cause of death. Dave had filled in the forms up to that part. The Catch-22 of all this was that the doctor was asked to positively determine the cause of death was heart disease, and in no way related to the diabetes.

Dave's answer had been marked through, and Ann had written over the answer. No" was changed to "Yes." *Damn,* Robert thought. *Why would she do that?*

There was no way that this patient's death could absolutely, positively be linked to heart disease only. If this was an essay answer on a test, Dave would have excelled at explaining the complex relationships between diabetes and the pathology in organs throughout the body. But the question required only a yes or no answer. No wonder Dave went crazy and killed himself.

"Bureaucrats," Robert muttered out loud, then reasoned: *Ann had simply marked through Dave's responses and written what she assumed the bureaucrat who would review this would want to know and would understand.*

Robert continued to plod through the stack of papers Ann had left for him. He shook his head in bewilderment. "Poor Dave. This is impossible! Those morons in Washington don't know anything!" he yelled. He threw a chart of a kidney patient who also suffered diabetes against the wall.

"Medicine is much more complicated than that. What simplistic crap presented in these stupid forms!"

He got up to get a beer. He figured he needed it. Opening the refrigerator door, he wondered whether all the work that had to be done to present the data to Mr. Castner and NHCO would be worth it.

He opened the beer and read on in disgust. None of these questions could be answered in the format presented. *How are we going to be able to present consistent findings to those Washington pinheads when the format presentation they provide us is this screwed up?* The complexity of the task at hand was beginning to sink in.

One thing that puzzled him was that Ann had denied autopsies to many patients with multiple pathologies. Yet some other patients with acute trauma or only one organ system disease were autopsied. That didn't make any sense. He knew that must have infuriated Dave also: the chance to study some significant pathology passed over for another autopsy on a patient who was obviously younger and healthier.

He got another beer from the refrigerator and reassured himself. *Ann knows what she's doing. She obviously knows what Mr. Castner feels will be important to present to Congress at the appropriate time.* Sipping on the beer, he attempted to complete another form. The patient had died of a stroke but had severe electrolyte imbalance, including an extremely low blood sugar. Yet the NHCO form wanted the physician, or whoever filled out the forms, to unequivocally state that the electrolyte imbalance had nothing to do with the patient's death.

This is bullshit! This'll have to wait until Ann gets back, because I don't know what these ignorant bastards want me to put in these forms, he thought.

Resigning himself to waiting for Ann's return to resume work, he decided to go to the hospital, where he could do some good. He parked the XKE in Ann's space. Elizabeth Johnson bounded around the corner after viewing him from her car.

"You're here. I thought you would stand me up."

Robert had become so infuriated and disoriented with the paperwork at the house that he had forgotten their date. He thought quickly and decided he should cover up his absentmindedness:

"I wouldn't stand you up." He shuffled his feet shyly.

"We're still on for seven o'clock then?"

"Oh, yeah, sure. Let's just meet right here at the car.

"Okay, unless you want a rain check...?"

"Oh, no, Elizabeth. I've just been buried in work with this new position. I don't have to be here as much. But all this administrative crap, it's a bitch. Seven o'clock. Meet me here."

"Seven it is then. I'll meet you right here."

They walked together toward the E.R., Robert thinking that his unconscious mind must have gotten him to go to the hospital that night, because his conscious mind had obviously buried his date with her in a far recess of his gray matter.

"Where do you want to eat?" she asked.

"How about Commander's Palace? I'm going to do some work up in my office, and then I'll meet you at the car at seven."

They stopped at the door to the E.R.

"By the way, Robert, you're not getting laid tonight." Elizabeth smiled broadly. "At least not by me!"

"You really, really are shy, aren't you, Betsy?" he said sarcastically.

She laughed and walked into the E.R. He heard her say "see you at seven" as she went through the doors.

Robert meandered to his office. Ann's image played in front of him.

I will be a good boy. I will be a good boy, he repeated over and over to himself.

Chapter Nine

Silas Arlington nodded approval as Dr. St. John escorted Elizabeth into Commander's Palace. He seated them at Robert's favorite table.

"Robert, I know what you'll be having to drink. What may I get for the lady?"

"Gin and tonic, please."

"My pleasure."

Silas turned to the bar for their drinks. Dr. St. John excused himself from the table. On returning from the restroom he crossed Silas' path.

"I admire your taste in women," began Silas, opening his eyes widely. "But does the other one know you're here with this one?"

"Silas, this is just a friend and colleague. It's nothing more than that."

"If you say so."

"Silas," Robert turned back toward him, "next time Ms. Finn and I are here, will you promise me you'll not tell her about this lady I'm with tonight?"

Silas made a zipping motion over his lips, then broke out into a laugh.

"Thanks a lot, Silas. Does that mean you're going to be my confidant?'

"Doc," Silas slapped him on the shoulder. "Go have a good time. What you do is none of my business. It's not my duty to tattle on you."

"Silas, you haven't changed a bit since we were at

Tulane." They both laughed.

The evening with Elizabeth went marvelously. Silas was his charming self, as usual helping to make the evening an especially memorable affair. Robert continued to remind himself to behave. Elizabeth was so beautiful that he knew that he would have to exhibit extreme self-control not to cross the line. When they inadvertently touched legs halfway through the meal, both of them shifted in their chairs in embarrassment.

Elizabeth had not driven to the hospital that day, so he drove her to her apartment, which was close to his new home in the midtown area. An embarrassed silence descended in the car during the drive. Elizabeth's posture and body language seemed to say, "I'm just as uncomfortable as you."

They kissed lightly on the front porch, a kiss reminiscent of a shy teenage couple's kiss on a first date.

"Good night, Robert. Thanks for a wonderful evening. I am really looking forward to working with you," she said quietly.

After they separated, she asked: "Will you help me meet some new friends here in New Orleans?"

"Of course, Betsy. You know I will."

"I'll see you at work then, Robert."

"Goodnight!" He had walked halfway down the sidewalk to his car when he turned to her. "Betsy?"

She stopped unlocking the front door. With the light over the porch shining on her, Robert thought she looked like an angel.

"What?"

"Can we do this again?"

"All you have to do is ask, Doctor."

He smiled all the way home. John Wyatt had warned Dave and him a long time ago that women could confuse the hell out of you.

Chapter Ten

Dr. St. John looked at the mountain of papers at the house. *I should have just stayed here*, he thought remorsefully, *and tried to update these instead of going out with Elizabeth.*

He had sworn that he was going to leave all of this until Ann returned. He thought, *I'm sure that's the last thing Ann will want to hear when she gets back, that I couldn't get through this stupid paperwork. Get through it, hell, I couldn't even finish three of the forms.* He looked down at the mound of at least four hundred.

He picked up another one, with a sigh. "Patient: Harrison Roberts. Age: 42." Awfully young. He leafed through the assorted questions and suppositions.

He sat down, reading on. "Curious, this patient had an apparent myocardial infarction. But his blood sugar was eight. This must be wrong. Outdated equipment at the hospital, or the blood cells had ruptured prior to these lab studies maybe," he muttered, scratching his chin.

He tossed the document back onto the pile of its cousins. He knew he should have kept his word to himself and waited until Ann returned.

In the middle of the night, a warm form he recognized as Ann slipped into the bed beside him. He realized with a start that he was glad the date with Elizabeth ended when it did. He snuggled closer to Ann, and slowly glided back to sleep.

The next morning he was awakened by Ann singing "Good morning, Sunshine" in the shower. He peeked at her through the hot mist. "You're in a good mood."

"Oh, hi." She brushed her hair out of her face. "Yes, I am in a good mood. The trouble in Washington was straightened out a lot more easily than I ever imagined." She stepped out of the shower, patting her hair dry with the towel he handed her.

"Good, that's great. Look, I want to show you something." He padded to the kitchen where all the paperwork was piled. He brought back the two patient charts that contained the extremely low blood sugars.

"Look at these. How can I fill these out completely, Ann? The premise of these questions is all wrong."

Ann stood silently, continuing to rub the towel over her body.

"These questions don't take into account the complexity of medicine," he continued.

"I know, Robert. Did you finish any of them?"

"No, I couldn't, Ann." He knew she was disappointed.

She sighed. "That's okay. At least I straightened out the Washington mess." She guided him over to the bed, and they both sat down.

"These monstrosities" she waved the patient papers in the air, "were put together by Washington insiders who know zilch about medicine. They were thrown together in two months. It's obvious there was no thought put into them."

She sighed again. "I'll complete these. I know what they want."

"But Ann, it's a Catch-22. There's no way to complete these documents and use the data they contain for any real purpose. How can the data that are compiled in this way possibly be used to influence future health care policy decisions?"

"They can't, Robert."

"Well, I'm glad you understand, but what's the reason to

even mess with this crap if it can't be used? That's the first rule of the scientific process. The data collected have to be able to be used in a reliable manner."

Ann got up off the bed.

"Robert, do you trust me?"

"Of course I do, Ann. You know I do."

"If New Orleans Hospital closes down due to lack of government funding, what chance do we have of implementing some of Dr. Guttierez's practices here?"

"I don't know."

She stamped her foot emphatically. "None. Zilch. Nada. Not a snowball's chance, Robert. We—I—will have to continue to complete these documents."

"But," he attempted to interrupt her. She held up her hand, signaling him to be quiet until she finished. "We'll complete these documents as best we can, for now.

She sat back down, patting his hand. "Robert, this is only temporary." She picked up the papers, flourished them, then flung them to the floor. "When the time is right, we'll change things. We'll change the whole damn system. We'll do a tremendous amount of good.

"I just came back from Washington. And I alone probably saved our funding." Her voice rose an octave with each declaration. "The hospital's special NHCO standing—the whole ball of wax. Trust me, Robert, we'll fix the system together. But right now I need your M.D. to sign off on these forms—it's a temporary thing."

She looked into his eyes. "I'm wealthy, darling, remember. I don't need this crap. I'm trying to help my fellow man. I've done my part. I'm sacrificing a lot. I could be in Mexico, lying on the beach and not having to deal with any of this bureaucratic bastardization of the American health care system. I'm still here because I know...that you and I," her voice rose again, "can change the system."

She snapped her fingers. "We can make mega-changes.

We can do it, Robert."

"I'll help any way I can," he conceded, feeling weak. "I think I know what Dave felt, Ann, and I've just been through a couple too many of those paper mazes."

"I know." She kissed him on the cheek.

"It's just not my style to sign my name to medical documentation that I feel is inaccurate."

"Okay." She got up, perturbed. "New Orleans will go broke—it'll go down the tubes—all the work—the transplants—"

"That's not what I said, Ann! I'll agree to help, but—"

She placed her hands on her hips. "But what?"

He pointed to the papers she had thrown to the floor. "Let's get a game plan—a time frame to replace those Mickey Mouse documents."

"Absolutely—that was one thing Mr. Castner and I discussed. See," she beamed broadly, "you and I think alike. We make a good team."

"We can't get into any trouble doing this, can we?"

"Robert, grow up. You know about NHCO security. Mr. Castner is going to protect us. Besides, have you read those forms all the way through? It is a Catch-22. You can't answer them correctly."

"That's the truth. I dare anyone to correlate the pathology of any disease within the forms presented and have it make sense to anyone except a Martian."

"Let's not forget the final goal and objective, Robert: to get the transplant process okayed for the American people."

"You're right, Ann. I'm sorry—I'll help any way I can."

"Great. Leave everything to me, sweetheart. I'm an old pro in getting around these bureaucratic land mines. I'll get us through it."

"I'm sure you will, Ann."

She hugged him. "Let's cook breakfast!"

They decided to take the rest of Sunday off. A game plan to attack the massive problem before them would be outlined over the next two weeks. They concluded they were both smart and ambitious. They could overcome any obstacle by brainstorming over the next month. They felt they would be able to devise an answer—or at least an alternative method of documentation that would be acceptable to the NHCO.

"Variables, multiple variables," said Ann. "When you're dealing with all the variables that are promoted in a complex medical use, and you have to prepare an entirely new method to present them in a logical, satisfactory manner—whew! It can be a daunting task."

"Good old American experimentation, Ann. We'll reinvent the wheel in this case. We can do it!" he enthusiastically concluded.

Monday morning arrived. They had to take separate cars to work because Ann had to stop by Touro Infirmary for an administrator's meeting. "The Touro," as everybody called the midtown Jewish hospital, was located only five blocks from Ann's house. They parted with a kiss.

Dr. St. John entered through the pediatric E.R. to see if any of his smaller patients like Martin and Marion had been in. Elizabeth Johnson plowed through the public doors leading from the trauma E.R., right past him. Her mascara had streaked down her face.

"Dr. Johnson," he called. She seemed not to notice his presence as she passed through the pediatric E.R. and up the flight of stairs leading into the main hospital

He followed her up the stairs. "Betsy, slow down." He caught up with her and grabbed her by the shoulder. "What's wrong?"

"Oh, Robert, you're going to fire me!"

"No, I'm not, Betsy." He held her by the shoulders. "Now, tell me what's wrong."

"After our date Saturday, I got a call from my service to admit a patient. Dr. Simms called me." She began to regain her composure as she wiped the mascara lightly away from her face with a tissue.

139

"And what happened?"

"I admitted the patient."

"What was wrong with him?"

"He was a young black kid, with juvenile diabetes. He was brought in by his family in severe diabetic keto-acidosis." She started crying again.

He continued to console her. "How old was he?"

"Eighteen." Composing herself, she took a deep breath and sighed. "When I left him Sunday night he was fine. Then I received a call from the I.C.U. at three this morning. He had suffered a complete cardiovascular collapse and died." She looked bewildered.

"Betsy, you're not going to get fired. You hydrated him well? You put him on a slow drip of I.V. insulin and potassium?" Robert looked at her expectantly.

Betsy nodded her head vigorously. "Yes, of course. We monitored his glucose. Blood gases were improving. His potassium was stabilizing. When I left the hospital last night, I told the family that their son was improving ,and then I got a call this morning from Sally Ortiz..." She just shook her head, confused.

"Betsy, it's not your fault! The mortality rate for people with diabetic acidosis that severe is still probably 10 percent, even today."

"I've lost two patients since coming here. This never happened to me at Duke!"

"Betsy, the patients we treat here at New Orleans are poor. They don't have the resources or the wherewithal to take care of themselves. Why was this kid so out of whack anyway? There's almost always a precipitating event when they come in this sick."

"The mother did tell me that her son wouldn't take care of himself. He wasn't following his diet or taking his medication."

"See, Betsy, it's not your fault."

"He was just regaining consciousness," Betsy continued. "His last I.V. bag of saline I hung myself. I even helped the nurse mix it, since she was busy with other patients. I decreased his insulin down to one unit per hour. The boy smiled at me a little, before I left."

"Do you want me to speak to the family?"

"Would you, Robert?" She was clearly cheered by his offer.

"Of course I will." He hugged her.

"Do you still like me, Robert?" she whispered, as she tried to choke back tears.

"Of course I do. Silly girl." She held her head against his shoulder.

"Look, Betsy, take the rest of the day off, okay? Go home. I'll talk to the family."

"They're still up in I.C.U. Nurse Ortiz is trying to explain to them how complex D.K.A. is to treat. I think I'll go home— I'm exhausted." She turned to go down the stairwell, then looked back up at him. "Thanks, Robert. You're a nice guy."

"That's okay," he responded reassuringly. "Go home!"

She stopped again before she pushed out the door to home. "I'll probably call Daddy," she said, laughing slightly.

He took two steps at once as he bounded up to the I.C.U. Sally was still talking with the boy's family. He could barely hear Sally speak over the whirl of ventilators, clicking of I.V. units administrating medicine and fluid and the BEEP • BEEP • BEEP of the cardiac monitors. When Sally noticed him in the background she motioned for him to come forward. She introduced him to the family.

"This is Dr. St. John. He's the E.R. director here at New Orleans Hospital. The E.R. director is a little different here than at other hospitals in that Dr. St. John oversees a lot of departments of the hospital." She turned to Robert. "I was telling Reverend and Mrs. Carter that diabetic keto-acidosis is a very serious problem."

"Yes, it is," Robert said to the group.

Reverend Carter stood up and shook Robert's hand.

"We don't blame the doctor or the hospital, Dr. St. John. We understand that sometimes these things are in the hands of the Lord."

The grieving family nodded in concurrence.

"I think you would like to know that the young doctor who took care of your son is very upset, Reverend Carter. She feels she has failed your son."

"Oh, no," protested the preacher. "Tell Dr. Johnson that we appreciate all she did for our Nelson—and God sees the good that is done."

The family nodded again in agreement, behind a wall of white handkerchiefs.

Dr. St. John excused himself, stating, "If there's anything I can do, Reverend Carter..." He shook the gracious man's hand, and he and Nurse Ortiz walked out into the hall. A New Orleans nun with a hospital ministry for grieving families passed by in the hall. Robert asked if she had time to visit with the family he had just left.

Turning to Sally, he asked for her assessment of what had happened to Nelson Carter.

"I don't know, Robert. Elizabeth's work is impeccable." She produced the copies of admission and progress notes. "As far as I can tell the kid just coded. Just went into cardiopulmonary arrest and died."

He looked through the charts, shaking his head. "Blood sugar coming back down to normal; blood gases stabilizing. Everything was done according to the book."

Sally looked puzzled. "Dr. St. John, the I.C.U. nurse is young and inexperienced...but look at the paperwork! This death shouldn't have happened!"

"Piss-poor protoplasm," he muttered, looking at the ceiling. "An eighteen-year-old kid!"

"Come on, Dr. St. John. Sometimes shit happens!" Sally practically shouted.

"Oh hell, Sally, D.K.A. is extremely hard to treat, but it's hard to accept that sometimes things just happen." He looked through the notes again. "What happened the night before Nelson coded?"

Sally stepped beside him, and they glanced through the sheets and the nurse's notations. "I.V. bag with normal saline; filled with ten units of regular insulin...so the patient would receive 1 cc per hour. Blood gases and electrolytes under control. And potassium was okay immediately afterward."

Sally shrugged. "A code was called in about thirty minutes."

"Could the I.V. have been administered too fast?"

"No," Sally said. "Fifty percent of the bag was still there, so he wouldn't have gotten too much insulin.

"Elizabeth mixed the bag herself," Robert added.

They looked at each other spontaneously. "Let's check the insulin stock!"

All medications in the I.C.U. were held under lock and key in a big glass cabinet in the back room of the unit. Sally and Robert inspected the boxes of insulin bottles. There were eight boxes, and only one had a broken seal. A box contained thirty 1-cc bottles of insulin. Ten were gone. The log book indicated Elizabeth Johnson, M.D., had removed 10 cc for Nelson Carter.

"So he didn't get too much insulin," Sally said.

"Yeah, even if he had received it all at once it probably wouldn't have hurt him," Robert said. "Piss-poor protoplasm," he repeated out in the hall as they walked from the I.C.U.

"I do know this," he said, turning to Sally. "Elizabeth Johnson sure is upset."

Sally shrugged. "It wasn't her fault."

"Yeah, well she's taking it hard."

"I'm sure," Sally agreed. "Thank God that kid had such a nice, understanding family."

"Yeah, really." Robert paused at the elevator. "I'm going down—where're you going?"

Sally sashayed down the hall, flipping her keys around the chain clipped to her belt. "To my office. Say hey to Ann Finn," was her parting quip.

Dr. St. John walked straight into the administrator's office. Jerri was busy buffing her nails while cradling the telephone under her chin. She saw Robert and put her hand up as if to say *stop!*"

"I'll call you back," she assured the caller on the phone. To Robert: "She's not in a good mood."

"Why, what's wrong, Jerri?"

I think you probably know, Doctor. What did I tell you the other day about men being dogs?"

Before he could respond, an enraged Ann Finn stormed out of her office.

"I'm going to Mexico," she snapped as soon as she saw him.

"Do you want me to go with you, darling?"

"Hell, no!" She gathered her bag on her shoulder. "She killed another one, you know!"

"Who?" he meekly asked.

"You know who," Ann bellowed. Jerri slid down in her chair, pretending to type. "That goddamned bitch."

"Elizabeth?" he asked, white as a sheet.

"Elizabeth?" she shouted louder. "What happened to professionalism? Don't you mean 'Dr. Johnson'?"

"Well, yes, Ann. But what happened?"

She walked straight up to him, putting her nose to his face.

"When I get back from Mexico, that little hussy better be gone!" She was steaming with rage. Then, in a lowered voice: "I'd do it now, but Mr. Levitz hired her and I can't fire her because of all the bureaucratic hurdles and crap, or I would. She's already killed two patients—"

144

"But Ann," he was beginning to protest when she hit him in the solar plexus with a clinched fist. He buckled over, the wind knocked out of him.

Ann stomped past him to the door. She paused just long enough to sputter: "And if you *ever* go out with her again..." She stopped and made the most horrible face Robert had ever seen, then spat the rest: "I will cut it off!"

She slammed the door so hard it cracked the glass pane in the corner. He imagined New Orleans Hospital rocking on its foundation.

Robert wobbled back over to the couch and flopped down. He looked at Jerri for sympathy. "I think she's mad..."

Jerri mumbled, "I told you so," as she turned away and picked up the phone.

Chapter Eleven

Dr. St. John got up and left Ann's office, closing the door behind him. He leaned against the wall in the hall. Breathing deeply, he attempted to regain his composure. *Hell hath no fury...*, he thought. He had had no idea what that really meant until now.

The operator's voice came over the intercom: "Dr. St. John, telephone."

He attempted to walk casually to his office, closed the door and sat down slowly behind the desk. He picked up the phone. "This is Dr. St. John."

"Hold for an outside call, Doctor."

"Robert? Robert St. John?"

"Yes, who am I speaking with?"

"This is Johnny Wyatt, Bobby."

Mr. Wyatt. How in the world are you?"

"Fair, Bobby, just fair."

"Why, what's wrong, Mr. Wyatt?"

"Bobby, let me tell you what's happening. Have you got a minute?"

"Sure," said Robert, still rubbing his sore abdominal area.

"I've had a heart attack. Massive."

"Oh, Mr. Wyatt, I'm sorry. When?"

"Two days after the funeral. The cardiologist says I need a heart transplant."

"Can't they do a coronary bypass?"

"You mean using the veins from my leg to replace my heart veins? No, Bobby, the doctor says there's been too much damage, and the vessels are clogged in too many different places. The only way I can live—five-year survival he called it—is to have a heart transplant."

"Oh, God. I'm sorry Mr. Wyatt. But the University of Tennessee hospital can do a wonderful job for you. You won't have to leave Knoxville."

"Bobby, there's a problem."

"What, John?"

"They won't do it. That's why I'm calling you."

"What do you mean they won't do it?"

"It's that damn card! That red, white and blue card! You know, with that eagle flying on the corner."

"The NHCO card, with the eagle hologram on the side?"

"Yes, that's it."

"What's the problem? You can get a heart transplant with it."

"No, I can't. Somebody else might can, but not me."

"Why not, what's the problem?"

"Something about the fine print in the card. There's five criteria that I have to meet, and I only meet four of them. It's my age. I'm 62. They won't give anyone a new heart over the age of 60."

"Yes," Robert interrupted. "But you're the youngest 62-year-old I've ever known. Are you absolutely sure, John?"

"That's what they tell me, Bobby. The way they explain it, because of the scarcity and the cost, they're rationing the transplants and they've never given anyone my age a heart transplant. That's why I'm calling you, Bobby. I thought maybe you could help me at your hospital. I know you're a big shot down there."

"I'm afraid we don't do transplants here, Mr. Wyatt."

"Call me John, Bobby. I don't know who you're calling 'Mr. Wyatt.'"

"Okay, John. I'll sure look into it for you. I'll do what I can."

"I'm sure you'll help me if you can, Bobby. I wouldn't even bother, I'd have forgotten about it, except for Dave's mother. I really don't care much about living."

"John, please don't talk like that."

"It's true, Bobby. But that's neither here nor there. Grace is truly upset. I'm really doing this for her. I promised her I would. She said she didn't think she could take it if we both died in the same year."

Don't worry, John. I'll do all I can for you. I'll need to talk with your cardiologist in Knoxville. Who is he?"

"Dr. Lonnie Thompkins. He's at U.T."

"I know of him. I'll call and talk to him."

"Thanks, Bobby. Call me back, will you?"

"I sure will, partner. You hang in there."

"Bye, Bobby."

"Good-bye, John."

Dr. St. John sat at his desk for a full ten minutes, staring at the wall. He decided he would call Dr. Thompkins in Knoxville. There was really nothing he could do for Mr. Wyatt at New Orleans Hospital. Transplants weren't done here. He snapped his fingers: Tulane Hospital did transplants, and he knew the staff there. Maybe he could work out something here in New Orleans before calling Dr. Thompkins. He decided to check with the Tulane staff.

The staff cardiologist and cardiovascular surgeon told him the same thing: there just wasn't enough money to perform all the procedures that were needed. The reason, as explained to him, was that it was a "poor investment" to put a healthy organ into someone that age. It was rationing, in their words, pure and simple.

"It's in the NHCO charter, no exceptions," the cardiologist explained. "The politicians had to come up with a way to pay for this huge federal bureaucracy and all of its promises."

This sucks, Robert thought.

Then it came to him: *I know where we can get the heart transplant he deserves.* He slapped himself in the face in mock disbelief. *You dummy, Hospital of the Americas—Dr. Guttierez. How could I have been so stupid? Ann and I will arrange this.*

He felt tremendously happy. "Don't worry," he spoke out loud to no one. "Mrs. Wyatt, you're not going to have to suffer anymore—not this year anyway."

Chapter Twelve

Flight 692 to the Cayman Islands will depart in five minutes "came the pilot's voice over the intercom. "We thank you for flying Delta. "

Ann Finn adjusted her seatbelt. She laid back and leaned her head against the head cushion for support. She double-checked the envelope in her breast pocket to make sure it was there. A small smile crossed her face as the paper crunched under her touch.

"Would you care for a drink, miss?" the stewardess leaned over the empty seat and asked.

Ann smiled, thinking about how much she liked flying first class because of the way they pampered you.

"Sure, I'd love a Southern Comfort."

"I'll bring one right now."

"Just a little ice," Ann added. The stewardess nodded affirmatively.

After finishing her drink she drifted off into a light sleep as the jet flashed toward the tiny Caribbean Island.

The stewardess had to gently nudge Ann to awaken her after landing.

"We certainly enjoyed having you on this flight, Miss Finn."

"You don't know me!" Ann snapped.

"I...I...I mean we at Delta are always glad to have repeat flyers..." the stewardess attempted to explain. "I didn't mean anything by it."

"Of course not," Ann lightly offered, "but you must have me confused with someone else."

"Grand Cayman is my regular flight," the flight attendant continued. "I thought I recognized you from previous flights, that's all."

"That's okay, "Ann interjected, "but I've not been to the Caymans before."

"Sorry," was all the flight attendant said as she continued to say good-bye to the other passengers.

Ann followed the line of passengers to the small terminal as they all got into line to pass through customs. When she came to the entry desk, she pulled out her passport and offered it to the young man there. He adjusted himself in the chair, drawing himself to his full height. She noticed him peering over her passport trying nonchalantly to get a better look at her breasts.

"Is anything wrong, sir?" Ann asked, in an attempt to get him to return his attention to the passport.

"Oh no, ma'am "he smiled. He continued in an accented speech that seemed to be of British origin. "I just wanted to be sure everything was in order."

"Well, is it?"

"Is it what?"

"Is everything in order?"

"Oh, yes…it most certainly is." The young blonde customs official took a long look at her body.

"I guess I'll go claim my bags then," Ann said, sharply.

"Yes," he said, as he stamped her passport.

"Good." She began to reach for her document.

"Just two things," he said as he teasingly pulled her passport away from her grasping hand.

"Now what?" She placed her hands on her hips and sighed in a disgusted manner.

"First, are you carrying any financial instrument of over $10,000—"

Ann began to shake her head no.

"I'm not through," he interrupted. "Let me finish."

She rolled her eyes in an exaggerated motion. He started waving the passport in front of her face.

"And are you free tonight to allow me to take you to the most wonderful restaurant on Grand Cayman Island?"

"To answer your first question, I only brought two postage-stamp—sized bikinis with me." She leaned forward against the counter allowing the full size of her breasts to bulge against her top.

"And to answer the second question, I'm spending my time in Grand Cayman with U.S. Cabinet Secretary Richard Castner, and he and your foreign investment minister, who I'm on my way to see right now, might want to know why you are hassling me!"

The young official quickly placed the document in her open hand and pointed to the turnstile leading to the baggage claim area.

Ann took the passport with her right hand and with her left reached under his chin and tickled him with her index finger.

He turned a bright shade of crimson. With his blonde hair he looked like a carrot.

"Don't worry, I'm not going to tell on you. Besides you're cute. The next time I'm here, I think I'll take you up on your offer."

He broke out in a big smile and watched her as she strode across the room to collect her luggage.

Customs officials in Grand Cayman rarely check tourists' luggage because they don't want to hassle their rich tourists. Ann gathered her two suitcases and passed through the inspection point quickly. She hailed a taxi outside the airport.

"Where to, miss?" the taxi driver asked.

"I'm going to the Hyatt Regency on Seven-Mile Beach, but first I need to stop at the International Monetary Management Company. Do you know where that office is located?"

"Yes ma'am, I do."

"Do you mind waiting for me there for about thirty minutes before I go to the Hyatt.?"

"Oh no, not at all. We in the Cayman Islands are very accommodating, you will see! The cabby chattered on about the history of the island as he drove the yellow Chevrolet away from the airport and headed toward Georgetown, the capital city of the Caymans. Ann nervously fingered the envelope in her pocket as he talked. Traffic became heavier as they approached the center of town. Off to the left of the road, the ocean appeared. A dock jutted out from the middle of the city, extending some 200 yards into the Caribbean.

Several cruise ships were docked out away from the pier, while hundreds of tourists mingled mindlessly around the shops that lined the bay-side street. Cars had to navigate the human flood. No one seemed to mind the way they carelessly strolled into the street. The taxi driver explained that his people and this island depended on the tourists for their livelihood, so the Caymanians tolerated a lot of their foolishness, even though it was frustrating at times.

"Here we are, lady," he said as he pulled up to a four-story office building. "I'll wait for you across the street." He gestured to a vacant space.

"Good, I shouldn't be more than just a few minutes. "

Ann entered the building and took the elevator to the top floor. Stepping off, she approached a door emblazoned with the title International Monetary Management Company. She walked directly in without knocking.

"Hello, Miss Finn," the secretary acknowledged her and pointed toward a large double door. "They're waiting for you. Go right on in. "Would you like something to drink?"

"Yes, yes, I would. Let me have some Southern Comfort on the rocks, please."

"Go right on in. I'll bring the drink in just a second."

Ann opened the door and was greeted by three men: Richard Castner, Carlos Levitz, and the owner of the International Monetary Management Company, Nick Sands.

"Hello, gentlemen. "she smiled triumphantly.

All three men rushed to her, attempting to shake her hand at the same time.

"Whoa, not so fast, I've got what you want," Ann said, patting her coat pocket. She shook hands with all three.

"Let's see it, "Castner implored.

"In a minute…" Ann said. "I've got a drink coming. I've had a long trip. That's just like men, you're in such a hurry to get to the climax…" Ann took the envelope from her pocket and walked around the room, waving it above her head, "that you don't savor the best part…the foreplay."

All three men groaned in protest.

"Come on, guys. Let the lady have a drink, and she'll show you more money than you've ever seen before," she continued.

Levitz sat down in a chair. Nick Sands hopped up on the desk. Castner simply faced the big window looking out over the Caribbean. The secretary brought Ann her Southern Comfort and left the room.

"Come on, Ann," the three men began at once.

"Okay, Okay, boys." Ann took a sip of her drink with her left hand and handed the envelope to Richard Castner with the other.

All three men grabbed for the envelope at the same time.

"I'll do it, I'll do it," all three said at once.

Ann grabbed the envelope, stamped her foot and placed her drink on the desk.

"I'll do it!" she snapped. "You're just like a bunch of teenagers." She deftly tore open the envelope, pulled a green certificate from inside and held it in front of her.

"A bearer's bond for $16 million, $4 million apiece."

All three men whistled loudly and gathered closely to inspect the money.

Ann continued. "All compliments of Raphael Guttierez, Hospital of the Americas, Robert St. John and…" she pulled out a credit card sized plastic object, "…this. She flashed the red, white and blue national health care card in front of them.

All three men laughed and clapped their hands.

"This calls for a celebration, gentlemen. "Let's join Ann in a drink," Nick Sands said. "What do you guys want?"

"Champagne, champagne, definitely," said Levitz.

"Good idea, let's break out a bottle," Nick replied.

Levitz and Nick went to the bar next to the window and began to open a bottle of Moet.

Ann and Richard Castner took the bond and walked over to the window overlooking the sea.

"Is everything going smoothly, Ann?"

"Yes, it is. But let's not discuss this here, Richard. Let's wait until we get to the Hyatt." I don't want these guys to know anything more than they know.

Hell, I don't want you to know anything. The less people who know what's going the better off we are. "

"You're right. Let's get some champagne. "

Ann and Richard joined the other two men in the celebration. Ann traded her Southern Comfort for a glass of champagne. They saluted one another.

"Cheers!" they all shouted in unison and took a sip.

Ann held up her glass. "To Mr. Levitz, $4 million for allowing me to run New Orleans Hospital any goddamn way I want. No questions asked."

Levitz held up his glass and toasted his fellow revelers: "Ann, I don't want to know. You do anything you want…as long as I get paid this kind of money."

Ann turned to Nick Sands and hoisted her glass again. "To Nick, for hiding all this beautiful green money for us."

Nick nodded his head in acknowledgment. "I don't care what you are doing to get all this dough," he said. "I'll help you anyway I can." He turned toward the ocean.

"Of course," he laughed, turning back toward them. "It helps to get paid this kind of money. With this kind of loot, you can have all kinds of friends."

"Mr. Castner gets his share," Ann said, again pulling out the national health care card, "because he helps me do my job by signing off on all those imbecilic autopsy forms. NHCO won't find out what's going on until we're living abroad with millions in off-shore banks."

"What exactly are you doing, Ann?" Nick Sands asked.

"Now, now, Nick, you know the agreement. No questions asked. It's better like that. You just take care of the money, and we'll all be wealthy."

"You're right, Ann," Nick offered. "I just got curious, that's all."

"Ann's right, Nick." Castner started, "Mr. Levitz and I

don't even know what all is going on. And let's keep it that way. So long as Ann produces this kind of money, who gives a shit anyway?"

"Get out of this woman's way!" Castner exclaimed.

"Here, here!" the three men cheered in a salute to Ann Finn. The four people continued to celebrate. Below them, hundreds of American tourists scurried about, totally unaware that the small plastic card they carried in their wallets was allowing a small fortune to be made by these revelers.

A few minutes later, Ann pulled Richard Castner to the door.

"Time to leave guys," she called back to Nick Sands and Mr. Levitz.

"What's the hurry?" Mr. Levitz asked.

"It's been a long trip, and I'm tired." Ann continued to pull the reluctant Richard Castner to the door. He simply shrugged.

"I guess it's time to go, fellas "

"If you need us, we'll be at the Hyatt," Ann continued as she tugged at his arm.

"I'm thinking of buying a villa at Brittannia, right next to the Hyatt," Ann explained as they stopped at the door. "If we don't see you guys again this trip, we'll meet again in two months?"

"Sounds good, Ann," Nick said

"Fine," Mr. Levitz concurred. "Keep up the good work!"

"Don't worry, fellas, it'll keep rolling in, because I'll do anything for money!" she laughed.

With that final announcement, she pushed Richard out the door into the hall, and her laughter slowly faded away.

* * *

"What is she doing to make all this money?" Nick Sands looked quizzically at Mr. Levitz.

"Nick, I don't know for sure, but it involves Dr. Guttierez

156

in Cancun, and of course Richard Castner. But to be honest with you, I don't want to know, and I advise you to just keep up with the money and forget where it's coming from."

"I know, I know." Nick shook his head in bewilderment. Its just that I don't really like to deal with dirty money. I'm doing this for you, Mr. Levitz. I don't like not knowing where my clients get their money."

"Look, Nick. You're getting four million dollars every two to three months to set up these numbered bank accounts! That's a hell of a lot of money. I wouldn't concern myself with where it comes from. If anyone is going to get into trouble, it's not you or me. It'll be Ann or Castner. I even leave the hospital so I don't know what's going on. If anybody goes down, it's not going to be me, it'll be them! I'll protest mightily that I knew nothing, which I don't. They'll take the rap, and I'll have all this money down here.

"No one will be able to trace it if you do your job. Besides, Castner is the head of the NHCO for Christ's sake. If he can't cover all of this up, no one can."

Nick Sands nervously paced the floor of his office. He rattled the ice in his glass as he walked to the large window where he continued rattling his glass. He looked out the window, a glazed expression on his face and his brow furrowed in worry.

"Let me tell you something…I'm a little bit afraid of that woman. She's too damn sure of herself." Again he rattled his glass, took a deep breath and sighed.

"Good lord, man." Levitz sputtered, "What in God's name is wrong with you? If you know something I don't, then you need to tell me."

Nick turned from the window and looked at Levitz. He continued rattling his glass.

"Will you quit messing with that glass!" Levitz walked over to Nick and took the glass from his hand.

"Okay, okay, there's nothing probably going to come of this. But after Dr. Wyatt died—and I begged him to keep his money down here in his numbered account, but he insisted that at least a portion be mailed to him back in New Orleans—well, the post office sent the last check back marked 'deceased.' It's our rule that any such account be sent to the next of kin."

Levitz slapped his forehead in disbelief. "You didn't!"

"I didn't," Sands fairly yelled. "I was on vacation!" He buried his face in his hands.

"You idiot!" Levitz ranted. Now he took the glass and began to jiggle it furiously.

"That's not all."

"Well, let's hear it!" Levitz looked at him incredulously.

"A week ago we got a letter from a Mr. John Wyatt stating he had been forwarded a check from New Orleans made out to his son for two million dollars. He wanted to know where his boy had gotten such a large amount of money. He also wrote that he had endorsed the check and had it deposited in First Tennessee Bank in Knoxville."

"Have you written him back?" Levitz quizzed.

"No, actually I was waiting to talk to you first." Nick shook his head as if confused about what he should do.

"You've got to understand that this is the only questionable money that I handle. I don't like not knowing where it comes from! But who can argue with the huge sums involved." Nick again shook his head.

"If I had only a different protocol in place. It's not my secretary's fault."

Levitz again swirled the ice in the glass and began to pace the floor. After a couple of minutes of this behavior he turned to Nick and said,

"I've got it !"

"What!"

"First of all, write him back and tell him the money is his rightfully to keep."

"Who wouldn't want that kind of money?"

"Secondly, no one wants to think that their son, the

158

doctor, is not on the up-and-up. Then all we have to do is come up with a reasonable way that his son made all that money in a legitimate manner."

"Yeah, but what is that going to be?" Nick asked.

"What else—let's tell the truth!" Levitz said.

"That he helped pioneer a remarkable new medical procedure being perfected in Cancun, Mexico?"

"Hell, that's the truth. And if he questions it, we'll have Raphael Guttierez write him a letter explaining the situation."

Levitz broke into a huge smile, very pleased with his sudden idea that would explain everything. Nick's furrowed brow immediately began to relax. He began to shake his head up and down affirmatively. Obviously he liked the idea.

"I'm so glad I waited till you got here to talk this over," Nick said. "I would have probably blown it."

"It makes sense, doesn't it?" Levitz posed.

"Yes, it does."

"And you know what?"

"We don't even have to tell those two."

"Here, here." Nick took the glass from Levitz's hand and offered a salute to the administrator.

* * *

Ann and Richard Castner crossed the street to where the cab driver was parked. He had fallen asleep while waiting for Ann. They approached the car and had to knock on the driver's side window to awaken him. He apologized profusely as he struggled to awaken. They entered the yellow vehicle laughing and joking, obviously pleased with the day's events.

"Are you ready to go to the Hyatt?" the cabby asked.

"Certainly," they responded, laughing.

The crowds of people surrounding the downtown shops prevented traffic from moving very fast. The cab driver talked aimlessly about the bargains that were available in the duty-free shops in Georgetown. The car inched forward, through the crowds. The cab driver apologized to Ann and Secretary Castner for the slow progress. His talking fell on mostly deaf ears as they were already deep in discussion.

"I feel very good about the money we're making and the smoothness with which everything seems to be proceeding," Castner said.

"Cool, Richard. All you have to do is keep NIH from looking too closely at the pathology reports from some of those autopsies."

"Don't worry, Ann, so long as those NHCO forms are signed by Robert St. John, or any M.D. for that matter, we're okay."

Ann snuggled up to Richard and purred, "Don't worry, love, I have that doctor wrapped around my little finger."

Castner adjusted himself some in the seat. "Be sure you do, Ann." A touch of sarcasm entered the conversation.

Ann sat straight up. "And what does that mean?"

"It doesn't mean anything."

"Go ahead, Mr. Secretary, I'm waiting." Ann was obviously perturbed. Richard Castner looked out the side window past the American tourists and toward the cruise ships docked in the bay. He sighed and turned back to her.

"I just don't want us to get overconfident, that's all. Everything is going so well. Dave Wyatt's suicide upset me. It might bring scrutiny to what's going at New Orleans Hospital and possibly in Cancun too."

Ann squirmed in her seat. It was her turn to stare outside the slowly advancing vehicle. A break in the tension inside the taxi was brought about by a young swimsuit-clad tourist. Trying to get past the taxi to get over the road to the beach, he simply jumped on the car's trunk, walked over the top and bounced off the hood. The taxi driver rolled down the window and began shaking his fist at the impatient traveler. The crowds around the young daredevil clapped their appreciation of his athletic feat. The taxi driver rolled up his window and muttered something about the tourists under his breath.

"I can't help it if Wyatt couldn't handle the pressure, Richard. He was a weak man. He had me and all the money he could want. All he had to do was continue signing off on the forms. I did all the work. All he had to do was provide his M.D. You and I know that those organs are never going to be missed so long as we keep the present procedures and protocols intact."

"I know, Ann, that's what you keep telling me. Do you think Levitz suspects anything like this is going on?"

"No, why would he?"

Castner shook his head. "Okay, but what about St. John?"

Ann laughed. "Robert thinks what I want him to think. When I left, I hit him in the stomach like a crazed, jealous lover. He'll do exactly what I want him to do."

"Then why did you and Guttierez show him the transplant process, for heaven's sake?"

Ann again seemed agitated, and again looked out the window down the beach to the crashing waves. "That was a judgment call. I understand your concern. But we need to be able to blackmail him if we should ever need to."

She noticed that the conversation had attracted the interest of the driver. She punched Richard lightly on the leg and pointed to the cocked head of the curious man.

"I'll discuss this with you at the villa," she whispered in his ear.

The rest of the trip to the Hyatt was slow. The driver seemingly forgot his passengers' presence as he again began a monologue that was meant to entertain them.

"If you people need a tour of our beautiful island, I'll be glad to personally be your driver. I even have an auntie who is originally from Haiti who practices voodoo."

"You're kidding?" Ann pulled herself over the back of the seat.

"Do you want to see her home and how she practices the voodoo?"

"Yes, I sure do!" Ann gushed.

"How about you, sir?"

"No thanks…I'm not a believer in such."

"Oh, come on, Richard. It'll be fun!"

Castner simply shook his head in disinterest.

"I want to go," Ann continued. She tossed her long hair in Richard's direction. "I'm not a fuddy duddy. I'll go tomorrow…say at 10 a.m.?"

The driver pulled into the welcoming station at the Hyatt Regency, jumped out of his car and opened the door. "I'll pick you up tomorrow here." He pointed at the ornate front door. "At 10 a.m." He turned to Richard: "If you change your mind, sir…"

"No thanks," Castner shook his head again as he tipped the enthusiastic driver.

"Okay, suit yourself." Turning to Ann he extended his hand. "I'm Sam, Miss…"

"Sam, I'm Ann, and I'll see you in the morning at 10."

With that Sam stashed his well-earned money in his shirt pocket, pulled the yellow Chevrolet out of the circular drive and headed to his next fare.

The concierge, a young Scottish girl named Sherri, welcomed the couple. She had the bellman take their bags to their private villa at Brittannia, which is behind the hotel, while she took them on a small tour of the Hyatt's gardens and pool.

"Part of the movie *The Firm* was filmed here at the pool bar," she told them. "We at the Hyatt Regency Grand Cayman are very proud of our role in that film."

"Yes, that was a good movie," Ann and Richard agreed.

"And over across the street is our world-renowned golf course. It plays as a short course at 18 holes or a 9-hole championship course."

"Hey, I've heard of this course. Don't you use a special

162

ball for it?" Richard asked.

"Yes, it's called the Cayman ball, and you use it to help lengthen the course."

"Ann, when you go on your island tour tomorrow, I'll think I'll head out to the course," Richard said, taking an imaginary golf swing, his upper torso ripping through the breeze.

"Sherri, where's the beach?" Ann quizzed, showing no interest in the rolling hills that sheltered the links.

The concierge pointed back over the pool. "World famous Seven-Mile beach is found just beyond our beachside restaurant, Hemingway's. Just follow the signs and you can't miss it. Is there any thing else I can show or do for you?" She looked back and forth between the two.

"No, you've been most helpful," Richard smiled and shook hands with the young concierge.

"Do you need a ride to your villa?"

"No thanks. We'll walk, if that's okay with you, Ann?"

"Fine," Ann responded,

They walked leisurely through the gently swaying palm trees to the privacy of their villa.

* * *

The Brittannia Villas are an assortment of private homes adjacent to the Hyatt Regency. They are leased out individually to affluent people who want the amenities of the vacation resort but desire and can afford the privacy of a spacious home. The landscaping and lavish architecture make the place a true island paradise. Their villa was Number 705, a 4,000-square-foot residence. The bellman had already deposited their belongings there.

"Ann, I'm dying to know."

"What are you talking about?"

"Why did you let Robert St. John see the operation in Mexico?"

"Blackmail, as I said earlier. Curiosity killed the cat, you know." Ann smiled, then became serious. "Richard, what is being accomplished medically in Cancun is absolutely astounding. What I'm doing in New Orleans to placate the damn NHCO bureaucrats, who are your employees by the way, is a necessity. And you don't need to know much more than that we are doing some organ donation—"

Richard interrupted her. "Damn it, I know all that!"

Ann held out her hands in a gesture for him to be quiet and not to interrupt.

"You're getting paid to sign those damn forms and keep Washington convinced that their little bureaucratic invention is running smoothly," she said. "And I'm paying Levitz to stay out of that hospital and leave me alone." She hesitated as she attempted to find the right words. "Well, let's just say that two million dollars every month or so is a lot of money!"

She became pensive as she thought. She tossed her long hair and let out a sigh. "Dr. St. John has a bank account in New Orleans that he isn't aware of," she continued. "I hate to say it, but if one of your bureaucrats stumbles on something that they shouldn't…well, let's just say I'm not going to be the fall guy.

"Our good doctor will have a lot of explaining to do. A large bank account…" She shrugged. "After all, he's signing off on all the NHCO autopsy reports, not me, or at least they're not in my name." She laughed. "But, Richard, I feel that eventually he has to be let in on the operation just as Wyatt was."

"Goddamn it, Ann, don't you think that's a decision all of us needed to make? Who gave you the right to bring him in on this?" Richard's veins stood out on his neck.

Ann exploded. "I'm doing all the dirty work for you bastards. You don't say much when I bring all the money down here!"

Richard shook his head, attempting to calm his own anger.

"Well , I hope you're able to prevent another fiasco like Wyatt's suicide."

"That wasn't my fault, goddamn it. He was weak. That was something no one could have foreseen. St. John is different, and I will control him, I *guarantee* it." She stomped her foot and slung her hair again.

"Well, see that you do," Richard retorted. "We all have too much to lose."

Ann stormed off to her bedroom, her hair swinging back and forth. She yelled back over her head, "I'm going swimming."

Richard headed straight to the mini-bar,

"I need a drink," he mumbled under his breath. After pouring a scotch on the rocks, he sat down on the sofa and took long deliberate sips.

"You know, Richard," Ann shouted through the closed door, "if you were nice to me and respected the work I do, I might sleep with you."

"Ann, don't flatter yourself. Besides, I don't sleep with people I do business with."

"Neither do I!" she responded.

"Huh...what do you call what you do with St. John, Wyatt, Guttierez...need I say more?" he snorted.

Ann enunciated her words more forcibly as she continued to yell at him through the door. "They aren't business partners," she sputtered. "They're just...boy toys!"

"Yeah, right."

Ann opened the door and walked into the room.

Richard bolted straight up off the sofa, spilling his drink. Ann was gorgeous! She was in a tiny bikini, her long hair pulled on top of her head. She appeared to be all breasts, legs, hair and blue eyes.

"Ann," he began

"I know," she interrupted. "You apologize." She twirled and revealed her back.

"A thong!" he sputtered as he stared at her bottom. He

took an uncertain step toward her.

She turned around toward him and held up a thin arm with an open palm, signaling him to stop.

"You don't sleep with business partners," she mocked.

"I'm going out to the pool to get some sun and check out the boys! I really don't think I'll have trouble attracting one, do you?"

A humbled Richard Castner said "no" in a defeated tone.

Ann walked out the door into the bright Cayman sunshine, slamming the door behind her.

Richard poured himself a drink, and walked to the villa window to look out over the pool. Sure enough, Ann already had two dark Latin types falling all over themselves trying to impress her.

He laughed. "I've got to stay away from this one," he said out loud. "When she goes down, I'm not going with her." He looked back out the window. Ann had taken off her top and thrown it at one of her new friends as she dove into the deep end of the pool.

He walked over to the phone to make a tee time at the golf course for himself the next morning, then lay down on the couch for a short nap. He was startled by a hand nudging his shoulder.

"Richard, Richard, wake up." He pulled his arm up over his face to shield his eyes. It was Ann.

"Mr. Levitz is here, and we need to talk about what Nick's secretary sent Dave Wyatt's dad.

"Wake up, Richard." The figure of Mr. Levitz popped up behind Ann's concerned face.

"What...let me wake up some." He stumbled up, walked to the kitchen sink, stooped and washed his face. He turned around and almost knocked both of them down.

"Whoa, fellas give me some room. What's up?"

"First of all, I think I've taken care of the problem," the silver-haired administrator began."

"What problem? And what did Nick's secretary do?"

Ann began to pace back and forth feverishly. She pulled at the sheer cover-up that clung to her still-bikini-clad body.

"Start from the beginning." Richard looked first at Mr. Levitz and then at Ann.

"After you guys left, Nick told me that his secretary had inadvertently mailed Dave Wyatt's check to his dad in Knoxville."

"What?" Richard stared at Mr. Levitz. "How in the hell did that happen?

"Oh, I believe it was an innocent mistake, but I wanted to run this by you and to tell you what I told Nick to tell Mr. Wyatt."

Ann stopped her pacing and ran over to Mr. Levitz and grabbed his arm.

"What did you tell him to say?"

"I told him to tell Mr. Wyatt that his son was involved in a pioneering medical project in Mexico and that he earned every penny of that money."

Richard and Ann looked at one another to see what the other's reaction would be. Both shrugged.

"That sounds reasonable," said Richard.

"I agree," Ann said. "Good deal, Levitz."

"The only thing I'm worried about really is Nick's reaction," Levitz said.

What do you mean?" asked Ann.

Mr. Levitz stumbled a little bit as he attempted to explain the panic that Nick had exhibited. "I mean this is not probably that big of a deal. After all, this is just some old guy in Knoxville, Tennessee, who's grief-stricken over the loss of his son."

Ann interrupted. "It sounds like you calmed him perfectly."

Richard Castner stood pensively and stroked his chin. "Yeah, it sounds like you offered a good scenario. I say let's relax and see if this blows over."

"In the meantime," Ann interrupted, "let's go get some

dinner at Hemingway's. We'll think more clearly after eating something."

"Sounds good to me," Levitz agreed.

"Let me clean up, and we'll go," Richard chimed in.

* * *

Hemingway's is located on Seven-Mile Beach. The northern trade winds wave over the apex of the restaurant's bamboo roof. Although the Hyatt owns the place, all of Grand Cayman uses Hemingway's as its celebrity showplace. Actors and the like frequent this open-air gathering spot, and people expect to see Gene Hackman or some other movie star while dining there.

Ann, Richard and Mr. Levitz walked over the sidewalk circling the hotel and leading to Hemingway's. Everyone stared at Ann as she entered the building. The afternoon sun had made her bronze complexion even more radiant. Quiet whispers of "Where have I seen her before?" echoed through the restaurant as she walked by.

They were seated in the outer row of tables that faced the ocean. After ordering mahi mahi, they quickly returned to the conversation of how to handle the Nick Sands situation.

"I think everything will take care of itself," Mr. Levitz said.

"I'm going to check him out tomorrow," Ann chimed in nonchalantly.

"What do you mean?" Levitz asked.

"I had planned to dive at Stingray City while I was here. I'll just ask Nick to take me, and I'll check him out personally. If he's panicked, I'll reassure him that everything is okay and that I'm in charge."

Richard Castner and Mr. Levitz looked at each other and shrugged their shoulders in acquiescence.

"I'll pay him a visit after my trip with Sam the taxi driver tomorrow," Ann said.

At the end of the evening, after leaving Mr. Levitz at the Hyatt entrance, Ann and Richard Castner walked back to the darkened villa. Both were deep in their own thoughts. They said goodnight and quietly retired to their separate rooms.

The next morning, Richard noticed that Ann seemed unusually quiet. She busied herself around the room, tending to trivial details. They spoke cordially but were noticeably distant with each other.

"Ann, I'm going out to the pool," Castner said.

"Oh, all right, Richard. I'm going to take my excursion with Sam and then go by and see Nick."

"I would play things down to him," Richard began.

"Goddamn it!" Ann interrupted. "I'm just going to see the guy. First of all I'm going to invite him to go scuba diving, and then I'll placate him about Dr. Wyatt's dad."

"Look, I didn't mean anything by it."

"Richard Castner, you're like every other man I know. Even though you're a doctor and a cabinet secretary, I produce everything and take all the risks and you *still* try to tell me what to do. Well, this is one woman who doesn't need the help!" Ann stormed around the room grabbing her bag and placing sandals and suntan lotion in it. "We only have two more days here before we go to Mexico, and I want to have some fun!"

"All right, go have your fun…I'll be right here."

"Fine, I will! " She walked out the door.

"Boy, if she didn't produce the way she does…" Richard muttered, shaking his head in bewilderment.

* * *

Sam had kept his word and was at the front door of the Hyatt at 10 a.m. Ann looked every bit the rich tourist, as she had stopped at the hotel gift shop and bought a broad-brimmed straw hat. Dark sunglasses, high-heeled sandals and short shorts accentuated the look. She elicited several second takes as she slid in the back seat of the taxi.

"Where to?" Sam grinned broadly as he welcomed her.

"I want to go to see the voodoo lady first, do you mind?"

"Of course not! As a matter of fact, that's what I recommend to all my tourist chums. Where's your gentlemen friend?"

Ann crossed her arms across her ample chest and slid back against the back of the seat. "I prefer that we not discuss him," she caustically replied.

"Sorry, we won't." Sam turned around and pulled the car out into the driveway, then headed for the street.

"Do you believe in the voodoo magic?" he asked. "Do you know much about it?"

Ann smiled and leaned forward over the seat.

"I don't know that much about it except what I've read in magazines."

"Oh, it's real, all right! And it is ba-a-ad news if you know how to use it! By the way, Miss, what is your name? Do you mind that I ask?"

Ann lit a cigarette and blew smoke throughout the cab.

"No, I don't mind. My name is Ann, Sam."

Sam smiled broadly as he looked into the back seat. "If you don't mind, I would like to pay you a compliment."

Ann laughed and took another drag off the cigarette.

"No, I don't mind. As a matter of fact, it would be nice for a man to appreciate me for a change."

"You look like a movie star!"

Ann laughed again as she looked out of the rear window.

"Thanks, Sam, I truly appreciate the compliment. Now, give me the full tourist treatment! Tell me about the island and how far it is to this voodoo lady."

"Gladly," Sam began to drone on about the location of the three Cayman Islands below Cuba, how after World War II the British government had allowed the Caymans to become a tax haven where people from all over the world came to deposit money in the many banks located there. He explained how Grand Cayman was also world-renowned for its crystal blue waters, which attracted scuba divers from all over the world.

"I'm a diver," Ann interjected. "And after we see this lady, I'll probably go."

"Good, I'll be glad to get you to the best dive captain on the island."

"Sounds good. By the way, what's the lady's name?"

"It's Miss Cassie, and we're almost there."

Sam began to slow down the car. Ann had not paid any real attention to where they had driven on the very small island. The row houses they had passed basically looked the same to her.

Sam pulled off on a small dirt indention that jutted from the asphalt into a patch of tall weeds. Ann instinctively flinched as Sam pulled straight into the middle of them. Instead of a crash as she expected, the foliage opened up to reveal a small, weathered house. Chickens loitered where the front yard was supposed to be. Ann sat upright as she inspected the ramshackle home.

"Sam," Ann began, "Miss Cassie needs to 'voodoo' herself up a nicer place."

"Don't be fooled, Miss Ann, Cassie has plenty of money! She just doesn't like to spend it. I'll take you in to introduce you, then she'll want to be alone with you."

They got out of Sam's car and crossed the yard. Chickens milled about around them expecting to be fed. One pecked Ann's sandaled foot, and she sent it flying with a swift kick. Sam looked back at her as if to sternly warn her not to mess with Cassie's chickens. The front porch creaked with their combined weight as they walked to the door.

"Miss Cassie," Sam bellowed as he knocked loudly on the door. "It's me, Sam. Are you home?"

Silence greeted them initially; then they heard a shuffling sound emanating from the back of the old house.

"A faint voice carried forward to them. "Sam, Sam, is that you?" A frail-looking black woman with a large red bandanna circled around her head appeared before them. She squinted against the bright Cayman sunshine, holding her hand above her brow.

"I'll be damned, it is you, Sam," the little lady laughed loudly. "Where have you been lately?" She opened the screen door separating them and gave him a hug.

"You know me, Cassie. I stay busy with my taxi service. I've brought someone here to meet you." Sam gestured with his hand toward Ann.

Ann smiled broadly at this woman who looked at least a hundred years old.

"This is Ann, Miss Cassie, she's from the United States. And she wants to visit with you for a while."

Ann stuck out her hand and gently shook the woman's.

Still squinting up at the brightness, Miss Cassie motioned for them to come in.

"I can't, Cassie, I'm going to do a few errands while Ann visits with you. How long do you want to stay, Ann?"

Ann shrugged and said, "I don't know, about forty-five minutes, I guess."

With that Sam backed out of the door and mouthed, "Don't worry, I'll be back shortly," and headed back to his car.

Miss Cassie took Ann by the arm and led her back into the darkness of the house. As Ann's eyes struggled to adjust to the darkness, she was surprised to see that contrary to the outside of the house, the inside was very well kept and clean.

She was led to a middle sitting room, where the old woman placed her in an overstuffed chair. Ann immediately took her hat off.

Cassie sat down in a small rocking chair. One small window provided the only light, and that shone eerily, framing Cassie's head as if she had no body.

The bandannaed head started rocking back and forth in the darkness. As Ann's eyes grew more accustomed to the darkness she could see clearly Cassie's kind and weathered face and could make out her body.

"So what do you want to see me about, young lady? It's not often that I get visitors from the mainland."

Ann stumbled around a bit explaining that she was interested in the different aspects of the Caribbean culture.

"Voodoo," Cassie interrupted. "When Sam brings me someone, it's usually the black magic of the islands that they're interested in."

Ann, at a loss for words, simply threw up her hands in frustration.

"That's okay, honey, I love receiving company. I love sharing what I learned from my grandmother way back in Haiti. Specially to such a young pretty thing like you. It's not often that the younger generations, black or white, take much interest in the ways of us older ones nowadays."

"Does it work?" Ann blurted out rapidly.

Cassie stopped rocking. She looked straight at Ann as if to size up this stranger in her home. "If you believe in it, honey, it works," she stated emphatically.

Ann stared back without comment.

Cassie slowly got up out of the rocker. She held up an old hand as if to say "stay put."

Ann watched her as she disappeared behind a brightly colored quilt, which served as a curtain separating the sitting room and a back bedroom. Cassie rummaged around for a minute and then came back holding a pewter plate with a pile of bleached chicken bones strewn on top. She slowly pulled her chair closer to Ann and sat back down.

"Now then young lady, what is it that you want to know?"

"Can you read my future?"

Miss Cassie shook her head and said, "It's possible, young missy, but what I've found is that it's not very—"

Ann interrupted: "I'm not talking about specific stuff...just general things."

"Like what?" Cassie tilted her head inquisitively.

Ann shuffled her feet over the floor nervously.

"I've come into a great deal of money recently..."

"And..." Cassie raised her eyebrows.

"Can you tell me if I will make a whole lot more and be worth millions?"

Ann flipped her tan arm in the air in a flamboyant manner. "Ahhh...you want to know if all your hard work will pay off!"

"Yes, exactly..." Ann agreed

Before she could say more, the old lady pointed a finger directly at her face and said, "And will it bring you *happiness*?"

Her bluntness took Ann aback momentarily. She smiled sheepishly and stated somewhat shyly, "Well, yes."

"Then look closely, Missy Ann!" Cassie exclaimed.

She picked up a handful of the bleached bones, shook them savagely in her frail right hand and then spat on the pewter plate that she had placed atop her lap. She then threw the collection of osseous poultry fragments at the plate violently.

Ann instinctively held her hands up to shield her face, but all landed in a tangle on top of the plate. Not one had missed the mark.

Ann brought her hands down and looked down at the floor.

Cassie laughed in a delighted manner. "Sweetheart, they're all here." She pointed to the shining collection on top of the pewter. Ann collected herself, leaned forward and peered at the mass of bones.

"What do they say?" Ann quizzed, so excited she had fallen back into her habit of bouncing up and down in her chair.

An old hand flashed in front of her eyes signaling "patience."

"Hmmm...interesting, very interesting!"

"What...*what*?" Ann implored seemingly unable to contain herself further.

Wham! Just as quickly as Cassie had thrown the bones onto the plate, she knocked all of them over the entirety of the darkened floor.

"Damn, why did you do that? Ann's tan face blanched from surprise.

Cassie threw up her hands in resignation.

"I learned all that they could teach!" She snapped her fingers in the dark so briskly that static electricity sparked from them.

"So…"? Ann continued.

Cassie relaxed back into the rocking chair and slowly began to push back and forth. Her head disappeared and reappeared in the window light as she rocked.

"You will have lots of money, Missy Ann, more than you can ever spend!"

"Great!" Ann clapped her hands excitedly.

"*But…*" The old woman held up a finger to temper Ann's enthusiasm. "You will *never, ever* enjoy it." She wagged her finger back and forth.

"Well, "Ann jumped up, "we'll see about that!"

The old woman cackled loudly, "Ohhh…Missy Ann…please don't be upset. After all, this is just the rantings of a silly old woman."

She smiled up at Ann and pointed toward the chair.

"Please," she continued, pointing, "ask ole Cassie anything else you like…I'll take care not to be mean to you again."

Ann thought for a second and slowly sat back down.

"There, there…that's better, what else do you want this foolish old woman to tell you?"

Ann took a deep breath, exhaled and pulled a cigarette from a pocket in her short pants.

"Mind if I smoke?"

Cassie extended her hand and signaled with her arthritic fingers that she wanted one also. She cackled that high laugh that had grown to irritate Ann.

"I'm not supposed to smoke," she began, "But my ole doctor, he up and died last year...so I guess it don't matter none." She took a light from Ann and inhaled deeply.

Ann looked directly into the old woman's eyes.

"There is something else, Miss Cassie." Ann blew a wave of smoke across the streak of sunlight.

Cassie took an equally deep drag off her cigarette and awaited the question.

"It really has nothing to do with voodoo...er...anything like that," Ann sheepishly began.

"It's my little cousin back in New Orleans. He's twelve years old, and he cleans up at the new aquarium there. Well...he's gotten all intrigued with these stingrays...and—" she hesitated as she spoke, stumbling over her words.

"When he discovered that I was coming down here he wanted to know if I would bring him something."

Cassie had been listening intently. She opened her eyes widely as if to ask "what already?"

"Pheromones, stingray pheromones. The stuff that makes them have sex. That's what he wants me to bring back to him"

Cassie nodded her head in acknowledgment. She again slowly got up out of the chair, shuffled over the floor, threw the quilt up out of the way and disappeared into her back room. Ann's eyes grew weary staring into the darkness, searching for her frail outline. Suddenly the red bandanna popped into view, followed by Cassie's smiling face. She held up a small amber container, occluded at the top by a big brown cork.

"Here it is, deary. I think the young man will appreciate this liquid potion. Just a drop, mind you, will get the most reluctant of 'rays to join." She waved the bottle in the air.

Ann reached to take the bottle from the old woman's grasp.

"Wait!" Cassie jerked the bottle away from Ann.

"Just a minute, Missy. A warning first!"

Cassie meandered slowly back to her chair and sat

down, exclaiming, "Oh my, Cassie has got too tired today."

"What warning?" Ann interrupted.

"This is mighty powerful," Cassie again held up the bottle. "It causes the 'rays to join, but...a few drops on a human being in the water..." Cassie let out a slow whistle. "It's sure and certain death!"

"Really? I had heard something like that from my cousin...but, of course, I wasn't sure if it was true."

"Oh yes, Missy, it's very true." Ann stuck out her hand to take the bottle.

"One more thing!" she said so loudly that Ann jumped.

"Woe be upon the person that causes another human being to die by the effect of this potion!"

"What do you mean," Ann asked. "Isn't it just an attractant...I mean to help people mate stingrays in captivity?"

Cassie slowly shook her head.

"Oh no, Missy Ann, whatever comes from ole Cassie is voodoo magical, and that magic is never to be used harmfully on another human being. The old one clucked her tongue loudly to emphasize her point. Ann rolled her eyes slightly.

"Here you take this, Missy, but you remember Cayman Cassie's warning!" The old woman cackled her high pitched laugh again.

"Knock, knock! Hello, is anyone there?" Sam's voice carried throughout the house. Ann picked up her hat and headed to the door, almost in relief.

"Yes, Sam, I'm here."

"Did you have a good time? Did you learn anything?" Sam asked, laughing.

Ann walked to the front door. She heard Cassie shuffling behind her.

"Yes, yes, I did," she said. "But I'm ready to go."

She turned to Cassie and asked, "How much do I owe you?"

Cassie laughed out loud again.

"The only thing you owe me, Missy, is to pay young Sam here well for his time."

"Are you sure?"

Cassie simply nodded her head. She patted Ann and the appreciative taxi driver on the arms. "Come back to see me." She reached up and quickly hugged Ann around the neck. "And be sure to remember what I told you," she whispered into her ear.

"I will," Ann whispered back.

"Let's go, Ann. And don't worry, Miss Cassie, I'll be back to see you no matter what." Sam gave the fragile old woman a big hug.

Ann and Sam continued to wave good-bye as they walked together back to the car.

"What did you think?" Sam asked as soon as they had gotten back into the car.

Ann fingered the top of the amber bottle and replied, "Interesting."

"Where to now?" Sam turned to Ann.

"I want to go scuba diving...but first...I want to go back to the IMMC building."

"Yes, ma'am." Sam turned back onto the asphalt road and headed back to Georgetown. Sam began his usual tourist banter, explaining the history of this side of the island.

Ann stared at the houses and palm trees flashing past her window. Approaching Georgetown the traffic slowed as usual. Ann surveyed the hordes of American tourists searching for bargains to take back home.

"Here we are, Miss Ann."

"This is fine, Sam." Ann noticed that he had parked in the same place across from the IMMC building as the day before.

"Wait here, Sam, please," she instructed. She hopped out of the car and headed across the street.

"Ann, Ann Finn." Nick Sands yelled at her from the

doorway of the building. Ann waved in acknowledgment, held her hand tight over her hat and trotted over to him.

"Hi, Nick. I was just coming to see you."

"Really, what about?" he asked.

Ann said in her best Southern drawl, "I want to go scuba diving so desperately, Nicky," and snuggled up to him. "And I don't know how!" she continued.

Nick puffed his chest out, somewhat flattered by the attention she was showing him.

"Why, Ann, I'll be glad to show you," he said, taking her in his embrace and walking across the street.

"Is that your cab?"

"Yes," Ann responded, starting to pull from his grasp and lead him to Sam's car.

"Sam, Sam," she began as they slid into the back seat. "This is Nick Sands, a business associate of mine. And we would like to go scuba diving!"

"Hello, Mr. Sands, I'm Sam," Sam began as he looked back at them.

"Nick, please call me Nick," Nick said, shaking Sam's hand.

"Always glad to be of service," Sam continued. "And as any good Caymanian Tour Guide, I have access to some of the finest diving boats in all of the islands.

"Great then, "Ann said. "Let's go."

Sam started the car and headed back through the masses that lined the streets.

"If we're lucky," Sam began, "we'll have the boat all to ourselves seeing it's this late in the day. Where do you want to dive?"

"Stingray City!" Ann clapped her hands enthusiastically.

Nick made a face, obviously not pleased to go to this tourist haunt where virtually tame rays and skates feed from people's hands.

"Let's make a wall dive instead," he offered, referring to

the great drop-offs surrounding the island. Experienced divers hover over these massive underwater precipices and experience a sensation of terror unlike any other on earth, fearing a slide into oblivion with one simple miscalculation.

"No, no, Nick, I'm a novice diver. That's too difficult." Ann moved closer to his side.

"Yes, she's right," Sam interjected. "That's much too dangerous a dive for an inexperienced diver. Besides, this time of day, there aren't any tourist dives scheduled out there."

"Okay, I understand," Nick agreed. "Let's go to Stingray City!" He made a motion with his hand as if signaling a cavalry charge.

Sam stepped on the accelerator and increased his speed. He fell into his usual habit of pointing out locations of interest, such as where movie stars had beach homes.

Ann crossed her long tan legs and began to engage Nick in chitchat. After several minutes of idle conversation, she began to quiz him about his business, turning the conversation to the subject of John Wyatt and the money that was inadvertently sent to him.

"Mr. Levitz came by and told us the whole story," she said.

"He shouldn't have burdened you and Secretary Castner with that!" Nick protested.

"Oh, don't worry," Ann began. "I'm just concerned that you're comfortable with covering this up...that is, if it comes up again."

A concerned look swept over Nick's face. "What do you mean?"

Ann's demeanor turned serious. She looked directly into his eyes.

"I mean, what are you willing to do if the heat turns up on our little project?"

Nick shook his head. "I'm not going to be the fall guy, if that's what you mean," he said tersely. "Especially since I don't know everything that's going on."

"That's what I thought," Ann muttered under her breath.

"What's that supposed to mean?" He responded, a somewhat puzzled look playing over his face.

Ann hesitated, adjusting the hat on her head and allowing one of her legs to nudge against his.

"Oh, nothing, Nicky…nothing. Besides, you and Levitz came up with the perfect solution. And, after all, we're worrying about nothing. That was just an unfortunate slip-up, and nothing is going to come of it anyway.

"Tell me about how we're going to dive today! It sounds so terribly exciting." She slipped back into her deep Southern dialect and flirtatiously batted her eyes at him. She followed this with a huge smile.

Nick smiled back, his brow unfurrowed as he relaxed.

"You're right Ann, we're worrying about nothing. Let me tell you about Stingray City. Have you ever been?"

Ann leaned forward, displaying a keen interest in every word the young financier uttered.

"Why no, tell me all about it!" she gushed.

Nick began to explain the underwater dive that was located in the natural habitat of literally thousands of stingrays and their cousins, the skates.

"You can feed the creatures and stroke their sandpapery underbellies," he said.

" Cool," Ann said. "I can't wait!"

"We'll be there shortly," Sam chimed in.

"What's the name of the boat?" Ann asked.

" The Stingray," Sam replied.

Sam had taken them to the northern tip of the Island. A dilapidated dock protruded into a small natural harbor, which in turn led out through a channel to the ocean. A large white diving vessel was moored midway out. STING RAY was painted in black lettering across the bow. No one appeared to be on the boat.

Sam parked his car next to the dock, directly in front of

the boat. They got out of the car and headed over to the rickety old pier.

"Be careful!" Sam warned as Ann and Nick walked gingerly on the old structure. He explained as they neared the boat that wood was scarce on the island and any structure still serviceable was used.

"No joke!" Ann yelled as she spread her feet on the old structure and began to rock it. It swayed precariously from side to side.

"Quit that!" Sam called out, enough sternness in his voice to stop her.

"Sorry!" Ann offered as she shyly peeked at him over her shoulder. She and Nick continued to make their way to the diving boat. Regardless of the condition of the structure to which it was attached, the Stingray was a fine vessel. A forty-foot-long runabout in appearance, it had been adapted to add a diver's station on the back.

"Hop on!" Sam urged, steadying the boat with both hands. The couple slowly climbed on board. Sam followed after unmooring the boat; he quickly made his way around the boat, checking air tanks and regulators. He threw face masks and flippers out of the way so their seats would be cleared.

"We're lucky. I share this boat with several other tourist guides, and sometimes they are really packed in here." Sam started the motor and pulled out into the harbor. He then climbed up into the small fly bridge above the main body of the boat.

"Settle in, folks. It'll take a bit to get out there."

Ann and Nick sat back in the stern and tried to make themselves comfortable. A wind was blowing up from the south, making the waters choppier. Leaving the harbor, Sam pushed the throttle forward and urged the bow through the waves.

Ann had to hold her hat down on her head as the wind whipped up over them.

"Let's get some sun before we get there!" Ann bounced up and headed down in the cabin. "We need to change into our suits anyway."

Nick turned red as he slapped his forehead.

"Geez, I forgot to bring a suit."

"Not to worry, Mr. Sands, There should be a bunch in the closet under the galley.

"I'll change first ,Nick, and then you can look for one, okay?"

"Yeah, sounds good."

Ann pulled the door behind her after she stepped down into the aft compartment to change. She pulled two bikinis from her bag, one the slight number she had worn the day before. She opted for a less revealing one that at least covered her backside. Although they weren't going to dive long, every little bit of body cover would help, since they weren't going to wear wet suits.

"Ta da," Ann pronounced, emerging from the cabin.

Nick slid past her in a rush to find a suit, seemingly oblivious to her grand entrance. He rummaged through the various trunks and chose a solid green, cut long at the knee.

Ann was oiling her arms and legs when Nick stepped self-consciously back on the deck.

"Cute!"

He didn't know if she was teasing him at first and instinctively began to apologize for forgetting his suit.

"I'm teasing you, Nick!" "Besides, who will see us anyway? Come on, sit down beside me and I'll rub you down." She held up a bottle of Hawaiian Tropic. Nick looked up at Sam in the bridge,

"How far are we from the spot?"

"Not far, but go ahead and have fun...I'll let you know when we get close," Sam replied.

Ann reached up and gently pulled him beside her. She plopped a generous amount of the coconut oil on her hand and began to rub it slowly on his shoulders.

Tension immediately began to leave his body, and he slumped back against her. "Feels good...Ah..." Nick sat with his eyes closed as she gently massaged his muscles. Turning to look at her, he caught a glimpse of her face.

"What's the deal with you and Castner?" he asked.

Ann waved her hand in front of his face, gesturing "nothing" with one motion. "Do you want to grab a bite to eat after our dive...or something?"

"Sure, I'd love it!"

"Wa-a-a-atch it!" Sam yelled from above. The boat suddenly veered to the right throwing them hard against the side. Nick's body penned Ann momentarily behind him. Gathering themselves, they separated and tried to regain their positions.

"Whoa." Nick shook his head, the jolt having made him lose his concentration. "What happened, Sam?"

"I had to miss some junk floating in the water. Sorry, folks, are you okay?"

Ann and Nick nodded in agreement. Nick fidgeted and dug at an object underneath him.

"What's this?" He handed a small amber-colored glass bottle to Ann.

"Nothing...er...oil...tanning oil." She grabbed the bottle from him and tossed it overboard.

"Let's talk about our date tonight," she said as she resumed massaging his back.

Nick turned to her slightly and sniffed,

"What's that sweet smell?"

"I don't smell anything. it must be the ocean or something." She rubbed his neck muscles strenuously.

"Where did you say you thought we should go?" Nick responded to the increased friction by allowing his head to lean back and rest on her cheek.

"There's lots of places."

"Almost to Stingray City, friends!" Sam's cheerful voice interrupted them.

Ann jumped up and headed to the galley underneath. Nick watched her bottom admiringly as she disappeared downstairs. He peeked over the cabin window to get a look at her. Curiously, she was scrubbing her hands with Comet cleanser.

Sam tapped his foot loudly on the bridge above him, and the big motor slowly began to wind down.

"We're here!" He bounded down the bridge ladder and then headed up to the bow, where he took the anchor and threw it overboard, snagging it against a piece of submerged coral and tightly secured it to the bow. Heading back to the storage areas, he got out air tanks, flippers and face masks.

Ann emerged from the cabin, headed directly to the collection of equipment and began to get ready.

"Without wet suits, you two will only stay down a few minutes," Sam said.

Nick began to work with a regulator and slid a tank on his back.

Ann tossed her long hair around in a loop and fastened it snugly with a rubber band, creating a ponytail that allowed her mask to fit tightly on her face.

After gearing up, the two walked around the boat deck like frog men.

Sam laughed and said, "I'll make sure the boat's stabilized so you can concentrate on having fun. Pet a ray for me" he added as he helped position them on the diving platform on the back of the boat.

"Looks like you'll be mostly alone." He pointed to the only other boat tied up in the area.

They jumped in simultaneously, splashing as they hit the water. They both gave him a thumbs-up sign as they adjusted their masks and began to dive. Bubbles floated to the surface slowly as they began the descent to the sandy ocean floor. They could see a wall of beautifully colored coral surrounding the "city." Nick pointed excitedly as hundreds of gliding stingrays circled below them. Ann had gently

185

pulled away from him and was descending on her own about twenty yards away.

One other couple was down on the ocean bottom feeding and petting the graceful sea creatures as Nick floated over them. Ann was descending at the same rate but had drifted further off to the side.

Nick did not see the first stingray that struck him. He was only fifteen feet above the other couple when two more left their paths on the floor and struck him with their venomous tails. The couple below him looked up in shock and swam over to where Ann had settled on the bottom. All they could do was look at one another in horror through their masks and point. Nick disappeared in a flurry of flapping water wings and a blizzard of sand stirred up by the thrashing of man and hundreds of stingrays. They attacked him with the tenacity of a swarm of African killer bees. Just as quickly as they had turned from calm "petting zoo" creatures to killers, the rays left Nick's lifeless body and floated back to their glide patterns just above the ocean floor.

Ann motioned to the couple to surface with her and they nodded in agreement. It was obvious that Nick was dead. There was nothing they could do. The threesome began to slowly ascend to the surface. Nearing the top, Ann shivered as she looked back at Nick's bloated purple body splayed across the ocean floor.

Their bubbles broke at the surface, alerting Sam that they were near. His welcoming smile turned into one of disbelief as he saw the two strangers with Ann.

"Where's Mr. Sands?" he shouted at the bobbing heads.

"He's *dead*, Sam!" Ann sputtered as she reached up to him with both arms. Kicking as hard as she could with flipper-covered feet, she slid up on the diving platform. Water choked from her mouth as she lay crying hysterically below Sam's feet.

The couple climbed up onto the platform with Sam's help. "We live in Florida," the man began, "and I've never seen or heard anything like it! They swarmed him…" He held up his hand, catching his breath.

"It could have easily been us!" his wife sobbed.

"What could have caused them to do that?" The man asked after catching his breath.

"Did he do anything unusual?" Sam looked at Ann.

Ann simply lay on the platform and shook her head.

The man helped his wife, and Sam helped Ann back into the boat.

"I've heard of other species doing this," the man said.

"Yes, but usually they were provoked!" his wife added.

"Nick wasn't doing anything!" Ann protested, undoing her rubber band and flinging her long wet hair out.

"Just goes to show that when you enter another creature's domain, by God, you can't take anything for granted!" the Florida man exclaimed as he covered his wife with a towel that Sam had gotten.

"I'll have to call the Caymanian Police," Sam said walking over to the radio and turning it on He spoke in a hushed tone attempting to contact the local authorities.

The threesome sat with downcast eyes, huddled close together draped with towels, and waited for the authorities.

Sam prepared his gear and tanks. It's my duty to help the police when they arrived to recover the body," he said. "After all, this man was a guest of mine."

When the authorities arrived, they towed the Florida couple's small boat and docked it next to the Sting Ray.

The Cayman police were very courteous and gentle as they questioned the three eyewitnesses. They too allowed they had not heard of a ray attack quite like this.

The other couple invited Ann to go inland with them as they were boarding their boat. Ann looked at Sam, seeking his permission.

"Go ahead, Missy Ann, it'll be better if you don't stay around to see this."

Ann hugged Sam, thanked the Cayman police officers

and then climbed on the boat with the couple. She waved at Sam as they pulled away from the Sting Ray.

Ann discovered that the couple, Jim and Cathy Natkins, were staying at the Hyatt and asked if they would mind dropping her off at her villa.

"Of course not," the woman sympathetically responded. "Did you know him well?" she stammered.

"Didn't know him at all," Ann answered, staring over the waves.

* * *

Not much else was said on the trip back to the hotel. Ann waved good-bye and headed for the villa. She passed the pool where Richard Castner was sunning himself.

"Hey, Ann!" Richard called.

Ann walked by in silence, disappearing behind the double-doored residence.

Richard jumped up and followed her into the villa.

"Ann, Ann, is anything wrong?" he called into her darkened room. He looked in and saw her sprawled out on her bed.

"Nick's dead," she whispered in a choked voice.

"What?"

"He's dead!"

Richard walked slowly to the end of her bed, waiting for her to move or acknowledge his presence.

"It's true. He's dead." She still didn't move.

"What are you talking about?" Richard sat down on the end of the bed, next to her tanned feet.

Ann sat up, her hair in a tangle from the dive and the drive home. She curled her feet under her and clasped her arms beneath her legs. She began to rock back and forth. A large tear formed under one eye.

"Nick's dead. The stingrays attacked him. It was awful!"

Richard moved closer on the bed, put both arms around her trembling body and held her tightly.

"I don't know what to say, Ann. How did it happen?" He continued to hold her as she shook.

She didn't respond at first. Slowly she lifted her head, shook her hair and tried to straighten it with a shaking hand.

"I saw him die. The stingrays attacked him for some reason.... The police and Sam said they had never seen anything like it."

"Are you okay, Ann?"

She reached up and hugged him tightly around the neck.

"Richard, let's go. I don't want to stay here any longer."

"We'll go, Ann, just as soon as I make sure the police don't need anything further from you and we visit IMMC and make sure our money is all right."

Ann looked up at him and nodded her approval.

"The cops won't need me for anything else, or at least they didn't say anything about it in the boat."

"Just to be sure, let me get in touch with them."

"Okay. But you don't have to worry about our money. In case of something like this it's automatically held in escrow at the Cayman National Bank until we claim it. No questions asked."

The shaken, trembling figure had been transformed back into the Ann he knew as she explained Cayman national law concerning funds such as theirs.

"If Nick's company isn't solvent or if there's some kind of problem, the funds are still safe," she continued. "Look, I had Levitz research the matter months ago before we transferred any money down here."

Castner shivered as he listened to her continue to explain how she had settled on the Caymans to stash her money. It was safe, and with the numbered accounts, an incident like this didn't jeopardize the fortune she had already amassed. Not once did she express remorse over the loss of Nick Sands.

"When Ann competed her explanation, Castner agreed that it would be best if they cut their visit short.

"Let's go to Cancun tomorrow, Richard. We can check

on things in Mexico. I need to talk to Guttierez about our cuts. I think we deserve more money."

"Are you sure, Ann? You've been through quite a shock."

"I'm sure. Will you arrange everything?"

Castner promised he would.

Ann finally lay down on the bed. He covered her with a sheet and encouraged her to go to sleep. After closing the door to her room, he called Delta and rearranged their flights. He called the Cayman authorities, who confirmed what Ann had told him. Nick Sands' death was a horrible accident.

Castner sat and stared at the door behind which Ann lay asleep. He crossed the room, tiptoeing so as not to wake her, and poured a large glass of straight Jack Daniel's. "When we get back, you're on your own, Ann," he whispered. "No amount of money is worth this. I'm staying alive!"

* * *

Ann and Richard flew to Cancun the next day. Castner was polite but reserved. At one point he looked at her and smiled. "Ann, how much money is enough?" he asked.

"I will never have enough!"

He smiled again. "That's what I thought."

"What's that supposed to mean?"

"Nothing. It's just that I have a lot to lose. Money only has so much value to me.

"I can't believe you said that"

"You don't understand. I'm a cabinet secretary. I don't want to screw things up, that's all.

"Don't worry, Richard." She patted his hand. "You just keep okaying St. John's work and leave the rest to me."

He was silent for most of the rest of the flight.

Julio met them at the airport.

"Did you make an appointment with Guttierez for me?" Ann asked as they loaded the luggage into her Mercedes.

"Yes, he's going to see you as soon as we can drive there.

I told him it was urgent."

"Good job, Julio. I can always depend on you." She patted him on the shoulder.

The drive to the hospital was essentially a one-sided conversation with Ann repeating the reasons she deserved more money. Julio and Richard sat in silence, listening quietly as they drove up the winding road overlooking the Gulf.

Julio pulled in front of the hospital. "I'll wait out here," he said as he opened the door for them.

"This shouldn't take long, Julio." Ann patted him on the shoulder.

Ann led the way down the marbled foyer. She didn't hesitate as she entered the administrator's office. Lupita smiled at them. "Go on in. Dr. Guttierez is expecting you."

Ann and Richard walked in.

"I'm glad you came by," Guttierez said. He shook both of their hands warmly. "Ann, Dr. St. John has been calling asking if you were here."

"What does he want?" she asked.

"Well, he wants to bring Dr. Wyatt's father down here to get a heart transplant. He's ineligible to get one back in the United States due to his age."

Ann's face turned red in anger.

"He knows better than that! What did you tell him?"

"I had Lupita to tell him that I wasn't available."

"Good! Let me get to the point of our coming here then." Guttierez motioned for them to take a seat.

"We think we deserve more of the money generated by these procedures."

Dr. Guttierez's face reddened.

Ann continued: "I provide 90 percent of the organs that you use. Richard masks the morbidity and mortality reports so no one is the wiser."

Richard Castner held up his hand in protest. "Hold on, Ann. It's you who wants more money. I'm satisfied."

Ann shot him a nasty look.

"Ann, I understand your position, and you have done a great job from your end, but..." Guttierez put his hands behind his head and leaned back in his chair. "I would pay you more. The problem is with my board. They would never go for it. They feel that since the procedure was perfected here we should receive the bulk of the money. The potassium storage containers alone cost over a million dollars apiece. You're doing a great job, but that's all I can say."

Ann jumped up from her chair. "I guess there's nothing more to talk about then."

Guttierez arose and offered his hand in consolation.

"I'm sorry, Ann. It's just business. We've all got a finger in the pie, and we're all making money. Let's make sure we stay friends so we can continue to work together."

"Let's go, Richard!" Obviously upset, Richard Castner shook Dr. Guttierez's hand and gave him a look as if to say, "Ann is just like that."

They walked down the hall.

"What are you going to do now?" Ann asked.

"I'm going to Washington, Ann. There's nothing more I can do here. Besides, we have a cabinet meeting at the White House in a few days."

Julio spotted them as they left the building and drove up to meet them. Ann opened the Mercedes door and said, "Julio, take Mr. Castner to the airport."

Richard Castner looked at her suspiciously. "What are you going to do?"

"You need to go home. As for me, I'm going to talk Raphael Guttierez into giving me more money!"

She patted Castner on the cheek, and wheeled around to go back into the hospital. She skipped back up the sidewalk and entered the building.

Castner closed the door of the car. "Julio, say what you will about your boss, she usually gets what she wants!" he said, laughing and shaking his head. "Take me to the airport."

Chapter Thirteen

nn Finn. The thought of his beautiful lover brought the exhilaration he was feeling crashing to the ground. Robert rubbed his stomach again. She was very mad at him when she left. He waved that thought away with a flippant pass of his hand.

She loves me. She'll do this for Mr. Wyatt. It'll make us both feel better to do something this great for Dave Wyatt's family.

He contacted the airline first. Delta would only say that she had taken a flight. After contacting their flight information number, he was informed that it was against airline policy to disclose passage information, but he surmised that she was probably on her way.

Did Casa del Mar even have a telephone? He remembered the phones on the night stand in the bedroom. What was the number? Jerri would know.

Jerri gave Robert the number. He assumed it would be a minimum of three to four hours before he could talk with her anyway. In the meantime, he should check with Dr. Thompkins to ascertain the urgency of the situation.

Dr. Thompkins reassured Robert that there was no way the 62-year-old Mr. Wyatt could be eligible for the transplant. The medical complications were as Mr. Wyatt reported: The ejection fraction—the amount of blood being pumped from the left ventricle, which was the main pump of the heart—was very low. Bypass surgery was not possible because of the nature of the diseased coronary arteries.

"He doesn't have long to live," Dr. Thompkins confided

to Robert. "He sure is a feisty fellow, isn't he? You know what the guy did?"

"No, what?"

"He brought in a certified check for two million dollars, saying he would pay us more if we would just do the surgery."

"Two million dollars?"

"We called the bank—it was good. What do you think about that?"

"I had no idea the guy had money," Dr. St. John responded, stunned. "Well, thanks for your time, Dr. Thompkins. Please call me at New Orleans Hospital if Mr. Wyatt's condition worsens."

"I certainly will."

Robert was confused. He had been raised with Dave Wyatt. That family didn't have that kind of money! He decided to go on home and call Ann in Mexico from there.

He telephoned Casa del Mar after propping his feet up at the midtown home. Julio picked up the phone in Mexico. He assured Robert that he would have Ann call him in New Orleans as soon as she got back.

He called Mr. Wyatt.

"Bobby, how are you? Thanks for calling me back so quickly. What did you find out?"

Dr. St. John explained that he had talked to surgeons in New Orleans and Dr. Thompkins in Knoxville and that they all told him the same thing. There were no exceptions to the age limit for organ transplants under the new health system. Robert could feel Mr. Wyatt's disappointment through the phone.

"But," Robert countered enthusiastically, "there may be another way, John."

"What do you mean, 'another way'?"

"I've promised someone that I won't talk—"

"Shoot, Bobby. I'm dying. Can't you lie this one time and tell me?" he said, laughing.

Robert laughed with him. "No, I can't. Not yet, anyway. But I can tell you that there are other doctors and hospitals in this world. I'll tell you about it as soon as I can. So tell Mrs. Wyatt not to worry— we're going to get you a new ticker!"

"Thanks, Bobby-Boy!"

"I'll call you back just as soon as I know something."

Robert called Casa del Mar five more times that evening. Julio swore each time Ann wasn't there.

"Where is she?"

Dr. St. John acknowledged to himself ruefully that Ann had been very mad when she left. He decided he would call once again in the morning. If Ann wasn't there or didn't answer he was going to go down himself. He would see Raphael Guttierez in person. If John Wyatt had that kind of money, it shouldn't be any trouble whatsoever to get him a new, healthy heart. The thought made him smile. He allowed himself to think of Dave Wyatt for the first time since the funeral, as he slowly dozed off to sleep.

* * *

"Hello, Julio. This is Dr. St. John again. Is she there?"

"No, Señor Doctor. She is not here."

Something in Julio's voice had changed. Robert sensed he was lying.

"Look, Julio, when Ann left the United States she was very mad at me. Please just tell me the truth. She's there, isn't she?"

"No, she's not here."

"Julio, this is very, very important. If she is there and you can't say because she'll get upset, tell me that the fishing is very good, and we'll catch another blue marlin when I come down."

There was a long pause, then Julio said, "The fishing is great now. The next time you come down we'll catch a bigger marlin."

195

"I knew it. Thanks, Julio. I'll see you in three or four hours."

"No, Señor Doctor!" Julio protested, but he was too late. Robert had already slammed the receiver down. He called Delta for reservations to Cancun and packed in less than five minutes.

The flight to Cancun was full of happy Americans ready to slosh on tanning oil, lie in the warm rays of the sun, and enjoy the beaches of Mexico. Robert rehearsed his pleas: the first to Ann—to forgive him for having a date with Elizabeth, and the second to convince Dr. Guttierez to perform a heart transplant on John Wyatt.

The second part shouldn't be very hard since Mr. Wyatt had plenty of money. The only drawback he could think of was that Dr. Guttierez did not want to include Americans in the preliminary group of recipients.

Getting Ann to forgive him, however, would be difficult. After tossing several ideas around in his mind he chose the best. He would fall on his knees and beg her forgiveness, then carry her to the bedroom and make passionate love to her. That should work.

The thumping of the big jet down on the runway brought him back to the present. Looking out the window, he surveyed the modest but efficient Cancun Airport. Leaning against the fence next to the passenger exit was a young man who looked a lot like Julio. As the jet pulled closer to the departure ramp Robert realized it *was* Julio. He grabbed his hand bag and stepped off the jet. He waved at Julio as he descended the portable stairs.

Julio began to wave and motion wildly to him.

What the hell? Robert wondered. Julio continued his very exaggerated motions. Robert waved back, entering the airport to claim his baggage and clear customs.

"You should not have come, Señor Doctor."

"Why not, Julio?" Robert grabbed the young man and physically held him to stop Julio from appearing to be a large

Mexican jumping bean.

"I just don't think you should go to the casa, Doctor. As a matter of fact the guards have been ordered to never let you in again."

"What? Julio, you don't know women as well as I do. Ann is mad at me, but I'll persuade her to forgive me, if she'll just give me a chance."

Dr. St. John picked up his bags and threw them in the back seat of the Mercedes.

"I'll get fired or worse if she even knows I met you here at the airport," Julio pleaded. "Besides, you won't be allowed into Casa del Mar."

"There's something you're not telling me, Julio. You and I are friends. Just get it out, man!"

Julio dejectedly walked back to the driver's side of the car. "Get in. I'll explain to you on the way."

They drove down the road in silence. Finally, Julio asked: "Robert, how well do you know Ann Finn?"

"Pretty well, I think. Why?"

"I'm going to take you the back way to Casa del Mar. There's a way to take the cliff and sit above the pool and hot tub without being seen. You and I can hide above the grottos and the waterfall."

"What the hell are we doing that for, Julio? I'm not going to slip around like a spy or a Peeping Tom."

Julio looked perplexed. "What's a 'peepingtom'?"

"Oh, never mind. Tell me what's up, Julio."

"No, you'll see for yourself. Then you'll thank your friend Julio."

Julio pulled the car off onto a side road that angled down toward the beach.

"What the hell?" Robert protested. "You can't take a Mercedes Benz down here—you need a Jeep or a Hummer."

Julio ignored him and continued to drive. The Mercedes crept over the crushed rock. The waves of the Gulf nearly crashed into the car at a spot where the road met a narrow part of the beach. The road then began to snake around back toward the summit. "I'll be damned," Robert exclaimed.

Julio stopped the vehicle in the road. Above them was Casa del Mar. The wall surrounding the house loomed all the way around. Julio turned to Robert. "Do you love her, Doctor?"

"Yes, I guess I do, Julio."

Julio just turned up the road and pointed. "Here is where we're going. Do you see where the rocks that make up the overlook over the sea extend up higher than the wall?"

"Oh yeah. I do."

"If we climb the rocks we can see everything in the pool and hot tub. We can hide and observe pretty much everything that happens."

Dr. St. John was looking at the wall he was supposed to climb. "Climb that!" he yelled. "Are you crazy? That looks like Mt. Everest. We'll kill ourselves."

"No, we won't, Doctor. My dad helped build this house. I played up there when he and the other men worked on it. It's easy—if you know where you are going."

"This is bullshit, Julio." Robert turned to head back to the car.

Julio grabbed him forcefully by the arm.

"You won't get in the house because of the guards. You have to go this way. It's not hard. I'll show you. There's something you need to see, Doctor. As your friend I'm going to take this risk in losing my job and maybe my life, because I don't want you to be hurt."

Julio's demeanor convinced Dr. St. John that he needed to follow him up the rocks and spy on Ann.

Chapter Fourteen

The climb was far easier than Dr. St. John had imagined. Julio had been right. The cliff's foreboding appearance disappeared with each move upward and forward. Each hard hold and pull up was followed by Julio turning to him and exhorting him onward.

Robert felt a like fool. Julio would not have brought him to this ridiculous precipice without just cause. In the short time he and Julio had gotten to know each other while fishing, they had come to trust one another.

"Here we are," Julio whispered. Robert pulled himself to the top of the overlook. The top of the fenced enclosure was a mere foot from where they clung precariously. From below, the rock wall and precipice had seemed impregnable. But here it was obvious that one need only know where to step. It was simply a matter of perseverance and trust.

"All we have to do is step onto the wall encircling the house, walk five yards, and step onto the rocks making up the waterfall." Julio pointed the way.

Dr. St. John nodded his head in understanding, then looked back over his shoulder the beach and the pounding waves below. "Julio, it's getting dark. Will we be able to make it back to the car without breaking our necks?"

Julio smiled. "Everything will be fine. Let's go. No one is in the pool area. Follow me."

With one deft step, Julio jumped to the top of the wall and walked the five yards opposite to the top of the falls. He leaped to the apex of the rock where the water emerged and began the fifty-foot descent into the pool.

Robert swallowed hard and duplicated the feat. Soon he joined Julio inside the compound of Casa del Mar.

Julio looked at him. "Jump exactly where I do."

Dr. St. John followed him in a series of six jumps, each one taking him four to five feet, until they reached a spot where they could hide and not be seen by anyone below. Directly to their left was the hot tub and pool furniture where he and Ann had made love. Embarrassment crept over him as he realized that someone could just as easily have been watching him from this very position.

"Julio," Robert hissed under his breath. "I don't like this one bit."

"Shhh, Doctor. Somebody will hear us."

They waited five minutes, crammed behind the rock and cascading waterfall that obscured their presence. The water exuded just enough mist to cool them from the heat.

The sliding door of the covered pool house slid open. Two voices from inside laughed. The noise of the cascading water made discerning the words distinctly next to impossible.

Twilight approached. Laughter continued to emerge from the opened doors. Ann Finn walked briskly out to the hot tub. She was completely naked. He would recognize her marvelous body even in the most faint of light. She laughed mightily, then appeared to beckon for the reluctant party inside to join her. Out walked the naked form of Dr. Raphael Guttierez.

Julio, anticipating Robert's anger, grabbed him just as he started to jump out from his hiding place.

"Wait," he said, as he pulled his friend back into their hiding place.

It was more than Dr. St. John could watch as Ann began to perform the same oral trick on the hospital director that she had done to him.

Julio whispered in his ear. "You don't have to watch, but

you've got to see what kind of person Ann Finn is. That she is betraying you is the least of what is important." Julio looked into Robert's eyes. "There's something else going on, Robert, and I'm not aware enough of what it is to understand. That is why I dragged you here—not to see her in infidelity— but to see if you can understand what they are talking about. Something is terribly wrong here, in this house and at that hospital."

Dr. St. John's rage had subsided. His conscience had been pricked by Julio's admonishment that something was terribly wrong.

Julio pulled him back to the edge. Ann and Guttierez had moved to the hot tub. They were raising champagne glasses in a toast and discussing money. Robert overheard "one hundred thousand dollars" mentioned amidst hearty laughter. He also made out "Fool!" and "Doctor!" and "transplantation." His face and neck bulged with anger as he realized those words were possibly about him

The sentences were mixed with laughter and clouded by the thud of the waterfall. He strained to decipher more but couldn't. He leaned back from the edge as the exultant couple suddenly splashed from the hot tub and ran into the house.

Julio turned to Robert. "Did you understand what they were talking about?

Dr. St. John shrugged. "No, let's get out of here."

"No, not yet. Let's wait until it gets darker."

Julio and Robert squatted in silence behind the rocks. As the sun set, the mist from the falls changed from heat relief to a slight chill.

Dr. St. John was so confused he couldn't think.

Julio tugged at him. "Let's go."

They retraced their steps down the slope. The approaching darkness made their getaway much more precarious than the climb had been. But, true to his word, Julio led him safely back to the Mercedes.

After Julio warmed the car to cut their chill, Robert

asked: "Julio, what do you mean 'something is terribly wrong'?"

"I don't know, but there is something wrong. Did you understand what they were saying, Doctor Robert?"

"No, not really. I think it's crystal clear that Ann thinks I'm a fool," he said with a mocking laugh. He felt anger returning at the memory of the couple.

Julio turned to Robert. "What exactly are they doing at that hospital, Doctor Robert?"

"Transplants, organ transplants. I came to Mexico to attempt to get a heart transplant for a very sick old friend. Now, I don't know…I promised this man's family that he would get one."

"I see," Julio stated reassuringly.

"I just don't think I should approach Ann now. Not until I understand better what is going on at that hospital here!"

"Doctor, there's something I need to tell you. My sister works for you in America, at the New Orleans hospital."

"Really? Who is your sister, Julio?" a surprised Robert asked.

"Sally Ortiz."

"Really? I see the resemblance. I knew Sally was from a large family, but I assumed they were in America."

"And there's something else, Robert. There was some trouble when Sally worked here in Cancun."

"What do you mean, 'trouble'?"

"I don't want to shed a bad light on my sister, but I thought you should know."

"What do you mean, Julio?"

"Oh, I don't really know all that was involved, but some patients were…well… Nothing was ever proven, but she left here and went to the United States to work."

"I'll be damned," Robert said out loud. "You and Sally— brother and sister." He put his arm around his new friend. "You're a true friend, Julio. You stuck your neck out for me."

"Do you want to go back to the airport?"

"Yes, Julio. There's no reason for me to stay in Cancun."

Julio took him directly to the airport. Robert was fortunate to get the last Delta flight, the 10:30 p.m. to Dallas.

"Julio, do you have a telephone at your home where I can contact you?"

The young Mexican wrote his number down and gave it to the doctor. Robert gave Julio the number to his office at New Orleans Hospital.

"If something unusual happens, or you need to talk to me, just leave a message at this number."

They walked silently to the gate.

"When did you notice something unusual here, Julio?"

Julio shrugged. "I don't know. I'm sorry, Doctor Robert. Maybe just knowing that Ann is not a good woman has made me fearful. I'm sorry you had to find out this way…"

"Do you want me to tell your sister anything when I get back? Do you want me to give her a message?"

Julio shook his head emphatically. "No, no. We are not on the best of terms."

"I understand," Dr. St. John said.

The last boarding call for the Dallas flight was announced. He embraced Julio. "I'll call you in a couple of days at your home, after I talk to someone."

"Who?"

Dr. St. John patted Julio on the shoulder reassuringly. "Someone you don't know, my Mexican friend. Police officer Sandy Elliott."

Chapter Fifteen

A depressed young doctor settled in for the red-eye flight back to Dallas, Texas, U.S.A. He, as other human beings, had been rejected and hurt before in relationships. The nature of this development was more than humiliating. It involved his sexual pride, of course, but he thought also of his professional aspirations. He had made this trip to obtain a heart transplant for John Wyatt, who had been his surrogate Dad growing up. That was up in smoke at least for now. And where would he live? Go back to Ann and her house? Not on his life! And yet he had no other choice at the present.

The image of Elizabeth Johnson popped into his mind's eye. He crossed his arms over his chest in disgust. How could he have used such poor judgment?

What did Ann and Guttierez mean by "one hundred thousand dollars?" Were they using the transplant process to make that amount of money for themselves? He probably was the doctor and the fool they had referred to. Or could they possibly have meant Dave Wyatt? He bolted suddenly up in his seat. Julio is a good guy—he knows something is wrong. But Elliott said Dave killed himself. He slid back into his seat as the shock of the thought of Dave Wyatt being murdered hit him.

He was puzzled and very tired. How did all of this tie together? What if Ann was just a frustrated girl and Julio had taken offense at her promiscuity? In Catholic Mexico, sexual adventurism is frowned upon much more than in post-'60s

America. Maybe Julio was just overreacting to that and that's why he took him up the cliff to spy on Ann. Julio had said something was not right at the Hospital of the Americas. But what?

The fatigue of the day began to weigh him down into the twilight time right before sleep overtakes one, but his mind still reeled. There were so many questions that needed to be answered. He considered that after all, he had been about as untruthful about Elizabeth Johnson. If it hadn't been for Elizabeth's virtue, he might have done the same thing with her after their date. He rubbed the bruise inflicted by Ann, winced slowly with pain and fell asleep.

* * *

"Sir, sir," a pert, attractive stewardess roused him from a deep sleep in which he was dreaming. Shaking his head to clear his mind, he had momentarily forgotten he was in flight from Cancun to Dallas.

The dream was hard to shake. He had seen Dave Wyatt standing above him on the cliff overlooking Casa del Mar. Robert was down on the beach. Someone pushed Dave from behind. Dave was clutching something in both hands. He couldn't make out what Dave was holding until he almost hit the rocks and surf below. Dave was holding pumping hearts in both hands. The organs appeared to have just been harvested and made ready for transplantation.

What a weird dream, he thought, shaking his head in an attempt to awaken. He left the plane, and passed through customs. A uniformed officer was inspecting everyone's luggage. The uniform reminded him that he wanted to go by and see Sandy Elliott when he got to New Orleans.

He was able to catch a commuting flight from Dallas to Baton Rogue and then New Orleans. The streets were hauntingly quiet as he left the airport, obliged to return to Ann's house. The clock on the wall in her uptown home caught his reflection as he stumbled into the ornate mansion. Four a.m. He had thought of staying in a motel, but figured Ann wouldn't return to New Orleans for at least twenty-four hours. Despite the confusion and deadening fatigue he was experiencing he pulled the number of Officer Elliott out and placed it on his night stand. He would call him as soon as he got some sleep.

The long shadows on the bedroom wall startled him. He couldn't believe he had slept until 4 p.m. Only the old standby—the hot shower—thoroughly cleaned out the cobwebs. He did not allow himself to think of the events of the previous day. He kept looking toward the front door of the house. Unrealistically, he expected Ann to walk through it, fall into his arms and all be forgiven. They would live happily together just as in the movies. Alas, his relationship with Ann, he finally acknowledged to himself when he inadvertently tripped over one of her shoes that had been left on her bedroom floor, was changed forever.

Sitting on the edge of the bed half-naked with a towel wrapped around him, he looked at himself in the mirror and began to weep. Part of his release was from the visual shock of seeing Ann with another person. Part of the it, he finally realized, was for the continuing grief he felt over the loss of Dave Wyatt.

The tears slowly ceased to flow after he again visualized Dave's dead body staring up at the ceiling fan in their former apartment. The reality of that vision brought a juxtaposed vision of Dave's dad, John. His sorrow, remorse, uncertainty and grief gradually, but unequivocally, began to turn to a gritty resolve.

Robert decided three things. If Dave's death was not a suicide, he would do his best to help discover and bring to justice whoever had done this to his friend. He would also make sure John Wyatt received a heart transplant. The man deserves a new heart, he concluded, remembering how diligently John had helped and encouraged both Dave and himself to become physicians. That East Tennessean had worked so hard and had unselfishly helped so many people. It would be no less than a criminal act not to do absolutely everything in his power to extend his life. Lastly, Robert would get to the bottom of what was wrong in Mexico. It couldn't have anything to do with Dave's death as far as he could see. Still, he knew something was wrong. Surely Ann would not do anything criminally wrong? Sex is one thing; breaking the law is another.

Julio's absolute steadfastness in his push to get Robert into a position to view Ann and his realization of the sum total of happenings during the tumultuous past few weeks solidified his desire to contact Officer Elliott. Dr. St. John halted as he began to phone the policeman. First, he had to help John Wyatt. His condition could not wait.

Chapter Sixteen

The Ford Taurus pulled into the parking lot of the Royal Sonesta. Robert couldn't believe his eyes. John Wyatt had driven the long drive from Knoxville by himself. The car door opened and an ashen John Wyatt emerged.

Robert helped John to his feet. They struggled up the front steps of the French Quarter hotel.

"I've got an adjoining room for us, John," Robert said as they walked past the front desk. "What possessed you to make that drive by yourself? It could've killed you!"

"I didn't want to bother anyone, Bobby."

"Good grief, John. It wouldn't do any good if you died on the way down here!"

Robert stopped his preaching and helped his old friend and his luggage. The room they would occupy was on the first floor, adjacent to the courtyard.

The Royal Sonesta had been a French Quarter landmark for many years, and Robert had chosen it for its proximity to the hospital and the dock where Silas and Isaac would pick them up for the trip to Mexico.

Dr. St. John had not told John Wyatt that to receive his heart transplant they would have to travel to Cancun.

The room was small and compact, which was the style when this hotel had been built. Robert had turned the room into a hospital room. He knew that John was extremely sick. Dr. Thompkins at the University of Tennessee Hospital had given him the prognosis. He had suffered a heart attack and gone into congestive heart failure. Without a transplant he would have six months to live. Accordingly Robert had an oxygen tank in the room. He also had a setup for an I.V., which could give anti-arrhythmic drugs and also serve as a conduit for Lasix, which would get the fluid out of his lungs if necessary.

Dr. St. John listened to John's lungs and decided to put him on oxygen and give him some Lasix, as his congestive failure had gotten worse as a result of his trip. Robert explained that he would feel much better after he treated him overnight.

"John, let me tell you something about your transplant."

"What do you need to tell me, Bobby?"

"You're going to get your transplant, just like I promised you." Robert stopped working on the equipment, took his old friend by the hand and sat him down on the bed.

"John, we're going to have to travel to Cancun, Mexico to get your heart transplant.

"Bobby, what are you talking about. The hospital is right over there." He pointed out over the courtyard.

Robert shook his head slowly. "John, do you remember three years ago when the nation's health care system was taken over by the government?"

"Of course, Bobby. I never did understand why you doctors allowed that to happen."

Dr. St. John laughed. "I guess we just weren't able to control all the political uproar. He shook his head in frustration. I'll get into that later, but now we have no choice but to travel to Mexico, by boat, to get this done."

"Whatever you say, Bobby. We're really going to go there by boat?"

"Yes, a friend of mine, Silas Arlington, and his brother, Isaac, are going to float you right down the old Mississippi to Mexico."

He patted John's chest and got a stethoscope and placed

it against the chest wall to listen to his heart and lungs.

"We're going to get you a new ticker." Robert never looked up at the older man's face. He was awestruck by his friend's faith in his ability to get him this life-saving operation. He had dreaded telling him that they would have to storm into this foreign country and steal a heart for him. It sounded too incredible to believe. But it was true. It was the only way he knew to get his old friend a heart.

"John, I have to tell you what we're facing. This is not going to be easy and it will be dangerous." He looked up from his inspection of John's heart and lungs.

John interrupted Robert before he could say anything further.

"Robert, if it's a matter of money, you know I have all that—"

"That's not it," Robert interrupted. "This is going to be very dangerous, and to be honest, I'm not sure if it's even possible or not."

John Wyatt put his hand around the young doctor's neck and patted him gently.

"Robert, I want to be sure that I pay your friends, Silas and Isaac, well for helping me. I have nothing to lose if we don't succeed at this..." he paused, looking Robert in the eye. "Hell, I'm going to die anyway," he laughed loudly. Turning serious, he continued, "Now I don't want you or your friends getting hurt. If this is dangerous..."
his voice trailed off.

"I've promised Isaac and Silas that we would pay them well. Besides this is probably not going to be nearly as bad as I've imagined."

John Wyatt looked up again with a smile creeping across his face.

"That's the spirit." Robert patted his friend on the leg.

John reached back into his back pocket and pulled out his billfold. He took out a large pile of thousand dollar bills.

"How much could they protest, Bobby? I've got over a million bucks locked in the car." He laughed loudly again.

"You brought all that money with you?"

John waved a few of the bills in the air.

"Yep, I sure did. My banker at First Tennessee threw a fit...but what the hell?"

"Maybe we should go bring it in."

"Naw, leave it. No one will bother it."

Chapter Seventeen

Robert and John received a wake-up call at 4 a.m. They were to meet Silas and Isaac at the First Street pier at 5 a.m. Isaac had agreed to provide his shrimp trawler to take them down. Although they would arrive unannounced at Hospital of the Americas, Robert was hoping that Dr. Guttierez would take John Wyatt's money and provide him with a heart. If not, Silas and Isaac Arlington, both big men, would just have to persuade him!

Robert checked John briefly prior to leaving the hotel. The older man's heart had been through too much. It could be helped along with rest and the appropriate medications, but without this transplant, he would die.

New Orleans was particularly foggy that morning. Robert had parked his XKE at the hospital the previous day, so they drove John Wyatt's Chevrolet down to the pier. Isaac's shrimp trawler, the Arlington, was docked waiting. Robert had "borrowed" all the necessary equipment—cardiac monitor with defibrillator, oxygen tanks, I.V. poles, bags of premixed cardiac medicines—from the E.R. and created a floating cardiac unit for John. Isaac and Silas were busy preparing for the trip.

The fog was even thicker right off the river, but John could see Silas and Isaac as they worked.

"They're black. These are black men!" John looked with wide eyes at Robert.

John Wyatt had been raised in east Tennessee where there had been few African-Americans. Consequently he had no real friends who were black.

"John, don't tell me that after all these years I find out you're a racist. Don't you remember all those talks you gave Dave and me in Little League back in Knoxville. You know, treat all people, regardless of race or creed with respect."

John Wyatt cleared his throat in embarrassment.

"Of course I do! It's just that when you said that some friends of yours..."

"John, these men are friends of mine, they're as good as gold and I trust them with our lives."

John Wyatt grabbed his suitcase of clothes and money and said, "Let's go meet your friends and get my new heart!"

They locked the car and headed to the boat.

"Silas...Isaac," Robert called out as they walked to the boat.

Silas saw the two men heading to them and jumped onto the pier to greet them.

"Good morning, Robert, it's okay to drop the Dr. St. John, isn't it, considering the circumstances?"

"No, Silas, you address me as Doctor," Robert teased. "Silas Arlington, this is John Wyatt, Dr. Wyatt's dad."

John and Silas shook hands.

"It's my pleasure." John smiled.

Silas took John's bag and led them back to the boat.

"You don't know how much I appreciate this," John began, his voice choking with emotion.

"You're welcome, Mr. Wyatt. Isaac and I are just glad to help. Besides, Isaac says shrimping is awfully slow now and he needs the money." Silas laughed.

"Well, about all I've got now is money." John pointed to the suitcase, his voice still trembling slightly.

Isaac walked back to meet them as the three walked over the gangplank to the back of the boat. Silas introduced his brother to Mr. Wyatt: "This is our captain, my brother, Isaac." The two men shook hands, and John Wyatt repeated his assertion of how much he appreciated the brothers' help.

Isaac laughed. "My pleasure. Besides this is a pleasant break from the shrimping business. You should see how the

good doctor has transformed this old trawler into a hospital."
He point at the cardiac monitor that was beeping inside the
cabin."

John Wyatt looked around at the boat and shook his
head in appreciation.

"Well, if you folks are ready, I'll get Silas to help me and
we'll shove off," Isaac said.

Robert took John into the cabin and began to show him
the equipment, including a hospital bed that had been set up
for him.

"Hey, this is really something, Bobby," John said.

"This was the only practical way we could come up with
to transfer you safely out of Mexico after surgery. A car or bus
would be difficult considering the inadequate nature of the
roads from Cancun to the U.S. A train couldn't be arranged.
The Cancun International Airport was potentially a problem,
so a chartered jet was ruled out. The only reasonable solution
was a boat."

Robert didn't tell John that Isaac had felt if they had to
make a quick getaway, the best way to slip back into the U.S.
undetected was by boat. Who would suspect a shrimp trawler
of being anything but a shrimp trawler? Robert hoped that
Dr. Guttierez would take John's money and perform the
transplant. But who knew how he would respond? He hadn't
returned any of Robert's calls. If Ann had anything to do with
it, she'd probably say no. He would plead for this transplant
if he could, but he knew it might be difficult because of the
secrecy currently surrounding the new procedures.

Isaac had turned the trawler out into the main channel of
the Mississippi. The outline of the Crescent City began to
appear as the rising Louisiana sun burned off the fog. This
would be a long trip due to the fact that the trawler traveled
only a few knots per hour, but Robert thought it would be
worth every bit of the effort if he could give his best friend's
dad a new lease on life.

"Look at that city," Isaac pointed at New Orleans from
the flying bridge above the cabin. Isaac's boat was unusual

for a shrimp trawler in that it had a large cabin that covered a good third of the boat and an observation deck above that cabin from which he could pilot the boat. Isaac stayed out in the gulf of Mexico for days sometimes in his quest for shrimp. He was a bachelor and virtually lived on his boat. He was known as one of the best shrimp boat captains around New Orleans.

Robert felt that this trawler would do just fine as a floating hospital. He knew that Silas and Isaac would do everything in their power to make this journey a success. Besides, they were big men. Silas had played football at Tulane. Isaac had been offered scholarships to play football at Alabama, LSU and Mississippi State but had decided to take over the family fishing business right out of high school instead. Robert felt that if worse came to worse in Mexico, it would be mighty helpful to have such strong friends along for insurance.

"Look, you can almost see everything downtown." Isaac pointed from atop the boat. The downtown New Orleans skyscrapers were beginning to peek through the haze that had settled over night. The Big Easy was beginning to wake up from its nightly slumber.

The trawler seemed out of place as it navigated slowly between large barges and other boats headed toward the Gulf of Mexico. An occasional horn blast pierced the fog warning all other ships to be careful because its owner had the right-of-way. In the dim light, all the boats and barges were traveling at a leisurely pace.

"Hey guys, " Isaac yelled from the bridge. "If you want to see something special, look over to the left bank."

A flying white boat zoomed by them, scarcely leaving a wake.

"Isn't she a beauty! " Silas shouted.

"Hey, I recognize that boat," Robert said as he watched the hydrofoil fly by. "It's Ann's." His jaw opened wide in amazement.

"Well, it's up in these waters all the time," Isaac said with his hands on his hips.

"I wonder what it's doing up here?" Robert said to no one in particular.

"Rumor on the river is that it's running some kind of illegal something or another," Isaac said.

Isaac and Robert looked at each other and shrugged their shoulders.

"Just another rumor," Isaac continued.

Robert and Silas went inside the cabin and began to check the equipment. John Wyatt had taken a seat inside while the other three men had been watching the hydrofoil. He was exhausted. The travel from Tennessee and the excitement of the upcoming trip to Mexico had taken its toll.

Robert immediately rolled out the oxygen and hooked him up. John began to look better almost instantaneously. Silas placed a stool under his feet to help him breathe easier.

"This isn't going to be easy, Bobby," John Wyatt looked up at Silas and Robert.

"We'll make it, Mr. Wyatt," Silas said. "My brother is the best pilot on the Mississippi and the Gulf. If he'd been in command of the Titanic, it never would have sunk."

John Wyatt laughed. "If you have that much faith in Isaac, then I do too."

Silas' comment as well as the unlikely nature of their voyage made them all begin to laugh hysterically. They laughed so loudly that Isaac stamped his foot on the roof to get them to quieten down.

The trawler moved cautiously down the river. Small homes dotted the riverbank. Almost everyone who lives on the Mississippi makes their living in some way or the other from the river. The day passed quickly and the darkness of night soon overtook them. Isaac decided to dock up for the evening. It would be safer.

The larger vessels and barges continued to mosey past them after they had tied up to a large water oak whose humongous limbs draped over the water. Spanish moss dripped from the tree, covering the majority of the shrimp trawler behind a curtain of gray.

Isaac and Silas prepared a dinner of shrimp and oysters, Cajun style. The galley was filled with good-natured ribbing during the preparation of the meal.

"You're a city boy now, Silas. Let me show these Tennesseans how real Louisianans eat!" Isaac teased his brother.

"Get out of the kitchen, country boy." Silas responded. "Your food won't be fit to eat."

They alternated between cooking, wrestling around the kitchen and singing the worst rendition of Hank Williams' "Jambalaya" Robert and John had ever heard. It was obvious these brothers were awfully fond of each other.

Dinner was served on an old oak table that had been bolted to the deck so it would stay stable during shrimping expeditions on the Gulf. Robert limited what John Wyatt could eat because all Cajun food is spiced with so much salt.

"I'll be careful on the trip down, but that means I can have extra helpings on the way back," John said.

"Did you gents notice the Chalmette National Battlefield that we passed on our right?" Isaac asked.

"No, I didn't," Robert said.

"Where?" John looked out the window upriver.

Isaac explained that they had passed the battlefield approximately five miles upriver.

"Our great-great-grandfather Arlington, who was a slave at the Arlington Plantation, helped Andrew Jackson fight the British there in the War of 1812," Isaac said.

"My great-great-grandfather was with General Jackson too!" John Wyatt told everyone excitedly. "He was a volunteer from Sevierville, Tennessee."

"Well, well, sounds like we need to offer a toast to the brave men who helped Andrew Jackson defend New Orleans from the British!" Silas stood up and headed to the cabinet above the sink. He pulled out a bottle of wine and held it up in the air.

"Wildberry wine from the bogs of Louisiana."

As he broke open the bottle, and the four men let out a

shout of hip-hip-hooray for the heroic men who fought alongside General Andrew Jackson in 1812. The wine pro-longed the celebration longer than was prudent consider-ing the cir-cumstances.

The sun had already topped the trees along the river when the Arlington restarted the long trek down the river. Its diesel engine scattered herons, pelicans and an occasional osprey in its wake.

It seemed that everyone on the river knew Isaac. All the boats and tugs blew honks of recognition as they passed. Isaac honked back.

* * *

"Robert, Robert, " Isaac shouted down from above.

"What, Isaac?" Robert looked up at him.

"You need to hear this weather report!"

Robert climbed the ladder up to the bridge. Isaac tuned the radio so he and Robert could hear clearly.

"The National Weather Service is cautioning all small vessels that a tropical storm has formed off the West African coast and according to computer projections will threaten the western Caribbean and possibly the Gulf of Mexico. Please be advised and take all necessary precautions," the weather report stated.

Isaac turned to Robert and explained that the National Weather Service never issued such warnings in advance unless there was a strong likelihood of danger.

"Isaac, Mr. Wyatt doesn't have much time. I'm not sure if this is even going to work, but it's his only chance."

Isaac pushed the throttle forward and his boat sped ahead, pushing an even larger wake against the banks. He didn't look at Robert but said, "Let's get this show on the road. It'll take a few days for that mother to get here, so let's beat it to the punch."

An already determined group became even more so with the prospect of poor weather possibly moving in. They began to continue the journey down the Mississippi with the prospect of battling the storm on the way back at the very least. What would be a perilous journey with a very sick postoperative John Wyatt would be almost impossible if they were battling a tropical storm.

Over the Geologic Eons, the Mississippi had carved itself a path through the Louisiana Delta. As riverboat captains through the ages could attest, its choice of direction was not the straightest one.

In times past Robert had loved the meandering ways of this mightiest of American rivers. Now he cursed its sluggishness. Time had become of the essence. He paced the deck, hoping he could conceal the worry that had begun to choke up in his throat. This was going to be difficult enough as it was. Now it seemed the river invented a new bend every few minutes just to delay their entry into the Gulf.

"Don't worry, Bobby." John's voice drifted above the hum of the big diesel engine. "I know this is a mighty risky venture, and I may not make it. I don't want you fellas to put yourself at risk just for me. As a matter of fact, if it wasn't for the missus back home in Knoxville, I wouldn't be here at all..." his voice trailed off.

Robert knew that the odds of this being a successful trip for John were not good. He, Silas and Isaac would probably be okay, providing of course that a hurricane didn't blow them away. But Robert knew that this could be John Wyatt's last trip anywhere. He had not told anyone at the hospital about what he was doing simply because he felt that they would talk him out of it. He decided to be as cheerful as he could be to John, because he felt the need to hide the truth from him. He cursed the bureaucrats in Washington who had blindly decided that John Wyatt was a number and because of his age was arbitrarily "deselected" as a candidate for a transplant in his own country.

"The U.S.A., richest country on the planet," he laughed under his breath with contempt toward Washington.

"What, Bobby? I couldn't understand what you were

saying."

"Nothing, John. I was just mumbling to myself. You know I wouldn't put us at risk, buddy, if I didn't think we could get through this alive and well." Robert put his best rah-rah attitude behind his words, trying to reassure himself as much as anyone.

"There she be," Isaac bellowed from above. "The Gulf!"

Sure enough the Gulf opened up wide before them. Silas looked at his worried friend in a reassuring manner. "We'll make good time now, Doc! We'll be there now in twenty hours max."

Both Robert and John breathed a huge sigh of relief. Any good news was music to their ears. Isaac tugged at the Arlington's horn in celebration of leaving the river and journeying into the Gulf.

"See, what did I tell you, John? These guys are going to get us there. No problem."

"No problem, mates," Silas mimicked, peering at the Gulf.

The boat continued to chug headlong toward Cancun. True to Silas' word, the trawler began to pick up speed. A large wake now began to trail behind them. The channel markers that had guided them through the Mississippi disappeared as they headed deeper into the Gulf. Behind them spread the coast line of the good ole US of A and ahead stretched open water and the Mexican shore.

Silas walked over to the open doorway of the cabin. John Wyatt sat inside.

"Mr. Wyatt, if Dr. St. John thinks he can help you, then I would quit worrying and just do what he says. As for getting you back," he gestured to his brother, his voice turning to a whisper, "Isaac can get you back, I guarantee." He gave a thumbs-up sign. "Just don't tell him I said so."

Every few minutes or so Isaac would blast his horn at another shrimper or fisherman; otherwise the skipper of the Arlington manned his post and was obviously intent on getting them to Cancun as quickly as possible.

"Hey, fellas, come look at these dolphins!" Isaac called.

John, Silas and Robert gathered at the side of the boat and saw a large group of porpoises jumping alongside the boat.

"That's the biggest group I've ever seen," Isaac said. "This is good news, Mr. Wyatt. They're guaranteed good luck!"

The trawler trudged forward through the continuous sea. Isaac never seemed to tire and asked for no relief. Robert checked John's heart and lungs so often that John finally jokingly said, "If I'm going to die before we get there, good riddance."

The sun began to set over the horizon. Silas explained that he and Isaac would split shifts during the night and that they should reach Cancun sometime tomorrow. All of them allowed that if a storm was on its way, it was a mighty quiet way for it to enter, as there wasn't a cloud in the sky.

"What do you guys want for dinner?" Isaac asked, peeking in at them after leaving the boat momentarily on auto pilot.

"I want a T-bone steak!" Silas teased.

"We're at sea, brother, be realistic."

"I'm just funning with you, Isaac, what about some mahi-mahi. Can we catch some fresh this far out?"

"Dolphin? Sure we can. Is that okay with you fellas?"

"I don't know if I could eat one of those Flipper fish, Isaac. I don't want to seem unappreciative...back home I eat squirrel and deer. But those little fellas...I just couldn't eat one of them." John Wyatt was serious.

Isaac and Silas looked at Robert, and they all three burst out in laughter. The more they laughed the louder they laughed. The more flustered and perturbed John Wyatt got, the more they laughed. His bewildered face brought on more howls from the three.

"You don't understand," John Wyatt attempted to explain further, "ever since I saw Flipper talking on TV, I just couldn't never, ever eat one."

That did it. The three hugged each other, slapped each other and rolled around on the floor laughing. Finally, an exhausted Isaac Arlington caught his breath long enough to explain to Mr. Wyatt that the fish he would attempt to catch was not "Flipper" or any of his relatives.

"What we'll be eating tonight is mahi-mahi, a fish which is real ugly. It doesn't look anything like the porpoises."

'Ohhh…that fish. I knew what you meant. I really did."

Isaac set out two fishing lines with ballyhoo as bait. "If we can't catch anything, I'll rustle up some grub," he said.

Night was beginning to fall when Isaac ran back to one of the lines and pulled the rod and reel from the holder. Line was singing from the reel.

"It's a chartreuse-colored dolphin," Isaac said.

The rod continued to bend forward as Isaac pulled back, fighting the fish. After Isaac pulled the bull-headed fish beside the boat, Silas gaffed it and pulled it aboard.

"Fifteen-pounder," Isaac said, lifting the fish up for all to inspect. It'll take me just a few minutes to clean it and then we'll have beer-batter-dipped mahi-mahi before you know it."

Silas went about helping his brother prepare the fish. The sweet smell of frying fish filled the entire boat. The foursome sat back around the now-familiar wooden table.

Now that they were in open water, Isaac could place the trawler on a type of auto-pilot. He could enjoy his meal and the company of his fellow travelers. On occasion he would scurry up the ladder to scan the horizon for boats or other obstacles.

Dark had descended over the Arlington, yet it continued to tug toward its destiny. John, Isaac, Silas and Robert settled back after completing dinner. The night turned the Gulf of Mexico into a shimmering pool of water lit by the moon. For an hour or so the men drifted about the boat.

Silas and Isaac tended to duties and chores, while John and Robert talked quietly among themselves. Inevitably their talk turned to Dave Wyatt.

"I still have not accepted his death" John Wyatt concluded, slowly shaking his head.

They had begun talking while leaning over the railing, watching the warm Gulf waters glide under them.

Robert began a long talk with his best friend's father. He attempted to explain the events leading up to Dave's suicide. But no matter how he attempted to analyze things he still couldn't bring a rationalization to the whole thing. What lent a surreal shadow to the whole episode was the fact that now he was responsible for an expedition to a foreign country to force a surgeon to perform major surgery on John Wyatt. It seemed impossible. Yet here they were.

"I've got all this money!" John Wyatt's mention of money brought Robert back to the present.

"I hope I brought enough to pay for the operation and to pay Silas and Isaac too," John continued.

Robert laughed thinking about John Wyatt lugging that amount of money around the country.

"John, you've got plenty of money. That's not a problem."

"What's the problem then?"

How was Robert going to explain that Dr. Guttierez might refuse in spite of money? He looked at the two brothers and reasoned that he had the manpower to force him.

"I think it's time to have a strategy session, fellas." Robert yelled up at Silas and Isaac. "We'll come up there."

Isaac motioned them to come up the ladder.

Robert and John walked around the trawler to the creaky old ladder and joined them up on the flying bridge. A magnificent view of the stars and the Gulf waters opened up in front of them. Silas had an old ivory pipe stuck in his mouth. He took an occasional long puff, which cast a red glow on his face.

Silas had taken over the wheel. He stared intently into the gleaming darkness.

"What's up?" Silas glanced over from his pilot's station.

"I think we should get a game plan for whatever might

come up in Cancun," Robert said.

"What do you mean, game plan?" John asked. "I brought all the money."

"It's not that simple, John. Hopefully, we'll walk in, Dr. Guttierez will take your money, you'll have your surgery and we'll leave. But..."

"But what?" John shot back.

"The problem is that they don't know we're coming," Robert whispered, lowering his head.

"What do you mean, they don't know we're coming!"

"This is a special procedure that they've come up with, John. They're not going to be thrilled to be sharing it with us."

"Shouldn't the money be enough?"

"I think they'll take care of us, but you don't know the restrictions these people have put on this procedure. It's strictly not available to Americans yet. They're waiting to present all the data to NHCO in Washington before they go before Congress. I may just be a worrier, but I don't think they'll be real happy about having a walking, talking advertisement back in the states saying, 'Hey, you don't have to die. I know a place in Mexico where you can get a transplant just like me.'"

"I don't understand. If this is all about money, why don't they just take mine and give me a new heart?"

"It may be that simple. I just don't know yet. We'll going to have to wait and see.

Another thing Robert was worried about was that after not getting through to Dr. Guttierez, he had left a message with his secretary that he had a special friend who needed a heart transplant ASAP. This had obviously alerted Dr. Guttierez as to what he wanted. Thereafter when he called, the secretary had given him the brush-off, and that was not an encouraging sign.

"I think regardless of what they may say, we'll get you a transplant if we stick to our guns and demand it," he said.

Part of him realized that the thought of demanding that Dr. Guttierez give John one of those stored organs would help his bruised ego.

"All we can do, John, is go down there and use whatever means necessary to get you this surgery."

"Whatever," John said and shrugged.

The diesel engine hummed constantly, drowning out the normal sea sounds. The four men sat in silence, staring out at the looming coast of Mexico.

"Why don't you people go get some sleep?" Isaac suggested. "It's going to be a long trip, and there's no need for all of us to stay up."

"Good idea," Silas agreed." Come on, guys, Isaac will keep watch up here tonight. He'll come trade with me later."

The three men thanked Isaac for dinner and for keeping the boat going that night. They all agreed that it would be smart to get to bed early as to no one knew what the next day might bring.

They all began to settle into their respective bunks. John looked over at Robert and Silas.

"Guys...I want to thank you for all you're doing. You don't know how much this means to me."

Silas tried to reassure him by joking, "Don't worry. Wait until you get the bill from Isaac and me," he laughed.

"Whatever it is, it won't be enough." John's voice showed emotion. "There's just one more thing I want you to promise me. I don't know how this will turn out. If I don't make it back home, please promise me to take care of my wife."

Silas and Robert looked at each other

"John, you and I have been friends for a long time," Robert said. "We'll get through this thing together. I'll let you take care of Mrs. Wyatt yourself when we get back to Tennessee." He patted John reassuringly on the arm.

"Let's all get some sleep," Silas said." We're going to make it through this, I promise.

All three men gave each other the thumbs-up sign as they turned over and settled in their bunks.

Robert was awakened by the brightness of the Caribbean morning sun. It strained and pushed its way into the trawler cabin finding him in his bunk. Isaac had been re-placed by Silas in the bunk opposite him. John Wyatt was still asleep. Robert quietly got dressed and joined Silas on the flying bridge.

"Good morning, Doc. Good to see you up so early." A lone seagull flew above Silas as he greeted Robert.

"How far are we from Cancun, do you figure, Silas?" Robert asked as he rubbed sleep from his eyes and stretched.

"Can't be more than thirty miles now. We should be getting a glimpse of land soon. What do you think will happen when we get there, Doc?"

Robert looked his old friend directly in the eye. "I honestly can't say for sure, Silas. It would seem to make sense for these people to take John's money and help him. But there is something strange going on and...I just don't know what might happen."

Silas continued to steer the boat. He looked far out into the Gulf, then looked at Robert and asked, "What on earth would keep these people from taking John's money and helping him?"

"I'm not sure exactly what all is going on this hospital, Silas. There's a lot of money being made. When that happens, the old saying 'money corrupts' is usually true. The main thing I'm suspicious about now is where all the transplant organs are coming from and why they want to keep this such a secret from the United States government. It makes sense in a way, but in another way it doesn't. Besides, Dave Wyatt is dead, and that doesn't make sense either."

Robert let out a big sigh. "I'm probably being paranoid. Dr. Guttierez is probably going to be glad to help. Sad to say, Silas, but my jealousy may play in some of my feelings of suspicion." Robert hung his head as he turned a shade of red.

Silas Arlington let out a laugh that probably carried over to the Mexican Coast. "That's okay, Doc. It's good to know that you consider yourself a flawed member of our human race." Silas laughed again.

"Look," Isaac pointed from below deck. "It's Mexico."

Silas' brother had just gotten out of his bunk and spotted the coast line.

Robert looked at Silas and said, "We'll find out soon enough now. When we spot Cancun, Casa del Mar will be off to the right. Julio will meet us at the boat dock."

"I just hope Ann Finn won't be there," he whispered under his breath. The thought of saying the right thing to her made him extremely nervous. He knew that she would not approve of trying to reallocate a heart for John Wyatt. He knew how much this project meant to her and how hard she could be. Ann knew what she wanted and seemingly always got it. Robert felt strongly that John deserved this chance, but it wouldn't be out of character for Ann to turn the request down. She would be concerned only with the project and the glory and money it would bring her. If John died, Robert would feel the loss tremendously. Ann, he felt, would not care one way or the other. That's why he hoped that she wasn't around. He felt that Dr. Guttierez would be more likely to help them, especially when he saw the suitcase of money John Wyatt had brought.

"Land ho...land ho..." Silas Arlington yelled out as he pointed to a now apparent beach.

Sure enough, Cancun lay straight ahead. It was just a small collection of elongated boxes on the horizon, but there it was. The trip down had been smooth enough; now came the hard part.

Robert surveyed the sky behind them. There was still no sign of a hurricane.

"Silas, Isaac, what's the latest weather report?"

Isaac leaned forward and whispered so John Wyatt could not hear him in the cabin. "They're still calling for one. It's just a matter of where it will go."

Isaac looked up at the crystal blue sky. He scratched his forehead and admitted, "It certainly doesn't look bad, does it?"

He skillfully maneuvered the Arlington toward the beach. They passed several small passenger boats, fishing boats and one large cruise ship.

"Look Isaac," Robert was pointing to a house hanging over the beach a few miles north of the main Cancun area. "It's Casa del Mar."

All four men gathered up on the flying bridge to get a better view.

"Where should I bring it in?"

Robert got behind Isaac's shoulder and pointed out the barely visible dock.

"We should be able to pull in there. Julio is supposedly expecting us. He assured me when I talked to him last week that he would hang around and be there to great us. He's the one who's going to take us to Hospital of the Americas."

It was obvious that John Wyatt was getting very nervous. He may have been having second thoughts about this whole thing. He tapped his foot repeatedly on the top of the bridge, looking around at the different boats nervously.

Robert patted his friend reassuringly on the shoulder. John responded by smiling weakly at everyone.

A small figure slipped down the hill from Casa del Mar to the marina. It was Julio. Robert waved wildly, reassured by the presence of his new friend. Julio's smiling face came clearer as the trawler slowly navigated the final stretch of water to the pier. The Hatteras was docked in its usual location. The hydrofoil had not made it back. Julio threw a line from the end of the pier to Silas, who began to tie the Arlington safely next to the fishing boat.

"Julio, how are you doing? I want you to meet some friends of mine." Robert jumped from the deck and gratefully shook hands with him.

"This is Silas and Isaac Arlington." The two brothers shook hands with the young Mexican.

"And this is the guy who needs your help, John Wyatt."

John grabbed the Julio's hand and shook it vigorously.

"You don't know what it means to me, young man, to have you help me this way." He continued shaking his hand.

Julio beamed when he smiled back. "Come on up to the

house, bring your things and we'll settle you in."

The men gathered some belongings and followed Julio back up the serpentine path that led to the house. John clutched his precious suitcase as he struggled up the hill. Robert walked beside Julio.

"Is she here?" he whispered, his heart pounding.

"No, she went back to the Cayman Islands. And since I'm in charge," Julio smiled, "welcome to the house."

Dr. St. John felt a strong sense of relief. He now felt that they would be successful in getting John's heart transplant since Ann wasn't in the vicinity. He was continuing to realize that Ann wanted only the money and prestige this medical procedure would bring and not the good it would do.

"Were you able to get all the equipment that I asked for?" Robert asked.

"Everything except the cardiac monitor," Julio replied.

"That's great, Julio! Good job. And were you able to set up the Mercedes with a cot and an oxygen tank?"

"Sí Señor!"

Robert smiled from ear to ear. Julio had been able to arrange everything as he had asked. He was pleased and impressed with his young friend.

"I suggest we get some rest and then pay our friend at the hospital a visit. The sooner we get this done and get back to the states, the better off we are," Robert said, addressing everyone.

They had finally arrived at the front of the house. John had struggled the whole way but had made it without assistance. The old suitcase was tucked tightly under his arm.

"Welcome to Casa del Mar, gentlemen." Julio swung the door open and gestured for them to enter. The guards eyed the quartet warily but didn't say anything as they entered Ann's mansion.

"Wow," Silas whistled. "No wonder you're impressed with this lady."

Robert punched him lightly on the shoulder. "Listen guys, I suggest we take a couple of hours to rest and then we'll go to the hospital. How does that sound?" Robert looked around at the others.

Everyone nodded. Julio then led them to their accommodations. An hour passed quickly, then another. Robert left his room and rounded up the others. His goal was to persuade Guttierez to okay the surgery today. Then with luck they could get the procedure done tomorrow.

Everyone seemed anxious, but none more than John Wyatt. He kept thanking everyone for their help.

Julio met them at the front gate with the Mercedes. A perfect ambulance it wasn't, but it would do for the transport of the recuperating John Wyatt.

"Looks good, Julio. I'm impressed," said an admiring Robert.

"Let's get going, folks. Let's get brother John a new ticker!"

John had continued to hold on to his suitcase for dear life. He squeezed into the car with the rest of them and simply stared out of the window as they made the trip to the hospital. Robert and Julio attempted to make small talk as the trip proceeded. The conversation turned to fishing and the type and size of marlin that had been caught recently. Robert realized the talk was strained and superficial, but he wanted to try to lighten John's mood. He continued to peek in the rearview mirror at John as Julio excitedly described a huge blue marlin that had been caught about twenty miles out.

John continued to hug the suitcase as he stared at the Mexican countryside.

"That's the hospital up ahead," Julio said, pointing to a cross visible above the hill before them. The car rounded the next curve and pulled within full view of the building. Robert cautiously looked back at the patient and was grateful to see John smiling slightly as he viewed the hospital.

Julio pulled up to the front door and let the others off.

"I'll park the car and meet you at Guttierez's office," he said.

Robert led Isaac, Silas and John to Dr. Guttierez's office.

A pleasant young lady greeted them.

"May I help you?" she asked.

"Yes, I need to see Dr. Guttierez. I'm Dr. Robert St. John."

"Do you have an appointment?" she asked as she looked through her appointment book.

"No, but I'm sure he'll see me if you'll ask him."

"I'll ask, but I'm afraid today is a very bad day. He's completely booked with surgeries."

She disappeared through the big oak door to the administrator's office. She took care to conceal the interior of his office as quickly as she could by closing it rapidly. Just as quickly, she reappeared, shaking her head.

"Out of the question! He's completely booked. You should have called and made an appointment."

Robert crossed his arms across his chest and began to tap his foot in an agitated manner.

"Out of my way," he cried as he pushed past the receptionist and into the administrator's office. Isaac, Silas and John followed him, each one incurring the sharp-tongued wrath of the now hysterical young woman.

Dr. Guttierez was sitting at his desk. As soon as Robert and the others got past the receptionist, he simply nodded his head to her and motioned her out the door.

"Dr. St. John, what a surprise!" he said.

"You've ignored my phone calls, Guttierez, and taken liberties with my woman." He immediately turned a shade of pink and regretted his jealous statement. Silas looked at him with big eyes.

"We have an emergency here. This is John Wyatt, Dr. Dave Wyatt's father." Robert pulled John by his arm over to his side. "He needs a heart transplant immediately, and we're not going to leave until he gets one."

Silas and Isaac stepped forward, shoving their chests out.

"Well, why didn't you say he was Dr. Wyatt's father when you called?" Dr. Guttierez smiled grandly, shook John's hand and patted him on the back. "That makes all the

231

difference in the world! We of course want to take care of Dr. Wyatt's family."

All the men were taken aback by this turn of events.

"John, I told you that everything would turn out okay!" Robert hugged John Wyatt around the neck. He then turned and shook Guttierez's hand, as well as Silas and Isaac's. He then went into a rapid discourse of how they had arranged for Isaac to turn his trawler into a floating hospital to facilitate the transfer.

"Don't worry, everything will be taken care of now," Dr. Guttierez assured them. "All we need to do is to check Mr. Wyatt into the hospital, get him prepped for the surgery and make sure after we do the donor match that we have an organ available to do his surgery."

"When will you know?" Silas asked.

"Yes," Isaac followed, "there may be a storm heading our way and we need to make plans."

"Oh, gentlemen, we at Hospital of the Americas will take care of all the transportation home if you wish," Dr. Guttierez offered magnanimously.

John Wyatt began to shake his head vigorously.

"No offense, doctor, but the only way I'm going is with my friends. If that's okay with you, Isaac?"

"John, we set up that trawler to be your lifeboat home and if that's the way you want it, that's the way it will be."

Dr. Guttierez shrugged his shoulders and looked at each of them. "If that's the way you want it," he hesitatingly replied. He stopped and looked directly at Robert as if to say "it's up to you."

"Well, the trawler is set up to take care of him. If that's the way you want it, John…" He looked from Guttierez to John Wyatt.

"I'd just feel a lot better if I was with my friends after the surgery, that's all," John explained to Dr. Guttierez.

"Okay, that's fine with us. Now let's get you set up and see if we can't get you scheduled for tomorrow."

He reached down to the intercom: "Lupita, will you

come in and take Mr. Wyatt to the prep area for surgery in the morning?"

"I'll be glad to, Doctor," came the young receptionist's voice. The usual set-up cross-match procedures?"

"Yes."

"I'll be right in."

"Hey, wait a minute," John interrupted, jumping forward with his suitcase. "We Wyatts pay our way," he offered as he opened the suitcase, spilling thousands of dollars on the doctor's desk.

Everyone laughed out loud at the manner in which he spread it over the glass top covering the desk.

"The only special request I have is to allow Bobby to assist in my surgery. I trust him." He patted Robert on the shoulder, his red-rimmed eyes beginning to fill with tears.

"Well, with that kind of money, I'm sure we can accommodate the good doctor. And we at Hospital of the Americas are glad to be at your service."

Another large laugh followed that remark by the humbly bowing hospital administrator

Robert exhaled a large sigh of relief. His huge trepidation of the past few days slowly faded. The guilt and uncertainty that had haunted him, especially after discovering Ann's infidelity, and the animosity he had felt toward Dr. Guttierez lessened.He smiled and allowed his laughter to easily join the other laughter that filled the room.

John profusely thanked Isaac, Silas, Robert and Dr. Guttierez as Lupita started to lead him out of the office. John had finally relinquished his suitcase, leaving its contents spilled on the desk. Dr. Guttierez assured him that he would see all of them in the morning prior to surgery.

"Wait a minute, I'm not going to stay in this place overnight." John shook his head mightily.

Dr. Guttierez shrugged his shoulders. "I don't imagine it's absolutely necessary, so long as you can be here early enough for the prep. And nothing to eat tonight after eight. You'll have to go now with Lupita to be cleared for surgery by the surgeon, Dr. Menendez, and to have lab work done."

He looked over at Dr. St. John, who nodded his okay.

"All right, I'll meet you guys at the car then."

Dr. Guttierez ushered him to the door. He then turned to the other three men and reassured them that everything would be okay. He would take care of everything. He walked with them half the way to the lobby, then excused himself.

"I'll see all of you tomorrow. I'm glad you brought John down. We'll take good care of him. Dr. St. John, you need to be here at 6 a.m. to scrub up, but John needs to be here at 5 a.m. I'll see you then."

All three men walked ecstatically out the front door. Julio was approaching them. "What happened?" he asked.

"A piece of cake, " Robert snapped his fingers.

Silas and Isaac both clapped him on the back.

"Way to go, Doc," Silas said. "You should have seen him, Julio. You would have been proud. Ole Doc here was smooth, real smooth."

"When is his surgery?" Julio asked as he got in the drivers seat.

"Tomorrow morning." Robert smiled proudly. "Everything is set up and ready to go. Turned out that I was worried for nothing. We've got the worst part behind us. We'll be out of here in just a couple of days.

Julio entertained them by asking questions about their lives in the United States. He was particularly interested in Isaac's work as a trawler captain.

After what seemed like hours, John came smiling out to the car.

"I didn't understand a word of the Spanish that the doctor spoke, but I'm at least going to get my new ticker. They're going to help me where none of those pencil-pushing bureaucrats back home would!"

"Let's go, Julio," Robert said.

Julio gave him a mock salute and pulled the car onto the main road. The Mercedes headed back around the winding road to Casa del Mar.

* * *

"Hello, international operator, I need Grand Cayman Island. I need to speak to Miss Ann Finn at the Hyatt Regency there. What? Yes, this call will be person-to-person from Dr. Raphael Guttierez.

Ann was at the pool outside her villa at the Hyatt Regency when a valet approached her with the message.

"Miss Finn, there's a person-to-person telephone call to you from a Dr. Raphael Guttierez. You may take it in your room, or if you wish I will bring an extension here poolside."

Ann looked up from her recliner. Bart, a young New Zealander who had been rubbing tanning lotion onto her naked back, sighed, not appreciating the interruption.

"No, I'll take it in my room," she said to the valet.

"I'll be right back, deary. Don't go away." She fastened her top and jumped up, skipping to her room.

"Raphael, what a pleasant surprise. Have you missed me so much that you had to call, sweetheart? "

Dr. Guttierez cleared his throat. "Ann, let me tell you what's happened. Dr. St. John showed up here with two black man and John Wyatt, the father of Dr. Dave Wyatt. They demanded a heart transplant for Wyatt, and I had to agree."

"What do you mean you agreed?" Ann screamed. "No American is going to get one, period. That's what we agreed on, Guttierez."

"I know, Ann, but it was your idea to let St. John in on this in the first place. Castner was right. You should have consulted with everyone first. This is as much your fault as anyone's. You knew he could spoil everything just like Dave wanted to!" he yelled back.

"Look, we can use that to blackmail him in the future if we need to. Besides, aren't I getting you 90 percent of the organs you use, pal? That's way above what I projected I could get out of that one damn New Orleans Hospital. Aren't you making a fortune? Don't you appreciate the little extra special attention I give to you...you macho Mexican!" she screamed. "Why did you agree to give old man Wyatt a transplant? Why didn't you tell them you didn't have a match?"

"Ann, Ann, listen to me. It won't help any of us to fight like this. We need to keep our heads now. I agreed to help them because I didn't know what else to do. If I had refused, St. John and the crew with him would have spilled the beans back home or...or...blackmailed us.

"You dumbass," she yelled. "St. John isn't going to do anything. I have him wrapped around my little finger..."

"I wouldn't be so sure about that," Guttierez interrupted. "But that's not the point. The guards at the house told me they came up in some rinky-dink shrimp trawler. I'm going to give them what they want, but they'll never leave the Gulf of Mexico alive. They'll join our buddy Nick Sands as shark bait. It's the only way. This way no one in America knows about anything about a heart transplant patient. All that will be reported is that four men were lost at sea during a tropical storm, which is now conveniently brewing in the Caribbean and headed our way."

Ann listened silently at the other end. Guttierez waited for some kind of outburst.

"Hmmm... I like it. I really do," Ann said.

"There's only one real problem, Ann."

"What's that, love?"

"Who will sign off on the NHCO forms if St. John is dead?"

"Oh, who cares about that? Castner can do a few until I can seduce someone else at the hospital. And as you know, that won't be a problem at all. Let me hear your plan for doing this. It sounds exciting." Ann curled up on the couch and lit a cigarette as she listened excitedly to Guttierez's plan.

* * *

Julio pulled up at the front door of Casa del Mar and let one of the guards drive the car back to the garage. All of the men noticed the dark clouds that rolled over the horizon.

"That's the storm rolling in," Isaac said, scratching his chin and furrowing his brow in worry.

A small Volkswagen beetle, the type that is no longer marketed in the U.S., came honking up the driveway. Lupita, Dr. Guttierez's secretary, waved at them from the car.

"Cousin Lupita, what's wrong?"

Robert, Isaac and Silas looked at Julio in disbelief.

"Cousin?" Robert asked.

Julio walked down to meet her. He reached the car and listened for a minute to the very animated young woman. He then walked over to the driver's side and attempted to get her out of the car, but it appeared she didn't want to get out as she repeatedly shook her head. Finally, Julio threw up his hands in disgust. Lupita pulled the car into the street and drove off, shifting gears rapidly and accelerating quickly.

Julio motioned to them. He pointed to the edge of the yard, the cliff overlooking the Gulf.

"What's up?' Robert asked.

"Bad news." Julio looked at John with saddened eyes.

"What? She left like she was afraid."

"She is afraid. She came here at great risk, or at least she thinks so. She didn't want to get out of the car for fear of a guard recognizing her. She says that after the surgery tomorrow, Guttierez is going to have you all killed."

"What!" Isaac, Silas, John and Robert said at the same time.

Julio shrugged and said, "I know, I know, it sounds crazy. But she said she overheard Guttierez talking on the phone with someone. He said the operation will be done, but after that he's going to get rid of all of you."

"Who was he talking to?" Robert asked.

"She couldn't make it out. But she was certain that he was serious by his tone of voice."

"Well, I guess this validates the worries I've had about this whole thing," Robert said.

"That does it then!" John said, "We're all going to load up on the Arlington and go home. You men have done enough for me already. I'm not going to have you subjected to more danger!"

"Nonsense, Mr. Wyatt!" Silas got in front of him. "We're not going to do any such thing. Robert says you'll die if you don't get a heart transplant. Since those bureaucratic fools back home won't get it for you, then these crooks down here are going to provide you with one. Hell, you've already paid them a bunch of money."

"Robert, do you think they'll do right by John in surgery?" asked Julio.

"Oh, I'll be right there, holding the retractor. I held a retractor in medical school so many times it's amazing that one didn't sprout from my hands. John, I'll guarantee you that the procedure will be done correctly. I saw enough done at Tennessee that even I could probably do one in my sleep."

"Besides," Robert continued. "Guttierez said his top surgeon would perform the surgery. He's not going to foul up his little business down here by telling his top man to screw up a surgery. If they plan to hurt us, it will be afterwards. What I suggest we do is surprise them. We'll get the surgery done, then we'll leave. When John is supposed to be in recovery, we'll wheel him out of there and straight to the Arlington. It's set up to like a hospital anyway. We'll be halfway to the States before they even know we're gone!"

Robert took his friend by the shoulders, looking him straight in the eye. "John, I'm not afraid of what those men might try to do. But us moving you that soon is dangerous. It's not the best thing to do right after a major surgery, but I don't think we have any choice if Julio's cousin is right."

"Bobby, Dr. Thompkins at U.T. said I was dead if I didn't get this transplant. At least this way I'll have a fighting chance. Besides, like Isaac said, I've already paid these sons of bitches a pile of money."

John's steadfast response drew a small round of laughter.

238

"Good, it's settled then. Julio, I'm glad I asked you to set up the car as an ambulance now. It looks like we're going to need it even more than I thought.

Robert looked at all of the men present. "Are we all in this together then?"

Each man nodded his approval.

"Julio, can you get us out of the hospital after surgery without being noticed."

Julio frowned. "I don't know about that. I do know the back way out. We can back the car right up to the exit there and load John into it without any problem."

"Okay, let's get rested up tonight and tomorrow we'll get out of here as soon as John hits the recovery room. I'll tell the recovery room nurse that there's some kind of complication and we need to wheel John back into the O.R. Instead, we'll just roll him out the back door." Robert laughed.

"Julio, you'll have to meet me in the recovery room and do some fast talking, because my Spanish isn't good enough to pull this off."

"Lordy, Lordy, I never meant for you boys to go through all this," John Wyatt ruefully shook his head.

"Good Lord, John! You're the one who's about to get his chest cracked open and have a new heart stuffed in it. We're just going to make sure you get to New Orleans safely," Robert said.

"I know, Bobby. Still..."

"Come on, everyone. I'll fix us some supper so we'll have plenty of stamina tomorrow " Julio said, herding the group into the house.

Isaac broke off from the group. "I'd better check on the Arlington," he said. "I'll work on the engine tonight to be sure that old trawler can get us back to New Orleans as soon as possible."

"Thanks, Isaac, I know you'll have me home faster than any other captain on the Gulf," John said.

Isaac smiled and headed down the path to the marina.

"Isaac, I'll save you a plate from supper," Silas called

after his brother.

Isaac threw up his hand and waved as he continued down the path. The rest of the group turned and quietly entered the house.

Julio fixed a meal for his companions. They ate mostly in silence, and any small talk they attempted was strained. The tension in the air was tangible.

Robert knew the task in front of them was formidable. What did Guttierez's men have in store for them? Maybe he was taking too much of a chance by hustling John away after surgery. But what choice did he have? If Lupita was correct, and Julio seemed to trust her, then he had no choice but to take this action.

He thought about everything that had happened since the night Sandy Elliott had taken him back to his apartment to see that horrible sight. All the events of the past few weeks seemed unreal. However crazy it seemed to take a sick man from his home and bring him to a foreign country to have a major surgery—well, all the strange things that had followed seemed to somehow make his actions seem reasonable. But one thing was certain. Without this heart transplant John Wyatt would die. So they had to go through with this despite the risk.

Dr. St. John knew these people wanted to protect their multimillion dollar enterprise. He had no doubt they would kill all of them if they viewed them as a threat to the project. Taking a man into a potential hurricane just after major surgery and trying to outrun an unknown enemy sounded crazy, he knew, but he was beginning to see that life *is* stranger than fiction sometimes.

He finished his meal and excused himself after Julio assured him that he would get him up plenty early in the morning. He went directly to his room. He was distancing himself from his compatriots physically simply because he did not want them to see the worry and concern on his face. He tried to shake the dread from his mind. He couldn't. There was a job that had to be done and he *had* to come through for

John Wyatt. If nothing else, he vowed to get this done for Dave.

Dr. St. John dressed for bed, then stood before the open window and watched the approaching maelstrom with amazement. The storm's lighting flashed crazily across the waters of the Gulf. The thunder began to echo throughout the room ,obscuring the sound of the waves pounding the beach below him.

Robert was not a particularly religious man, in the sense of going to church every Sunday. But he prayed everyday to the higher being that had given him life and blessed him with the wonderful career he had in medicine. Tonight he would pray on bended knees in front of God's most powerful exhibition in nature, the hurricane.

He was afraid. Not for his own life necessarily. And he was not as concerned about John Wyatt's. Sure, he wanted to get John back healthy and well to Tennessee, but he was sure that John had made his peace with God. And John realized that without this surgery his life was over. He really didn't have a whole lot to lose. If he didn't take this chance, he wouldn't live much longer anyway.

Robert thought of young Martin and Marion, Silas' sons. He worried that he had brought their father and uncle into a dangerous situation. A situation that neither of them bargained for. And Julio—he was just a boy. On his knees, Dr. Robert St. John begged for God to protect them all, especially Julio, Isaac, and Silas.

Perhaps it was God's way of answering his prayers because he slept as soundly as he could ever recall. He was awakened by Julio at 5 a.m. He rubbed his eyes, took a deep breath and said, "Let's get John and Silas and go to the hospital. Isaac needs to say with the boat and have it ready to shove off."

Julio and Silas joined John and Robert as they got into the car. Isaac walked cautiously through the increasing winds back down to the boat.

It was a quiet but determined group that left in the rain

that morning.

"What should Silas and I do?" Julio asked.

"The only thing you can do is have the Mercedes in position ready to go. I'll come and let you in the back door as soon as John is in the recovery room."

"Okay, Doc, we'll be ready."

"No one will suspect that we would move John so soon after surgery if we act cool." Robert snapped his fingers. "It should be a snap."

John's mood seemed to be lifted by Robert's observation. He turned to his friends. "You all have to promise me that if something goes wrong, you'll get out of there. I'm a big boy and you're giving me a shot at life that I wouldn't have. I'm thankful. I just don't want any of you getting hurt."

Robert felt a surge of sympathy sweep over him for his friend. John had shown what a truly humble man he was. This trip had to have been agony for him but all he seemed to care about was the safety of everyone but himself.

"Okay, folks, here we are," Julio announced as he pulled up the drive to the hospital.

"You and Silas pull the car to the back. If everything goes well I'll motion for you to help me about eleven."

The men shook hands and wished each other luck.

Silas and Julio promised John before he got out of the car that they would get him back to New Orleans safely. He simply nodded.

Robert and John slowly walked through the increasing rain and wind to the front door. As they entered the building they were greeted by a couple of nurses, who led them in opposite directions, John to the O.R. prep room and Robert to the surgical suite scrub area.

Dr. St. John was met there by two Mexican surgeons. They introduced themselves, but they spoke so rapidly he did not understand what they said, much less what their names were. Maybe that was on purpose, he reasoned. He followed them into the scrub room and washed up. His Spanish was poor. He had thought he would be able to follow what they said, but he couldn't. He wished that he had Julio with him to interpret.

The three men stood around and attempted to make small talk but eventually the two Mexicans began to converse between themselves. Robert attempted to discuss the remarkable new organ storage ability that they had pioneered here. They looked confused and shrugged. Maybe it was his poor Spanish or maybe they just didn't want to discuss this amazing discovery with him. He felt like he stood out like a sore thumb.

The nervousness and anxiety he had felt prior to meeting them disappeared. Eventually he came to recognize that these two men were laughing and gossiping with one another just as surgeons back in United States do. This was just another patient to them. Nothing ominous was happening at all.

Dr. St. John began to feel foolish. Perhaps Lupita had misinterpreted what she had heard. Besides, why would these people use such a valuable commodity as a donor organ on a man they intended to kill. Why not just kill us and get it over with? He was going to stick with the game plan, but he admitted to himself that he was getting confused.

The surgical suite sprang to action as John Wyatt was wheeled into the operating room. Dr. St. John was glad. Now he could get his mind off his worries and do something positive by helping in any way he could to bring new life to his old friend.

The scenario for the surgery was exactly as in the United States. The anesthesiologist had put John to sleep. The surgical nurses were scurrying about readying the patient for surgery. Meticulous sterile procedure was being followed just like at home. The heart-lung by-pass machine was whirring. Before long Dr. St. John became engrossed in the whole event.

Betadine scrub covered John's thorax. His chest was opened, revealing his heart. Blood began to flow through the tubing of the machines. One of the surgeons had pulled him over and handed him a surgical retractor. It was *déjà vu* as he was taken back to his medical school days in Memphis.

The surgeon attempted to include him in the discussion around the operating table. He nodded as if he understood, but that was a lie. He was exchanging smiles and nods, but he felt isolated due to the language barrier.

John's heart was removed and the tedious nature of replacing it began. His new heart was removed from a stainless steel container full of a purple solution. As the surgeons worked with the new organ, Robert was impressed with the skill of the team. *This equals any in the States,* he thought. *Surely these gifted men aren't killers.* He began to seriously doubt the sanity of his plan. Then his mind flashed to the image of Dave's dead body and he steeled himself to trust his instinct.

One of the surgeons said something in Spanish. Everyone backed away from the table. Instinctively he did also.

"Pop!" The distinctive sound of electrical paddles shocking life back into the human body was unmistakable. John Wyatt's new heart began to beat life-giving blood through his body.

Everyone in the room looked at him and smiled, sharing the incredible feeling that always accompanies miraculous events.

The closing of the chest wall flew by. Robert's heart began to beat rapidly. It soon would be time for him to act. The sense of camaraderie he perceived in the surgical team again lessened his belief in their plan. But when those waves of doubt washed over him he forced himself to visualize Dave. He again summoned all his courage to trust his instinct and to act.

He rebuffed the obvious invitation the Mexican surgeons were offering him to join them after the surgery. He pointed to his friend and motioned that they go on. He helped the nurses push John into recovery. Robert's pulse quickened. John was on a respirator and would need to be weaned. Moving him now seemed cruel.

Trust your instinct, trust your instinct, he repeated over and over to himself. *The car and boat are well prepared to handle this patient, that is if all the moving and jarring doesn't throw him into cardiac arrest.*

Dr. St. John quietly slipped down the hall to the back entrance. Julio almost fell on him as he opened the door.

"Hurry, let's get moving," he hissed.

""There are two cars of men out in the parking lot—federales," Julio said explained as they scurried down the hall.

Silas lugged the portable respirator with him. "Yeah, and those are some serious-lookin' dudes," he whispered.

"Okay then, Julio, you go act hysterical in front of the recovery room nurse. Tell her to get the doctors and meet us in the surgical suite again. We'll roll John back down there for her. Tell her I suspect he's bleeding around the aorta."

"Silas, John can live for only a short period of time without this respirator functioning absolutely normally."

"You just tell me what to do, Doc!"

Julio deserved an Academy Award for his recovery room performance. He had the nurse so upset she ran into the wall while trying to leave to find a surgeon to meet them back in the O.R.

Robert and Silas pulled John and his bed down the hall, connecting tubes and oxygen as best they could. They would have laughed at themselves if they weren't scared to death.

"Here, fold the sheet under John as we leave the bed outside. We'll put him on the cot in the back seat," Robert instructed.

They pulled John into the car with what seemed like one movement. His respirator and oxygen filled up the whole floor. Julio pushed the hospital bed back down beside the hospital.

"Julio, get us out of here...but slowly and calmly," Robert said.

Julio pulled the car back out into the parking lot behind the two dark cars parked there. Robert didn't dare look at them.

When they had made it back on the main road Julio said, "I don't think they noticed us!"

"They'll be on our tail in just a few minutes when they discover he's gone," Robert warned.

Julio constantly checked the rearview mirror for any sight of the federales. None could be seen. The road from the hospital wound down the hill leading straight to Casa del Mar.

Julio turned off the main road and stopped at the edge of the path that led down to the marina.

"Silas, you and Julio grab the sheet and carry John down to the boat," Robert said. "I'll carry the equipment. We can make it easily if we work together as one."

The three men struggled against the weight of John's body and the elements to make it down the steps to Isaac and the Arlington. They kept him as dry as possible as they shuffled to the boat.

"How is he?" Isaac shouted as they approached. All of them nodded okay. They were too breathless to respond otherwise. Exhausted, they made one final push to get him aboard and get him attached to the more adequate set-up in the cabin.

Robert checked ventilator settings and oxygen pressures. When he was satisfied that everything was at least reasonably correct, he shouted above the rising wind and surf, "Let's shove off."

Julio was helping to loosen the moorings.

"Julio!" Robert took his young friend by the shoulders. "You've got to stay here!"

"No way, Doc! I'm going." Julio shook free of his grip and continued to work at freeing the rocking boat.

"Julio, you've got to understand—we need you to try and divert these people from us. You're not involved with this. You can come to visit me in New Orleans when this thing cools down."

Silas had come to stand by Robert, showing his support

for this decision.

"Hey, guys," Isaac yelled at them from the bridge. "The weather is getting seriously bad. We've got to go!"

"Okay, okay." Julio conceded. "Get on, I'll push you off from the dock."

"Look, look!" Isaac's panicked voice drew their attention to him. He was pointing at the steps at the start of the path down to the marina.

About a half-dozen darkly dressed men spilled out of two cars and began to stream down the path toward them.

"Go, go, go!" Julio screamed.

Isaac slammed the trawler in reverse. He backed away from the pier, straightened the boat's nose into the force of the wind and headed out to sea.

Julio bounded up the steps and motioned the men back to the house. They ignored his directions and ran to the Hatteras still moored at the marina.

Dr. St. John ran into the cabin and checked on John. Blood pressure and heart sounds were all normal. The rocking boat hindered everything he tried to do. It was a miracle but John Wyatt was alive and doing well. Now Robert was going to have to try to wean him off the ventilator in the middle of a hurricane and without benefit of blood gasses.

He double-checked all the equipment one last time, and put on a yellow rain slicker he had found and headed to the bridge.

The Arlington was bucking against the waves and wind. Robert had not realized how violent the storm was becoming. The natural harbor of the marina at Casa del Mar had sheltered them from the brunt of the storm. Now that they were in the Gulf, they were subjected to its full fury.

Dr. St. John struggled up the stairs. One look at Isaac's face sunk the hope that had sprung up in him.

"Silas and I want to let you know, Doc, that it's only 50-50 that we can beat this thing to New Orleans," Isaac shouted.

"Yeah," Silas yelled. "That is if we can beat those guys!"

He pointed back to the marina. The dark-suited men

were boarding the Hatteras.

"That Hatteras isn't the fastest thing in the water, but it can beat us in the long haul in this kind of weather. The only advantage we have is that we sit lower in the water," Isaac explained.

"Nobody can beat this storm," Isaac said. "The National Weather Service is calling this Hurricane George. It's now a category-two hurricane, and they say it may strengthen to a category three before it hits land. We're somewhere outside the main wall—"

A huge blast of wind knocked them all off balance momentarily.

"I'm going to head directly toward that wall," he continued, "then attempt to cut directly north to New Orleans behind a rain squall. With the low visibility, hopefully we'll shake our friends." He nodded to the bobbing boat that was about a mile behind them.

Dr. St. John strained to see the Hatteras behind them. It seemed to have gained on them in just the few minutes they had been talking. "What if we can't shake them?" he asked, looking first to Isaac and then to Silas.

"We'll shake them," Silas said, facing straight ahead into the storm just like his brother.

"How's John doing?" he asked.

"All right," Robert conceded, "but he isn't out of the woods by any means."

"Doc, go down and check on John. We had faith in you. Now you're going to have to have faith in us." Silas patted him reassuringly on the shoulder.

"You're right. It's just that I've never been out in a hurricane on a shrimp trawler with a heart transplant recipient on board before." The absurdity of it all caused them to break out in a laugh.

Isaac stood up behind the wheel and yelled, "Come on, George, give us your best shot!" pumping his fist in the air and whooping and yelling like a cowboy riding a bucking Bronco.

"Go on back down and check on John," Silas repeated.

Knowing there was nothing he could do up there, Robert gingerly groped his way down the ladder and back into the cabin. He could tell immediately that John was fighting the respirator; his body was shaking the effects of the anesthesia. Robert felt he had no choice but to pull the tube from the trachea and see if he could breathe on his own. He steadied himself and pulled with constant pressure on the tube.

John coughed and hacked violently. Robert was amazed at how well his friend had pulled through this. Still only semi-conscious, John fought and flailed with his arms. Robert proceeded to tie them down as best he could.

A large wave seemed to turn them almost sideways. Robert could see through the porthole that the Hatteras had gained on them. He felt his heart go up into his throat. These men were serious if they were following them out into this type of storm. He prayed again that Isaac could pull this off. *If we don't get to that squall line and turn north soon, they'll either capture us or we'll sink,* he decided.

The waves and wind picked up. The trawler seemed to only inch forward. The sky darkened. John seemed to be resting comfortably even though the boat seemed to be on a Nantucket sleigh ride, riding waves up and then crashing down on the other side. Robert decided to go back topside.

The storm's fury had definitely intensified. He didn't know at first if he could even climb back up the ladder to rejoin them.

"Sit down here between us, Doc!" Silas shouted. "How's John doing?" He could barely be heard above the howling wind.

Robert gave the thumbs up sign, then checked the boat behind them. "It's gaining!"

Isaac and Silas both nodded. " We know."

"Look ahead," Isaac shouted. "A hurricane has a definite configuration to it. Everyone knows about the eye, but that ahead is the outer wall of the storm. We get there, scoot behind that black curtain and scoot north to New Orleans."

Robert smiled at Isaac's confidence.

"That's if it doesn't tear the boat apart first." Isaac looked at him slyly and winked.

An eternity passed before they entered and passed the wall. Darkness fell and everything turned black. Robert looked behind him for the Hatteras. He couldn't see it. Rain pelted them, stinging like BB's.

Without warning Isaac violently turned the wheel of the boat northward.

Robert thought they would surely capsize. They bobbed back and forth like a cork. Suddenly, they caught the storm from behind and it seemed to propel them forward. The knot in Robert's throat eased a bit.

As they blasted forward away from the storm, he began to believe that they might make it back home. They emerged from the northern edge of the curtain of the storm into an area of lightness. They could see actually each other. Squalls of rain and wind seemed to propel them further from their adversaries. All three men broke out into huge smiles. They were drenched with rain and sea water. They were exhausted. And they were still scared. They looked around them. The Hatteras was nowhere to be seen.

"Oh damn! Look!" Silas pointed directly behind them.

There was the Hatteras! No further than 100 yards behind them and seemingly closing fast. It had appeared like a pirate ghost ship. Their hearts sank.

Robert was almost positive that he recognized the slim form of Dr. Guttierez holding onto the bow, urging his federale mate to catch the Arlington.

"Better be prepared," Isaac said.

What happened next was unclear. The Arlington and the Hatteras had emerged from the northern wall of the hurricane. Squall lines, tornadoes and water spouts are frequently spawned at the cutting edge of any hurricane. The men of the Arlington heard a roar the sound of which tore through the constant grinding noise of hurricane George. A large tornadic water spout flashed directly overhead. They instinctively ducked as it mercifully passed. It skipped twice on the water directly behind them, sucking up monstrous quantities of water wherever it touched down. The Hatteras had closed to within fifty yards.

Robert looked back at the fishing boat directly behind them. On the bow, he saw Guttierez gesturing at them as if he were Ahab cursing the white whale. He never knew what hit him. The Hatteras was there, and then it exploded. Literally. The negative pressure inside the funnel cloud caused the whole boat to simply splinter skyward into a million pieces.

There could have been no survivors. Silas, Isaac and Robert huddled together fearing some of the flying shards from the doomed boat would hit them. They sat in silence for another ten minutes or so. Suddenly, as if a miracle, the clouds parted a little and the rains lessened.

"We've topped the northern edge," Isaac shouted jubilantly.

Silas hugged his older brother around the neck. "You did it!"

They acted like crazy men, whooping and hollering at the top of their lungs. They pounded each other on the back and sang a few rounds of "Barnacle Bill the Sailor."

"I'd better go check on John," Robert told the jubilant brothers. The weather was still severe but much less so than just a few minutes previously. He still had to take care as he worked his way down the ladder back to the main deck. He entered the cabin.

"John, John!" he shouted so loudly that Silas immediately began to follow him to the cabin.

Silas jumped down the ladder and ran through the door. Robert was frantically giving a blue-tinged John mouth-to mouth resuscitation.

"Pump his chest!" Robert shouted, clearing vomit from John's mouth. "He aspirated, Silas! He was doing fine when I left him to go upstairs with you!"

Silas began to methodically push down on his heart through his chest wall.

"It's my fault, Silas!" Robert sobbed. "I shouldn't have left him."

"It's not your fault, Doc. For Christ's sake, we were in the middle of a hurricane."

A quick wheezing sound escaped from John's mouth.

"Hold it Silas! Let me see if he has a pulse." Robert held his finger over John's carotid artery."

"Yes!" he exclaimed, giving Silas a high and low five.

"He must have gotten sick and vomited when we were in the worst weather. If he had been like that for a few more minutes I doubt we could have revived him."

John began to cough and moan. Robert placed an oxygen mask over his face, administering the much-needed gas.

Silas bent over him. "We're here, Mr. Wyatt, and everything is okay."

"Where am I?" John Wyatt groggily asked.

"We're heading to New Orleans. We're almost home."

"Where's Bobby?"

"I'm right here, John." Robert responded. "I'm just drawing up some lidocaine, which I'll give to you through an I.V. It'll keep your heart from going into a crazy rhythm."

"Oh," was all John could muster through a cough and wheeze.

"Thanks for the help, Silas," Robert said as Silas headed out the door to rejoin his brother.

Silas saluted Robert. "Glad to help, Doc."

The rest of the trip into New Orleans went smoothly. Amazingly the sun broke through the overcast, casting hot rays down upon the trawler. The hurricane spun itself toward the Mexican coast, leaving them a clear path back into the Crescent City.

John gradually gained some strength. Robert planned to transfer him to Touro Hospital in the Garden District. His old friends and mentors Dr. Kaplan and Dr. Goldman, who practiced there, would take good care of him. With all the crazy shenanigans going on, he didn't feel comfortable putting him in New Orleans Hospital.

John kept telling Silas and Isaac that he would send them a suitcase full of money. They both laughed and said it wasn't necessary.

They stopped for the night about five miles after they entered into the mouth of the Mississippi. Robert constantly checked on John. The levity of the trip down had been replaced by a feeling of tremendous satisfaction.

Later that night Isaac, Silas and Robert sat around a fire on the bank. The popping and hissing fire illuminated the vast stretch of the river where they had stopped. Silas and Robert praised Isaac's seamanship, allowing that no one else could have guided them through such a storm in such a fragile boat.

Isaac modestly deflected the praise to the family heirloom, the Arlington. Isaac allowed that divine providence was the reason that they made it and that the tornado had put a direct hit on the Hatteras. What else could it have been?

Before they retired in their cots in the cabin, Silas and Isaac volunteered to contact their congressman to try to get the NHCO to relax at least some of the ridiculous rules that had caused them to go off on this adventure in the first place.

Dr. St. John mused that it might be best to dismantle the whole bureaucracy.

A muffled "Amen" came from John Wyatt. That brought the loudest laugh of the night. Exhaustion finally overcame them and they fell asleep with the gentle nocturnal noises of the Mississippi in their ears.

Chapter Eighteen

Code Blue in the I.C.U., Code Blue in the I.C.U." the voice over the intercom blared.

A flurry of activity immediately overtook all of the hospital.

"Get going!" Dr. Henry Simms instructed Dr. Elizabeth Sheridan Johnson.

Elizabeth dropped the patient's chart she had been writing on and ran down the hall toward the back of the E.R., joining a throng of nurses heading up the stairwell.

As Elizabeth exited the stairwell she saw head nurse Sally Ortiz standing in the hall outside the I.C.U. She was sending all personnel back to their permanent stations. She had called the code. It was Elizabeth's patient.

The night before Officer Sandy Elliott had brought in a young Hispanic youth who had been in an altercation involving drugs, and Elizabeth had admitted him.

"I'm not *believing* this, "Elizabeth shouted, slapping her hands against her cheeks. Sally walked up, put her arms around the young doctor.

"It's not your fault, Dr. Johnson!" Sally attempted to console her.

"I don't know what's happening." Elizabeth shook her head. "He was a healthy boy! He had a knife wound! We were just going to keep him overnight and let him go today."

"Who knows what happens to these people," Sally comforted, patting her back. "These people are all on drugs. It could be anything. Wait until we get the autopsy report back, Doctor."

"Yeah, but with all the reports going to NHCO in Washington, Dr. St.. John says we won't get the autopsy results and morbidity and mortality reports for months!" Her voice trembled as a large tear fell from an eye.

"What am I going to do? All of my patients are dying, and I can't figure out why. I'm going to get fired!"

"Robert wouldn't fire you, sweetheart," Sally tried to console her.

"No, but Ann Finn will!"

"No, she won't! We're too short-handed as it is! Besides, Dr. Johnson, this is a *hospital*...people die! Go on now, go on back down to the E.R. I'll take care of the paperwork. I'll take care of everything for you. Don't worry about Ann, either. I'll take care of it."

Elizabeth hugged Sally. "Thanks. You know I want everyone here to think I'm a good doctor, especially Dr. St. John."

Sally rolled her eyes a bit as she hugged the attractive young physician.

"Go on now! Go back and help Dr. Simms in the E.R. I'll take care of everything up here." Elizabeth released her grip on the head nurse, wiped a tear from her face and headed back downstairs.

Sally checked in at the I.C.U. and ran down the hall to the administration office. Jerri waved her into Ann's office.

Sally made sure the door to the office was locked and then picked up the telephone. She dialed a number and hopped up on Ann's desk.

"Hello." Ann Finn's voice came quietly over the receiver.

"Ann, this is Sally. Listen, I have some news."

"Well, let's hear it. I know it's not good news or you wouldn't be calling me."

Sally took a deep breath. "Dr. Guttierez is dead!"

A long silence followed. Finally, Ann said, "But I just saw him…I just…I was just…intimate with him a few days ago."

Sally rolled her brown eyes at Ann's frankness.

"Lupita called me from Hospital of the Americas. He was killed pursuing Dr. St. John. They had just transplanted a heart in John Wyatt—"

Sally winced as she heard Ann swearing and breaking things.

"I told *those idiots* to kill those fools! Serves Raphael right! He disobeyed me," she shrieked.

"I hate to bring this up now, Ann," Sally whispered. "But we're almost out of insulin. And Lupita said she didn't know if they would send us any now that Guttierez is dead."

"Well, is there *any* good news?" Ann asked.

"Yes…yes, there is. Our new doctor, you know, Dr. Johnson, just…uh…how do we say…killed another one a minute ago. Or at least she thinks she did."

"Well, at least that's good news. Did you call for the hydrofoil yet?"

"Not yet, but I will."

"Good. That is very good news. And hey, listen, don't worry about the insulin. I'll go get some myself if I have to. And Sally?"

"What, Ann?"

"I'll be coming home to New Orleans, and *I'm going to take care of business*!"

* * *

As soon as Dr. St. John reached New Orleans, he decided to take action. Fumbling for the receiver of the telephone, Robert knew that confiding in Sandy Elliott would start him down a path that in all probability would be painful.

"Hello, this is Officer Sandy Elliott."

"Sandy, this is Dr. St. John."

"Dr. St. John, good to hear from you. How can I help you?"

"I'm not sure, Officer."

"Why did you call then? And by the way, call me Sandy."

"It's like this, Sandy: If I give you a scenario, even one that sounds absurd or crazy, or makes no sense—if I were to explain some things to you even though they're not making any sense to me, would you be able to see, through your experience I mean, if there was something bad going on?"

"What the hell are you talking about, Doctor? Have you been drinking?"

"No, I'm sober. Do you like beignets?"

"Yes, I do. But not at five o'clock on a Sunday afternoon, which just happens to be my day off."

"I've got to see you, Officer Elliott."

"Again, call me Sandy, Doctor. May I call you Robert?"

"Sure Officer—I mean, Sandy. Please—I won't sleep until I talk to you."

"Go ahead then, shoot. You've got me on the telephone."

"No, it's not the same. You've got to understand the implications of what I'm going to tell you. Plus, you've got to see my face to know how seriously concerned and worried I am."

There was a long pause, followed by an even longer sigh, which Robert recognized as one of quiet resignation. Officer Elliott must have realized that he might as well meet with this guy and get it over with.

"Good, let's meet at Cafe Du Monde in the Quarter."

"Why there?"

"Don't ask me that either! All I can say is that it's a public place and our meeting would be construed as just a chance meeting. Besides Cafe Du Monde is only for tourists anyway."

"You're right about that."

"In a half-hour then?"

257

"Make it an hour. I have to clean up and drive all the way from west New Orleans."

"Thanks, Sandy. You're great. Hopefully you can set my mind at ease during this little rendezvous and all my suspicions will prove unfounded.

"Well, why go to all the trouble then?"

"Please, Sandy. One hour, okay?"

"Okay, Doc. Order me a beer and beignets if you get there before me."

Cafe Du Monde was an old-time, circa-1894 doughnut stand. At least that's what most Americans would call beignets—a deep fried doughnut with an outside covered with powdered sugar. The place was always packed with tourists.

Finding a parking place where his Jag would not be dented by a carelessly opened door was a feat in itself, considering the crowd. Pushing past the tourists, Robert arrived at the open-air restaurant.

Searching the cafe and satisfying himself that he had arrived before the police officer, he located a table and ordered biscuits and coffee for himself and beignets and beer for Sandy. The thought of the officer's requested combination of beer and beignets was enough to nauseate him if he allowed himself to ponder it.

Robert held up his hand high to attract Sandy's attention after he had picked him out of the large crowd. To Robert's consternation, Sandy had brought his wife and toddler-age son.

"This is my wife, Connie, and my son, Cody," Sandy said. "Cody's three years old. Don't worry, Robert, they're going to Jackson Square to shop, so we'll be free to discuss your concerns."

When Connie tarried, cleaning off the table and putting them on notice not to drink too much beer, Officer Elliott jumped up and produced his billfold. "Do you need some money, darling?" He offered her two twenties from his wallet.

She took the cash, saying, "If need me, I'll be just two blocks away."

"Thanks for allowing us some privacy, and for letting me take your husband away from the family on a Sunday afternoon," Robert said.

The red-haired Mrs. Elliott responded, smiling: "Oh, I'm used to it by now, Doctor." She headed toward Jackson Square with Cody in tow.

"We New Orleans cops don't make much money. At least those few of us not on the take. The missus is too polite to ask for money unless I offer." Sandy smiled with obvious pride. "So what's up, Doc?" He took a big bite of a just-fried beignet and chased it with a swallow of beer.

"Look, Officer Elliott—"

The officer held up a hand covered with powdered sugar. "Sandy, please!"

"Sandy, let's get to a place a little more private. I didn't think this many tourists would be here like this on a Sunday afternoon."

Elliott held up a beignet and took a bite, obviously biding his time in order not to show his loss of patience. Realizing this, Robert waved for the waiter to bring the check and paid the young man without ever looking at the bill, simultaneously asking for to-go cup for the officer's beer. He whisked the officer out the door toward the Mississippi River.

"Let's go over toward the river and the docks. I'll be able to share my thoughts with you without being embarrassed."

The officer, who had brought three of the sweet confections with him, took small bites followed by beer and seemed not to pay much attention to the doctor. Robert decided not to say much until they reached the river. *He must be concentrating on what he has to say*, Robert thought, noting Sandy's indifference.

After arriving at the edge of the brown-tinged water,

Sandy brushed the white powder from his hands, trousers and mustache. He threw the plastic cup into the river's current. He mimicked a curious doctor's opening question to a patient:

"What's ailing you?"

"Where do I begin"

"The beginning?" Elliott looked at him impatiently.

"Yes," Robert sighed deeply. "The beginning. Do you remember a question you asked me on the morning you pulled me over on St. Charles Avenue?"

"You mean the morning you attempted to 'play chicken' with an ongoing street car? Yes, yes—I believe I do." Officer Elliott feigned a bare remembrance of the drunken stunt.

"I remember you saying you didn't think Dr. Wyatt had committed suicide and you were searching for the truth because you were a good cop," Robert said.

Sandy Elliott looked at Robert, showing no emotion.

"You may remember how much grief I felt—which does not excuse my driving stunt but perhaps does explain it. Deep down I felt like you—or maybe I was yearning for a type of explanation—that Dave was a victim of an accident or even murdered. Not that it would bring him back, but it would restore my belief that Dave was the strongest, most resilient person and doctor I'd ever known.

"After the autopsy proved no evidence of abnormalities, I'm assuming we both pretty much laid aside any idea of foul play and thought this was just another suicide. Like you said, sometimes the guy you least suspect is the one who commits suicide. You just never know."

A large group of barges pushed past them down toward the Gulf.

"I had pretty much come to accept the idea of Dave's suicide until my world was turned upside down," he continued.

Sandy interrupted him. "Let's sit down on the levee."

The two sat down and angled their feet toward the

water. It was obvious the doctor had captured the officer's attention with his sincerity.

"I had to question even things about myself I thought I was certain of," continued Robert. "But…" he paused a full 15 seconds to make sure he used the correct words. "Something that's happened has precipitated the very, very sure feeling again that Dr. Wyatt couldn't, wouldn't and *did not* kill himself.

"I guess that belief was just pushed under the conscious surface, and the events of the last few days brought it back out into—" He held both arms and hands open and extended skyward "—the truthful surface."

Sandy Elliott had not wavered from his intense concentration on Robert's story.

"The things that have happened will take some sorting through maybe even writing down in a list before their significance becomes apparent. But I am convinced that they will become crystal clear in the light of understanding, just as surely as the Mississippi empties into the Gulf of Mexico."

Robert paused. Sandy Elliott said, "Go on."

"There are a lot of other things that don't add up and that I think might tie into this. But the one thing I am positive of is that Dave Wyatt did not kill himself."

Sandy Elliott dug into his pocket and pulled out a penny. He threw it skipping into the river.

"I'll tell you something," he said, looking back at Robert. "Evidently a lot of things have happened since we met, Doctor."

"Yes, they have, and I can explain—"

Officer Elliott interrupted him before he could go any further. "Before we get into those events, tell me what one thing has happened that has absolutely convinced you of this."

"Do you remember when we first met and you told me that I wasn't a suspect? Do you remember that?"

"Yeah. So?"

"You first told me that it was because I told you so by my behavior and you trusted me or something to that effect."

Sandy again nodded.

"Listen, you knew I was innocent. Just like you kept up your investigation of Dave's death, even though your supervisor told you not to—because your knowledge of people made you sure of yourself."

Sandy again nodded affirmatively.

"The exact same thing happened to me. A Mexican kid who I barely know stuck his neck out for me. I thought at first that he was trying to protect my feelings by showing me something that hurt my ego really badly.

"But that wasn't it. And then he told me that something was terribly wrong. He didn't spell it out for me and he didn't even know exactly what was wrong. But he sacrificed his job and maybe more. A poor Mexican kid with a lot to lose.

"And you know something? He was 100 percent correct. I know people too, Sandy. And it's like a veil has been pulled off my eyes. There's something else...I can't tell you everything...but there is something else...

Sandy looked at him curiously,

"What is it, Doc?"

"I think I've broken a bunch of laws...international laws maybe."

Sandy looked at him. "What are you talking about?"

"It's a long story, but I didn't know what else to do. John Wyatt needed a heart transplant...

And Dr. St. John started to retell the story of how he and the Arlington brothers had gone to Mexico to save John Wyatt's life. When he had finished Sandy Elliott just looked at him.

"Well, say *something*!" Robert implored.

"You are one crazy doctor! Do you know why Dr. Guttierez would want to kill you?"

"No."

"Can you point a finger at anyone else?"

"I'm not sure yet. But I do know this—Dave Wyatt is dead, and he sure as hell didn't kill himself! And Dr. Guttierez tried to kill me, and now he's dead!"

"I see." Sandy Elliott looked at Robert for what seemed like an eternity. "Listen, I want you to elaborate on a lot of the things that have happened. But first, remember when I said the autopsy didn't show anything abnormal on Dr. Wyatt?"

"Yes, what about it?"

"I want to ask you something. Is there anything suspicious about his glucose being low?"

Robert jerked. "How low? Tell me how low?"

"Sixteen."

"Good Lord, yes! Now that doesn't necessarily mean anything, but it's something that shouldn't be ignored. Wait a minute! Remember me telling you about Elizabeth Johnson having two or three patients die unexpectedly? I looked up the lab work to see if there was any correlation, and they both had low insulin levels."

"Who does the autopsies at New Orleans Hospital?"

"It depends. Since NHCO, a lot of them, believe it or not, are done by techs."

"Techs? You mean by lab techs?"

"Yeah, or more correctly, autopsy techs. An autopsy is no different from a lot of other things that really require just a modicum of technical skills."

"But the interpretation of what you see?"

"Yes, there's a huge difference in being able to detect the subtle things: the cause of death, the pathology."

"Who signs off on the autopsies over there?"

"I do now."

"You! You're an E.R. doctor."

"I know it's crazy, but those are the rules under NHCO."

"You want to know who signed off on Dr. Wyatt's autopsy? Richard Castner of NHCO."

"Damn!" Robert blurted. "That is strange."

"No joke, Dr. Sherlock. Let's do this, Robert. We need to

go and pick up the wife and baby. Is it possible that we could observe an autopsy done over there?"

"Sure. After all, they do what I tell them to."

They walked back over to the Cafe du Monde. Mrs. Elliott and Cody were eating beignets.

"I thought you two had fallen into the river or something," she said.

"Naw," said Sandy. "Just goofing off."

Robert picked up the bill out of appreciation and they headed for Robert's car.

"Connie," Elliott stopped his wife when they reached the XKE. "Listen to Robert just a second. You know how you can always pick up on stuff between men and women?"

Robert looked around, somewhat embarrassed.

"It's okay, Doc. This is just a little test. It saves me a lot of time. Tell Connie about seeing Ann and the other man, and then she's going to ask you a question."

"Hell no! No offense, Mrs. Elliott, but that's extremely personal!"

"Robert, Connie has a sixth sense about things. She's never wrong!"

Connie Elliott shifted her body from her right to left, trying to look blasé.

"Sandy, I don't want to!"

"Robert, if you want me to help, you will give her a brief synopsis of what happened. Nothing graphic." He nodded toward the three-year-old. "And then I'm going to whisper a question to her which she will in turn ask you."

"I come to you for help, Officer Elliott, and you're going to depend on 'women's intuition'? I'm a man of science, Officer, and I don't believe—"

"Do it, or I walk!" Sandy replied, turning as if to leave.

"Okay, okay." Robert gave Connie a brief, censored version of seeing Ann and Guttierez, blushing as was his custom.

"Poor baby." Mrs. Elliott patted him with her free hand.

Sandy Elliott bent over and whispered into his wife's ear. She nodded and began: "Do you think her betrayal of you is linked to what happened over the past week?"

Robert looked at Sandy. "I don't believe this!"

"Answer the question, Doc." Sandy tapped his foot, awaiting the answer.

Connie repeated the question. "Be honest," she implored.

Robert took a deep breath. He really hadn't thought about it in that way. "Honestly?" he asked, looking at them both.

They both repeated, "Honestly," awaiting his answer.

"Yes, I think so. But so much has happened…

"Sandy added, "Yeah, Connie, you wouldn't believe some of this stuff."

Robert looked at them to see if they believed him.

Connie handed the squirming Cody to Sandy, looking at both men.

"He's telling the truth, Sandy," she said, nodding her head.

Sandy handed Cody back to his wife. "Then we have a lot of work to do." Sandy and Connie began to walk together down the street, looking for their parked car.

"Wait a minute! Is that it?" Robert held out both hands in front of him in amazement.

"No," Sandy turned and looked at him. "Can you arrange for us to see an autopsy at the hospital tomorrow?"

"You bet, if there's one to do."

"Good. After we observe that, you and I have to go to Washington, D.C."

"Washington? What for?" the doctor yelled out at the officer.

"We have to visit Secretary Richard Castner."

"Wait a minute." Robert ran up to Sandy. "What does he have to do with anything?"

"There's a rumor in the ranks that there's something

wrong over at your hospital, pal!" Sandy moved closer to Robert, now barely talking above a whisper. "Something is being sent by a very fast boat to Mexico."

Robert looked at him in amazement.

"The rumors are concerning some kind of narcotic smuggling, but after the story you just told me—what if it's something else?

"Body parts?" Robert asked.

"That would have sounded loco before what you just told me. That's why I want to see an autopsy done tomorrow."

"And what if Ann comes back?" Robert asked.

"Pal, from a social point of view I can't tell you what to do, other than be sure to wear a condom!"

"That's not funny, Sandy."

"It wasn't meant to be funny, Doc."

"That's not what I meant. Should I talk to her about this?"

"No! Hell no! Until we get more information, let's keep everything to ourselves. Okay?"

"Yeah, let's do that."

"Listen, you call me first thing in the morning. You've got my number. Let's see if we can see that autopsy."

Sandy walked away. Robert shouted: "Wait a minute! You didn't tell me, what would Richard Castner have to do with this?"

"I don't know." Sandy got into his car and paused as he rolled the window down. "Why would a man of Castner's stature go to some obscure doctor's funeral in Tennessee? You tell me about some crazy new transplant procedure pioneered in Mexico, and some people trying to kill you, maybe because you know about it. Add that to the wild rumors going around the police department about something going out of the country to south of the border, and then when I look up the autopsy report on your dead buddy..."

Robert interrupted, talking in a slow but understanding

manner. "And the autopsy is signed by Castner."

"That's right, pal!" Sandy began to roll up the window. He furrowed his brow. "And that's why we're going to Washington."

* * *

Ann didn't return home that night. Dr. St. John was glad. He wanted extra time to prepare his act. He had a fitful sleep. He half anticipated Ann's return. Once he thought he felt her presence. Sitting up, he realized he was just dreaming.

The next morning he called Sally at the hospital. She informed him that an 82-year-old patient with pneumonia had died and was scheduled for autopsy. Robert was tempted to ask her about her brother, Julio, but decided against it. He hung up with Sally and called Sandy to tell him the news. "Meet me at my Jaguar, in the hospital parking lot."

"I'll be there in thirty minutes."

They met as scheduled and walked toward the hospital.

"Have you ever witnessed an autopsy, Sandy?"

"No, never wanted to, Doctor."

"We've got an 82-year-old man scheduled this morning. He died of pneumonia. It's a pretty cut-and-dried case, pathology-wise, but we might—"

Sandy caught Robert by the arm. "We're not here to study pathology, Doc. We're here to see who performs the autopsy, who interprets the protocols, other things that might clue us in on something. I mean, why would Castner sign off on an autopsy of a patient even if he was a colleague of sorts—Dr. Wyatt?"

"I see what you mean, but ever since NHCO took over the country's health care several years ago, lots of things that would have seemed unconscionable before—"

"Like?" Sandy asked.

"Hell, autopsies being performed not by an M.D. but a tech. But at many of the hospitals, New Orleans for one, autopsies are videotaped and are signed off on by a doctor."

"So that might explain why Castner signed off on this one?" Sandy asked.

"Yes, I guess. But damn, there's a hospital of doctors here. Why one in Washington, D.C., who doesn't even practice medicine?"

"That's why we're going to observe. Do they always perform these things—autopsies?"

"It depends on the presumed cause of death. Let's go see. I've got a stack of autopsy reports at the house that we can go through after we finish here. Maybe we can learn something from them too."

Dr. St. John had never spent much time in the morgue and adjacent autopsy chamber. The morgue was located in the basement of the Old New Orleans Hospital Addition. It was damp and reminded Robert of a dungeon. He would prefer to never spend any time down there. He had always wondered why anybody would go into forensic pathology.

They entered the morgue and crossed over the cave-like hallway to a small, white room labeled AUTOPSY. They knocked on the door. No one responded. They pushed open the door and peered inside. The body of the deceased, an 82-year-old black man, lay naked on a granite slab in the middle of the room. They walked warily toward the corpse.

"You go first, Robert. You're the doctor."

"Boo!" They both jumped at the sound. An old, white-haired man leered at them from around the corner desk that was obscured by a white partition in the back of the autopsy room.

"What do you boys want?"

"Good Lord, man. You scared us to death," Sandy protested.

"Heh, heh." The guy was dressed in a surgeon's smock and cap. He lit a cigarette and walked toward them. "What're you afraid of?" he asked, grabbing the deceased's arm and waving the hand at them. "He won't hurt you."

Robert attempted to grasp control of the situation as he regained his composure.

"I'm Dr. Robert St. John, and this is Sandy Elliott of N.O.P.D. We're here to observe the autopsy."

"Ah, Dr. St. John." The old autopsy tech jumped forward and began to pump the doctor's hand. "I've heard a lot about you. But what are you doing down here? You doctors quit coming around after they passed that health care thing a few years ago."

Leaning forward and whispering behind the back of his hand, presumably so Sandy couldn't hear, the tech said: "They quit paying you guys to come down here, I understand. But, hell, I guess that's why they pay me."

Elliott said, "We're here to observe the autopsy and ask you some questions, okay?"

"Fine," the tech responded, turning to the autopsy slab. "Ask the questions first. These old ones smell some, so you want to fumigate the room as soon as possible afterward." He patted the old man's belly. "All that lactic acid," he explained. "I know your names. Do you want to know mine?"

"Yes, of course," Robert said, attempting to be courteous.

"Elmer Badeaux, and I'm pleased to meet you," he said in a Cajun accent." I've been working down here since 1934. Long time, huh? Since I was fourteen years old. Started in the Depression." The old man crossed his arms across his chest. He mumbled over the cigarette. "You know, Huey Long had this hospital built at the height of the Depression. The common folks loved him." Ashes fell from the hand-rolled cigarette onto his stained lab coat.

"Excuse me," Elliott said. "Thanks, Elmer, but we really need to ask you these questions, so..."

Robert interjected: "Did you do the autopsy on Dr. Dave Wyatt?"

"Yes, I did."

"*You did*?" Robert asked, shocked. "Sandy, why didn't

you tell me?"

"Lieutenant Sheldon transferred the autopsy here," Elliott answered.

"Yeah," Elmer piped in. He held up a copy of the NHCO form. "See, here's his signature."

"Why?" Robert asked.

"I don't know why," Elliott said. "I didn't tell you at the time of the autopsy because at the time I thought it didn't matter."

Elmer Badeaux interrupted. "What's up here? What's wrong?"

"Nothing, Mr. Badeaux," Robert responded.

"Well, when I did the autopsy on Dr. Wyatt, Lieutenant Sheldon came by and personally escorted the body to the mortuary for cremation."

"Cremation!" Robert shot back incredulously. "Hell! I was at his funeral! There was a casket." Sandy and he exchanged confused looks.

Elmer shrugged his shoulders. "That's what he told me."

"Maybe that's what they wanted the official documentation to say," Sandy offered, looking at both men.

Elmer continued: "I don't know about that, but Castner personally called from Washington to make sure I mailed the NHCO form to him. I felt like a pathologist, or someone important for awhile. Like I said, these past few years, I usually work down here alone."

"Let me ask you this, Mr. Badeaux. Was there anything unusual about the Wyatt autopsy that you noticed?"

Looking up and drawing a long draw on his cigarette: "Yeah, yeah, I'd say so. He didn't kill himself the way they said he did. I don't know how he did it, but it sure wasn't an inhalation of natural gas. And I may not have a degree from medical school, but I've probably done more autopsies than any other living person in America." With that assertion, he nodded knowingly, flicked his ashes into his hand, and dumped the contents of his hand into the trash can.

Both men followed behind him to his desk. "How do you know all this?" Robert asked.

Elmer sat back in the chair at his desk, smiling. "Because, when I opened his lung there was absolutely no hint of smell of butyric acid, the smell they add to natural gas to make it stink. He may have killed himself, but not that way."

"Couldn't the smell have dissipated?" Robert asked.

"Nope! In sixty years I've seen one other supposed suicide from gas inhalation that had no gas smell upon opening the lungs." He propped his feet on the cluttered desk and struck a triumphant pose. Smoke curled above his head as the cigarette dangled from his lip. "Turned out to be a murder! His old lady did him in. He was already dead when she turned on the gas, therefore the gas smell wasn't there. That was 1954. I noticed the same thing with the autopsy on your friend."

Sandy looked over at the doctor. "I know what you're thinking, Robert." He glared at him with a determination Robert had not seen before.

"Impressive," Robert said in a subdued tone.

"Why didn't you tell anybody about Dr. Wyatt's autopsy?" Sandy asked.

"I did," Badeaux responded, pulling his feet off the desk and letting them plop down on the floor.

"Who?"

"Richard Castner at NHCO. I mailed him the forms just like he asked."

"That son of a bitch!" Dr. St. John growled.

"Let's go," Sandy said. "We definitely have to go to Washington ASAP."

"Wait, Sandy. Let me ask Elmer a couple more questions."

Elmer said, "Sure, go ahead, but I've got to get started on this guy. He had a pneumonia, but I'm going to cut the skull open first and remove the brain for inspection." Robert suspected the old man was being so graphic for the policeman's benefit.

"Great." Sandy blanched. "We've got to go."

"Sandy, wait. Don't you guys see gory stuff all the time?"

"Yeah, but not like this."

"Mr. Badeaux," Robert began as the old autopsy specialist tested out a skull saw, preparing to open the cranium. The saw roared to life as the old man turned toward the corpse. "Have you noticed anything unusual since the autopsy on Dr. Wyatt? Anything at all?"

"Yes, as a matter of fact I have. It may not mean nothing, but..."

"But what, Mr. Badeaux?"

"Since the lady administrator came..."

"Ann Finn?" Robert asked.

"Yes, I guess. The real good-looking one."

"That's her," Sandy chimed in.

"Well it's probably nothing, but since then, we get a lot of NHCO requisition forms for whole organs to be sent iced to them. Here's one." Elmer pulled a form off the cork board above his desk.

"What do you mean, 'whole organs'?" Sandy asked.

"Let me explain." The smock-covered man smiled, revealing a mouth with no teeth, not even dentures.

Badeaux continued: "I'm going to autopsy this old bird laying here. I'll remove the brain. After I remove it, I'll weigh it. I'll observe it for contusions or ecchymosis—that's 'trauma' and 'bruises' to you." He looked at Officer Elliott. "Then I'll slice it into sections to reveal the pathology." He hesitated.

"So?" Sandy exhorted.

"We do a lot of whole organs. Now...*them*...I don't slice. I remove them, ice them, call this number." He showed them a local number. "It beeps."

"So it's a beeper." Sandy interrupted.

"I guess," he continued. "And someone picks it up—and I mean in a hurry! The boxes all go to the NHCO. He picked

272

up a set of NHCO autopsy forms and waved them in the air.

Robert looked at Sandy. "Incredible."

Robert shook Mr. Badeaux's hand. "You've been most helpful, Elmer. Thank you so much."

"Glad to have helped. Aren't you going to stay to see me work?"

"Can't." Robert looked at this watch. "We're late."

Sandy was motioning to Robert to leave.

"Robert, before you go, will you promise me something?"

"What's that, Elmer?"

"Will you come see me work sometime?" He held up the saw, revving up the motor. "You might learn something."

"Yeah, sure will."

"Let's go to Washington *now*," said Sandy."

"That old guy may be crazy, but he sure made some valid points," Robert said. "We can discuss them on the plane."

The two ran up the labyrinth-like hallway toward the main area of the hospital.

"Wait a minute, Sandy!" They stopped at the top of the steps. "What if Castner isn't there? Don't you think we should at least phone first?"

"No, surprise is the key element here."

"Well, if he's not there, we're not going to surprise anyone."

"I know. But we'll break into his office."

"Are you crazy? You have no jurisdiction in Washington!"

"No. But I've never been wrong about a gut feeling before. Remember, I told you that. I thought this might be the first time, Doc—" Sandy was standing two inches from Robert's face. "But that old coot convinced me that my instincts are right again." He opened the door into the main part of the hospital. "Dr. Dave Wyatt didn't kill himself!"

Chapter Nineteen

Dr. St. John! Dr. St. John!" Sally's voice was overheard above the din.

"Run," Robert said to Sandy. "She'll be impossible to get away from."

Sally, noticing that they were breaking into a trot to get away without talking to her, yelled, "It's about Dr. Johnson, Doctor!"

"Okay, but I don't really have time to talk," he said, turning to see what she wanted. "What is it with Elizabeth?"

"She's lost another patient, and she's hysterical."

"Do you remember Officer Elliott?"

"Yes, I do. Hello, Officer."

"Sandy, can you wait for me just one minute?"

Sally pleaded, "It's important, Officer."

"Okay. But hurry. We've got to get to Washington."

"She's in your office, Dr. St. John. Hurry!"

They ran up the stairwell. "Washington?" Sally implored. "Why? What's up?"

"I'll explain when I get back."

They rounded the corner leading to his office and found Elizabeth Johnson sitting at his desk with her head in her hands.

"Thank God. At least you've calmed down," Sally remarked, crouching by the young doctor, putting her arms around Elizabeth.

Elizabeth wouldn't take her head out of her hands. "I just don't know what I'm doing wrong."

"Another young patient—this was an endocarditis—probably secondary to drug abuse, suffered cardiovascular collapse, evidently overnight, and died," Sally said.

"How old?" Robert asked.

"Twenty-three."

Elizabeth still didn't look up.

"Have our mortality rates suffered recently?"

"Probably," Sally retorted. "But with all the reports forwarded to that NHCO bureaucracy in Washington, who knows?"

"That's right!" Dr. St. John snapped his fingers in recognition. "Since NHCO implementation, all data is sent to Washington for the Central Data Bank."

"Precisely. We review it when it returns—eight months later!" Sally said in disgust.

"And have you reviewed the forms they return?"

"No, but I can imagine they're as indecipherable as hieroglyphics."

Yeah, if they're anything like the NHCO forms I have to send in for review on the autopsies."

Elizabeth finally opened the fingers on her right hand so she could peek out with her right eye: "So, what are you saying?" she asked.

Robert crouched next to Elizabeth and Sally. "I don't know what we're saying, Elizabeth."

"Is there a reason why you're going to Washington with Officer Elliott?" Sally asked again.

"I can't get into that yet. But Sally, you know, if there was some sort of investigation going on, the way you described the mortality reports, quality assurances...we'd never know. Especially in the time frame of eight months."

Sally's eyes opened wide. "What do you mean, Roberto?" she asked excitedly, starting to switch to Spanish.

"Nothing!"

"It has something to do with Ann, doesn't it?"

"No, Sally."

Elizabeth uncovered her face.

Robert continued: "No! Now listen to me, both of you! Elizabeth, I will personally review this case when I get back."

He turned directly to Sally. "I do not want to start any rumors flying around this hospital." He pointed his finger at her. "And you will not say a word to *anyone* about where I'm going, or who I'm going with! Do you understand me?" He briefly pierced her eyes with his.

"Sí, Señor Doctor! There's plenty of rumors going around this hospital anyway," Sally responded, standing with her hands on her hips. "Like, how come we've got so many unexplained deaths? Dr. Johnson isn't the only M.D. who's noticed. And it started when Ann Finn came in."

"Is that true?" Elizabeth asked.

"No. I promise we'll bypass NHCO procedures and get to the bottom of this when I get back from Washington. That's why we're going to Washington," he lied.

"Then why do you need a police officer to go with you?" Sally asked.

"Look, you two guys just keep doing as good a job as you can until I return, okay? And Sally, I love you to death—you're like a sister to me. But if you start some vicious rumor about—whatever —" he sputtered, "—I swear I'll —" He couldn't think of what he would do to her.

This prompted Sally to say: "Piss-poor protoplasm!"

Exasperated, Elizabeth blurted, "You guys keep saying the same things. But a lot of people are noticing we are losing a lot of awfully young patients!"

Robert sighed deeply. "I'll be back tomorrow or the next day. Are you okay, Elizabeth? Will you be all right until I get back?"

She was peering through her fingers again. "I'll be okay now. Thanks for caring and for coming by to see me."

"I'll see you two when I get back." He ran downstairs to find Sandy. "Let's go!" They got the XKE and sped toward

New Orleans International Airport.

The flight was tedious, and the two men didn't say much. They both knew Castner would hold the key. Finally, Robert turned to Sandy with a solemn look. "You have no jurisdiction in D.C."

"Doc, I'm just going to talk to the man. I'll find a D.C. cop to arrest him if he needs to be arrested." He laughed.

"I see," said Robert. *That's right,* he tried to convince himself. *We're just going to talk to the guy. This is probably nothing. Yeah, right, then what are we doing?"* As he began to lose confidence in their actions, he looked over at Sandy Elliott, whose arms were crossed over his chest. Robert crossed his own arms, mimicking him. He hoped this gesture would give him as much confidence in their pursuit as Sandy obviously had. *We're really stepping over the line doing this.*

Sandy stared at the bald passenger in the seat in front of him. When he began to speak again, he spoke in a low, measured voice, never looking at Robert. "The whole New Orleans Police Department is supposed to be on the take, as you probably know. We don't make much money. I do my job well, just like most of the other cops who are clean. But something like this—a death covered up as a suicide, illegal shipments of *something* from that hospital to Mexico." His hands waved over his lap. "All of this would have to involve the police or some kind of conspiracy."

He finally looked at Robert. His gaze had softened. "We both know that Dr. Wyatt's autopsy was a joke. Castner signed off on the whole thing. By God, let's go to the horse's mouth and find out what he knows.

Robert nodded his head in concurrence. The stewardess offered the pair something to drink. They both ordered Diet Coke because they didn't want anything to dull their senses. They clinked the plastic cups together in a salute. Robert smiled weakly at Sandy, attempting to show solidarity in their mission. He just hoped they weren't making a colossal mistake. *Sandy is used to this cop and robbers game,"* he sighed to himself. *"I'm just a Doc along for the ride."*

They landed at Dulles International Airport. They had decided not to pack. If they needed anything, they would buy it.

"Okay, let's go and find out what's going on," Sandy asserted, as he walked briskly off the plane and directly to hail a cab.

"National Health Care Organization headquarters," he said to the cab driver.

"Where's that? Never heard of it."

"It's probably in the Health and Human Services building," Robert said.

"Okay, guys. I know where that is."

The driver droned on about area sights of interest.

Ignoring the driver, Robert asked, "What are we going to do when we get there?"

"Ask the man for the truth. We're going to find out what's going on."

"And what if he doesn't tell us?"

Sandy crossed his arms again. "We'll cross that bridge when we come to it."

"Here we are, fellas. It's the big white building just to the left."

Sandy said, "Pay the man—you're the rich doctor."

He started walking toward the huge building. Robert paid the cab driver as directed, then scurried to catch up to Sandy.

"What are we going to say?" He had seemed very certain at the hospital of what they were doing, but as they got closer, he wasn't as sure. "We don't have an appointment."

"Follow me, and do as I tell you," Sandy shot back, as he bounded up the steps.

"Okay, whatever you say." They entered the large marble foyer and walked over to the huge directory.

"There," Robert pointed to a name. "Dr. Richard Castner, NHCO, Fourteenth Floor."

"Just follow me and do as I do."

Upon entering the office, the two gentlemen strode to the receptionist's desk.

"I'm Officer Sandy Elliott, and this is Dr. Robert St. John. We'd like to see Secretary Castner."

"I'm afraid he's Castner is in meetings all day. He could see you tomorrow at one o'clock, if you'd like a brief appointment, say five minutes. What's your business?"

"That's fine." Sandy pointed to a large oak door. "Is that the office there?"

"Yes, but he's not in right now."

Sandy had already walked over and opened the large door.

"Sir! Sir!"

"I see he's not in, is he?" Sandy smiled back at the receptionist.

"As I said, you can see him tomorrow. He likes to see as many people as he possibly can."

Sandy closed the door behind him. He smiled again at the receptionist. "We'll see him tomorrow. Let's go, Robert."

Robert followed him out the door to fourteenth floor lobby. "What was that all about, Sandy?"

"Just checking out the place." He headed down the stairwell to the first floor and the exit. "We'll come back tonight when no one is here."

"Wait a minute, pal! That's breaking and entering."

"Chill, good buddy. I'm a cop, right? We're not going to steal anything. Just have a look around the good doctor's office. I just wanted to make sure I could get in the locked doors."

"What are you talking about, Sandy? That's against the law."

"The guy wasn't there, Robert. He's not going to tell us anything unless we have some goods on him. I'm just going to look around his office and hope I find something to refresh his memory."

Robert stopped on the Washington street. "I may not go then."

"Yes, you will go, because I need your help! We've come this far—we need to see it through. This guy is involved in something down at the hospital, and we're going to find it."

They found a small motel only three blocks from the office building. They decided to forego any sightseeing once they had checked in.

"Sandy, I should just go to Castner tomorrow and tell him we have some suspicions about Dave's autopsy."

"And what?" Sandy interrupted. "I'm a cop, Doc I know what I'm talking about. He won't tell us anything. Let me rummage around and see what I can find tonight. Most of these federal office buildings don't close the entrance doors at night. It should be easy to get into his office and have a look-see. If I find something incriminating, he'll talk to us tomorrow."

Robert shook his head in disbelief. "Oh, hell! I just don't like the way this is coming together."

Sandy Elliott grinned. "Trust me. I'm a cop!"

Chapter Twenty

Night fell. From the small room they could see the top of the Washington Monument. Sandy seemed as cool as ice water, puttering around the room. He had put together a collection of knives, a couple of coat hangers and a fingernail file. He actually seemed to be enjoying the subterfuge. Dr. St. John was sweating nails.

I shouldn't do this, he kept saying to himself. But he kept seeing Dave Wyatt's body and face. He knew he must do it if the truth was ever going to come out. He finally girded himself to do the job at hand no matter what the consequences.

Ten p.m. came. Eleven, twelve midnight. Finally at one a.m., Sandy said, "Let's go."

They walked down the dark side streets of the nation's capitol until they came to the massive building again. Sandy was right. The front door was open! They took the stairs to the fourteenth floor.

Sandy slipped a knife and file into the lock and opened the hall door. He winked at Robert. They crossed the large room, and Sandy opened Mr. Castner's office just as easily. The office was large and impressive. Moonlight illuminated the entire room. Sandy walked over to the desk and whispered, "I've found if a man has something to hide, he usually keeps it close to him."

The large files locked in the desk were again no match for Sandy's burglary skills. He produced a penlight to see well enough to work his magic on the lock.

"Presto," Sandy said as they both jumped forward to inspect the desk's contents. When they opened the files, NHCO forms were everywhere.

"What did you expect?" Sandy said sarcastically. "This is the NHCO."

"Yes, but look," Robert pointed out. "They're all from New Orleans Hospital."

"Yeah, that's right. Every one of those autopsy reports."

"Look, they've all been signed by Dave Wyatt."

"Look, there's another locked door behind all the forms—it's another storage vault. Can you pick it, Sandy?"

"Hell, yes," Sandy smiled. "Here, hold the light."

Sandy again opened the lock with ease. "I was a troubled kid," he explained.

Upon opening the back lock, they found a large photograph and a small, locked bag. Sandy brought both articles to the top of the desk.

"Look at this photo. Who are those other people besides Dr. Wyatt?"

"It's Ann, Guttierez, Dave and Castner. They're at Ann's place in Cancun. Open this box! Hurry!" Robert was ready to leave. Viewing the pictures of Dave and Ann gave him a lot of bad feelings. "Get what we need, Sandy. Then let's go."

"Check stubs, receipts—that's all that's in here, Robert."

"Let me see." Robert looked at them. "All are from Hospital of the Americas in Mexico. Hundreds of them."

"Look, each has a name and the amount of the check. There's a lot of money here. And look, each verification is for at least $20,000! Let's get out of here and see if we can figure out what it all means.

"Listen, Sandy!" Robert whispered in near hysteria: "Someone's coming!"

"Hide under the desk!"

They didn't have time to replace the objects in the desk. They could hear muffled laughter in the main office.

"I think they're coming in here!" Robert was now hysterical.

They both crouched under the desk. The laughter grew louder.

The door pushed open into the room.

"Don't turn on the light," a woman's voice said. Then a loud giggle, followed by an unzipping noise.

"Where's the couch?" a man's voice asked.

"What should we do?" Robert whispered to Sandy.

"Let's get up and turn on the lights and confront whoever it is. I'm a cop remember?"

Before Robert could answer, Sandy bolted for the barely visible light switch.

"Who's there!" the man's voice shouted. Simultaneously, Sandy flipped on the light switch. The woman shrieked, pulling her tight skirt back up. The man, also in a state of undress, began to struggle with his pants.

"Who are you?" he demanded. "What do you want?"

Sandy flipped his badge open. "Officer Sandy Elliott, investigating a report of a burglary. Robert hid under the large desk, mortified. The man sputtered, "I'm Richard Castner, head of the NHCO. This office is under my jurisdiction."

Castner then noticed the rifled desk and receipts and check stubs that had been left on the desk.

"Hey, wait a minute! What's going on here? What are you doing?" He turned to the lady. "Here, darling," he said, giving her a hundred dollar bill. "I'll call you tomorrow."

She picked up her shoes and ran out of the room.

Sandy closed the door and locked it behind him.

"Robert, come on out."

Robert shyly pulled himself out from under the desk.

Castner recognized Robert. "I know you! What's going on here?"

Sandy slowly waved the badge. "Castner, we have a few questions to ask you."

Robert's courage had returned somehow. "What is happening at New Orleans Hospital? You're sure receiving a lot of money for something." He pointed at the pile of check stubs. "And what's the connection with Hospital of the Americas?"

Castner began to regain his composure. "You guys are in my office! I'm not going to tell you anything! I'm calling the police." He walked toward the phone on the desk.

Sandy Elliott beat him to it and violently cut the cord from the wall with his knife. "We need some answers from you, sir." He stood with the entire phone in his right hand, held high as if he were ready to strike Castner.

"Hold on!" Castner was taken aback by such a bold move. "What do you mean?" He backed away from Sandy.

"That's a lot of money you've received," Sandy said, lifting the telephone higher. "And I want to know why you're receiving it."

Before Castner could say anything, Robert, emboldened by Sandy's actions, walked to within a hand's length of the NHCO chairman:

"Did you kill my friend, Dave Wyatt?"

"What—? Whoa! I haven't killed anybody!" He looked excitedly and from Robert to Sandy, who was still holding his New Orleans badge in his left hand and the telephone in his right hand.

"Then who killed Dave Wyatt? We've talked to the man who did the autopsy, and he says that Dave's case was no suicide!"

"Wait a minute, guys," Castner began to protest. Robert stopped him. He didn't know why. Maybe it was Dave's picture; maybe it was Ann's. Maybe it was the way this Washington peacock had responded. Maybe it was the lifeless face of Dave Wyatt gazing at the rotating ceiling fan that flashed into his mind's eye. For whatever reason, a slow rage welled up within the doctor. Suddenly, and without hesitation, he struck Castner with his open hand.

Castner dabbed at the blood trickling down his nose.

Robert said, "My best friend is dead! And I want to know *who* killed him and *why!*" Robert looked straight into Castner's eyes with deadly seriousness.

Sandy, who was still holding the phone aloft, interrupted. "We're going to call CNN, CBS, NBC and ABC and let them know you're getting a lot of money from a foreign entity. They'll want to know why."

Robert slapped the man again. "That was for Dave!"

"All right, all right! I'm not doing anything, really. And I'm not associated with murder." Castner tried to stand taller. "All I do is get the NHCO forms from Dave..." He lowered his eyes and dabbed his nose again. "All I do in this office is okay the autopsies so NIH doesn't get suspicious."

"Suspicious of what?" Robert slapped him again, knocking him back against the couch. "That's for President Andrew Jackson."

"Quit hitting me!" Castner protested. "Okay, okay, I'll tell you. But no CNN, ABC—nothing! Just between us!"

"Okay," Sandy agreed. "Tell us the truth. If you haven't killed anyone, then you don't have anything to worry about. We just want to know what's going on, and why. And no news. No Dan Rather."

"The transplant program at the Hospital of the Americas is using some of the organs harvested at New Orleans Hospital," Castner said.

"That's it. Remember what the old man said about the special carrier and whole organs being removed?" Robert said.

"But why?" Sandy asked.

Castner just stood there. Dr. St. John had gotten used to hitting him, so he did it again. "That's for Elvis."

"The money," Castner said, finally getting up off the couch. "But this is bigger than me and the hospitals. The administration—they know about this. They look the other way. They're looking for a giant leap in technology. But I haven't killed anybody!" he protested.

"You're off the hook for now, Castner." Sandy put his badge right on the bridge of the man's nose. "If you try to stop us from finding out who killed Dr. Wyatt, I swear we'll be back and we will destroy you. We'll call all the news agencies and totally blow your cover. You'll be run out of town!"

"I'm just the paperwork guy," Castner responded. "I don't know anything about the operation, and I sure as hell didn't kill anybody."

Robert stepped forward as if to strike the cowardly figure again. Instead, he and Elliott turned and walked out of the office. They began to run back to their motel, somewhat giddy with their mission accomplished.

"We've got to get out of town, Robert."

"Yes, I agree," Robert confirmed.

"How long do you think Castner will be quiet?"

"I don't know. Look, we'd better take the Greyhound bus out of town—nobody will expect us to be traveling that way."

Robert asked, "Do you think we're in trouble?"

"Hell, man! You just slapped around a cabinet secretary. He's got to have powerful friends and allies."

"Yeah, I know. I got carried away. I snapped, I guess. But we got the information we wanted."

"But what was that shit about Elvis and Andrew Jackson?"

"State pride, I guess. Something for me and Dave."

Sandy looked over at his doctor-partner. "You've got quite a right jab, but you don't pack that heavy of a punch, Doc." They stopped to catch their breath at the adjacent street corner. "He sure sang awfully easy, though."

"What do you mean, 'sang'?"

"He gave up the information easily!"

"Well, I think I hit him pretty hard."

"Yeah, I know. Let's get out of town."

They were obscured by the shadow of another large government building. The two slipped through the shadows

286

and returned to the hotel. At last they felt safe.

"Should we get a cab to the terminal?" Robert asked.

"Hell, no! We're better off walking."

* * *

There was hardly anyone at the old bus terminal downtown. Sandy and Robert slipped onto the bus after buying their tickets. They determined their trip would take twenty-eight hours and eight stops. "It's still the safest way home," Sandy said. "Let's go."

After settling in, Sandy looked at Robert in the adjacent seat. "They've got to have a contingency plan," he said. "They're making lots of money doing this thing, and they're smart people. They knew this would or could get uncovered eventually, so someone may be waiting for us in New Orleans."

"Could be," Robert conceded. "Listen, we've got to think of a way to trapping the person responsible for Dave's death."

Sandy said, "It'll be tough, partner. All we've got is the word of an old run-down autopsy tech. He would be our only witness other than John Wyatt and the Arlingtons. Not much to go on."

"I know, but you and I know the truth."

"Yes, we do."

The lights of Washington began to fade behind them. Soon they were both asleep. The bus trudged on its circuitous route to New Orleans.

Robert had a fitful sleep trying to get comfortable in the lumbering bus. He finally drifted off into a deeper sleep and had a dream. Dave Wyatt and he were children again. They were fly-fishing in a small stream outside the Smokies that John Wyatt had taken them to. After they had caught some fish, Dave turned to Robert and said, "You know, when we're older, a real pretty lady will kill me. She will give me a big

shot of something and I'll die." Dave just looked at Robert
after he told him this, and then walked up and hugged him.
"Let's go eat these fish," he said, holding up the stringer, but
the fish had mysteriously changed from bass to large barra-
cuda. Robert awoke as the bus was approaching the old
Confederate capital of Richmond, Virginia. He was sweating
profusely. A smallish white-haired lady sitting halfway up
the bus was staring at him. He smiled slightly at her as he
attempted to shake the cobwebs from his head.

It was still jet black outside. There was no sign of daylight when he began to punch Sandy. "Wake up, listen to
this!"

"What?" Sandy sleepily looked around him. "Almost to
Richmond?"

"Listen to this. I just had this weird dream. I think I have
a way to trap the person responsible in New Orleans."

"What?" Sandy repeated again. "Go back to sleep, Robert."

"No, listen to this. I have a sister in Oak Ridge, Tennessee."

"That's good, Doc."

"Strontium-90. That's what we need."

"What are you mumbling about Doc? It's not even light
out yet."

"I'm pretty sure who is responsible for this—maybe
even Dave's death."

"Ann?"

"Yes, how did you know?"

"Robert, I'm a police officer. It's pretty obvious she had
a motive—money! And she probably had the opportunity."

"Yes, and I think I know how she did it—and how to
catch her."

"How?" The bus rolled toward the terminal, slowing to
a stop.

"Strontium-90. It's an isotope produced at Oak Ridge
National Lab."

"Never heard of it."

"Listen, sit over here. Let's get a plan. This just came to me in my sleep."

"I don't know who's goofier—you or me," the officer groaned.

"Strontium-90 is a short-acting isotope that is relatively harmless but highly volatile. I think whoever is responsible for Dave's death probably has instigated some premature deaths at the hospital.

"Think of it," he continued. "We've had a bunch of unusual deaths. The mortality rates, quality assurance reports, and last, but not least, autopsy reports are essentially in Castner's hands. They're all bogus.

The driver announced on the loudspeaker that the Richmond stop was over. "All passengers on board. Next stop: Knoxville, Tennessee."

"Remember the low glucose on those people, including Dave?"

"Yes. So?"

"Insulin!"

"Insulin?"

"Sure. Insulin is not really detectable in an autopsy. It's relatively common in any clinical setting. And given inappropriately, in much larger doses than needed, it could cause death. It would cause a hypoglycemic crisis that in susceptible patients could lead to stroke, heart attack—you name it!"

"Would Ann Finn have access to it?"

"Yes, of course. As the hospital administrator she could make routine stock checks periodically."

"What's this about the strontium-90 stuff?"

"If she is tampering with the insulin—say 10cc dosages were doctored or changed to 100 units per cc, this would cause the type of problems I described. And it also could be exposed with strontium-90. Whoever used that vial would show up as radioactive by a Geiger counter."

"What? Explain this to me like I'm a cop, not a doctor."

"Okay, let's say I get Sally Ortiz to lock up the good insulin, and only she has the key to the cabinet. All personnel would have to contact her if they need insulin."

"Wouldn't people get suspicious?"

"No. Just say it's a conventional policy. Stupid stuff happens all the time now under the NHCO rules. We could doctor a few vials of insulin, leaving it not locked up, with strontium. Administration wouldn't be told. Then if anyone replaced them or tampered with them, that stuff is so volatile it would get all over their hands.

"Ann Finn, you mean."

Robert's heart sank. "I hope I'm wrong, but this would be a foolproof way to prove it if my theory is correct."

"It's so stupid it just might work, Doc."

"Stupid? It's brilliant. Only the perpetrator would be exposed. There would be no excuse for even touching the insulin, unless it was tampered with."

"So we could check the insulin she tampered with for what?"

"I think, I really think, Sandy, that she's replacing normal doses of insulin for concentrated doses. Like I said, it's nondetectable and would precipitate a lot of crises and probably deaths."

"If she's got strontium-90 on her hands and the vials are replaced with stronger dosages, it wouldn't convict her of Dave's death. But we could bring her up on a lot of other charges if we can get the autopsy reports, not doctored, on a lot of these other patients."

The bus started to meander through the Appalachian mountains and then Knoxville. The two men continued to plan how to trap their suspected foe.

"Can you get any of that stuff?"

"Yes. I've got a sister who works at ORNL. She surely can get me 1 cc or so. It wouldn't take much."

Okay, when we get to Knoxville, we'll rent a car for the

rest of the ride to New Orleans. We'll see if we can get some of this stuff somehow."

The bus station in Knoxville was in the part of town called the Old City, a rehabilitated section of buildings built before the turn of the century. They both scanned the outside of the bus. Dr. St. John halfway expected the Washington police to be there to arrest him for assault and battery.

"Let's have a drink, and I'll call my sister, Susan," Robert suggested to Sandy as they got off the bus.

Patrick Sullivan's Saloon was one of those 1880 buildings that had been returned to its former glory. It had actually been a saloon in old Knoxville, prior to prohibition. The building had been in a state of disrepair for years until it was restored and the good times began rolling again in that part of the city. Sandy noted, as he walked into the door of the establishment: "Hey, this reminds me of New Orleans in a way."

"For the first time since leaving Washington, I feel comfortable," Robert said.

"Yeah." Sandy nodded in agreement. "I know what you mean. I hated that bus. Do you want a beer?"

"Sure do. I'll call Susan at the pay phone and see what we can do about that strontium."

Susan St. John had studied chemical engineering at the University of Tennessee at Knoxville and then taken a job at ORNL after graduation. Robert hadn't seen her since Dave Wyatt's funeral.

"Susan."

"Robert, how are you?"

"Susan, we're in Knoxville."

"You're kidding, why didn't you call?"

"It was an unexpected trip. Susan, can you come see us at Patrick Sullivan's?"

"Who's 'us'? Is it the pretty lady from the funeral—Ann?"

"No, it's Officer Sandy Elliott from the New Orleans

Police Department.

"Police department? Are you in some kind of trouble?"

"No, no. Can you come down here to talk to us?"

"Yes, I guess. I never miss work, but okay, I'll be there in thirty minutes."

Robert returned to the table. "She's on her way."

"Will this work, Robert?"

"It will if someone is committing these murders as I suspect."

"What will you tell your sister?"

"I think I need to tell her pretty much the whole story. She loved Dave when she was a kid."

They drank their beer in silence. The restaurant was basically empty except for a couple of old-timers at the front of the bar.

"Will Sally Ortiz help us catch Ann, if that's who it is?"

"Hell, yes, Sandy. She hates Ann."

They sat silently nursing their beers until Susan St. John skipped through the door, obviously happy to see her brother. Robert hugged her. "Hi, Sis. This is Officer Sandy Elliott of N.O.P.D."

After several minutes of pleasantries and a minor gossip exchange, Susan asked what was up. "What's this about strontium-90? Why do you need it?"

"This is the idea. We intend to catch a potential murderer, perhaps Dave's killer."

"Really?" Her eyes misted "I thought Dave committed suicide!"

Robert and Sandy shook their heads.

Susan sipped her Coke. "That's unbelievable. Tell me more."

Robert began to tell the tale of the Hospital of the Americas and his trip to get John Wyatt a heart transplant. He took a deep breath and continued, telling her about the autopsy tech, Mr. Badeaux; their suspicions that people were being murdered by insulin overdose; and their need of the strontium to catch the perpetrator.

"Why don't you just watch the supply?"

"It's not that simple, if it's Ann."

"You mean your Ann? That pretty lady?" Susan was in disbelief.

"I know it sounds incredible," Sandy conceded, "but I think that's what's going on."

They told her about their recent trip to Washington and the confrontation they had had with Richard Castner. Sandy described Robert's actions to Susan. "He thinks he's Muhammed Ali," he said with a laugh.

"That's not like you at all, Robert."

Robert turned red and shrugged his shoulders. "I just lost it. The thought of Dave and all."

"I've got to go to the little boy's room," Sandy declared, clearing his throat and allowing his buddy to collect himself.

"Straight back past those swinging doors." Susan gestured to the back of the bar.

Sandy walked past two men sipping on drinks and disappeared in the men's room.

As soon as he had left, Susan looked at her brother with huge open eyes. "What are you doing? Strontium-90 won't do what you're saying." She held up a finger and wagged it in front of his face.

"You can't fool me, Robert St. John…and that trip to Mexico to get John Wyatt a transplant…are you *nuts*!"

"Listen." Robert hushed his sister in a low voice. "Sandy Elliott, I trust. But I don't trust all of the New Orleans Police Department. If I'm right about some of this, there's someone corrupt around him. I don't want Sandy to know that strontium 90 won't do all this…. He'll tell a superior or something and we'll be screwed. So please, Sis, just play along. All you have to do is get me some sterile water from ORNL. I'll do the rest!"

Susan St. John's eyes stared at him. Her eyes softened.

"So you saved John Wyatt's life." She shook her head

and laughed lightly. "Okay, I'll do it. But you have to be careful. Dave's dead. You can't bring him back."

"Shh, shh." Robert squeezed Susan's hand as Sandy strode through the swinging doors.

"Well," Susan said as Sandy approached them, "I don't know if I can get the strontium or not. It's not super-classified or under lock and key, but they do a twenty-four-hour supply check."

"Could you replace it with a false bottle, or could you check any out?" Robert asked rather loudly.

"I probably could switch a sample for a bottle, or—I know. I could say I broke a small vial!"

"Perfect," Sandy said, sitting back down. "That way no one would get into trouble."

"Yeah, I guess that's the way then, Susan."

"Okay, gentlemen. I'll do it. But on one condition."

"What's that?"

"You both have to come up next fall for the Tennessee-Alabama football game."

Robert laughed. "Sandy, Susan is a bigger Tennessee football fan than I am—if that's possible!"

"Well, okay then," Sandy said. "I'll be glad to. But then you'll have to come to New Orleans and eat at Commander's Palace."

"It's a deal," Susan replied, as she shook Sandy's hand. The threesome left the old building, leaving the old-timers to drink by themselves.

"Susan, can you drop us off at the Hertz rental place so we can rent a car to get home? Robert asked. "Then we'll follow you to Oak Ridge to get the strontium."

"Can you get it today, Susan?" Sandy asked.

"I don't see why not."

"Let's go then," Sandy said.

They walked out to Susan's Porsche 911.

Sandy asked, "What is it with you guys and these cars?"

"We both like fast cars." Susan smiled. "It's a family

tradition."

They headed to the National Laboratory. Sandy decided to tell Susan about the night he followed Robert down St. Charles Avenue and saw her brother almost crash into a street car.

"Uh, don't tell her that, Sandy."

"Yes, tell me, Sandy." She laughed and guided the Porsche down the interstate toward Oak Ridge.

Sandy had just finished the story when Susan pulled up to the guard outside the gates of Oak Ridge National Lab. The guard looked at her I.D. and let her pass. She pulled in front of a large red brick building with a swirling atomic symbol on the facade.

"Well, here goes nothing. Wait here." She strode confidently into the building, flashing her ID in front of another security guard.

In about forty-five minutes she came striding back out to the Porsche and the two waiting men. "Got it."

"How did you do it?"

"Just like I said. I replaced a vial, soon to be accidentally broken, and sneaked this one out." She pulled a two-inch cylinder from her purse and held it up. "After this thing is opened, your culprit has only three days to be exposed. It vaporizes that quickly."

"Now let's go to Hertz," Sandy demanded. "And take it easier on the acceleration, okay?"

Playfully she zoomed them out of the parking lot, then sped toward the car rental agency.

"Are you in any danger?" Susan asked her brother.

"No, not at all," he lied.

Sandy chimed in. "The people who should worry are the ones who are facing the Dynamic Duo!"

Robert laughed at that, remembering himself hiding under the desk in Castner's office, and then turning into a junior G-Man by slapping him around.

"That's us," Robert laughed. "The New Orleans Dynamic Duo."

Susan pulled the Porsche up to the Hertz rental office. Sandy went in to get a car. She turned to her brother with a serious expression: "Be careful, Robert. This might be dangerous, no matter what you say."

Robert hugged his sister. "Someone has to stop these people, Baby Sister. I guess Sandy and I are elected."

Officer Elliott brought out the keys to a Ford Taurus.

"Bland, I know." He pointed toward the white Ford. "But I don't have a need for blazing wheels like you two. Besides, anything is better than that damn bus."

Susan hugged his neck. "Remember, you're coming to the ball game next fall."

"I'll be there, Susan. Thanks so much for your help."

The two men with a mission in New Orleans left her waving good-bye.

They planned the set-up on the Interstate. Sally Ortiz would lock up all the insulin without strontium. If a nurse needed some she would have to check it out through Sally. Two or three vials with the strontium would be left in the I.C.U. If anyone replaced a vial, or added or replaced anything in a one, the volatility of the strontium would be on the criminal's hands. The culprit couldn't be tried for previous murders, but attempted first-degree murder of another patient would be good enough.

Even though it was dangerous for Robert to be alone with Ann, it was decided that he would act as normally around her as possible.

"It will only be dangerous for you, Doc, if Castner has forgotten our threat, gotten bold and informed her."

"If he has," Robert stated explosively, "I'll work him over even better the next time!"

"Well, she may still be in Mexico, pal," Sandy said as they crossed the Louisiana state line. "We'll soon know."

"What will we do if we get suspicious of Ann or whomever, Sandy?"

"We get a Geiger counter, read them their rights, then see if they've been exposed. Then we'll arrest them." He threw his head back and laughed gleefully. "I'm a cop, you know!"

"That's a favorite little saying of yours, isn't it, Columbo?"

Sandy raised his eyebrows in an exaggerated fashion and gave his best Sherlock Holmes imitation: "The game's afoot!"

They both became quiet as the car approached New Orleans, crossing the Mandeville Causeway.

After a long silence, Robert asked, "If Castner was so easy to get information from because they figured someone would catch on and had a backup plan, what do you think they have in store for the people who found them out?"

"You mean us," Sandy replied. "Well, they're going to try and kill us."

Robert's only response was "Really?"

"Good Lord, Doc, they've killed before. And they've already tried to kill you once. They certainly don't give a damn that you're a doctor. They'll just see a person attempting to get in their way." Sandy paused. "They'd kill us and never lose a minute's sleep, while they transplant our livers into two fat, rich European SOBs."

"A sobering prospect, Sandy. But there's no turning back now."

The causeway came to an end, and the tall buildings of downtown New Orleans grew in size as they approached the city.

"Let's go in and plan the whole scenario with Sally," Sandy said. "I'll also call Lieutenant Sheldon and fill him in. He's going to kick my ass, but at least my gut instinct was true, again! He would kill me if he knew I went to D.C. and did that to Castner." Turning to the doctor: "Let's never tell him."

"You don't have to tell Sheldon, Sandy?"

Sandy looked at Robert curiously. "Yeah, pal, I have to.

But it's the end of my career."

Robert looked at Sandy and smiled weakly. His face turned slightly pale. He looked over the New Orleans skyline and bit his tongue. "Okay. Mum's the word," he agreed. "So long as my trip to Mexico is kept secret too."

Sandy nodded okay as he drove on.

All the lights were on in New Orleans Hospital as they turned into the parking garage.

Sandy said slowly, "Doc, if Ann is here, you've got to be cool. She may try to seduce you, and you've got to be strong."

"Don't worry, Sandy. I remember too much to allow that to happen."

"Partner," Sandy lazily replied. "I've seen too many humans in action. You be careful. This is a dangerous woman."

"I will. You too, Sandy."

They shook hands, and Sandy took the vial into the hospital in his vest pocket. They entered the hospital through the emergency room.

The E.R. was bustling as usual for a Saturday night. Elizabeth Johnson waved from a back cubicle, where she was closing a laceration.

"Let's go up and see if Sally is in I.C.U.," Robert said after seeing that she wasn't in the E.R. Taking the stairway, they entered the hallway leading to the I.C.U.

"Sally!" Robert noticed her in the back of the I.C.U. "Come up here." He waved toward the front.

She said something to the nurse with her, locked up the medical cabinet and joined them up at the front of the I.C.U.

"Let's go to my office, Sally. You remember Officer Elliott."

"Certainly," she said, shaking Sandy's hand. "What's up, guys?"

They walked into his office and locked the door.

"What's wrong?" Sally's asked. "What happened in Washington?"

"Listen, we need you to do something for us," Robert

began.

"What?"

Sandy brought the vial out of his pocket. "Lock up all the insulin except for three vials. Place equal amounts of this substance—strontium-90 into the vials. Your job is to notify all nurses who need insulin for their patients to come to you for the insulin. If someone tampers with these vials they'll be marked radioactively."

"You're joking," Sally said.

"No, and we suspect—" Sandy began.

"Ann Finn," Sally blurted out.

"Possibly," Officer Elliott responded. "Will you help us?"

"Of course."

"Okay, then," Sandy began, "let's make the change."

"Sally, go get us three vials of insulin: two long-acting and one regular. Also get three 60cc syringes," Robert instructed.

The nurse left and returned almost immediately. In her hand she had the syringes and vials of insulin, which she held out to them.

"Okay, Dr. St. John is the only one to handle theses vials. Make the switch, Robert," Sandy ordered.

Robert drew the insulin from each of the vials and carefully poured the marker liquid strontium-90 into each one. He then capped the needles and placed the syringes in his white coat pocket.

Sandy looked at Sally and Robert. "Now go ahead and place all the other normal vials in the locked cabinet. Then inform the nurses and even the pharmacist—"

"We don't have a pharmacist anymore, since NHCO took over the hospital," Sally interrupted.

"Okay then, let's go. Sally, you go first. We'll follow."

Dr. St. John held the three vials tightly in his hands. The medicine cabinet was in the I.C.U. The threesome entered nonchalantly and walked to the back of the unit where the large cabinets were located. The nurses in the unit looked up and smiled as they walked past. They were basically alone in the back of the room. Sally unlocked the cabinet and removed the unmarked insulin. The medicine was placed and locked in the cabinet where only morphine and other narcotics were stored.

"Done," Robert and Sally exclaimed at the same time.

"All right. Now who would legitimately need to use insulin, Sally?" Sandy quizzed the nurse.

"Only the charge nurse on the floors and the I.C.U. charge nurse—a total of four different nurses per shift."

"It's imperative that you inform each and every one of those nurses to check with you on the insulin."

"Okay, Officer. Anything else I can do?"

"Just be sure to notify us if anyone tampers with that insulin. Dr. St. John and I will be around and I'll have one of the patrolmen in the parking garage at all times in case he needs to run up here."

"What do we do, wait?" Sally asked.

"Wait." Sandy responded.

"Check the vials periodically and watch for adverse reactions in patients," Robert ordered. "I'm going home. When I get back tomorrow, I'll replace you."

"Okay, Dr. St. John," Sally said. "I'll do my best, guys. You know I will. But please explain to me what's going on."

"Sally, I will tomorrow," Robert promised. "Just trust us tonight!"

"Good," Sandy said. " Now if you need anything at all, or are suspicious of anything, call this number and then push #9. It's our beeper. Got it, Sally?"

"Got it. Leave it to me," Sally answered, smiling. "We'll catch whoever it is."

Sandy looked at Robert. "Let's go."

"Call me," Sandy reiterated to Sally as they left.

"Robert, be careful when you go home," Sandy admonished as they approached the rental car in the garage.

300

"It's just a matter of waiting now, partner." Robert smiled.

"What should I do if Ann is home, Sandy?"

"Act normal. I don't know if I would sleep with her." Sandy gave him a sarcastic look.

"Don't worry about that." Robert laughed.

"Wait, let me check with Sheldon before we get you a ride home."

Sandy walked over to the car, opened his jacket and pulled out his cellular phone. Robert could make out some of the conversation, but not all. He could tell Sandy was getting agitated.

"Nobody has seen her, Robert."

"You mean you've had somebody looking for her?"

"Yeah, I called from Washington while you were asleep," Sandy said. "But if she shows up, act normal. Contact me ASAP. She may be dangerous—you'll have to be careful."

A patrol car pulled up next to them as they were talking. "He's going to take you home. I'll be here tonight."

"Great." Robert got into the car with a thumbs-up sign. "See you in the morning."

"Watch yourself," Sandy repeated as the patrolman sped away with Robert.

Sally Ortiz watched as the two men turned down the hall toward the stairwell. She turned to her office and ran to the privacy it afforded. She closed and locked the door. Clicking on a penlight she fumbled for the telephone. Holding the small light in her mouth, she dialed a number.

"Ann! They're back!"

"What do they know?" Ann asked.

"I'm not sure," Sally responded. "Probably everything! They've got *me* watching the insulin!" They both laughed. "Yeah, and they've spiked the available insulin with some kind of radioactive marker, hoping to catch the culprits."

"And they let you in on it?" Ann howled incredulously. "Those morons! Where are they now, Sally?"

"Robert's gone to your house and Sandy is waiting outside for a signal from me."

"You know what we have to do, Sally?"

"Look," Sally sputtered, "I've already stuck my neck out more than anyone—overdosing all those patients with insulin. I don't want to do any more!"

"Shut up, Sally!" Ann's stern voice commanded. "You're in over your head already! You know we've got to kill them both. You've forgotten that I killed Dave—shot him full of insulin—while we were in bed! And Nick Sands...don't be telling me what all you've done. Remember what all I've done! You're not the only one who's got blood on her hands!"

"I know that the role I've been playing of not liking you is part of the game plan, but you know," she slipped into a Spanish accent, "it's not really much of an act, Señorita!"

"Shut up! We're not in this because we like each other. We're in it for the money, Señorita!" Ann spat back.

"Okay, what do you want me to do?"

"Come over here and help me get rid of Robert. I'll call Sheldon—surely he can take care of Elliott!"

Sally hung up the phone. As she left the office a couple of student nurses saw her locking her door.

"Hello, Nurse Ortiz," they chimed. She jumped straight up in the air. "

You scared me to death!" she snapped.

"Sorry," they both exclaimed as they ran giggling down the hall.

Chapter Twenty-one

The fog on the New Orleans waterfront was heavy. A bright white Sea Ray hydrofoil bobbed up and down in the water at Dock #30.

"Lieutenant Sheldon," Sandy Elliott called out to his boss. "Are you here?"

Not a sound was heard except the lapping of the Mississippi River on the side of the concrete dock.

Sandy Elliott had received a call on his cellular phone to report to the dock immediately. Reluctantly, he had left his post at the hospital to find his boss on the waterfront and help him if he could.

"Sandy!" A voice that Sandy recognized as Sheldon's called out of the mists.

"Over here," the voice continued, "next to the boat."

Sandy carefully stepped through the pea-soup fog toward the just-visible outline of the boat.

"Lieutenant Sheldon?" Sandy asked.

"Over here, Sandy."

"Where?" he asked again, searching for his boss' outline.

A large form grabbed Sandy from the side. Before he could respond, he had been placed in a choke hold. Sandy felt himself slowly begin to lose consciousness. With a huge amount of effort he elbowed the burly lieutenant in the ribs.

"Whumph!" The wind was knocked out of Sheldon's lungs. He loosened his grip. Sandy broke the hold and stepped back. Both men pulled their revolvers and pointed at each other in a Mexican stand-off.

"You shouldn't have gotten involved in this. I told you to back off," Sheldon growled.

Elliott spat at him disgustedly. "What do you mean, fatso? People are being killed!

"This is bigger than you and me—" Sheldon began.

Sandy interrupted: "Nothing is bigger than the law, Sheldon. And the law is being broken."

"You fool." Both men had pulled their revolvers and begun to slowly circle one another. They each had a direct bead on the other.

"Put it down, Elliott!" the lieutenant commanded.

"Never!" Sandy yelled. "You put it down." They continued to circle one another.

"So, it's true," Sandy spat. "A cop *is* in on this thing."

"We're helping humanity in the long run, Elliott!" Sheldon continued to level the barrel of his.38 at Sandy's heart.

Sandy scoffed. "And if you have to kill a few people along the way?"

"Huh? You mean that street trash that goes to that hospital for free medicine?" the portly lieutenant shot back. "You've got to be kidding if you're concerned about them."

"Who made you God, pal? And for a few measly bucks!"

"Oh, it was more than a few bucks," he laughed in response.

"So, let's see," Sandy quizzed as the two men continued to slowly circle with their revolvers ready. "So Ann killed them."

"Ann and that nurse buddy of hers."

"I thought so," Sandy mumbled, suddenly realizing he had put Robert in harm's way, big time!

"That's right, fool. The Mexican and the good-looking administrator loaded 'em up with insulin. Hell, we even had the NHCO secretary to okay everything with goofy forms."

Sandy overcame his momentary loss of composure. He knew that Robert was in trouble, but he couldn't do anything about it right now. Maybe he could distract Sheldon and spring some sort of surprise to get the upper hand.

They continued circling each other, crouched down, taking a direct bead on each other.

The lieutenant continued to gloat. "You good cops make me sick, Elliott. Who cares? The public! Hah!" His fat face rolled with his laughter.

Sandy checked his back momentarily, then decided to stall.

"Took their body parts and sent them through the Gulf down to Mexico, eh?" he continued, glancing behind him to make sure of his footing.

"That's right, smart guy. We used this boat right here. And I okayed every delivery with the Port Authority. It was a piece of cake They were told those refrigerated cartons were vital medicine, all approved under NAFTA. They never suspected a thing."

"So another New Orleans cop gets rich while on the take," Sandy continued, his eyes glancing back and forth, looking for an opportunity to make his move.

"That's right, Elliott. I wanted a piece of the pie."

"And what about Dr. Wyatt? What did he get?"

"Look, Sandy. I didn't kill anybody. He wanted out. It was the bitch Finn. She killed him and left the gas on to make it look like a suicide. That was her idea."

"So, I'm the fly in the ointment, huh, Sheldon?"

"Yeah, you and that dumb hick Tennessee doctor St. John should have left this all alone." The overweight officer had been circling all this time in a stooped position. Now he began to straighten out. "He's probably dead already. Just as dead as you're going to be in a minute." Sheldon cocked the hammer on the service revolver. He had circled to where his back was to the boat.

Suddenly Sheldon grabbed Elliott's throat. His eyes bulged. Dropping the revolver to the dock, he clutched frantically at the back of his neck. He began to walk awkwardly backward, making unintelligible gurgling sounds.

This so startled Elliott that all he could do was follow the man backwards to the boat. "What the hell?" he muttered.

The outline of Julio with a deep-sea fishing rod and reel appeared on the side of the boat. He had hooked Sheldon with a large marlin hook, right in the neck, and was reeling him backward to him.

"Biggest catch I've made in a long time..." he nonchalantly offered.

Sandy regained his composure. He whipped out his handcuffs and cuffed the still bug-eyed catch.

"You're under arrest, you cocksucker. I'll read you your rights later," he said as he secured Sheldon to the side of the dock.

He looked at Julio: "You must be a friend of Dr. St. John's."

"Yes. He's in trouble, sir," Julio responded. "I'm Julio, from Cancun. I came up on this boat." He pointed to the hydrofoil. "Robert is in trouble, sir! Ann Finn is here."

"I know, I know! Let's go, then!"

"I'm going to leave you here, Sheldon..." He patted the policeman's belly. "I'm sure someone will unhook you...sometime."

Sandy and Julio left the hooked lieutenant tied up at the dock and rushed to Sandy's car.

"I'm going to call for backup, then you can fill me in on everything, Julio," Sandy said, pulling out his cellular phone. He instructed dispatch to send a car with backup to Ann's midtown home. "And have an ambulance there just in case," he added. "Call New Orleans Hospital and let them know Dr. St. John is in trouble."

He and Julio sped to the sight. "I hope Doc is okay," Julio began. "I feel responsible. My sister is in on this."

"Who's your sister?"

"Sally Ortiz," Julio responded.

Sandy slapped the steering wheel and slammed the

accelerator to the floorboard. "I hope we're not too late," he shouted.

*   *   *

Robert had just opened a Jackson Brewery beer and put his feet up on the living room sofa. He reflected on the events of the past month. *Never in my wildest dreams would I have imagined this.* He shook his head.

"Darling, I'm home." The front door flew open and Ann Finn walked in with her suitcase.

"Ann!" Robert dropped his beer on the floor. He picked up the longneck and patted the spill with a paper napkin.

She ran up and kissed him. "Have you behaved yourself while I was gone?"

"Yes, I suppose," he mumbled.

She lugged her bag to the bedroom and tossed it on the bed. When she returned to the living room he was still standing in shock. She patted a spot beside her as she sat down on the couch. "Come and sit with me on the couch."

He felt sure his knees knocked as he sat down beside her. He had felt somewhat confident before, when talking to Sandy, that he could act normally around Ann. Now he wasn't so sure.

A frantic knock came at the front door. Robert jumped up like a rocket. "I'll get it," he said as he ran to open the door.

Never had he been so glad to see Sally Ortiz in his life. His face contorted to try and communicate to the nurse that Ann was there and to act nonchalant.

"Why, Sally, what a surprise. What are you doing here? Come in."

"Ann," he continued. "Look who's here, dear. Sally Ortiz." He knew that Ann wouldn't like Sally's presence.

Ann stood defiantly, her hands on her hips. "Why, Nurse Ortiz, what a surprise!"

Sally strode directly toward Ann.

"Now girls," Robert began, moving between them, his back to Sally as he faced Ann with his arms spaced outward.

He felt a sharp sting in his neck.

"Ow! Jesus Christ!" he yelled. "What is that?" He reached up and pulled a 30cc syringe and needle out of his neck. Blood began to pump from the wound. He started to feel lightheaded and reached for the sofa, collapsing on it. Looking up toward the two women, he mouthed "What the hell?" as a slow, strong blackness descended on him. He could barely think and could not move his limbs or body at all.

So this is what it feels like to die, he thought as he lost consciousness.

"How much did you inject, Sally?" Ann gasped.

"A thousand units of fast-acting insulin, Ann. Enough to kill a monster at Mardi Gras."

"Yecch!" Ann said. "He's still bleeding from the neck."

"Oh yes, Ann. I hit the carotid artery. It'll still take a good twenty minutes for him to die."

"Well, let's stop the bleeding and get him out of here." Ann placed her hand over the arterial wound. "He's making a mess." She looked at the bloodied couch.

"Yeah, we'll have to clean this up," Sally noted coldly, as she wiped up some of the blood. "But we'll have some time. Lieutenant Sheldon has taken care of Sandy Elliott."

"Good," Ann said. "Those Keystone Cops should have known to mind their own damn business!"

Ann pulled Robert's body onto the floor to keep the blood off the couch as much as possible. "Too bad. He was a good-looking guy, and a good lay."

"With the money you'll have, Ann, you can have plenty like him."

* * *

Sandy and Julio's car screamed up from First Street and the docks and screeched onto St. Charles. They nearly collided with two patrol cars and, trailing not far behind, an ambulance dispatched from New Orleans Hospital with Dr. Elizabeth Sheridan Johnson inside.

They arrived at the antebellum house simultaneously. Sandy and Julio jumped out of the car and bounded up the steps to the house. The officers in the first patrol car went around the back of the house at Sandy's orders. He screamed at the others: "Bring the battering ram."

Hearing all the commotion, Sally and Ann ran out of the house into the backyard.

The ambulance crew was bringing a stretcher. "What do we need?" Elizabeth yelled.

"I don't know," Sandy screamed. "Hopefully, he's just drinking a beer. But better safe than sorry." He took the battering ram from the officer. "Robert!" he screamed as he pushed through the door with one blow.

Robert's body was wrapped in a sheet in the middle of the living room. He appeared dead. Blood soaked through the sheet at the neck wound.

"Bring everything you've got, lady!" Sandy screamed. The emergency crew ran into the house, where the paramedics and Dr. Johnson ripped the sheet from Robert's cold body and began resuscitation procedures.

"Pulse?" Betsy screamed.

"Faint," came the paramedic's response, as he covered the still oozing carotid wound. "It's faint and weak, but he still has one!"

"Get a line in him, and let's get EKG leads on him *now*!"

Sandy and the two police officers searched the rooms of the houses for Ann and Sally. Julio stood helplessly over Robert.

Sandy peered out of the bedroom as he searched the house. "Hey!" he yelled to Elizabeth. "They're killing people with insulin. Maybe they gave him that!"

"Glucose 50 I.V. push!" Dr. Johnson yelled. "*Stat*! And get a baseline now!"

The paramedic I.V.-pushed a bottle of the glucose. Almost immediately, Robert St. John stirred some, then dropped back motionless."

"Push another glucose, and get a blood pressure."

"He's breathing, no need to intubate," one paramedic said, as the other administered oxygen by mask.

"This glucometer must be wrong," the paramedic yelled. "It reads zero."

Sandy screamed from the kitchen, "No—give him a lot of it—whatever they're using is strong stuff."

"Do it again and start him on a drip—wide open until we get some kind of reading on the glucometer!" Elizabeth demanded.

"Out here!" Two officers in the back began yelling. "Halt! Police officers!"

A shot rang out. Sandy and the other officers inside immediately rushed outside to the back yard, where the shot had come from.

Inside, Robert began to stir.

"EKG normal, breathing shallow but regular. Pulse is the same but blood pressure coming up. Blood sugar still reads low…real low, 15," whistled the paramedic.

"God, he got one hell of a dose of insulin." Elizabeth shook her head in disbelief. "Can you get me a hematocrit?" she asked the paramedic.

"Sure," the paramedic responded. "But now that he's stabilized, do you want to get him to the hospital?"

"Good idea," Elizabeth said. "Let's transfer him to the stretcher and get him to the E.R."

They made their way out of the house toward the ambulance. As the glucose pushed through Robert's veins, he slowly began to regain consciousness.

Dr. Johnson patted his face. "Hang in there, Robert," she said as they elevated the stretcher into the ambulance.

Sandy Elliott had helped surround Ann and Sally. The

back yard's fence had prevented their escape.

Sally and Ann had kept up the front of not liking each other to camouflage what they were doing. In reality it wasn't much of a front. As soon as they realized they were trapped, they turned on one another.

"You skinny bitch!" Sally yelled. She pointed at Ann. "She killed Dave Wyatt! Screwed him and injected him with high-powered insulin from Mexico!"

"Shut up!" Ann swung at Sally as hard as could. "This fat little Mexican has been injecting patients at the hospital with the same stuff...killing them!" They jumped on one another, temporarily immobilizing the police officers between them.

"Pull them apart!" Sandy yelled. "Pull these thugs apart and throw them in the tank!"

It took three officers several minutes to pull the two apart. The struggling, screaming, spitting, scratching pair of arrestees were taken to separate police vans and placed in the back seats. Sally was speaking in Spanish only.

"I want my attorney! I want Secretary Richard Castner called immediately!" Ann yelled.

"Oh, don't worry, Ms. Finn, we're going to have a very long talk with Secretary Castner. Me and the FBI." Officer Elliott said, folding his arms across his chest.

Julio simply shook his head at Sally and Ann and asked Elizabeth, "May I ride in the back of the ambulance with you and Robert?

"Come on in," she said, smiling.

Julio hopped into the ambulance, and it sped toward downtown New Orleans.

Chapter Twenty-two

The scene at the hospital E.R. that night was typical: rushed. When Elizabeth wheeled a semi-alert Dr. St. John into an open cubicle, every nurse and doctor in the E.R. flocked to his side.

"Let's wheel him up to the I.C.U.," Elizabeth suggested to Dr. Simms.

"Sure, you got it. Let's go."

"Doc's hematocrit is 20, his glucose is 35," the paramedic noted while helping push the stretcher into the elevator. "No wonder he was out cold!"

"Type and cross four units of blood when we get up to the I.C.U.," Elizabeth instructed. "No blood and no go-juice!"

Elizabeth pushed the hair off her forehead, smiling at Robert. He smiled weakly back at her.

After arriving in the I.C.U., Robert was given several I.V.'s to continue to run glucose and a slow infusion of blood. After an hour of therapy, his body replenished with blood and vital glucose, he began stirring.

"What happened, Elizabeth?" he asked.

"I'll explain later. You try to rest and relax now," she said, smiling at him.

Sandy Elliott and Julio walked into the I.C.U. When they reached his bed, they immediately began to tease Robert.

"Two women beat you up!" Sandy laughed.

Julio just smiled.

"Go easy on him, Officer Elliott," Elizabeth said. "You

too, whoever you are."

Julio shook her hand. "I'm Julio, a friend."

"What went wrong?" Robert asked weakly.

Sandy smiled. "I trusted Sheldon. He was bought off, and nearly killed me." He leaned over to him. "Julio probably saved your life, and I know he saved mine."

"Thanks, Julio," Robert said.

"Sally was in on it, too," Sandy said.

"What?" Robert tried to rise up until Elizabeth pushed him back onto the bed. "That's right!" He remembered touching the neck wound. "Who would have guessed?"

"Sorry, Robert. She's my sister. What can I say?" Julio shrugged.

"I guessed it, Doc. I suspected her." Sandy confessed. "But I did something stupid. I felt strongly that Sally might be in on this, because who else had access to the medicine? And who else could cover up some of the patient's deaths? That's regardless of where the autopsies were performed, and where the morbidity and mortality reports were formulated and compiled."

"And Dave?" Robert wheezed.

"Ann killed him with insulin. She turned on the gas when she left. Those locks on the downtown apartment could be tampered with. She was lucky no one saw her leave, but that's the chance she took."

"Why?" Robert asked.

"He may have wanted out, who knows? He could have had a guilty conscience. Maybe he had just disowned what was going on. Sorry I left you dangling, buddy. I meant to go to the house to watch out for you after intentionally letting Sally in on what we knew."

"You thought Sally was in on this thing and you sent me into that house with those wild women?" Robert couldn't believe his ears.

"I thought I would get there in time. I had no idea that

Sheldon would lure me to the dock to try and kill me!"

"Why didn't you tell me that Sally was involved?" Robert asked. "Did you suspect me too?"

"No! But I didn't think you could hide the fact from her. She knew you too well."

"Well, congratulations, Officer Elliott! You almost got me killed!"

Elizabeth tried to calm him. Dr. Simms walked into the room and joined everyone at the bed.

"Well partner, I've got one for you," Robert looked up and winked. "That wasn't strontium-90 at all. It was sterile water. Susan helped me with that one. I didn't think *you* could pull it off, Elliott, so take that!"

"I'll be damned! What were you doing then, Doc?"

"Trying to flush out the killers."

"And if you two boys had trusted each other better," Elizabeth interrupted, "maybe neither of you would have nearly gotten killed."

Robert and Sandy Elliott laughed at her astute observation.

"Never trust a cop!" Robert teased.

"Huh!" Sandy snorted. "It's you doctors who can't be trusted! You make too much damn money!" They both laughed.

"I'm just teasing, Sandy."

"Me too!" Sandy conceded.

Sandy reached over and shook Robert's hand. "All's well that ends well, I suppose."

"I guess so." Robert smiled back.

"You folks are going to have to clear out now." Elizabeth got up and began to flush them out of the room.

"See you, pals," Robert said, waving to his departing visitors.

Everyone said good-bye and walked out of the I.C.U.

Elizabeth sat back down next to Robert.

"I liked you anyway...I mean as a girlfriend," Robert began to sputter.

"Be quiet, Dr. Robert St. John. You say anything and I'll pull all of these I.V.'s out of you, and then you'll be in the same shape you were when we found you today."

She bent over and kissed him. "Now you get well. I've got to take you to Atlanta for some of my mother's fried chicken."

He smiled and said, "Thanks, Elizabeth. That sounds great. Let's go tomorrow."